T

AWAY

THE COMPLETE POST-APOCALYPTIC SERIES

(PARTS 1 – 7)

GLYNN JAMES

First published 2019 by Glynn James

ISBN: 9781092804295

For John

PART ONE
In a fallen world

He sensed them in the darkness, all around, moving quickly through the building, room by room as they searched. Every few minutes the silence was broken by loud crashing sounds as they broke into another area, the clatter of broken wood scattering across rotten floorboards and cracked concrete, or the terrible, grief-stricken and desperate cries of those who had been found, their hiding places uncovered. He could hear the thud of boots sometimes, echoing through the corridors, or the creaking of the building's very structure as it protested against the abuse.

Centuries old and given to spontaneous collapse, the tenement buildings of the outer zone had ceased to be safe long before any of their current residents had been born, but the crumbling ruins were the only real shelter for many of the inhabitants of the zone, the only place to hide from the danger on the streets or the often unforgiving weather.

Most of the dangers lay outside of the crumbling walls - things that wandered the streets at night that were far from human, but the hunting squads from the city travelled deep into the darkness of the buildings, seeking those who would avoid capture. Finally, the noise that everyone dreaded could be heard in the distance - the rising hum and the sharp crackling buzz as a stun rifle was fired.

Jack sat in silence, listening, willing his nerves to calm and his heart rate to slow. The sounds were getting closer now, and he knew they were in a nearby corridor, possibly just a few rooms away. He heard boots shuffling along the floor, and the crash of rubbish as it was kicked aside - the barrier that he had built outside provided no protection, was merely an inconvenience for the heavily armoured troopers whose faces had never been seen, at least by anyone who remained to tell of them.

Jack had never known where the raiding parties took the captured, for no one ever returned. There were always tales, and rumours of course, but no one that he had ever met had confirmed any of them.

The corridors of the sprawling, old building were littered with the junk and debris of decades, most of it useless and left there because there was nowhere else for it to go. But the trash also acted as a territorial marker, a sign of neighbouring borders, of marked out claims. Often it was piled up to waist height, to act as a makeshift defensive barrier, and a way to slow intruders down or ward them away. Folks who lived in the area would know to stay away, and recognise the barrier for what it was, but the Hunters saw it as a sign of life, of someone to capture and drag away to their prison vehicles. The vehicles had no windows on the sides or the back, and Jack suspected it might be completely dark inside them, but that was something else that no one had confirmed. No one ever came back.

His heart thumped harder in his chest and he doubled his efforts to control his breathing, to remain silent, but a cold trickle of sweat heightened the twitching of already ragged nerves as it ran down his neck. Jack knew there was a chance, if only very small, that they could pass him by.

The Hunters might enter the room, their pinpoint searchlights flickering over the walls, passing over the cracked paint and the curled and mould-ridden wallpaper, skittering over the rubble and litter covered ground and not stopping as they zipped past the broken wardrobe that was his hiding place. Even if they did look into the wardrobe, they could still miss him as he lay huddled in the bottom, covered by rags and old clothing. With this thought, he crouched lower and did his best to *be* a pile of discarded junk.

It was possible. But maybe this is my time? He thought. They could pass you by, like before, but they are smart, not stupid, and you know that they see more than you think they do, don't you? What if they did take you?

He tried to ignore the thoughts. From his hiding place he could only see a tiny slice of the derelict room beyond. Both doors of the wardrobe were still attached, even if they did hang at odd angles, and he had pulled them as closed as they would go. It only left a few inches in between the doors, so his vision was limited, but his hearing was sharp, and when the first Hunter stepped into the room Jack slowed his breathing to almost nothing. Instinct kicked in and he lay there, perfectly still and silent, not knowing how long he could keep it up, but hoping that the search would be over quickly.

Slow and shallow, slow and shallow, he thought. Repeating the mantra in his mind, over and over. If he could just keep this up long enough, and if he made no noise, they would go away, wouldn't they? The old man that Jack had once travelled with, so very long ago, had taught him how to hold his breath and stay perfectly still, had even beaten him with a stick until he got it right. And so, over the years, he had done this before in many other places and not been found.

But I've also never been this close to them, he thought. Not this close. Just a few feet away. They can see through walls - that's what some folks claimed, and they can see you in the darkness. His breathing wavered very slightly at this thought. If they could see him anyway, wasn't he just delaying the inevitable, waiting and waiting only to be taken like all the others? But what choice did he have?

The same choice you had back then, he thought. You have your machetes. But what good would they be against the armour of the Hunters? If you had the guts to use them, you would have done it back then, back when it really mattered.

The Hunters never searched thoroughly, they just swept through an area like a hurricane, raiding entire buildings in just minutes, satisfied if they found someone to stun and carry away. Jack would hear the buzz of a stun rifle and the thud as a discovered victim hit the ground, and then heavy boots clomping away as the Hunters carried their latest catch to the vehicles that awaited them in the street - the vehicles with no windows.

Sometimes there would be a struggle if the Hunters found a group of people together, but the fight was always over quickly. There was little defence against the weapons that the soldiers used. Sticks, knives and metal pipes were no match for reactive armour and a stun rifle that could knock you out cold, at fifty yards, with one shot. Fists were useless against a shock stick that could render you unconscious with just one strike, twitching and writhing on the ground as the electrical pulse surged through your

4

nervous system. And if the resistance was too high then they would just throw in a grenade and stun everyone in the room. One loud *thump* and it would be over. Except the grenades didn't always stun - sometimes they caused more damage than that. Sometimes there would be bodies left behind.

The outer zone of the city - the area beyond the glowing barrier - was massive. Thousands and thousands of square miles of ruined, crumbling decay. Endless desolate streets lined with empty shells that had once been buildings - their windows shattered, doors long taken for firewood, bricks and stone cracked and collapsing, leaving holes that looked like gaping wounds. It was among these ruins that the destitute - the people not allowed to live on the inside of the barrier - were forced to make their homes, to scavenge and scrape some form of life from the remains of a fallen world. These people were never permitted within the confines of the barrier, but for some reason that no one had ever discovered, the people on the inside were capturing the ones on the outside, and in large numbers.

Where were they taken? This was the question everyone wanted an answer to, but one that was never given. There were places that were left alone - larger outer zone communities, workhouses - anywhere that had a dense population - these weren't raided. Maybe there was too much risk involved attacking such heavily defended locations? He didn't know. What he did know was that to claim your own pitch in many of the bigger hovels was a fight that most people couldn't win, so they were forced to live in the surrounding ruins. Those were the ones who would be hunted and taken.

It had been nearly three months since Jack was last in an

area targeted by the Hunters. With such a vast city to search, it was rare to even see them in the distance. They only came down from the inner city once every few weeks, that much he did know. But knowing where and when they would strike next was an art form that very few had mastered, a total mystery to most.

And it was so fast when it happened, the huge Dropship soaring across the sky at a speed that was dazzling for such a massive behemoth of a vehicle. It would land within seconds of appearing on the horizon, the huge black shape plummeting towards the ground as if it were about to crash. But it never did crash. Seconds after the blast of jets were unleashed, the Dropship was on the ground, spewing out a torrent of fast-moving armoured carrier vehicles that burst through the clouds of dust kicked up by the beast's arrival. The vehicles quickly sped through the streets at a terrifying speed, and when they arrived at their target location, dozens of armed squads would jump from the trucks, surging into the ruined buildings in search of vagrants. In search of prey.

Jack tried to recall the first time that he had seen a raid, and the picture came to him almost immediately, blanking out the sounds of the Hunters moving in the darkness around him. There were several of them in the room now, scanning, searching, but even with capture in such close proximity, his mind still drifted away, seeking a place to escape to.

Just once

Many years before...

How old had he been at the time? He had been very young, seven years old at most, and life in the ruins was still a thing of terror for him - a time spent hiding in dark corners and shadows, avoiding the folks that searched the ruins. It was a time of catching rats or mice and scratching for life, even though it was one spent in near constant starvation. That he had survived those days was a miracle in itself, for many others that he had known hadn't. He tried to wipe their faces from his mind and think back to the one scene that might ease him.

So many of them lost, he thought. So many friends, and some not so much friends. It didn't matter which, though. They were all gone, now. Taken was taken and dead was still dead, unless you were one of the things that roamed the streets at night, and no one really knew much about why they were still there.

The building Jack had been hiding in the first time he'd experienced a Hunter raid, all those years ago, wasn't in the block that the soldiers had targeted.

Lucky, that's what you were. Others hadn't been as lucky as you.

He remembered hiding for a while, curled up in the

corner of a bathroom, high up in the crumbling shell of an abandoned apartment building. He had been tired, almost completely exhausted, and had huddled inside the recess behind the cracked sink to sleep for a while. He'd found the spot a few days before, as he entered the bathroom in search of water. Some of the pipes and taps in the old buildings still gave occasional bursts of fresh water. No one knew how or why, but the old man that taught Jack how to slow-breathe also said that some of it came from hidden water springs, deep under the ground, and that it would occasionally overflow into the old water systems.

The hole behind the sink was almost unnoticeable even from a few feet away, and Jack certainly hadn't spotted it immediately, and probably never would had he not also been searching for metal to trade as well as water. A scavenger group living not far away loved their metals, and plumbing pipes were still the most abundant source, if you knew where to find them. As he had crawled behind the sink to see if any of the original piping was still there, he found that the area opened up into a small compartment just big enough for him, and a little left over to stretch his legs if need be.

Hiding places such as that would serve him for many years.

That first experience of the noise of the incoming Dropship was the most terrifying. The roar was louder than anything he had ever heard, and since he was unable to see its source, it sounded like some huge beast was about to trample the whole city. But the noise stopped in an instant, and the sound of smaller engines cut through the quiet. Jack had crawled from his hiding place, curiosity overcoming his fear, and peeped out of the broken window just above the sink.

The streets were buzzing with large grey trucks, and he could see soldiers dressed in grey armour rushing into the buildings nearby. They carried weapons that he had never seen before - large black rifles that looked heavy and awkward, and long black sticks with tips that glowed blue in the darkness.

He watched, struck motionless with fascination, as a group of people in a building just two blocks away were roughly ushered into the back of one of the vehicles, and a surge of fear hit him. What if they came to his building? Still, he watched from the window as the vehicles came and went, and once he realised that they weren't coming into his building, he tentatively crept closer to the window and watched. He still kept to the shadows, fearing that one glimpse of a person in a neighbouring building would set the hounds upon him and the few vagrants that lived in the lower levels, but he couldn't help but watch. Some morbid fascination kept his eyes glued to the chaos just yards away as more soldiers piled from the backs of vehicles and ran into the surrounding buildings.

Heavy boots kicked down doors, and long black sticks smashed through windows. Minutes later they reappeared, dragging the unlucky people that they had found, throwing them into the back of their trucks. This went on for ten minutes or so, until finally a group of four soldiers approached the front of a dilapidated and crumbling storefront opposite the tenement building he was hiding in.

Then the real chaos started.

The old store was where the gang of Scavs - scavengers - had been holed up, and Jack estimated there had to be at least thirty of them in there. They were inoffensive folk, if a little rough, but they left him alone, never harassing him or any of the other dwellers in the area. It wasn't their way. They weren't territorial, and would be gone in a few months, maybe even weeks - that was how the Scav clans worked. Jack had met their kind before on the few occasions when he ended up near the outer circle - the furthest parts of the city from the centre. It was usually where their kind lived. Except they moved around a lot, never staying in one place for more than a few weeks, scouring the area for metals to salvage and then moving on.

But he had no idea just how heavily armed Scav clans could be until the moment the four Hunters headed for the front door of the store.

The streets were silent, except for the distant crashes of doors being broken, and the cries of the discovered. Most of the search was over and many of the trucks were already filled with those unfortunate enough to have been found. When the four soldiers got to the door of the store, and the first lifted his foot to smash a way in, the doors burst open, both swinging wide. The first Hunter, one boot lifted in the air and now off balance, fell backwards, struck down by the force of the door, and that was what saved him from dying with the other three. Even as they started to raise their stun rifles, a deluge of weapons fire erupted from within the building. Jack had never heard such a tremendous and destructive noise. Flashes of blue light rocketed out of the double doors and tore into the three soldiers. All three fell to the ground, their bodies torn apart.

The Scavs weren't using weapons that just stunned.

The fourth Hunter rolled to the side of the doors,

jumped up and started to run from the store, but then the Scavs were flooding out of the front doors, most of them carrying bags and sacks as they turned and ran, but the first half a dozen were armed with heavy, black weapons. The fourth Hunter got maybe twenty yards before they gunned him down in the middle of the street, flashes of blue energy thundering into him, tearing the limbs from his body.

In the distance, a klaxon sounded - an alarm from the direction of the Dropship, and Jack crouched down, further into the darkness, watching as more armoured vehicles sped through the streets, heading in his direction. He looked down at the store below, and saw the last of the Scavs grabbing the Hunters' rifles and pulling belts and other equipment from the dead bodies before they ran, moving swiftly into the darkness of the surrounding streets.

By the time the half-dozen armoured trucks arrived, the Scavs were long gone and all that was left were the four dead, stripped bodies.

It was the only time Jack had ever seen or heard of someone putting up a fight and winning.

Hunted

Now, sitting in the wardrobe, pretending to be a pile of rags and holding his breath, he wished he had one of those weapons, in case the Hunters, just feet away, managed to detect him, and that he'd had one of those Scav guns a few years ago.

Then it never would have happened...

...and there it was, again. The ever-haunting memory he wished he could remove. But frustration had once again brought the memory rushing back, his brain desperate for distraction.

Jack had been furious at the boy for drawing in his magazine, so angry that he had stood there, towering over the child, shouting angrily at him. Until he saw how small the boy was, the tiny figure looking at the floor, his rounded face bright red with the shame of what he had done. They were Jack's things. His magazines. His way to learn about the past. The boy had known that, and should have known better than to de-face one of them. Jack had been so angry with him that he hadn't heard the Dropship approaching until they barely had the time to react - so little time to hide.

On that day, because of his scolding, the boy looked as fragile as he had the day they'd met.

They took his shoes

Three years before...

The boy had been sitting at the side of the road the day that Jack met him. The child's scrawny arms were wrapped around his knees, his head bent low as he shivered. It wasn't too cold, but then the child wasn't wearing the extra layers that Jack was. Where Jack had two shirts underneath his heavy leather coat, and black overall bottoms pulled over his jeans, the boy was dressed in a torn and filthy t-shirt and a pair of thin, ripped trousers.

You saw *things* almost every day in the outer zone - people in doorways, huddled against the weather, their eyes dark and tired, their faces gaunt, but you just moved on. Life was harsh and deadly, and to even attempt to help others was considered a foolish way to shorten your own life.

Jack had just been to The Crossing, a walled and defended section of the ruins that had grown over many years into a dangerous but necessary marketplace. It was a hovel - one of the small towns that the Hunters ignored. There were many such places dotted around the outer city, thriving hubs of activity where people had gathered and built defences against the world outside, ramshackle shanty towns filled with all manner of folks trying to survive and not wanting to live on the streets of the dead city. But to hold on to a place in one of the towns you had to have resources or weapons, something to ensure that you could keep your pitch. The Crossing was a place that Jack visited regularly, the centre of everything for miles around. That also meant that it was the hang out for every thug, gang or would-be overlord in the area.

But it was also a place to trade. If Jack found something while scavenging, something that had a value to someone, then it was to The Crossing that he would usually take it. Metals, ammunition, paper, plastics, food - anything that could be traded - was wanted by someone there.

He was trudging along the highway, on his way out after trading some lead sheeting he had found in an old factory, for a dozen packets of dried biscuits and a bottle of oil, and he had only made it a few hundred yards out of the gates when he crossed another intersection and saw the boy.

Anyone with any sense of self-preservation got off the road, hid away in a building, or just kept moving. The roads going into The Crossing were a place to get yourself killed in a second if you hung around too long. In the shadows of the buildings that lined the street, prospective scavengers lay in wait, watching from their hiding places, just for the moment where someone passed by or stayed too long. Jack had seen many a body in the gutters, stripped of all belongings, throats slit, skin turning pale.

And yet here was this small figure, sitting on the edge of the sidewalk, rocking backwards and forwards.

Jack slowed as he approached and glanced at the gaping hole in the side of the nearest building. It could be trap, he knew - the child sent outside as bait to draw in some unfortunate victim looking for an easy take, or a fool thinking of offering help. But there was no movement from inside the crumbling building, no eyes watching from the corners, no shadows shifting.

Still, he gripped the handles of his two machetes tightly as he started making his way around the swaying figure, keeping his distance and moving quickly. Yet every few steps he couldn't help but glance at the child - his thin arms, the dirt that covered every inch of him, his body heaving as he sobbed. These were good tricks for a baiter. But then, as Jack started to move away to leave the boy behind and move on, he noticed that the child had nothing on his feet, and that they were bloodied.

The hairs on the back of Jack's neck started to tingle. Why was he stopping? Why did he find himself standing, turning to face the small figure, and taking a step towards him? It made no sense. Even if he hadn't seen watchers in the building, that didn't mean they weren't there.

Right now there could be a dozen of them creeping around, surrounding him, and preparing to rush in for the kill. He could stand his ground against one, two, maybe even three, but a large gang - the kind of gang that employed baiter tactics to catch foolish, weak hearted folks that might stop to offer help - no, he wouldn't be able to fight that off.

But there he was, still moving closer. Then he was just a few feet away, looking down at the huddled figure that still hadn't sensed his presence.

"Why are you sitting here?" Jack asked him, but was rewarded with no answer. The boy just sat there, rocking and murmuring. Yes, Jack could hear the murmuring now… or was it singing? He listened, peering at the child through narrowed eyes, straining to understand. Didn't he recognise the words from somewhere?

Five green bottles sitting on the wall...

Some sort of saying, or a poem.

One green bottle, should accidentally fall...

The tune was familiar, vague, but familiar. Something from Jack's childhood that he didn't want to remember, but he did remember it.

We used to sing it in nursery school, he thought. The recollection was there, even after all these years, but not clear enough for him to picture it.

And he didn't want to hear it any longer.

"Boy!" he snapped, and the small figure jumped at that, almost falling back as he fumbled to steady himself. The child stared up at Jack, eyes wide and full of terror, his tightly closed lips trembling. At the sight of his fear, Jack's irritation with the song vanished, and he spoke again, more softly.

"What are you doing in the middle of the street?"

The boy looked at him, eyes still wide, and tried to speak, but for a moment nothing seemed to come out but a quiet squeak.

"They took my shoes," the boy finally said, grasping his bloodied feet with pale hands, his eyes bright with tears.

Jack wanted to ask if the boy was a baiter, but knew it was a pointless question. If the child was bait for a gang's trap, it was already too late. Jack would already be caught in it. But there was still no movement in the buildings surrounding them, and no noise but the howl of the wind and a repetitive squeaking noise. A few feet away a rotten sign hung over a door that would once have been the entrance to a shop. The wind blew it backwards and forwards with the same rhythmic motion as the boy's, as he had rocked backwards and forwards just a few moments before. The screech of the plastic, rubbing on the pole that jutted out of the broken brickwork was long and drawn out, a noise that grated at Jack's nerves.

The boy was still staring at him, his expression weary. He had dark bags under blood-shot eyes, a stark contrast to his pale skin. The boy looked severely malnourished and quite sickly, and those eyes spoke of many nights of missed sleep.

"They took my shoes," the boy repeated.

That was three years ago, he thought.

Hunted

The Hunters were so close now that Jack thought he could hear their breathing. Pinpoint spotlights continued to flicker across the room, tracing the corners, the places of darkness, the door opposite, and then the window. The thud of boots on the floorboards. He thought for one moment that he heard talking, muffled and low. The soldiers wore helmets that covered their faces completely, and even at security stations near the inner city, he had never heard one of them speak or seen their faces. Their armour and helmets made them look like robots, almost inhuman. Whatever conversations they were having must have been via radio, and private, only among themselves.

Through the narrow slit that was his only view of the room, Jack saw the dark shape move, slowly sweeping the area and peering through the two openings that led into the other two rooms in his small, rubbish-littered hideout.

He knew that these places had once been called apartments, and he guessed that centuries ago they would have been homes for people, couples, or even whole families. This much he had learnt from the remnants of magazines and books that could occasionally be found among the ruins and from the signs that he had seen on the stairwells of many of the old buildings. If you took the time to look around, evidence of the old days - from before the world collapsed into the chaos that he'd seen for most his life - was everywhere. Tatty old posters, half worn away by the weather, still clung to the walls, depicting people in some of the strangest clothing he had ever seen - bright and sparkling costumes that surely couldn't have been every-day wear.

Books lying in tattered heaps in the corners of old buildings were also a treasure of tales of the old world. Most of them had been burned for fuel, but occasionally he would come across them, sometimes hidden away where someone hadn't looked. And the magazines and old newspapers - he loved them the most - not only could he learn about things from the long gone, but there were pictures that showed him what things had looked like back then.

Once, in a run-down office building many miles across the city, out near the Ashlands, he had found an article about the very street that he was on. Some sort of horrible act had been committed. A murder, he thought, but it wasn't the scene of uniformed soldiers that had interested him. It had been the buildings in the background of the picture. He could clearly see the very building that he was in, and next to it the vast thing that had once been called The Grand Theatre. Jack didn't know what one of those was, but by the size of the place, he thought it must have been something important.

Two huge towers rose on either side of the main entrance, and a massive board with bright white lettering stood as a bold centrepiece. There were hundreds of people queuing outside the entrance, just yards from a cordoned off area patrolled by men in uniforms. All of those people were waiting to be allowed admittance into the vast building that he knew was now, centuries later, just an empty shell.

Jack had been in there before he discovered the offices nearby, and wondered in awe what the huge room, with the cracked and weathered carpets, was for. In the magazine there was a picture of the interior, with rows upon rows of seats, all filled with smiling people as they waited for whatever spectacle happened at The Grand Theatre. He had presumed that it was some kind of meeting place, and that the stage at one end of the room - now just a hollow hole in the ground with a twisted set of metal stairs leading up to nothing - was where someone important would stand.

So much was hidden away, waiting to be found by those with an eye for searching. So much still left behind but unnoticed. A keen eye could spot the clues that many had missed, and Jack had collected a few almost intact magazines over the years - something considered valuable just for the paper. And as he sat in the wardrobe, watching the figure of the Hunter move through the room, his gaze stopped on the small pile of magazines across the room in the corner, where he had left them, and when one of the tracer lights passed over them, stopped and went back to settle on the top magazine, his heart started to thump harder.

Stupid.

He had left them out in full view, an obvious sign of at least recent occupancy.

The dark shape of the Hunter moved across the room, rifle sweeping backwards and forwards, covering the door, the windows, and the dark recesses as the soldier approached the corner. The figure moved out of Jack's slice of vision, but he could hear the rustle of paper, pages being flicked through, being disturbed. And then the sound of the same boots again, thudding across the boards, the shadow moving swiftly out of the room and then heading away. They were leaving, treading heavily on creaking floorboards as they moved off down the corridor.

Jack breathed again, still keeping as quiet as he could, but his lungs had been close to forcing the breath out of him, screaming to inhale more air, and it was a relief to exhale and fill them again. Stupid, he thought. Part way through the raid he had stopped regulating his breathing and held it. And he'd held it so long that it was too late to exhale without making a loud noise. If the soldiers had been there for a minute longer he wouldn't have been able to keep his breath in, and right now he'd be in the back of their vehicle, on his way to wherever they went.

The urge to look out was almost overwhelming. He needed to see if they had taken his magazines. They were his most prized belongings, picked up here and there from various hidden treasure troves across the city - at least a dozen of them, including the one that the boy had left behind. The one the boy had drawn pictures in.

Now Jack felt the ache in his chest, a pain that he had tried to keep at bay for two years, but sometimes it crept over him at the most unexpected moment. He couldn't think of that right now, mustn't drift back into self-loathing and thoughts of the past that was lost.

He just stayed there, still, impatience burning in his guts, the urge to burst from his hiding place and scramble across the room almost unbearable, knowing that any noise could bring the soldiers back. He cursed his own foolishness. Why had he not just put them in his rucksack? That was where he normally kept them. He had taken them out to look at, and to add his newest finds to the leather sleeve that he kept them in to protect them from damage. Three new magazines to add, and yet he hadn't put them away afterwards. Instead he had drifted off to sleep, leaving them in a pile, and only waking at the tremendous noise of the approaching Dropship. In his panic to hide he had forgotten about the magazines and had just run for the wardrobe.

Now he couldn't see if they were still there, and couldn't see if the Hunter had taken any of them. The paper was worth money to the right buyer, but not as much as their sentimental value to Jack, and nowhere near as much as that magazine with the boy's drawings.

There was no price on that one. Could never be. He had scolded the boy, told him off for defacing what was precious to him, and yet, now, the one with the drawings in it was the most valuable thing to him.

The right choice

Three years before...

The boy had no shoes on the day Jack met him, and kept repeating that fact as Jack stood there, considering what to do next.

This isn't my problem, he thought. This is just stupid of me, staying here in full view for too long. I'm an open target. I need to move on.

But what about the child?

I could help him if I chose to, if I was willing to take the burden. Or maybe I could at least take him to The Crossing, and find someone who would want a boy to work for them.

There was no one who could be trusted. Jack sighed. Finally, he decided to just walk away. This was a problem that he didn't need. But then a memory from his own childhood came to him, because Jack had lived on the inside of the barrier once, but that was so very long ago.

Only two tickets

Many years before...

Jack could only have been six or seven years old - he couldn't recall exactly - and all of his memories of those days were remembered like a small child would remember them. He was very young when he stopped living on the inside of the barrier and found himself walking in a line, following other children. He wore no shoes and they were walking over the hard, gravelled ground, out of the security gates and into the crumbling ruins that was the *outside*.

The day before he had been at home, in the warmth, playing with his toys and reading his books. His parents had been packing up everything in the house, or at least most of it. He had peered into his parent's bedroom and saw his mother putting things into a large plastic container that looked like an over-sized suitcase. It wasn't one of their normal suitcases, the purple ones under their bed. This was different. His mother was putting things into it, and then taking them out, and he thought that she seemed to be choosing what to take with her.

They had gone on what his father called vacations, sometimes. It meant leaving, and it meant travelling on the sub-train for a long time, and then arriving at a place where there was sand and lots of water. They would stay there for a few days and then go home again. But this time had been different. All the furniture was covered with plastic sheeting, and the cupboards - which were normally filled with food - were now empty.

He'd gone back to his toys, not paying attention, preferring to use his crayons to draw stick men with guns shooting monsters, or huge dinosaurs eating helpless victims. But then he heard raised voices from his parent's room. They were arguing, he'd thought. It wasn't a frequent thing. His parents were both quiet people, prone to long periods of silence. He couldn't hear what the argument was about, but vividly recalled one phrase that his mother said.

"But there are only two tickets."

Those were the only words of the conversation that he'd caught, and it was the last thing he ever heard his mother say. A short while later he heard the front door open, and then shut, and then two men were in the room with him, ushering him out of the house.

Jack knew now that his parents had made some kind of decision that day, all those years ago, and the choice meant that he would go somewhere else. He'd figured that much out for himself. There were only two tickets to whatever journey his parents had gone on, and therefore, he couldn't go with them. Forty years must have passed, and he still didn't know where they'd gone. He always thought that you came back from a vacation.

As he'd walked in line with the other children, fear building in his chest as he saw the massive walls that protected the inner city - which had been his home for the entirety of his life - becoming more distant, further behind them with every step that they took out into the ruins. He remembered that his feet hurt on the gravel, and they bled, just like the feet of the boy as he sat at the side of the road that day.

A choice had been made a very long time ago that led to Jack walking barefoot away from every comfort he'd ever known, into a life much more precarious, harsh, and dangerous.

Let's get moving

Two years before...

Why had he made a decision, right then, to not leave the boy without first offering to help? Had he seen something of himself there, sitting on the side of the road? Had he seen that the boy was like him?

"Come on," Jack said, looking around, scoping the streets and the abandoned buildings for movement. If the boy had been bait, the attack would already have been upon him.

But that didn't mean they were safe.

Jack started to walk along the sidewalk, his machetes still drawn, eyes flickering over every possible hiding place. But when he stopped at the intersection and glanced back, the boy hadn't followed him. The child was standing, but not walking. He was just standing there, his tiny, round face screwed up with indecision.

The kid is terrified, he thought, and can't trust me. He couldn't blame the child for being cautious or afraid, but alive was always better than dead, and if the boy stayed where he was, he would be dead before morning. Maybe the kid didn't realise that?

He sighed, impatient but reluctant to leave the boy to his fate.

"I've got food," Jack shouted. "And... we'll try to find something for your feet."

The boy's expression changed at that, a flicker of hope removing the wide-eyed fear from his eyes.

"New shoes?" the boy asked as he took a single, tentative step forward.

"Yes!" Jack said, already beginning to regret what this offer would cost him. "But let's get moving." He waved his arm, indicating the buildings around them. "You think losing your shoes is bad? There are worse things that folks will do to you if you stay here too long."

Jack headed off down the street, deciding if the boy followed him he would help him, at least for a while. But if he didn't follow, then it was his choice, his life. Jack was already putting himself out, he thought. If the boy didn't come, then fate would decide what would happen to him.

But the boy did follow, and was soon jogging along beside him, not complaining even once. If his feet hurt him as they travelled away from The Crossing, the child didn't make it apparent.

Jack's hideout at the time was a long walk away, at least four miles from The Crossing, and he didn't stop to rest. It would be dark in a few hours and he wanted to be barricaded in by then, hidden away from what prowled the streets at night.

As they walked, he glanced over at the boy, realising for the first time just how small the child was. He couldn't have been older than six years old, about the age that Jack had been when he had escaped from the workhouse.

The workhouse

Many years before...

Even considering all the difficulties of life on the outside, among the ruins of the outer zone with the dangerous things that haunted that skeletal landscape and the gangs of vicious and cold-hearted folk that prowled and picked at the debris for anything edible or salvageable, Jack's short time in the workhouse near the border had been worse.

After the long walk through the ruins, following the other kids in the chain gang led by a dozen armed and rough looking men, they had arrived at what would be his home for six months.

It was a sprawl of several buildings, most of them crumbling and dangerously unstable, housing over a hundred kids and their captors. For Jack, the place was a shock beyond anything he had experienced in his short life. There was little care taken for those that were held captive and made to work in the derelict warehouse and machine facility, barely a mile from the pulsing barrier that protected the wealthy and the fortunate. Most days were spent working on huge machines, the purpose of which Jack had never really known, and most nights were spent on the cold, hard ground, trying to sleep through nightmares and wondering when the next meal would come.

Jack remembered spending hours upon hours shovelling

dirty, black rocks called *coal,* from the mountainous piles that the delivery ships would dump on the open grounds outside of the main building, into rickety wheelbarrows that were then rushed away by other children. There were no adults working the dumping ground. A few sat around the outside fence, their arms folded, watching intently for a child that wasn't working as hard as the rest.

He remembered aching constantly from the strain of the work. The small muscles of a child were never meant to haul the loads that they were forced to manage every day for almost the entire time that the sun was in the sky. And on top of the muscle-draining work of lifting shovel after shovel, there was the panicked and rushed moment when a new Dropship would arrive and no one on the ground knew where it was going to dump its next delivery load. For a frantic couple of minutes, the hundred or so children in the yard would stand and watch the sky, waiting as the ship slowed to a halt. And when it released its load, those underneath would run as fast as they could.

Why had it been that way? he wondered, as he always did when memories of the workhouse came back to him. Surely the guards could have called the kids away from the open area while the ship had delivered the next mountain of coal? Surely it would have made much more sense to do that? Then there wouldn't have been the accidents. People could be cold and uncaring in the outer district, and many were cruel, but none as bad as the men who made the yard workers stay out in the open when the coal was delivered.

He had seen them, the guards, making bets, and had heard names mentioned, though fortunately never his own. Who would be the next to go? - had been the subject of the money exchanged. Who would be the next child killed by falling coal?

The day that he escaped, along with many others, had been one of the times that someone had died under the avalanche of the black rocks. Except on that day it hadn't been a child that was killed, but one of the guards. No one planned for it to work out how it had, and he thought that not a single kid in the yard had expected the ship to drop early, and so close to the edge of the yard. Maybe it had been a mistake by the pilot, or the crew in the cargo chamber of the ship. Someone could have pulled the lever before they were supposed to and *whoosh*, away went the entire contents of the cargo hold, plummeting to the ground a hundred feet below.

One moment the guard had been sitting there, smiling, watching the fear in the children's eyes as they stood, dotted about over the open ground in the yard, looking up at the huge ship approaching, their shovels in hand, waiting to run. The next moment the ship had stopped, and the smiling guard had vanished under a hundred tonnes of black rock which hit the ground and churned out a cloud of thick dust that spewed for yards in every direction. Then the guards were shouting and running towards the fence where their co-worker had been.

That was when he had looked back at the other children around him. Some were looking at him, and some were glancing at the fence, just yards away.

Jack remembered the realisation that crept far too slowly into his mind. No one was watching them. Thirty yards away, the dozen or so guards were either shouting at each other, or pointlessly trying to move some of the coal, even though Jack knew - everybody knew - that the man underneath was dead. Very dead. He'd seen the mess left behind when someone had been crushed.

Among the yard workers was a one-eyed girl that everyone called Squint, though not to her face. She was older than most by maybe two or three years, and had a temper that would spark and explode at the slightest thing. Jack had seen a fair few younger kids hit the ground after a swift slap from Squint, and often for something trivial. You didn't mess with her, you didn't cross her, and if she told you to do something then you sure as hell did it.

On that day, Squint yelled just one word at the top of her shrill voice.

"*RUN!*"

And then she took off in the direction of the fence, a second or so before every other kid. Even before Jack started to run, she was going full tilt, sprinting as fast as she could, and when Jack got to the bottom of the fence and started climbing, she was already over the top and running for the ruins.

The memory of what happened after that day was fuzzy, a blur of starved, feverish moments and nightmares, but Jack clearly remembered the last time he saw Squint alive. She turned back, just before running into an alleyway, grinned at him, and shouted. "Good luck, kiddo!"

Kiddo. She'd called everyone kiddo.

Jack still wondered what had happened to Squint, wondered if she was still alive somewhere in the outer zone.

Talented

Three years before...

As the distant memory of his escape faded, Jack glanced over to the boy once more, and wondered if the child had also escaped the workhouses. There had once been a few of them dotted around the landscape not too far from the barrier, but they were all gone now, so if the boy was from a workhouse it had to be somewhere else. Jack had been back to the workhouse that he'd escaped from, many years later, only to find it deserted, though the open ground at the back of the compound was still, after years, covered in a thick black stain from the coal.

He'd often wondered why the workhouses disappeared, and thought that maybe someone had decided to move them after the mass escape that he had been involved in happened.

The boy could still have been from a workhouse, though, maybe one much further away, Jack thought, and he almost asked the child if he was an escapee, but figured that the kid would probably rather not talk about it.

The boy was called Ryan, Jack discovered that first night, as they sat opposite each other, huddled around a small campfire built from the broken remains of a door that had fallen from its hinges and lay in the middle of the floor, not far from the entrance of their new, and possibly temporary, camp. They'd moved on a dozen blocks away from Jack's old camp, as he had insisted. He liked to move regularly, but the building they found wasn't ideal, with at least three entrances open to the wind. Thankfully, the room at the back still had a door that could be shut, which allowed him to light a fire without the light being visible out on the street.

Jack had no idea where they would find new footwear for the boy, and he had nothing of a value even close to the cost of shoes to trade, but he did have some old sack cloth, which he cut and wrapped around the boy's feet. They both slept after a meagre meal of salted rat meat which Jack had traded back at The Crossing, but it took a while for Jack to drift off.

Instead he lay there, watching his new companion, listening to the boy snoring, and wondered what the hell he was going to do with the child. This was the first time in his entire life that Jack had the responsibility of another person on his shoulders, and if he was honest with himself, he didn't have the slightest idea how to behave. Was he supposed to teach the kid? Help him learn how to survive out here, like the old man had done for him? Obviously the boy hadn't done so well by himself, but then, when Jack thought back to his own childhood living rough, he hadn't always been lucky himself. Sometimes he had barely scratched his way through, nearly dying at least a dozen times that he could recollect. Probably more, if he actually tried to remember them all.

Maybe he *should* take the kid back to The Crossing? Maybe he should try to find someone there to take him in… no, that was utterly pointless. There wasn't a single soul in that place that wouldn't use the boy for some low purpose. Sure, there were folks there that were less terrible than most - some even showed concern for other people occasionally - but Jack could count on one hand the number of people he thought may actually try to help the kid, and not even one of those was a guarantee. The boy was his to watch over, whether he liked it or not. He could always tell Ryan to scram, to leave, but he knew that wouldn't happen, either. He'd already made the mistake of starting to warm to the boy.

It was with these troubling thoughts that sleep finally took him, drifting in on the howling wind and muffling the worry of what to do next.

In the end it turned out that he wasn't going to need to *do* anything. Only a few days in the boy's company and Jack had already gotten used to him being around. Before Jack had even realised, an entire month had passed as they moved from place to place, each time finding a good camp spot that was well hidden and then scavenging among the ruins nearby.

The boy turned out to be one of the keenest scavengers Jack had ever met, even if his first impressions of the boy's abilities were all disappointments. The kid was clumsy to begin with, not really knowing how or where to start looking, how to search a place and spot the signs of possible buried treasure. He constantly walked straight past obvious places to check, and was always surprised when Jack pointed them out. But that soon passed, and after the fourth day, while staying overnight in one of Jack's regular hideouts on the way to The Crossing to find a trader for a rubber tyre that Jack had hauled out from under a pile of collapsed masonry, Ryan crawled out from a hole underneath a smashed up kitchen unit, with a can opener in his hand.

A real, working, not even slightly rusty, can opener. The damn thing was a rare treasure, and Jack stood there for a full five minutes, turning it in his hands, inspecting the clasp joint and the circular blade. It was in perfect working condition.

"You found this... down there?" he asked, with an incredulous expression.

"Yes. Just down there," said Ryan, pointing at the hole in the floorboards that Jack wouldn't have even considered trying to squeeze into - *hadn't* considered investigating the few dozen times he had holed up in the very same room.

They were on the third floor of a derelict apartment building not too far from where Jack had seen the Hunters for the first time, an area that had been picked clean over centuries. Most days it was impossible enough to find decent salvage of any kind so close to The Crossing, and this place was less than two miles away. Collecting enough wood for a fire was a hopeless task in such a populated and over-picked area, and finding stuff like this just didn't happen.

And yet here he was, holding something that was impossible to find anymore, ever. A relic from an era that was three centuries dead.

And that wasn't the end of it.

Jack looked at the can opener, turning it over in his hands, checking for rust spots. There weren't any.

"This should be rusty," he said, frowning, and then glancing at the boy. "Just lying around in a dark, probably wet place, all this time. I mean years and years. It should be rusty."

"It was in this bag," said Ryan, reaching for a clear, plastic bag lying on the floor. The bag had been ripped open, and a guilty expression crossed the boy's face. "It was in this bag, but I opened it. Sorry. I found it in the box in the wall."

Jack's eyes widened.

"What box?"

"Well. Not a box," Ryan backtracked, looking a little flustered or even embarrassed.

The boy thinks he's done wrong, Jack thought, frowning, but he let the boy continue.

"It's like a big square hole in the wall. You can't see it from the floor below. I looked. But under there," Ryan pointed at the hole in the boards, "you can crawl to the bit above the wall, and the top of the box is a bit open. The wall is cracked. I think there's more stuff in there but I can't reach any further in."

"What do you mean, there's nothing in the room where the box is?"

"I'll show you," said Ryan.

Jack followed the boy down the stairs, avoiding the piles of trash. Underneath the kitchen, on the floor below, was a large open room that Jack had walked through many times. There were two entrances, one to the stairs and the other to the front foyer of the building. But the walls were completely bare apart from occasional scraps of faded but colourful plaster.

Ryan stopped in the middle of the room and pointed at the north wall. "Right there," he said.

Jack walked over to the small hole that the boy was indicating, and peered up into the kitchen above. The same rotten and faded green cabinets could be seen through it.

"This hole wasn't here before," said Jack. "I would have seen it."

"Ah," said Ryan, looking sheepish."It kinda gave way when I first climbed inside". The child walked over to the wall below the hole, reached up, and tapped the plaster. "The box is right here, I think."

"It's hidden?" asked Jack.

"Yeah. You can check both sides. If you go under the stairs the wall is bare there as well. But the box is there. I felt it. The top had cracked open, I think, but only a little bit." The boy held up his hand, using two fingers to indicate a three inch gap. A gap just big enough for a child's hand to squeeze through. "I felt inside and it was all dry, but I couldn't pull any of the other stuff out."

Jack took out his machete and tapped the wall with the back of the blade. The sound was dull. He tapped the area a foot away, and the sound changed.

It was hollow.

"My god. There must be a safe hidden in there."

And there was. After five minutes of hacking at the aged and softened plaster, which crumbled and fell away in large chunks, Jack took a step back and stared at the secure door of a metal safe, his mouth open. He didn't know what to say, and was utterly dumbfounded. No one found stuff like this anymore.

Ten minutes later and they had used Jack's wrench to pull the kitchen cabinets from the wall on the floor above, and pull up the floorboards, then prised open the top of the safe. The metal was a colour that Jack had rarely seen before. New metal. And worth a lot to trade for. It might take a while for him to pull the damn thing out of the wall and break it up, but metal that wasn't rusty was valuable.

The safe turned out to be mostly full of paper. Currency from centuries ago that was absolutely worthless now, except for the material it was made of. But inside they also found boxes of marker pens that still worked, a bunch of wax crayons, and some faded photographs. But on top of the pile of paper, pinning everything down, was a box of tools. Screwdrivers, cutting knives, a hammer, a chisel set, and more - all of them in immaculate condition. Jack sat in the middle of the room, the tools in his hands, speechless once more. This hoard of treasure was the most valuable he had ever found.

That night they moved camps again, away from the place that they had made so much noise when Jack first hauled the safe out of the wall and then broke it apart. They hid in the cellar storeroom of a collapsed shop two blocks up, hoping that it was far enough away that if someone went looking and even found the recent disturbance, they wouldn't be able to track who had made it.

When Jack awoke the next morning, there were scrawled crayon pictures across the back wall of the cellar, near where Ryan was sleeping - stick men of various colours, and there in the middle was one tall figure and a smaller figure, holding hands.

Hunted

The thought of those pictures stirred something, a hurt that hadn't gone away even after nearly two years. He couldn't wait any longer, and quickly struggled out of the pile of rags, pushed aside the wardrobe doors and fell out onto the floor. He smashed his shoulder on the ground and winced with pain, but then ignored it as he lay there, staring across the room at the corner where the magazines should be, at the spot that was now empty. He stumbled forward, scrambling in the darkness, hunting for anything that may have been left behind, but the corner was empty, the magazines gone - including the one that Ryan had drawn his stick men in the day that *they* had taken him.

Jack had always worried - back then, when he had been travelling with the boy - that one day they would be caught in a raid. He'd worried about how the boy would react, if he would cry out in fear and give them both away.

And he'd tried to explain to the boy.

If they come

Two years before...

Months before, during the cold season when they were sitting around a low burning campfire in a warehouse in the old docklands, he had told the boy how to behave if the Hunters came and found them. It was bitter cold on that night, and they were both wrapped up in dusty, mould-riddled chunks of carpet, stripped from an office two floors above. The carpet stank of the ages, but it kept the chilling breeze, which gusted in through the massive holes in the building, at bay.

The fire was barely alive, smouldering, but still managing a visible glow that lit the interior of the tiny loading bay area that Jack had chosen. Lighting a fire anywhere else would alert passers-by that they were there, but the overhang of the bay, and the metal stairs that they were huddled under, hid the light of the fire well enough. Jack still barely slept through the night, unhappy that they hadn't found somewhere to barricade themselves away, but he had to admit the warmth of the fire was a rare gift during the winter months.

He didn't know why he chose to speak of the Hunters for the first time on that occasion. The boy had been with him for nearly a year and the subject hadn't come up at all. But then - they hadn't seen Hunters in all that time. Moving

41

from place to place in search of salvage or food further out in the outer zone did have its benefits, even though they were often weighted against dangers.

"If they come," he had said, and paused for a minute, wondering if the boy even knew about the raids. "If the Hunters ever find us, you are to stay hidden, and quiet."

Jack didn't look at the boy as he spoke, but he could sense his gaze upon him. Even after nearly a year he was still a quiet child. Sometimes he would talk, but it was always about what they had unearthed that day, or what they could make out of the things that they found, even though the boy knew that their goal was mostly to trade the stuff in for supplies. When he did get going he would chatter non-stop for a while, and big plans of constructing flying ships or boats, or fortresses, would spill out.

But most of the time he was quiet.

"Do you understand?" Jack asked, finally looking up at Ryan.

Ryan nodded, but didn't speak. His gaze shifted between Jack and the wavering glow of the fire.

"Do you know who I am speaking of?" Jack asked. "The Hunters. The soldiers that come in the great ships and take people away. Do you know of those?"

"Yes," Ryan finally replied. "I've seen them."

"You have?" He was curious. The boy had never spoken of where he had come from before, even though he had asked questions. Ryan always clammed up, stopped talking, and Jack had taken the hint after a few attempts to at prising the information from the child.

Ryan smiled, but it wasn't a cheerful one. "Before the

people who took my shoes," he said, "I hid from the soldiers in the street, but they weren't in a big ship. They were in a truck. I don't know who they were looking for, but they found someone and took them away. I was hiding over the street and they saw me. I ran and ran, and that's when I ran into the people who took my shoes."

He looked down at the boots that they had traded for. After finding the stash in the safe, Jack had made it a priority to get the boy new shoes, and it had cost dearly, but had been worth it.

"These are much betterer boots," said Ryan. "They keep my feet warm."

"Better. Not betterer," Jack said, with a grin.

"Better," Ryan echoed.

"Well, then you know what they do. The Hunters? They hunt people down and take them. And if they find us - find me - you are to stay hidden and quiet. Do you get that?"

Another nod.

"You can't give yourself away, or cry out. If you do that then they will find you, too."

They sat in silence for a while.

"Then I would be alone," Ryan said, which took Jack by surprise. He hadn't considered that a child so young could think of such things.

"Well, you'll be alone one day anyway," Jack replied before even thinking about how morbid and pessimistic it would sound. "I'm much older than you, and I will get very old, one day. Too old to travel any longer."

More silence.

"You hide," Jack repeated. "And you stay hidden if they come. No noise, and maybe they won't find you."

Hunted

After two years, Jack still preferred *betterer* to *better*.

He sat in the dust and mould of the apartment, staring at the blank space where the magazines had been just a few minutes before, and listened to the distant sounds of the Hunters heading back to their vehicles. He could feel anger building up, burning in his gut.

An urge to follow the Hunters and take back what was his.

But what good would he achieve? he thought. They will just take you. He knew that no matter how angry he felt, how vengeful, he wouldn't get up and follow them. He wouldn't because he hadn't done it before. He knew that he was a coward, just as he had been *that* night.

Lost

Two years before...

Jack stood over the boy, towering above him, his voice raised, as he let the anger flood out. He didn't hit the kid, even though for the briefest of moments that urge surfaced. How dare he? This child that I've taken in and fed, and kept alive? How dare he draw his damn stick men in one of my magazines?

Jack looked down at the magazine, at the colourful pictures of the streets of the city whose glory was three centuries dead, and at the stick men that now stood in the street, crayon drawings that Ryan had probably thought would make the place look more real.

And he shouted, not even trying to be wary of others nearby, and the risk of drawing attention.

But then, after a few minutes, he stopped. The boy was staring at the ground, his face flushed bright red with shame. Jack didn't know what had possessed the child with the idea of drawing in his magazine, but he could see clearly that the boy regretted it. As the flush of anger passed, Jack suddenly felt foolish. What was he doing? Why was he shouting at the one person in the world that trusted him and would follow him anywhere? All over a damn magazine? Hell, it was the latest in his collection, and *the damn boy had found it for him*. He had come running out of the

46

ruin of the old shop with a huge grin on his face.

And there he was, scolding the child. Suddenly the foolish feeling turned to shame, much stronger shame than the boy must have been feeling. He put his hand on Ryan's shoulder and spoke just two words...

"Sorry... I..."

...before the roar of the Dropship engines cut the air around them, and the *whump* of the boosters almost rocked the building they were standing in as it hit the ground nearby.

Jack remembered panicking and darting for the darkened room behind them, heading for their makeshift bolt-hole to hide, expecting the boy to be right behind him. But as he heard the crashing of the doors on the floor below them as they were kicked in, and the smashing of the one remaining window, Jack turned and saw that the boy was not there.

Where the hell had he gone? Where was the *damn* boy? Jack panicked, looking around, but then he heard the thud of boots on the stairs and realised that the Hunters were upon them, and that in just seconds they would both be caught.

He turned and ran for the bolt-hole, hoping that Ryan had found cover and was already hiding, but Jack didn't make it to the hole in the floor of the small side-room as the door to the main room crashed open and grey-clad Hunters burst in. Jack darted to the side and crouched behind the rotten and torn sofa at the back of the room, knowing even then, as his hands went to his side, ready to draw his machetes, that the Hunters would find him.

But seconds passed, and the Hunters didn't come into the side-room. Jack could see around the edge of the sofa that they had moved into the back rooms, where the old pantry and kitchen were, where Ryan must have run.

Don't let them find the boy, he thought. Please don't let them find...

A Hunter emerged from the room, pushing Ryan ahead of him. The boy was hustled into the middle of the room as the four Hunters encircled him.

Now, thought Jack. Go now, while they aren't looking. Attack them from behind. You'll get the drop on them, and there's a chance, isn't there? There's a chance that you could take one of them out, grab his gun, and shoot the others.

But you don't know how to fire the gun, do you? he thought. You won't be able to fight them all off.

He watched, hesitating, hopelessly not acting at the one moment that he knew he should.

But then the boy was shaking his head.

They're talking to him, he thought. They're asking him something. What are they asking him?

He heard a voice, low, one of the Hunters. "No one else here? Are you sure?"

The boy shook his head again.

And then it was too late. The Hunters ushered Ryan out of the room and into the hall, and were gone.

Seconds too late, Jack jumped from his hiding place behind the ruined sofa and ran through the rooms of their hideout, rushing down the hall as he drew his machetes, hurrying out into the street only to see the windowless vehicle heading away at an incredible speed, then turning a corner a block away.

Then it was gone. And so was Ryan.

Time to go

And the boy did exactly as you told him, didn't he? He didn't give you up, he kept quiet. When all along you thought that your instructions might keep him alive if ever you were caught, that he would stay silent and hide, you never expected it to be the other way round, did you?

You didn't act that night because you were a coward, Jack told himself. You didn't act and the boy was taken - Ryan was gone - leaving you to stew over it again and again, every night for two years, to wake up sweating, crying like a fool.

What were you expecting after he was gone? That you could get over it?

In the darkness of the room, in the spot where the magazines had been, Jack finally realised what it was he must do. He'd waited too long - much too long - even though he'd always known what his only real option was. Two years ago the boy had been taken by the Hunters, and for two years Jack had tried to reason with himself, screwed his head up with thoughts of what he could have done - should have done - on that night, but he had never, until that moment, accepted that there was a choice he could make that might give him a chance to get back what was lost.

Jack Avery stood up and walked towards the door.

Pickup

Corporal Markell stood watch at the rear of the Armoured Personnel Vehicle as the last of the new workforce recruits were pushed inside. The corporal then nodded at the last squad as they passed by with no new prisoners in tow. They wouldn't be berated for not bringing someone back this time. This whole trip out had been low-yield, as her superior officer, Lieutenant Cray had suggested it would be.

It was pointless going back to the same area after such a short amount of time, and Cray had said as much when the target location had been announced an hour before. But they all knew that disputing the target was pointless, and even if they did it would be them that would catch the blame for the lack of worker harvest.

Markell closed the back door and turned to head for the side of the vehicle, glad that the day's fiasco was over and that they could all go back to their dorms and watch TV, and maybe get drunk.

But there was a figure standing just feet away, in the middle of the street - a man that shouldn't have been there. Markell frowned, and slowly raised the Assault Rifle.

The man lifted two machetes from his belt, held his hands out, and just as Markell was about to fire, the man - who looked tired and weak - dropped the machetes to the ground.

The man was giving himself up. It was a ridiculous notion, Markell thought. No one ever gave themselves up.

"We have another prisoner," stammered Markell into the radio, still not quite accepting the man's actions. Was he mad? He must be - had to be - to make such a stupid choice. It just wasn't done. Seconds later, the last squad rushed around the truck and encircled the man as Markell opened the back of the vehicle and watched, stunned, as the man voluntarily walked forward, heading for the open maw of the truck.

Markell frowned again as the man stopped at the back of the truck and turned. The man said something, but Markell couldn't hear him clearly. The words were muffled by the helmet's padding.

No one ever gave themselves up willingly, Markell thought again. Why would they? Even life out here in the ruins was better than the short life of a work slave, Markell knew that. Yet, here was this man doing just that, the first to do so in seven years of Markell's military career.

Markell felt a sudden urge to speak to the man, and it was uncontrollable.

I must know why.

Into Darkness

Jack stood at the back of the prison vehicle, about to step up into the open door, but then he turned to the nearest Hunter, the one who had been at the back of the truck as he had approached. He looked at the Hunter directly where his eyes should be - or Jack's nearest guess - and asked. "Who are you people?"

Then, to his shock, the Hunter reached up and tapped the side of his helmet, which immediately gave a hiss of compressed air before the entire front visor opened upwards.

Staring back at him, from within the armour of a Hunter, was the face of a young woman. He couldn't guess her age exactly, but thought she could be no older than twenty-five, thirty at most.

Then the Hunter spoke, and she sounded as he had expected, just like a young woman. This wasn't a robot, or something worse. Hunters were just people.

"Why give yourself up?" asked Corporal Lisa Markell, ignoring the furious chatter on the radio, and the orders to raise her protective mask, *immediately*.

Jack hesitated, and then looked at the woman. "I have to find a boy that you took from me," he said, just before he was pushed into the vehicle by one of the other Hunters.

The back doors of the prison vehicle closed and he was

plunged into darkness.

I was right, thought Jack. You can't see out of these things. Shame I can't tell anyone that.

Why

The vehicle sped through the streets, rapidly heading towards the Dropship, and in the middle compartment - the section of each vehicle that contained the recruitment squad and their equipment - Lisa pulled off her helmet and threw it to the floor.

"Are you mad?" asked Johnson, another corporal in her section. "You *never* take your helmet off. 101, man!"

"I had to know why," answered Lisa.

Johnson looked confused. "You'll be lucky if they don't demote you for it," he said.

"I had to know why he gave himself up," Lisa continued. "It just didn't make any sense. No one does that. *Ever.*"

"Of course not," said Johnson. "Even the irradiated scum out here isn't *that* stupid."

Johnson paused for a moment. "Why did he do it, anyway?" he asked.

Lisa looked over at Johnson, and smiled. "He wants to find a boy that was captured."

"Oh. Well, tough luck on that one," said Johnson, shuffling in his seat and then roughly snapping the safety belt into place. "They all die within a month or two, anyway."

PART TWO
Into the Junklands

Caught

Complete darkness surrounded Jack as he sat on the hard ground inside the back of the prison vehicle. Around him he could hear movement, and a soft whimpering came from somewhere nearby.

Over near the back of the compartment, he thought.

Other prisoners.

Some of them afraid like you are.

All of them afraid like you are.

Jack took a few deep, rhythmic breaths, calming his nerves and attempting to steady himself as the vehicle tore along the streets, leaving behind everything he had known.

He wondered if he would ever see the ruins again, ever visit The Crossing, and he realised that he didn't really care if he did. The life he was leaving behind held nothing for him anymore, probably never had. It had been a life and that was all it amounted to.

Survival.

Except some parts, and all of that was either gone forever, dead, or somewhere, he hoped, in his future.

This.

This was all that was left.

His search for Ryan had resumed. After two long years of wondering, he had finally given up and actually done something. He'd taken a step towards the unknown but he knew this was where Ryan had gone and where he needed to go, even if he never found the boy again. If this turned out to be a journey that ended only in his death, then at least he would know something, wouldn't he? At least he could die knowing that he had tried, even if it had taken him two years to commit himself to act.

Jack sat in the darkness, listening to the noises around him, and swore that as long as he lived he would task himself with two things only - he would find Ryan, and somehow, he would make up for failing the boy when he had been needed most. Jack knew that he could have done little when the Hunters took Ryan, and he knew that he would probably have died in the attempt, but somehow that seemed to him to be better than sitting there and just letting them take him.

This was what he went through, back then. What Ryan went through after he was taken, and you were left standing in the road, just watching the vehicles speed away.

The darkness, the frightened noises made by the other prisoners, and the not knowing where the truck was heading to.

Now you know this much.

The vehicle turned a corner, violently throwing everyone stuck in the dark prison at the back onto the floor. They sprawled over each other, grasping out at nothing, at anything, just trying to steady themselves. Hands pushed into faces and feet kicked up as people struggled desperately. There were cries of fear as the vehicle swerved again, skidded and then continued on a straight path. For a few seconds the heaving mass of bodies writhed over each other until finally everyone had settled back on the floor again.

Jack tried to picture the streets outside in his mind, playing back the turns they had made, and the directions they were travelling in, and estimated that they were now four blocks from his hideout, four entire blocks in what? A minute? The confusion as the vehicle had turned the corner had thrown his orientation out for a moment, but his mind raced to catch up, to estimate their location.

The roar of the engine brought more cries of fear from the other passengers around him. He tried to guess how many people were in the back with him but it was impossible. The darkness inside the armoured truck was absolute. There was not even the slightest glimmer of light that might allow his eyes to adjust. He could see no shadows or other figures but he could smell them, and that wasn't very pleasant.

Most people living in the Outer Zone, in the ruins of the old city, didn't get to bathe very often. Some of them never. Fresh water was a rare commodity and was more than often used for drinking. There were water springs in various places, but they were guarded by gangs, or were in the centre of one of the hovels that littered the ruins, and never out in the open or in a place that was accessible to just anyone. Of all the things that were considered valuable in the Outer Zone, clean water was among the highest.

And right then Jack would do anything for a drink.

He thought of Ryan again, and how the boy must have felt making this journey. This was frightening even to Jack, who wasn't disturbed by many things after such a long time in the ruins. But to a boy, this must have been terrifying.

Someone shoved him onto his back and Jack felt a large figure move past him, as whoever it was struggled to their feet, and then there was a roar of annoyance.

"Where the hell am I?" boomed the gruff voice of a man Jack figured must have been unconscious for the journey so far. Jack couldn't place it, but way back and hidden in his mind somewhere, that voice was familiar.

When no answer came, the man pushed forward, and though Jack couldn't see what was going on, he heard others crying out as the man unleashed his fury on them. Jack was just sitting up when a heavy weight landed upon him. Another man - or a woman - struggled and rolled over him as Jack pushed them off, trying not to push so hard that he would injure the person. It wasn't a courtesy that most would give but he saw no reason to increase the suffering of those around him. It was as bad for them as it was for him. Worse even.

At least he had volunteered.

"Let me out you—" the man bellowed, but he was cut off as the vehicle swerved sharply around another corner. Jack heard a loud thud on the side of the vehicle, and then another loud thud, a grunt, and then silence. Jack thought that in the second impact he had heard a cracking noise, like small bones breaking.

Unconscious again, thought Jack, as the vehicle quickly

swerved, this time to the left. The fool, whoever this man with the familiar voice was, had been standing with nothing to hold on to, and nothing to counter the gravity of the swerving vehicle. At least he wouldn't beat on anyone else for a while.

He went back to the movement and speed of the vehicle. Trying to adjust his bearings once more.

We're into 342nd Street. And now we're passing the old rail station.

And still the vehicle sped onwards.

We're getting close to the old pits and the open ground not far from the rail station.

And that was where once, when Jack had been much younger, the slave baron Jagan had kept his camp. It had been where the pit fights, a dark time in Jack's life, had taken place. A time he tried hard to forget about.

The vehicle slowed, then almost halted, but then Jack's stomach lurched as it shot upwards, as though climbing a hill.

No hills here. So where were they going now? Had he missed something?

But he wasn't sure. His mind scrambled over the terrain, recalling everything in the area, searching for a section of high ground. But he knew there was nothing for the vehicle to climb up like this, unless...

We're going into the dropship.

We must be. There are no hills in this area, only pits. Pits full of the bones of Jagan's Gladiators. That would be a good place for something as large as the dropship to land.

All that open space.

The vehicle moved slowly now, as though navigating narrow lanes with care, turning left, then right, and then finally stopping. There were more cries of fear from the other passengers, but Jack sat in silence, thinking only of Ryan.

If the boy could survive this, get through it all, then I can. All I need to do is keep my nerves steady, stay calm.

Breathe.

Whatever happens next, none of it matters if it means I end up in the place where Ryan is, or at least where he was two years ago.

They won't kill us, surely?

Would they? It was possible, wasn't it? But that would be ridiculous. Why would they go to so much trouble to round up people only to kill them?

Unless they did kill people, maybe the weak ones, he thought. That was also a possibility.

But you're not weak, are you? Maybe some of these others are, and they will die, but you're still strong. Getting older, and prone to coughs in bad weather, but still strong. And the boy had been strong, always had been, even though he was slight of build. Ryan had proven time and again that he wasn't as weak as Jack had first thought when he saw him sitting on the sidewalk the day they met. As soon as the boy had been fed a few times he'd started to become less gaunt and more human. And even though he was still thin, there had been a grittiness to him, a stubbornness that wasn't just in his attitude.

A thought cut through the silence.

Ryan would be nine years old now. He wouldn't be as small as he had been back then. He could even be a foot taller. He'd surely be more lean and muscular. He always was a strong kid.

As a hissing noise filled the darkness around him, and a faint mustard smell entered his nostrils, Jack's mind went back once more looking for somewhere to hide, to a time when they had been together.

Like a father and son. That's also what he had thought the day they celebrated Ryan's birthday that first time.

Ant Soup

They'd celebrated Ryan's birthday on the anniversary of the day that Jack found him. It was the only day that Jack could use, because Ryan couldn't remember when his birthday was.

"My parents always told me when my birthday was," Ryan had said when Jack first asked him as they sat on the flat edge of a warehouse loading bay. "I never thought about it."

It seemed that an even colder winter than usual was on its way. At least that was how it appeared to Jack. The bitter, cold wind was early by several weeks, and although they had supplies stashed it wouldn't be enough to last the entire three months of bad weather to come. Jack had known then that they would have to resort to trading something that he didn't want to part with or they'd be hunting rats. But it wasn't turning just yet, not quite.

He thought, as they sat there looking out over the expanse of ruins that was the Far Reaches, a place further out from the middle of the city than Jack liked to go, that they'd manage, they would get by, and he was determined to enjoy the last of the fading summer before the snow drifts came.

Every year, when the weather was just turning cold after the blistering weeks of heat that marked the summer months, the ants came out. It always happened at the same time of year. They'd come bursting from the ground, spewing tiny piles of dirt along the gutters and out of the cracks in the broken roads. And there were millions of them. For a day or so the air was filled with flying ants. They got everywhere, even in his clothes and his hair.

Their arrival marked the end of the hot weather and the creeping in of the autumn and the long winter that would bring about the deaths of so many. With little fuel, and nowhere to hide from the chilling winds and the unforgiving snow that would follow, many in the outer areas of the city would perish. Two days before he'd found the boy, he'd been heating a pan of squashed ants over a fire. It had been that time.

You'd think they'd taste foul, but they don't, he thought. With a bit of added mint and some water, they made a broth that tasted as sweet as the sugar that he remembered from his childhood, though Jack knew that memory was probably not as accurate as he believed.

The first time that he'd eaten ant stew, sitting next to a similar fire, many miles away and a lot of years before, he'd turned the offered cup away, finding the idea foul and the withered old man sitting opposite him even more disgusting. The old man had laughed at him, calling him a fool and telling Jack that he'd soon change his mind. And that old grisly fellow had been right.

Jack was amused to see the very same reaction from the boy even as Jack gulped down a whole cup of the dirty, brown, steaming broth. And he was even more amused a few minutes later when Ryan's growling, empty stomach made the boy change his mind.

It had been just the same for me, thought Jack.

As he'd watched Ryan grimace with the first sip, then look surprised and gulp it down, an idea hit Jack. It was almost exactly a year that they'd been travelling together, which meant it was sort of Ryan's birthday.

And that meant that there needed to be some sort of celebration, somehow. Jack had no clue what he would do for the boy, but he was damn sure that he was going to do something.

Caught

The memory of that day faded as the mustard smell filled his nostrils. He tried to cover his face but knew it was pointless. There would be no vent in the back of the vehicle and he already knew that.

Gas, he thought. This is what they do to people that they've caught. He knew that at some point they would want to take everybody off the vehicle, and other than forcing them to move and possibly using violence, the easiest way would be to gas them all out. He wondered for a moment why he was even bothering to cover his mouth. The gas was so thick in the enclosed space that there was no escaping it.

Around him, the cries of fear returned, and the sound of coughing pierced the darkness as people succumbed to the gas. Yet he still held his breath, thinking the same mantra that the old man had taught him, over and over. Slow and shallow. Slow and shallow. He pushed his hand against his hood, using it to filter the air. And he knew it was working, to some degree, but not enough. Bright sparkles of light flickered across his vision, stark in contrast to the darkness around him. He started to feel faint and slightly sickened. He wouldn't throw up but the dizzying effect of the gas made him feel drunk.

Eventually the coughing and the cries of those around him ceased, and he knew that he was the only one still conscious. Everyone else in the back of the truck had fallen. And there was something else familiar about all this. He tried to recall when he had felt it before.

Just as his eyes started to close, and his body began to collapse into a deep unconsciousness, Jack remembered the sharp sting of the dart that the slaver had used.

The Pits

Jagan was a name that for many years struck terror into the hearts of every living soul that lived in the Outer Zone. He went by other names, but Jagan was what the people of The Crossing had called the slave baron who ruled from his throne in the open grounds east of 342nd Street.

Jack had seen him from a distance, several times during his days in the pits, and was always in awe of the man's imposing figure. He was easily seven feet tall and was a mountain of pale muscle covered with armour that Jack thought may have been captured from the Hunters. He wore his bright red hair tied in a single braid that hung down his back, and even from a distance you could see his angry eyes glaring outwards at those he commanded.

The day that Jack had been caught, back when he wasn't even twenty years old, he had left The Crossing after trading and was heading out into the ruins to find a new spot to set up. He'd turned a corner and found a dozen heavily armed men walking towards him. Their armour was hotchpotch, made up of some pieces of the grey battle gear of the Hunters and mixed up with battered pieces of metal. The leading man, who had to be as tall as Jagan himself, wore armour that Jack thought was made from cut up street signs, and he carried a long heavy metal pole with the word

STOP on the metal plate at the end.

He remembered seeing the wagon behind the men, pulled along by a dozen or more gaunt figures, but that was all he'd managed to see before he felt the sharp sting in his left shoulder. He'd looked down and seen a throwing dart sticking out of his clothing, and then he looked back up at the approaching group.

When he awoke he was in the back of the wagon, tied to the metal railings. He had been stripped down to just the t-shirt he wore under his coats and the bottommost pair of jeans. Everything else was gone.

Glass Half Empty

Corporal Lisa Markell stared down at the plate of food on the table in front of her and decided that she wasn't hungry. It wasn't that the food was bad - quite the opposite in fact. The RAD - Reconnaissance and Acquisition Division - the section of the Inner Zone's armed forces that was tasked with the security of all salvage and workforce recruitment operations, and of which she had been a member of her entire adult life, fed their people well.

Too well, some said. The plate in front of her was loaded with carbohydrates and high protein, including meat, which was a rare treat, even for the wealthy who lived inside the barrier, and she felt a pang of guilt as she pushed it away.

"You not eating that?" a voice asked, and Lisa looked up to see Johnson eyeing the plate hungrily. They'd only been sat down for a few minutes and his plate was already empty.

"Help yourself," Lisa said and pushed the plate across to him.

Her thoughts had been miles away, not paying attention to the hum of activity around her as hundreds of RAD officers and troopers huddled around the long tables in the mess hall, ravenously filling their stomachs. Or more specifically, her mind had been back in the Outer Zone, where she was standing behind the truck as the troopers in her squad climbed back into the armoured personnel carrier after finishing the task of loading the small catch of recruits.

And the man had come out of nowhere, she thought, just appearing a few feet away from her. He stood motionless, watching her and looking behind her into the back of the truck where the captives were.

That had been half an hour ago, and she was still mulling it over. It bothered her. There was something about the way the man looked past her into the darkness of the back of the truck that unnerved her. Unlike almost everyone captured by their raids, this man hadn't been afraid of her or her troops. She had seen it in his eyes. No fear. And he had just walked up to them, silently, and given himself up.

He'd volunteered.

It had been a first for her, and from what Johnson and the other corporals had said, it was almost unknown for someone to just give themselves up like that. She imagined what she and her troops must look like to those who lived in the ruins. Grey armour over black jumpsuits, a black visor blocking all view of the person inside. When Lisa had first looked in a mirror after donning her battle gear, she had thought that she was looking at someone else. The armour was made to strip all individuality from the person wearing it and was customised to fit. Male, female, thin, bulky - none of those features were obvious from the outside.

The armour was even made to look imposing - frightening even. And it worked for the vast majority of those facing off against them. Sure, sometimes a group of Scavs or some remnant of the old Slave Empire would be among the buildings they were raiding, and they would fight back, but even they had learned to fear the RAD raiders.

Yet this man had calmly given himself up and even climbed into the back of the truck without being pushed or forced. And he'd had the nerve to speak to her.

And she couldn't get that out of her head.

"What's eating you?" asked Ellard, another corporal, currently sitting to her right.

Across from Lisa, Johnson stopped eating and grinned. "She got spooked by one of the recruits we picked up."

Lisa looked up, narrowing her eyes at Johnson.

"I didn't get spooked," she said, frowning with irritation.

Johnson shrugged and went back to eating, but Lisa wasn't letting it go that easily. He'd annoyed her. She turned to Ellard. "This...recruit... He just walked up to us and gave himself in."

Ellard frowned. "No way," he said before shovelling in another mouthful of food. "Must be a crazy."

Possibly, thought Lisa. But she had seen the man's eyes. And she had caught a lot of crazies in her time, and this guy wasn't one of them. There had been determination there, she had seen it.

Lisa stood up, pushing her chair back, and left the rest of her comrades to their meal. She knew she'd have to be ready for the Dropship to land at the base in twenty minutes, and be ready to process her catch at the import facility, but that still gave her a few minutes to head back to squad's ready room. And there would be no one else there.

Two minutes later she shut the door behind her and

72

walked over to the console on the wall at the far end. She hit the catch on the wall below the computer terminal, waited for the seat to pop out of the wall, and sat down. With one tap the terminal came to life, flickering a few times before displaying the identification screen. A flash of green light swept across her face as the terminal identified her before the familiar view of dozens of info panels appeared.

Lisa stared at the screen.

What the hell am I even doing? She thought.

He'd been looking for a boy.

Lisa tapped the screen and pulled up the roster of recruits, shaking her head as she wondered why she was even bothering.

27, 334.

She narrowed the search, selecting filters for juvenile, and male.

5,723.

Lisa stared at the number and frowned. Had there really been so many captured? More than five thousand? Lisa narrowed the search again, selecting only those still alive.

2341.

More than half of them were dead.

Again she questioned what she was doing. There was no way she was going to find the boy that the man was looking for. Stupid, she thought. I don't even have a name or age.

The door at the other end of the ready room opened and several of the troops in her squad filed in. Lisa tapped the screen, quickly logging off, stood up and hit the button on the wall that would tuck the console and the seat back into the wall.

As the noise of her fellow RAD members resounded off the walls, she thought about the numbers again.

More than half were dead.

Caught

The huge man hit the ground with a grunt, kicking up a cloud of sand and dust from the dry earth. And then he lay there, twitching, as three of the Hunters circled him and then began to drag him away.

Jack squinted, his eyes trying to adjust to the bright sunlight while still attempting to take in the utter chaos around him. Hundreds of captives were standing in groups dotted around the massive yard, most of them, like him, still groggy from the gas, and most of them still and placid. But the huge man in his group, the one Jack thought had become rowdy in the back of the carrier, was now sporting a smashed nose, which looked like someone had hit him with a hammer, and was not co-operating at all. No sooner had he come round, just after Jack, than he was up, roaring and bellowing, and charging towards the nearest Hunter.

Must be an ex-slaver.

The man was smaller than Jack had estimated, probably only a few inches taller than he was, but he was broader in the shoulders and far more muscular. Jack was impressed. The man even managed to get a hit in on one of the Hunters, smashing his fist into the side of the trooper's helmet and knocking him down, before the buzz of stun sticks cut through the air and three other Hunters descended on him, jabbing at him with the crackling weapons.

As Jack's eyes began to re-adjust to the bright sunlight, he managed to take in his surroundings. They were in some kind of port facility. Huge, grey concrete buildings rose around them on all sides, and the ground was mostly dry dirt apart from the concrete platform that the dropship had landed upon.

Jack looked back at the armoured vehicle they had just been dragged from and along the line of other vehicles. There were a lot more of them than he had expected, and he estimated that at least thirty of the armoured carriers had driven off the dropship.

And so many Hunters, he thought. There had to be hundreds of them.

He watched as other groups of captives were dragged, unconscious, from the backs of the carriers and unceremoniously dumped on the dry dirt. Some of the other captives were starting to come round, easing slowly out of their drugged state and standing up, looking around and appearing as confused as he felt.

Jack's gaze drifted back to the huge angry guy being dragged away. The three Hunters hauled him a hundred yards across the hard ground and then dumped him onto some kind of moving, metal platform. The unconscious body lay still as the moving platform carried it away into one of the buildings. He looked up at the sign at the front of the building, which read Conversion Screening Facility, and wondered what that meant.

Then Jack noticed the Hunter watching him from ten yards away and he lowered his head, staring down at the barren ground.

Don't give them any trouble. Just stay silent and still,

unassuming. But he glanced up one last time at the building where the big guy had been taken. He didn't like the sound of conversion, even though he had no idea what that meant.

The Hunter was still watching him intently, and Jack felt himself involuntarily clenching his hands together, shifting uncomfortably, and looking around at the other people in the same group. He recognised only two of them, an older man and woman that he had seen several times entering or leaving the same building that he had been staying in when he had surrendered to the Hunters. They were a couple, he thought, and lived somewhere on the upper floors of the building. Dozens of others had lived there, each staking their own claim on one of the floors in some corner where no one else was, but just like everywhere else, they tended to keep to themselves and protect what was theirs. Apart from places like The Crossing, where he often went to trade, there were very few communities in the Outer Zone.

No one trusted anyone else.

"Everybody up," said a metallic sounding voice from a few feet away. Jack turned and saw that it was the Hunter that had been watching him. At that command, several other Hunters approached and encircled the group, which Jack could now see was actually only made up of twenty or so people. The Hunters were waving their stun sticks and pointing in the direction of another large building directly ahead of them. As they started walking forward, guided by the rough hands of the Hunters, Jack noticed the other groups lined up in the yard were also being told to stand. But his group was the first.

It wasn't the Conversion Facility that they were heading for, and Jack was grateful for that, but as the troop of bedraggled refugees was ushered through the massive concrete doors of the building and into a large open space with white painted markings on the floor, Jack began to feel uneasy.

There were twenty or more entrances leading off one side of the room, and every one of the led into a tunnel that was lit with bright lighting. In front of each entrance was a booth with another Hunter sat in it, and next to that, some kind of metal platform roughly three feet across. The Hunter that had been watching Jack pushed him forward so that he was the third in the queue that was now forming.

In front of him were the old couple, and as Jack watched, one of the Hunters urged the man forward. The old guy was hesitant at first, but the Hunter pointed at the platform and, with a flick of his wrist, the stun stick in his hand hummed to life. Next to Jack, the old woman cried out, telling the old man to go, but the man looked back at her, worried.

"Go," she said, her voice shrill. "Or they'll hurt you."

The man stepped up onto the platform and stood still, looking around at the hundreds of captives now being forced to stand in lines in front of the booths and platforms.

A flash of light almost blinded Jack as the platform flickered to life. Blue lights flowed around the base of the metal panel, swirling clockwise around it until, a few seconds later, the lights turned green. From nearby came a buzzing sound, and Jack looked over to the tunnels that led out of the huge hall. Two tunnels along from where they were queued, a tunnel had lit up green, matching the colour on the platform.

The old man still stood on the platform, confused, and Jack could empathise with him. What the hell did all this mean? What were the platforms for? His heart jumped as the old man was pushed off the platform. The old guy looked at the Hunter that had pushed him, both fear and a hint of anger, maybe even defiance, crossing his face, but the Hunter pointed at the green-lit tunnel, and the old man looked back at the old lady once more and then started to trudge towards the tunnel.

Next, the old woman stepped up onto the platform, and no sooner had the blue lights started flickering than they changed to a flashing red. At this, the Hunter nearest the old woman pointed towards the corridor next to the one the old man had walked down. The old woman stepped off the platform and started to walk towards the second corridor, but as she approached, she looked back and then quickly headed towards the same corridor that the old man had taken. Two Hunters rushed forward and blocked her path, pointing her to the red corridor. She hesitated, but in the end she complied and started to walk down the red corridor.

As Jack stepped forward, heading towards the platform, he glanced across the line of corridor entrances, and saw that they alternated in colour - green, red, green, red and so on. People were being led into a corridor depending on which colour the platform indicated. As he stepped up onto the platform, Jack noticed a young man being directed down the green corridor, and on the next booth another older man, who could barely walk, was being sent down the red.

Jack heard a buzzing noise and felt the platform under his feet vibrate for a moment, and he looked down.

A young man and an old man had gone down the green corridor. The old woman and a nearly crippled man had gone down the red. This had to mean something, thought Jack. Was the platform some kind of decision maker? A technology that could somehow choose who went where? And what were the criteria? Two healthy people down one corridor, and two unhealthy ones down the next.

As Jack looked down, he hoped that the platform would be lit up green and was relieved when it was. He stepped off the platform and started walking towards the corridor with the green archway, and since none of the Hunters tried to stop him, or guide him the other way, he thought that he must have guessed correctly.

The corridor went on for roughly a hundred yards, and was lit on both sides by bright fluorescent lights spaced ten feet apart. The ground was smooth and worn, like many feet had trodden the path that Jack now walked, and he only looked back once as he headed along it. Ahead of him, roughly fifty feet away, was the old man who had gone into the tunnel first and beyond that, near the end of the corridor, he saw the back of the young man moving swiftly away. He had stopped and was leaning against the wall. As Jack approached, he slowed down and stopped next to the man.

"You okay?" he asked. He found it strange to be asking after someone else's wellbeing for what seemed the first time in years. Other than when he met the boy, Ryan, Jack hadn't given much thought to others. After all, no one ever did for him.

The old man was breathing heavily and clutching his chest. My...chest." said the man, his voice strained. "It hurts."

Jack stood there for a moment and then looked down the corridor in the direction that they had been heading. It ended roughly forty feet away, at a metal gate. Two Hunters were standing the other side of the gate, watching them. Neither moved to help the old man.

I guess I'm not the only one not used to helping folks, he thought. Then leaned forward, about to help the man. But then he caught sight of something that made him hesitate.

Blisters and pustules on the man's skin. Bright yellow sores surrounded by red, peeling skin.

Plague, he thought. That's Ratters Plague.

Over the years, Jack had seen many types of illnesses. In the Outer Zone there were few people who could heal, and even fewer who were willing. At The Crossing was an apothecary who sold herbs and salves that could help, but for serious illnesses such as Coughing Fever, Sweats, and Ratters Plague, there was no help. You either died from it or you lived.

Most died.

But Ratter's Plague was contagious. And Jack had seen just what it was capable of doing when he was barely twenty five years old.

This Old Town

Just twenty miles from The Crossing, out near the ruins of the Great Stadium, there had once been a small, growing community. Over the years, Jack had seen it expand from the first few settlers, who struggled to fight off bandits, wild animals, and night creatures, to dozens more who started to build defensive walls. They had a water source there, or so it was said, and had even started to run their own market. Then, one summer, just after the cold weather had abated and Jack had found a particularly good haul of junk, Jack realised he was in that area of the new community and decided to go there to trade instead of travelling further to get to The Crossing or Dartston. Both were roughly equal distance away and would take a whole day, maybe more, to reach. But the new place, which folks were now calling New Stadium, was only a couple of miles away and he realised he could be there before dark. He'd been there a number of times before but only because he had been passing. This time he had a reason to head directly there.

But he'd noticed the change even before he got near the outer wall. It was dusk, and the sun was barely a slither on the horizon, and yet the gates were wide open - a thing unknown with all the dangers lurking outside.

And there were no sentries atop the wall.

Jack remembered standing outside the gates, just ten yards from the wall, and staring at the utterly lifeless street beyond.

"You don't wanna go in there," said a voice from a short distance away. The wind was howling heavily, a stark contrast to the early breeze he had experienced during the day, and he only just heard the warning. Jack had turned to see a stranger - a man - sitting at the side of the road, outside a shop front on the corner of the street just beyond the gates to the new but now seemingly abandoned settlement. He noticed that he man was wearing a cloth around his mouth, and he also noticed that he carried an axe.

Jack had slowly reached to his side, to touch his machete, but the man had seen it.

"I've no bone to pick with you, if you don't wanna go that way."

And Jack hadn't. His hand lingered at the machete for a moment, but then he took it away and started walking over the broken ground to the stranger.

"What happened?" he'd asked as he got closer. He stopped twenty feet away, judging that if the man changed his mind and leapt for him, he'd still have time to draw and be ready.

"Plague," said the man. "Someone in there, guy called Harris, took to ratting just before I last came by here, bout two weeks ago. Well, I bin in there just now and seen them. It seems they all done caught themselves a nasty rash."

Jack stood silently for a moment, just staring at the gates.

"Just a rash?"

The man shook his head.

"Much more than a rash."

"Is there no one left in there at all?"

The man nodded.

"Sure," he said, placing his axe on the floor and reaching for a pouch on his belt. He started rolling a cigarette. "Three, maybe four left. They're all infected. So I left them. I asked if they wanted me to, you know, end it, but none of them even recognised that I was there. Only one crazy guy throwing stones. Reckon I should have put them out of their misery, but they didn't answer me, so I couldn't bring myself to do it."

The man finished rolling his smoke, and then, surprisingly, held out the pouch.

"Take one if you want, just go easy on the weed, okay?"

Jack had accepted and a few minutes later the two men were sitting at the side of the road, smoking their cigarettes.

As Jack sat there, slowly smoking the harsh, dry tobacco, his gaze drifted over to the gates once more. He didn't know if it was some form of morbid curiosity, or just a random uncontrollable urge, but he found himself struggling to resist going into the town even with the stranger's warning.

He stood up, nodded at the man and then started to make his way over the road towards the gates.

"You'll regret it," the stranger called after him, but said nothing more. The man must have realised that there was little point trying to stop somebody when their mind was made up, or maybe he just didn't care.

The gates were built from sheets of hammered car body parts, and as Jack approached he could clearly see the outline of several car doors, a roof, and dozens of hood panels, all hammered flat and then secured together with bolts. The wall itself was mostly more cars, turned on their side and propped up by piles of broken up masonry. Even though it had been centuries, there was still an abundance of abandoned vehicles littering the streets if you went far enough out, away from the sealed off city. The people who built this town had laboured for many months to collect the materials for the wall, Jack thought, realising that he had never considered it before. Scrap metal was low on the list of items he searched for when scavenging.

As he passed through the open gates, Jack looked to his left, to where a rusty old caravan was propped up on bricks just a few yards from the gate. The town folk used it as a gatehouse of sorts, and on the few times that Jack had visited there had always been a guard or two sitting outside the caravan, watching the entrance. Now the spot was devoid of life, and the door to the caravan was wide open.

He looked down the long street that was the main part of the settlement and saw no one, not a single person moving around. The settlement was quite small, and comprised of one long main street and a few alleyways that had been blocked up. Most of the buildings had their windows boarded up on the outside, and the alleyways were built up with salvaged bricks from other nearby buildings so that the outer buildings along the street also made up part of the defensive wall that surrounded the place on all sides. There were probably twenty houses in total, all facing into the street apart from the few farm buildings at the far end.

As Jack moved towards the first house, he noticed something at the end of the street that hadn't been there the last time he had visited. He walked half way along the street, stepping over cracks and weeds, but then stopped a hundred yards from what looked like a huge pile of dirt. Next to it was a hole, and even from the distance he was at he could see something that made him think twice about going any further.

The people from the settlement had dug a large hole just a few dozen yards from the farm plot, and there, sticking up from among the weeds and grass, was a foot. From where Jack was, that was all he could see, but his own imagination had told him far more than was visible.

It was a mass grave, just like the ones that had been dug on the outskirts of 342nd Street during the reign of Jagan and his pit slavers.

Jack stopped, took a step back, and was about to leave when he heard a noise to his right. Adrenaline kicked in, and Jack turned quickly, both hands going to the machetes on his belt, ready to draw and fight if need be, cursing himself for not just carrying them ready in the first place. But he didn't draw.

He didn't have to. The man that had made the noise wasn't going anywhere fast.

In front of him was a single story building with a porch that was half missing. Most of the wood had probably been stripped away years ago, to be used as firewood, but some of the decking planks and a section of the railing on the right side of the house was still there. The front door was wide open now, and swung further out as the figure - a man dressed in what appeared to be rags – first leaned on the door frame, and then stumbled out onto the deck to collapse onto a bench that was placed against the front wall.

Jack narrowed his eyes, watching the man intently as he struggled to right himself, one hand fumbling to push himself up. Eventually the man leaned back and gave a rattling sigh, and that gave Jack a better view of his face. He was covered in grey and brown pock marks, and his eyes were swollen and puffy.

"Take whatever you want," said the man, lifting his arm slowly and waving his hand around, indicating the building around them. "Ain't no one needing anything around here no more. All dead."

Jack stood there for a moment, his hands wavering over the hilts of his machetes, but then he took his hands away. There was no threat of violence here. Only the dead or the dying.

"Everyone's dead?"

The man nodded. "Ayuh. Everyone who stayed. Just me alive now, and I'm for the dirt soon, I reckon."

Jack's thoughts zoomed back to the last few times he had been at the settlement. There had been families there and several children, probably fifty people in total, maybe more. He vividly remembered a young girl and boy, both maybe five years old, playing in the street.

"Even the kids?" he asked, not sure if he wanted an answer. He glanced along the road again, at the naked foot sticking up in the air, poking out of the grave. Was that a child's or a woman's? He couldn't tell.

"Nah. They got taken off when the first of us caught the pox. That would be Tall Al and his wife Susan's kids. Al packed up and left and took them all with him. Don't know where they went. But they dint catch it, I'm thinking. I hope so, anyway. Hope they got away before it caught them."

The man coughed loudly, and then the cough turned into a heaving fit, until he leaned over and spat out a glob of grey mucus spotted with blood. Jack grimaced. The man looked up and laughed.

"How about we do a bit of trade here?" the man asked.

Jack frowned and opened his mouth to speak but then stopped. He was puzzled. What the hell could the man want? He was a day at most from dying. If any scavengers wanted to raid the village, they could just walk in and take whatever they wanted.

"A deal. If you can manage."

Jack peered at him warily. "What kind of deal?"

The man coughed again, then he took a few deep breaths, his chest rising rapidly with effort. "Got me a nice weapon back in there, locked up. Single barrel shot and thirty rounds, but the damn thing is in a case and I can't open it. My hands don't wanna work the lock. I gave up trying. Look. If you can take the key and take out the gun, you can have the damn thing."

"And what do you want out of it?" Jack asked.

"An end to this," stated the man.

Three minutes later, Jack walked out of the main gates and glanced over the street to where the stranger had been. He was still sitting there, and as Jack walked across the street towards him, he saw the man's hand reach to his belt, to something metal there.

Jack stopped, and raised his hands. "I still don't want

any trouble," he said.

The stranger watched him for a moment, his gaze jumping from Jack's face to the shotgun in his hand.

"I heard the shot," said the stranger, relaxing once more. "Thought that you must have gone into that crazy fellow's house."

Jack smiled. "You met him already?"

The stranger nodded. "Yeah. I went in there, took a look in a couple of houses and got to his. Damn crazy ass only started throwing rocks at me from his window. Missed, thankfully. He was raving and waving his arms in the air. So I took off. Figured I'd wait him out instead of risking getting smacked on the head."

Jack stopped at the side of the road and looked at the shotgun in his hand.

"And you figured if I went in I might save you the trouble?"

The stranger looked up.

"No. No. I did warn you."

Jack smiled and the stranger smiled back.

"No foul?" the stranger asked.

Jack nodded. "No foul."

"Good," said the stranger.

"I'm Jack."

The stranger grinned. "Drogan," he said. "Pleased to meet you."

Caught

Drogan.

The thought of his friend from way back then made Jack feel a pang of nostalgia for the days that had passed and times that would never return, but right then, standing in the tunnel, Jack knew he had to do something about the old guy with Ratter's Plague before a lot of other people were dead.

He turned away from the man and started forward, hurrying towards the three Hunters that waited at the gate at the end of the tunnel. As he approached, one of the Hunters turned his head toward Jack, then nodded at the other two and slowly drew his stun stick. He stood there, the other side of the gate, watching Jack.

Jack slowed as he got to the gate, and then turned and pointed at the old diseased man, who was slowly making his way down the tunnel. Behind the man, Jack could see several other captives in the tunnel, and a few of them were catching up to the old man.

If any tried to help him, Jack thought. If anyone touches the guy, they're as good as dead.

"That man," said Jack, talking to the Hunter that had drawn the stun stick. "That old guy has a disease."

"Move through," Jack heard. The voice was metallic and emotionless. He turned back and saw that the Hunters had opened the gate and were stepping aside. The one with the stun stick drawn flicked the glowing bat, indicating that Jack should go through.

"But the guy," said Jack, turning back again.

"Move through, immediately," said the voice. Again it was emotionless and flat. Jack turned back to the Hunters and glanced at each of them in turn, realising that they weren't even listening to him, and started forward, moving between the three armoured figures and out into the room beyond. He glanced back and saw that the nearest captive behind the old man caught up, glanced briefly at him, and moved on, walking past and away from the old guy.

He sighed. It's not even in people's nature to consider helping when it could save them too, he thought. He turned back, looking into the room ahead. I would have done the same a few years ago, he thought.

Before you met the boy. That was how things were. You would never have stopped to help the man. But he couldn't help but feel a little resentful towards both the man who had just passed the stricken old fellow and the Hunters at the gate. Emotionless, all of them. Just like you were, once. If you hadn't met the boy, and hadn't learned to care, would you have just walked by the old man? After all, that is what you did anyway. You didn't try to help him. But he's diseased. You could have caught it, and then where would you be? You'd be exactly where the old guy will be a week from now. Dying, or already dead, or bleeding from everywhere, just like the man on the porch had been. Bleeding out of your nose, and your eyes, and your ears.

Jack closed his eyes and tried to force the feelings of guilt to pass. You killed him. With his own shotgun. But he had asked you to do it. Yes, he had asked, but you didn't even hesitate. But that was before. Before. Everything changed with Ryan.

And anyway, it was merciful, wasn't it?

Ahead of him was a platform of some kind, maybe thirty yards long, with a metal rail along the edge. Beyond that he saw a row of windows lining something that was painted a bright white. He recognised it from somewhere, and tried to think how.

A picture you've seen? But when? What was it?

In the middle of the platform was another booth, just like the ones in the huge chamber where people were being... Sorted. That was what they had been doing, Jack thought. They were sorting us. But this one wasn't. This was different.

A group of three more Hunters stood at the booth on the edge of the platform. One was next to what looked like a metal seat that had wheels on the bottom. Beyond that was a door-shaped opening in the wall of windows.

Jack walked forward and stopped at the booth. The first Hunter indicated the seat, and Jack complied, wondering what was coming next. He had just noticed that all of the windows on the wall next to the booth were blacked out when he felt a sharp stabbing pain in his shoulder. He looked down, staring at the spot where the pain had erupted, and saw another of the Hunters withdrawing a needle of some kind.

It's just like the pain from the dart. The one that Jagan's slavers shot you with.

A wave of dizziness swept over him and he felt his feet

begin to tingle. The tingling sensation spread rapidly along his legs, up his body and into his arms, then his neck and his face. As it flooded over his cheeks Jack felt the world slipping away.

Will they put you in a fighting pit? He thought.

No. He didn't think so.

The Pit

Jack threw his weight to his left, hit the floor and rolled. Behind him, he heard a sharp clang as something hit the ground, hard. He pushed himself up, jumping to his feet, and spun around, instinctively swinging the wooden bat in his hand around in an arc as he came up. But his opponent wasn't there. Instead, the man was away across the other side of the pit, hopping from foot to foot, almost dancing as he swung the flail around his head.

The crowd above roared their enthusiasm, and Jack made the mistake of glancing up. Above him, maybe fifteen feet from the floor of the pit, was a metal railing attached to a barbed-wire fence, and looking down at him were dozens of faces, all of them wide-eyed, many of them grinning. A cacophony of voices assaulted his senses as the crowd shouted words that he couldn't decipher.

And it was a mistake to take his eyes off his opponent. Jack felt, more than saw, the man rush forward, and he sensed the flail - a ball of stone attached to a handle by a long chain, swing towards his head. He threw himself sideways again, rolling away, as rush of wind brushed past him.

"Oh! It looks like we found a lively one!" came a booming voice, seemingly from all around him. But Jack

94

was too busy avoiding the man with the flail to locate the speakers that the voice bellowed out from.

He gripped his bat too tight, his fingers turning white from the exertion, and once again threw himself away from his opponent, coming up across the pit again.

This time the man facing him stood still for a moment, his head cocked to one side as he scrutinised Jack.

He's weighing you up, Jack thought. He's looking for a weakness. Well, he shouldn't have much trouble. There are enough of them.

The fight was obviously unfair and intentionally so. Jack had heard of the pit fights, and how those that were part of Jagan's clan used them as entertainment, and he knew that he was meant to die there. His opponent was armed with a more lethal weapon, and wearing a leather jacket and trousers, but he was also wearing a motorcycle helmet with a mask attached, and some shoulder pads made of a material that Jack didn't recognise. Was it metal? Reinforced plastic? A lot of Jagan's men wore armour scavenged from the ruins or made from scrap metal. Jack, on the other hand, was wearing what he had left when they brought him in, just the t-shirt and a pair of ripped jeans.

Jack stood there, breathing heavily, as the man started to circle around, edging towards him, and still swinging the flail.

One hit from that thing and it will all be over, he thought, also considering his own weapon. It was a wooden bat, and thin. If he tried to use it to hit the man over the head, against the motorcycle helmet, he may dent the helmet, even stun the man, but the bat would most likely break. It already had some cracks in it.

And then the choice was taken away from him as the man lurched forward, jumping the distance between them and swinging the heavy stone ball down towards his head. Jack stumbled, falling backwards, but still he tried to bring the bat up, tried to defend himself. He felt the wind rush out of his chest as he hit the floor, and then felt a jolt in his arm followed by the sound of wood cracking. He rolled sideways, and only just in time as the heavy stone flail came swinging in for a second strike. Again it missed him by inches and bounced off the floor where he had been just a moment before.

Jack pulled back the bat, about to attempt a strike, when he saw that half of the weapon was lying on the floor a few feet away. All that was left in his hand was a foot-long splinter attached to the rubber grip.

His opponent came on again, swinging the flail around his head, and all Jack could do was back away towards the wall. His shoulder hit wood and he realised, with certainty, that he had gone as far as he could. The next lunge would be his end.

And then it came. The man stepped forward and swung the flail low, coming in from the side, and faster than he'd expected, but Jack, unarmoured as he was, was faster. He fell sideways and felt the heavy stone of the flail hit the wall. And then the man's eyes went wide as the ball smashed through the wooden barrier and stuck there. Jack's opponent had just half a second to attempt to pull the flail out from the wall, and he heaved on it, wood splintering and cracking, but the flail didn't move. It was stuck fast in the dirt behind the barrier, and Jack saw his moment. Just as the man let go of the flail, and reached for the knife at his side, Jack lunged forward and rammed the sharp end of his broken bat at the man's neck.

Luck, it seemed, was with him. The wood splinter burst through the leather around the man's neck and into his throat. Jack pushed hard, but then let go of the bat, his hands jarring with the impact, as he stumbled back and fell to the floor.

He gasped for breath, heard the crowd above the pit roaring with enthusiasm, and watched as his opponent grabbed hold of the bat and stumbled. Blood poured down the man's chest and down his arms.

"We have a winner!" came the bellowing sound of the match's commentator. The crowd above roared.

"Bring him on up!"

But the world around Jack darkened and spun, and he fell forward into the dirt. He was vaguely aware of boots on the ground around him for a moment, but then he passed out.

That had been the first fight, but not his last.

Caught

The darkness of unconsciousness after the fight felt much the same as what Jack now experienced. Except this time, as the world came back in a swirling lack of colour, he wasn't lying on the floor of a cage, but on a metal bed attached to the wall of a chamber even smaller than the cage he had spent most of his time in down in The Pits. But the walls of this new prison were solid, grey metal, and the only light came from a circular disk in the ceiling.

It took him a while to sit up, and he rubbed his forehead, trying to alleviate the throb of the headache that now pounded on the inside of his skull.

How long have you been out? An hour? A day? It could be any amount of time and you wouldn't know.

At least the cage in The Pits had a view of daylight.

There was something else. Something, as he sat there on the bed, looking around at the room that was void of any furniture apart from the bed, that bothered him. His stomach was churning and his head felt light.

Motion, he thought. It's motion sickness. That's what I'm feeling. I'm moving. Or rather, the chamber that I'm in is moving.

A Trans.

That was what the windows had reminded him of.

The picture that he had once found of the strange, amazing construction that had been created by the people of long ago, and used, somehow, to travel great distances. The magazine from bottom of the dumpster in the old factory north of The Crossing and out towards the Ashlands. It had a picture of such a thing, and a long story about something called a Trans. That was what had been next to the booth in the last hall, and what he had seen before they made him sit in the wheeled chair and injected him.

I'm on a Trans.

But where am I going?

Promotion Demotion

Lisa sat looking at the window of the Trans carriage. Outside, a beautiful sunset raged over the forested hills. A deep orange glow, sliced with yellow and red, covered most of the landscape and highlighted the endless sea of spruce trees that covered the land. Except none of those trees were alive and Lisa knew it. Even if the land above had once been covered with trees, it would be difficult to look at them through the window she faced.

The Trans hummed along the track, barely making an audible sound as it swept along. It was nearly two hundred feet underground, rather than up on the surface, and the dazzling view of sunset was actually a screen display to make the enclosure of the carriage less stifling.

Lisa looked away from the screen and back down to the display pad in her hands. There, in bold type, were her new orders and her new assignment. She sighed heavily and closed her eyes for a moment before continuing to read.

The last few hours had been the worst of her career so far. That something could change so quickly, and for a misdemeanour that she considered so small, was beyond her. And yet, she thought back to the meeting that she had been called to attend with the Section Governor, a big, bearded man called Alderton, and she realised that it was only she that thought it minor.

"So, Corporal...Markell. You were reported for removing your faceguard while out on duty. Do you have anything to say on the matter?" the tall man had said, and Lisa could tell that he was not impressed, and that he wouldn't treat the incident lightly. But even so, she hadn't expected it to go as far as it had.

"Your record is exemplary. Top performance, high discipline record. Excellent. Not so high a delivery record in the last couple of months. Hmm...not so good, but that's common at the moment, so we can overlook that."

Alderton hadn't offered her the chance to reply and had merely continued to rattle on.

"We can't ignore the misdemeanour of removing your face guard, though. I have been advised to use the highest discipline in accordance, but I'm not an unreasonable man, and considering your record, I think the best choice will be to reassign you to a new duty. Take you off the recruitment operation. The alternative is to discharge you, and I'm sure neither of us wants that."

And apart from some formalities, that had been it. After two minutes of listening to Alderton, she had been dismissed and told to go and wait in her quarters for her new assignment.

That had been just two hours ago, and her new assignment was waiting for her on the system when she got back to the barracks, with instructions to be packed up and waiting at the Trans terminal in twenty five minutes.

Twenty five minutes. That was all they had given her. And the rest of her squad were out of the barracks and on duty, not to return for at least six more hours. She didn't even get to say goodbye to them. Instead, she had quickly packed her few personal belongings and hurried out of her room, heading to the terminal and arriving with just five minutes to spare.

Guard duties at the NE7 Resource Recycling Facility.

She'd heard of the place before. It was where they sent a huge number of captives after they were sorted into possible abilities at the terminal. In fact, Lisa knew that on the very Trans she was on, there would be fifty or more new workers heading for that very facility.

Resource Recycling Facility. That was a joke. The place was a rubbish dump, far, far out into the Ashlands across the dead waters. It was a place that killed most of the workers sent to work there. There were stories from many years before, from a long time before Lisa was born, that said the NE7 zone was used as a rubbish tip for the city, a place so far away that it wouldn't matter what they dumped there. And yet it was now used as a salvage area, where captured workers would sift through the rubbish to find anything of use.

A promotion, the assignment had been called in her note from Alderton. She was now promoted to First Corporal, and would be in charge of expedition security.

And what the hell was that anyway? Expeditionary? It was a damn demotion is what it was, she thought. Bastard decided to get rid of me, send me out into the far away, into the ashes. And probably only because firing a trooper was not the done thing.

Lisa sighed again and wondered what her parents would think when they found out, or her brothers. Her position and pay were the mainstay of her family's tickets on the next transport off-world. She hoped to hell this wouldn't damage their chances.

Her thoughts were snapped back to the Trans as a light went on at the far end of the carriage, followed by a repetitive buzzing noise that grated at her nerves. She had been alone in the large, spacious compartment for over two hours, for most of the journey, but now the far doors hissed open and two Trans staff stepped swiftly into the room and sat down in the nearest seats.

"All passengers please be seated for deceleration," came a metallic voice from the speakers above her head. The voice echoed somehow, or maybe it was just her imagination. The message repeated a dozen times and then stopped. Then there was a loud sound of rushing air from all around her. Lisa felt her stomach lurching, as though it didn't want to stay where the rest of her was.

The display panel to her left switched off for few seconds, the beautiful forest scene vanishing from view, and Lisa felt a strange pang of regret. But there was no time for her to mourn the loss of a fake scene, for the screen flickered - as did the others in the carriage - and then an image of a very different place appeared, this one very real.

And First Corporal Lisa Markell got her first glimpse of a place that she wished she had never had to visit.

Caught

Jack forced his hands up to the wall, trying to prop himself up as the Trans began to slow down. There had been no warning. One moment he had been sitting in the middle of the room, staring at the blank wall, and the next his stomach had heaved and he slid across the polished floor to bump into the wall. Realising that raising his arms to sit himself up was only going to make him feel worse, he lay flat on the ground and waited for the motion sickness to abate.

Had Ryan laid on the cold metal floor when he travelled here? If he travelled here. That had bothered Jack from the moment he'd watched the huge man being dragged off to the Conversion Facility, to a different place. And then the sorting of people, and the different corridors that led to...wherever they all led. He'd presumed that all captives went to the same place. But the possibility that he would be sent somewhere completely different had become very real.

But maybe he was wrong to think so, maybe Ryan had sat in the very same chamber, wondering where he was going. Jack lifted his hand and traced the outline of a stickman and then a smaller stickman next to it.

All you managed to get the boy for his birthday was a pair of crayons. Sure, they were colours he didn't have, but it wasn't much, was it? Had Ryan sat here and drawn his stickmen on these walls?

It was foolish to think that, of course. He knew that. Whatever reasons the Hunters captured people, they would be different for each person, surely? Grown adults who were healthy would be sent to work somewhere, and the sick would be...well...he didn't know where they would go.

He estimated that it took two minutes for the Trans to stop. Jack had presumed that the other corridor, where the limping man and the old woman had gone, would lead to the place where they dealt with that, but he'd been sent down the same damn corridor as a man sick with Ratter's Plague. As for children, they would surely go somewhere else.

Jack sighed and tried not to dry heave, but his stomach wrenched with spasms as the motion of the slowing Trans reached its most violent. For a moment, he thought that he would actually be sick, or maybe pass out, but then the feeling was gone. The Trans had stopped.

He lay there for a few seconds, his head spinning, before taking a deep breath and sitting up. His stomach growled loudly enough for him to hear it.

How long is it since you ate, anyway? Three days at least. Has to be. The wheat bread you traded for with those nails, wasn't it? Damn that stuff had tasted nasty. And that had to be three days, unless you've been out cold for longer.

And how fast had the Trans been travelling for it to take so long to stop?

Stupidly fast.

Jack sighed, and sat there in the dim light, wondering how long he would have to wait before the door opened and they ushered him off to somewhere else.

Almost as though someone was listening to his thoughts, the door at the other end of the tiny compartment hissed open and a green light flickered on above it. Jack hadn't noticed the tiny panel above the frame of the door and cursed himself for it.

Years ago you would have spotted something like that. But he wasn't given long enough to properly berate himself before a metallic voice spoke from the panel.

"Immediately exit the compartment and turn right."

Jack frowned.

No guards?

He waited a moment, wondering just what would happen if he sat there and ignored the voice.

"Immediately exit the compartment and turn right," repeated the voice, and as Jack watched, one of the other captives shuffled past the doorway. The man looked confused and more than a little dazed.

Pretty much how you feel.

Jack rose to his feet, deciding that he wasn't really so keen on finding out what would happen if he didn't do as the voice said, and then started to walk towards the door. The old man passing by the door glanced at him.

I know him. That's the guy with Ratter's Plague.

Jack stopped, watching the man from the middle of the room. He'd expected to never see the guy again, expected them to cart him off to somewhere, wherever they dealt with nasty diseased people.

Probably a pit.

But then he noticed that the man's skin was no longer

mottled with red pock marks.

Jack frowned, and looked the man in the eyes.

"I'm not sick no more," said the old man, raising his hands to look at them, his expression that of a child seeing something unknown for the first time. Then he touched his chest. "It don't hurt here no more," he said, a grin spreading across his grizzled and scarred face.

"Immediately exit the compartment and turn right," repeated the metallic voice, but this time it continued. "Ten seconds to purge."

Purge? What the hell is purge? That does not sound good.

Jack hurried forward. Ratter's Plague or not, purge sounded a lot worse. He stepped out of the room and stood next to the old man, who although apparently clear of the nasty blotches that came with the disease, still stank like a three-week-dead dog.

The corridor was filled with people now, a few of whom Jack recognised from their brief gathering in the landing area, and as he looked up and down the corridor he saw dozens of open doors spaced a few feet apart.

Then he heard the protests.

"I'm not going anywhere!"

Whoever the man was, he was a few doors up from Jack's compartment, and on the other side of the carriage. In front of the door, a woman stood frowning at the open door.

"Get out of there, you idiot," she said, and gestured to the space in front of her.

"Five seconds to purge," said the metallic voice.

"I said...I'm not going anywhere."

The woman looked around at the other captives, and then back at the door. No one responded, and Jack could see that she was hesitating.

Was she actually considering going in there after the guy? He hoped not.

And she didn't, but she wasn't giving up. "Don't be a fool. Get out of there."

But it was too late.

"Purge commencing," said the metallic voice. And in response, every door along the corridor hissed closed.

"What the hell kinda joke is this anyway?" came the muffled voice of the man now trapped in his compartment.

A second hissing sound filled the corridor, but Jack didn't see any doors opening. What he did see was a thin wisp of smoke, or steam, coming from under the doorway of the room that he had just left.

There was a short, loud scream from the compartment with the man trapped in it, but that was cut off barely half a second later, and then silence. The captives looked round at each other, none of them – including Jack – knowing what to say. All of them terrified.

No kinda joke is what this is.

Light flooded the corridor, and the sound of more doors hissing open, and the metallic voice was speaking again, urging everyone to exit the Trans through the open doors.

A Trans. That's what it was called.

Jack trundled along with the others, not sure if he was

looking forward to being back outside or if he was dreading what he would see there.

This is the place they take them to. This is where it starts. If they brought Ryan here, then this is where you get to begin looking for him.

Jack stepped out of the Trans and headed down a long ramp, his eyes fighting to adjust to the bright glow of daylight, straining to focus on his surroundings. And when he finally did, he wondered if he would have been better off just staying in his compartment and dying like the other fool.

End of the Earth

Lisa stood on the platform, almost oblivious to the crowd of people being ushered from the prison compartments just twenty yards away, and stared, drop jawed, at what was in front of her.

The facility itself was probably a square mile in size, the Trans station rose from the ground, higher up than the rest of the facility by maybe fifty feet, and that elevation was enough to see beyond the outer walls. Because it wasn't the rows of prefab buildings that caught her attention. They were common enough in the work facilities across The City and she had seen enough of those in military camps before, including the camps outside of the barrier wall.

It also wasn't the massive warehouses on the far side of the facility, though she hadn't expected to see anything quite so big out here. She knew she was being posted out in the middle of nowhere, but the Outer Zone was as far as she had ever gone, and the sprawl of ruins outside of the barrier was familiar to her now but this place was something almost alien.

Outside of the perimeter fence, which was a thirty foot high wall with solid concrete towers and barbed wire that looked like it was maybe three separate fences rather than just one, was an endless mass of junk.

An endless mass that went on and on to the very

horizon.

Instead of rolling burned grey hills, like she had seen at the edge of the Ashlands, this landscape was made of trash. Ruined buildings stuck up from the junk here and there, dotting the landscape every few miles like broken teeth inside a rotten mouth, but they were few and scattered randomly.

This was where she had been posted. To watch over mountains of trash.

The histories and rumours that she had heard had been right. It had to have been a dumping ground of some kind, maybe centuries back, but how was there so much of it? This wasn't just a few square miles of junk. No, this was endless miles of it, and most of it looked like it had just been dropped from a great height to fall in piles that now sculpted the hills on the landscape.

As she stood watching, she became aware of movement around her. Troopers were forcefully guiding prisoners from the other compartments near the back of the Trans and pushing them in droves down the slope towards the first building, a hundred yards across the dusty ground.

And then she noticed a single figure nearby, on the edge of the crowd. The man wasn't moving. Instead he stood looking out at the junk landscape with an expression of hopelessness.

And she recognised him.

It was him. The man she had picked up just hours before. The damn fool that had walked up to the back of her truck and spoken to her. The one she had lifted her helmet to reply to, cursing herself to be sent out here in the process.

He was here with her.

Both of them sentenced to live at the end of the Earth.

PART THREE
Recycled

Junk

Six Months Later…

"Avery!" called an impatient voice.

Most of the workers ignored the tall, stocky trooper dressed in grey, ablative armour as he paced across the dirty floor of the warehouse. They were all too busy keeping their heads down and hoping to be ignored, and busy sifting through the massive piles of junk that littered the huge open space, sorting out the recyclable bits from the trash that needed to be thrown away.

And there was a lot of it to wade through. The warehouse was the biggest building in the NE7 Resource Recycling Facility, and easily stood seventy feet high and several hundred feet across in both directions, and it was probably the only original structure that was still standing. If *standing* was what you could call it. Every fifty feet or so a thick stone pillar jutted up from the floor, and they certainly weren't part of the old building, but constructed to stop the rusted and cracked roof from collapsing in on everyone.

The rest of the buildings in the two square mile Recycling Facility were prefabricated, and looked a lot newer, even if they were just as dirty. The original settlement teams had salvaged what they could of the surrounding buildings, but most of them had been smashed into the ground and new prefabs brought in and built on-site. Most of those were enclosed, and some even had air conditioning, but the Goods In building was open to the elements and the polluted air.

The thousands of square metres of cracked concrete ground inside the Goods In building were overflowing with piles of junk delivered from the transport dock at the other end of the building - where the dumpers that made the journey out to the salvager camps each day would deliver whatever they had recovered. There were ten delivery bays and every evening, just as the sun was setting, the trucks would come roaring through the gate, pull up at the back of their designated bay, and unceremoniously drop their contents onto the ground. The next morning, new piles of scrap greeted the weary workers of the sorting crews.

The guard paced around a pile of rubber tires, glared at the worker hauling another tire over to the pile, and called out a second time.

"Avery! Where the hell are you?"

The worker dropped the tire on the pile and pointed down the far end of the warehouse. The trooper glanced in the direction that the worker indicated, seeing only darkness in the corner and piles upon piles of scrap. He frowned, but started over towards the corner. As he rounded a particularly large pile of scrap metal, he spotted a man hunched over what appeared to be a trolley of some kind.

"Avery," he said, the irritation in his voice obvious.

The man stopped what he was doing, turned, and stood

up, scratching his head. The trooper grinned as he noticed the man's expression turn from one of puzzlement to that of nervousness. He could almost smell the fear and he thought that was good.

Let the scum be frightened, the trooper thought. He'll be more frightened soon. Look at him. He's a wretch anyway, covered in dirt and crap like the rest of them.

"You Avery?" asked the trooper, glancing down at the card in his hand that bore the man's name and designation.

Jack nodded. "Yes…yes, sir," he stuttered, wondering what the hell one of the guards wanted with him. He'd learned a lot in the last few months that he had been a worker at the Recycling Facility, and one of the most important things was to remain unnoticed, to just get on with what you had to do, and keep out from under the eyes of the guards. People who drew attention tended to disappear and not re-appear.

"Got your re-assignment card here," said the trooper, holding out the card.

Jack felt a further twinge of fear creep up his back. Re-assignment. That wasn't good. Where he was, in the sorting plant, he was relatively safe. The area was radiation free – well, low radiation anyway – and he was fed and had a place to sleep. It wasn't the easiest of jobs, hauling the scrap that came back from the expeditions each day, it was hard work, and he often went to bed at night exhausted beyond that which a normal man could cope with. But at least he wasn't gradually rotting from poisoning, or out in The Junklands, avoiding a million deadly insects and vermin.

"We have a new vacancy on the north side salvage expeditionary, and lucky you, your number came up."

The guard stepped forward, stuffed the card into Jack's hand, and turned to leave, but he stopped few feet away and turned back, grinning. Jack thought there was zero friendliness in that smile.

"Report to the bay in five minutes. They leave soon, and if you aren't on the truck you can follow them on foot. You'll need to pack down your gear from your bunk and take it with you. No sleeping in the main compound for you anymore. Good luck with the scabs," said the trooper, and then turned and walked away, leaving Jack staring down at a card that he suspected might be a death sentence.

He'd seen the condition of most of the scabs. They were the ones who went out on the trucks each week, the ones whose job it was to search among the mountains of trash and debris outside of the facility, trash that had been dumped there over centuries by not only the protected central city, but the cities and people that lived even before the world started dying. The scabs were tasked with bringing back resources, which meant salvage, and because of that they spent most of their time outside of the facility, out in the wastes where radiation could easily spike up and be unnoticed until, well, until it was too late to do anything about it. They were mostly quite sick individuals, covered in scabs, scars and burns, with their hair and teeth quite often falling out. He been told many times by other workers that when the scabs died, the body would be left out in The Junklands, discarded to rot wherever the poor individual fell, and then someone from elsewhere in the facility would be required to replace them.

No one wanted to be a replacement, but there had been at least twenty replacements made in the six months that Jack had been at the facility, and he was also convinced that

116

some of those who replaced the fallen had also gone on to die of sickness.

He rubbed some of the oil from his hands onto his tatty jeans, glanced at the trolley full of machine parts salvaged the day before, and thought of the drying blood he'd found on one of the parts. It had sharp edges, and looked like some sort of blade for a large machine. Whoever had salvaged it had cut themselves, maybe. Was that the drying blood of his predecessor?

Five minutes was all he had, and he had to go fetch his stuff from his bunk or lose it. He headed across the warehouse, towards the western entrance to the sleeping compound. He could see the guard already exiting the warehouse at the other end and followed.

As he walked across the building, he tried not to take notice of the glances that were cast in his direction by the other workers. He knew they all meant well. They felt sorry for him but were thankful at the same time. If he was going, they were off the hook for maybe one more week before another scab died. He'd felt the same. He tried not to think about it and just kept his head up and walked quickly across the open ground.

Jack squinted in the bright sunlight as he stepped out of Goods In and onto the roadway that led around the perimeter of the facility. Across the dirt track was the compound, and he made his way there, stepping around the deeper puddles.

Two minutes later he stepped back out into the light with his sack over his shoulder. It was every possession he still had, though most of what he'd carried with him when he originally surrendered to the Hunters six months ago had been taken away from him, and he knew he wouldn't see any of it ever again.

Breathing heavily, he took off at a jog towards the expedition building, which was three hundred yards along the dirt track, past the repair centre. Now that would have been the job to get, he thought as he passed the repair centre. The workers in the mechanical department were treated far better than anyone else, and Jack had heard that they even had their own rooms. But, of course, the workers in there, as few of them as there were, were highly skilled, and were able to fix just about any problem with vehicles or machines, and they were also responsible for the upkeep of the entire facility's electric and water, even the air conditioning in the admin building and the troop barracks. Meaning that the troopers and admin needed them.

Scabs, of course, were treated like what they were – dead men walking.

Five minutes, he thought, probably about two now. And if you don't get your ass over there they'll make you walk the road. And that was basically sending you out to die. Everyone knew from talking to the scabs that the trucks travelled ten, twenty or more miles out of the facility each time, and there was no knowing exactly where they were going until the truck stopped. If he didn't make it, and the guards made him go on foot…well, he didn't want to think about it. He picked up pace, jogging along the centre of the roadway, and arrived at the expedition compound just as the garage doors of the truck bays were opening.

Six months before, when Jack had stepped off the train and out into the open air of The Junklands, he'd been horrified at the sight. Even the Outer Zone of the city had looked more inviting than the tall, fume-spewing towers that lined the horizon, the sprawl of dirty buildings, and the lines of workers moving to and fro. It had looked like a slave camp, and effectively that was what it was. One of many slave camps in the Salvage Zone. All of those tall, filth-spitting towers were processing plants of some kind, or power stations, or other machine facilities. Everything that the city didn't want happening near them was out here, manned by armed troopers and worked by kidnapped Outer Zone prisoners. Back in the Outer Zone, no one knew where they took people, and that was because it was thousands of miles away, in a place that no one from the Outer Zone could ever get to, and no one was coming back. Not even when they died.

They're better off not knowing, Jack thought.

Now he ignored all the sights and ignored the fact that the sky was dark and filled with fumes. It wasn't worth the worry. He was alive, at least for now. And he hadn't seen a single sign of Ryan in the six months he'd been at the facility, so maybe that was a good thing. That was what Jack told himself. Maybe being sent out of the place was a good thing.

Jack approached the compound, watching the garage doors open and the trucks being driven out onto the gravel courtyard. A group of four troopers came out of the small office next to the building, and Jack turned and headed in their direction. As Jack got closer, one of them stepped forward and held up his hand.

"Identify yourself," she said, her voice slightly muffled. Unlike the Hunters that had stalked the Outer Zone, the troopers in the Recycling Facility didn't wear full helmets that covered their faces. Instead, they wore breathing masks. This meant that you could see their faces, and even after six months Jack still struggled to get used to it.

"Jack Avery," mumbled Jack. "I've been re-assigned."

The guard lifted her hand to her ear, tapped something on the side of her communicator, spoke a few words, waited, and then stepped towards Jack.

"Arms out straight. I have to check you," she said, waiting for him to comply. Jack did as he was told, and stood there, bemused, as the guard took a small device from her utility belt, switched it on and started to move the gadget over his chest and down his arms. The device bleeped when it reached his waist.

"What is that?" the guard asked.

Jack frowned, and then looked down. "Oh," he said, and then unclipped a small wrench from his belt, holding it out. "Just tools."

"Take it off and dump it in your sack," said the guard.

When he had dropped the belt to the floor the guard nodded at him.

"You got your assignment card?" she asked, her expression impatient. As he stood there, searching his pockets for the card he had been given, he thought for a moment that the trooper was sizing him up somehow.

Jack held out the card, and the woman took it, glanced at it, and then turned to the trooper standing next to her. He was a tall man, easily half a head above Jack, and he had to stoop down to peer at the card. The man read the details, then glanced at Jack, his eyes squinting.

"They take these goddamn photos and then expect us to

recognise these people after months in the dirt," he scoffed. "Yeah, sure, he'll do."

The female trooper grinned behind her breathing mask.

"Go into the compound, through the main doors, then turn left. Find room E2, that's your new assignment group," she said. "There's an empty bunk in there. Dump your stuff and get straight out here. We're leaving in fifteen minutes, and I presume you know what happens if you're not on the truck when we go?"

"A long walk," said Jack, nodding.

"A very long walk," she said, then she saw how he was frowning and must have read his expression. "Your stuff will still be here when you come back," she said. "Now get."

Room E2 was smaller than he had imagined, containing only six sleeping cots, five of which were ruffled and looked slept in. The sixth, right at the back of the room, was stripped of bedding, and even missing a pillow. Jack presumed that this was his, and dumped his sack on the empty frame and glanced around the room. There was a lot more stuff in there than the sleeping compound at the warehouse. Boxes and cases were piled up in corners, all of them shut, and bags of various sizes were stuffed underneath the cots.

These guys get to keep stuff, he thought, and he considered this unusual, considering how little the workers that slept in the main compound were allowed to own.

The room smelt like wet dog and was warmer than Jack expected. There was a window at the far end – furthest from his cot, he noticed – and several air vents in the ceiling, again something more than what he was used to. There was also a large metal box in the middle of the room with what looked like half of a door lying on top of it. The surface of the makeshift table was littered with empty cans and bottles, and a deck of cards that looked well used. Half a dozen crates surrounded the table.

I don't have time for this, he thought, and turned to leave, ignoring his natural instinct to investigate. He was curious about the contents of every box and bag in the room, and wondered why his bunk was completely bare. The dead man, or woman, must have had possessions, surely. They would in the least have had some bedding.

He hurried out of the room, shutting the door behind him, and headed back out into the courtyard where the carriers stood. The engines were humming now, and dozens of scabs were jumping into the backs of the vehicles through the open doors. He glanced around, wondering which of the dozen or so trucks was the one he should be on, and then saw the female trooper standing a few carriers away, beckoning him towards her.

Jack hurried over, moving between the hurried lines of people jumping into the trucks.

"Get in and buckle up," shouted the trooper, her voice barely audible over the roar of engine. Jack heard the slamming of heavy, metal doors as the trucks were closed up, locking in their passengers.

He stepped forward, grabbed the overhead bar just inside the back of the truck, and squinted in the dim light. As he stepped up and into the back of the truck, he heard a creak and a bang as the doors behind him slammed shut. The engine roared even louder, and Jack's heart jumped a beat as he tried to find an empty seat.

"Over here," a voice said, cutting through the noise of the engine, and as Jack's eyes adjusted to the lack of light, he saw five faces looking back at him, and there, just to his left, an empty seat. He stepped forward, turned, and plopped down into the seat just as the truck lurched forward, almost throwing him onto the floor, but he managed to grab hold of the seat as the truck started to move away, his hands searching around him for the safety belt. He thought he could hear laughter from nearby, but ignored it.

"The buckle's near your head, you eejit," said a voice, this one different from the first. Jack reached up and found the belt, and feeling a little stupid, he pulled it down and snapped it into place.

Then he breathed a sigh of relief.

"Well," said a voice next to him. "Talk about a dramatic entrance."

There was more laughter, this time from multiple directions.

"You certainly cut that a bit fine," said another voice, this one right next to him. It was deeper than the other voices.

Jack looked around, and found that his eyes had begun to adjust to the light. There were no windows in the compartment, just a trio of dim, blue lights at the front, and they cast a cold light across the faces that he now saw watching him from the darkness.

Sitting to his right was a very large man, with dark skin and long, dirty, plaited hair that Jack recalled were called dreadlocks. He wasn't sure where he had heard the term, maybe it was something Drogan had said. The man had a burn scar across one side of his face, and Jack could see that one eye was covered with a small patch made of some kind of plastic.

Directly across from Jack was a much older, frailer man, who Jack thought wouldn't have even been as tall as his own shoulders. The man also had long hair, but his was grey, almost white in places, and he had a beard that almost reached his waist. The man was grinning at him, and Jack could see that he had just four teeth, two on top, and two on the bottom, and the humour in that grin made Jack smile.

There were three others in the back of the truck. A heavy-set of about Jack's age, or so he thought, who wore a furry hat with long flaps that covered his ears and looked as though it was meant for winter rather than the heat of the Salvage Zone. Another man was entirely bald, with piercing grey eyes and thin, almost chiselled features, and lastly, a man with the strangest face that Jack had ever seen. Everything about the man was disproportioned in so many ways. One of his eyes seemed larger than the other, his bent and crooked nose sat too low down on his face, and his chin appeared to be wider than his forehead.

"So, what's your name?" asked the dark skinned man with the dreadlocks.

Jack was quiet for a moment, still considering his new companions, and presuming that these were the men that he would be sharing a room with.

"I'm Jack," he said.

The dreadlocked man nodded, and smiled. "I'm Tyler,"

he said. "This fellow over from you is Higgins, the oldest damn scab alive." At that several of the men laughed.

"Old as the junk around us," said the man wearing the winter hat.

"You can laugh," said the bearded old man, "But I'll be here when you're all gone, and who will be laughing when I get divvies on your gear?"

That brought even more laughter.

"Fellow over there," Tyler indicated the man with the winter hat, "is Locks, and not because he has fine hair."

"Nothing wrong with my hair," said Locks.

"Apart from you ain't got much of it under that damn hat," said Higgins. The old man started to chuckle to himself.

"That over there is Rick," Tyler said, indicating the gaunt, hairless man at the far end of the cabin. "He's our watchman. And, lastly, that's Boots over here. And don't mind that he looks like he's been smacked around more times than a pit fighter."

"Meet ya," said Boots, twitching his head to one side several times then, almost immediately, his head fell forward and he fell fast asleep.

"He does that a lot," said Tyler, sighing loudly. "Damage to the brain. So. Seems like you'll be joining our little band of freaks. At least for a while."

Jack frowned. "A while?"

Tyler laughed. "Well, we'll see if you can last it out salvaging. Not everyone can."

Jack was silent for a moment, while he tried to take it all

in.

"What happens to those who don't?"

Tyler's cheerful expression turned cold, the smile gone in an instant. "They become a vacancy," he said, then the grin was back, and he burst into laughter.

Jack sighed, feeling a little out of his depth among these new people. He had not been outside of the facility in the entire six months since he stepped from the transport, and had no idea what to expect. All he had seen so far was the rolling hills of junk and the smog-producing towers in the distance. Now he was in the back of a truck with five strangers, heading out of the facility and miles into The Junklands.

He looked around at the other men.

Strangers.

Strange was certainly the key here.

A View from the Top

A Week Before

First Corporal Lisa Markell blinked in the bright sunlight and looked back through the viewfinder. From the platform on top of the armoured carrier, perched high upon a mound of debris and junk, she could see for miles. Not that it gave her much of an advantage.

She could see even more trash, and that was about it. Endless huge piles of the damn stuff, stretching out into the distance.

It still amazed her, nearly six months after arriving in the Salvage Zone, just how much trash had been dumped out there. Centuries of the stuff, most of it broken machinery, the remains of torn down buildings. A lot of it was rusted metal, dumped there by the civilised world back when there was one. Now that world was long gone and the production of new resources was at a historical low. The Inner Zone officials had decided that it was time to salvage what mankind had scrapped. She'd been told all about the Salvage Zone, and how that entire area of the world had been sectioned off many centuries ago and used as a dumping ground. She had nearly nodded off in the briefing.

She knew that the ark ships, which launched once a year, sending tens of thousands of new resettlers on their fifty year cryo journey to New Earth, needed mountains of metal to construct, and so here she was, overseeing the salvaging operations that made it possible.

Dotted across the landscape were more armoured vehicles, just like the one she now commanded this particular expedition from, and as she watched, one of the vehicles stopped, unloaded its crew of troopers, and then sat waiting for them to return.

Scans, scans and more scans, she thought. The flyby scan had covered an area nearly ten miles across, and had come up with no life signs, but she knew that meant there could still be some. So they had to do it again on the ground, in person, just to make sure. The Junkers were out there somewhere, probably even watching her right now from within their hidden nests, and she had to do whatever was necessary to secure the area before the salvagers arrived.

About a quarter mile away, Lisa spotted a vehicle with its hatch still down, even though the troops had been dropped minutes before. She squinted and frowned, wondering why the hatch wasn't shut.

"A3, this is Markel, what is your status? Over."

There was a moment of silence as she waited. And then just as she was about to ask again, a voice replied.

"This is A3. We have a mechanical problem with the door hydraulics. Over."

"Received, A3. Is the rest of the vehicle functional? Over."

"Yes, ma'am. All other functions nominal. Over."

"Okay then, just keep an eye on your entrance, A3. I don't want any unwelcome visitors. As soon as you are all hands on-board, get back to the service truck and get that sorted out. Over."

"Affirmative, ma'am. We have two of the squad in the back of the truck keeping watch. Over."

"Acknowledged, A3. Keep it tight. Out."

Damn inferior machinery, she thought. It had been something she'd noticed almost within a minute of stepping off the Trans into the Recycling Facility. The equipment sent to them from the Inner Zone was almost always the most decrepit, the cast off trash that had most likely been replaced with something shiny and new. And the vehicles weren't even the same reinforced armoured craft that they used on the Outer Zone raids. No, these things were Inner Zone standard, and would be unlikely to withstand a hit from an automatic weapon without the crew inside being peppered.

Thankfully the only ones with automatic weapons of any kind around here were her people.

Lisa turned to Reece, her second in command, who was standing just a few feet away, staring out at the vast expanse behind them.

"Are we secure?" she asked.

Reece nodded. "Yes, ma'am," he said. "We had some movement a few miles out, which was picked up by the drone, but whatever it was scattered soon after. Thermal scanning hasn't picked anything up."

Lisa nodded and looked back out at the vehicle with the faulty door mechanism. The troopers were back, and getting into the vehicle. A few seconds later the last trooper jumped on board and the door swung clumsily before slamming shut.

"Good," she said. "Let's get the hauler in and clear a staging area. We've got a dozen cans of salvagers due in about four hours and I want this ready."

"Yes, ma'am," said Reece.

"And get that APV with the crappy door booked in with the maintenance crew."

"Yes, ma'am," said Reece.

Lisa turned to head towards the hatch in the middle of the platform, but stopped. "Where are we next, anyway?"

"Ahhh...let me check." Reece took a hand-held, touchscreen device from his utility belt, turned it away from the bright glare of the sun, and tapped it a couple of times.

"Facility reclamation mission," he said. "The Picking Factory that was raided by Junkers about ten months ago, over near the blast crater."

Lisa looked relieved. "Nice. We might actually get some activity for once."

Junk

As far out as you can go.

Jack sneezed as the cloud of dust hit him in the face. He squinted, straining against the bright glare of the sun, as he jumped down from the back of the transport vehicle. Even though he was near the back, he was the last one out, after struggling with his safety belt for more than half a minute. As he'd tugged, and tried to reach for the clip, the others filed past and jumped out into the bright sunlight.

Now he found himself standing on dry, dusty ground in a large clearing, maybe two hundred yards across. Where the clearing ended, the flat dry ground finished abruptly at a wall of junk. All around them, piled tens of feet high in some places, was a mass of trash. Most of it was rubble from broken buildings and large sheets of rusty metal, but as his eyes adjusted to the glare of the sun, even from fifty yards away Jack could see all manner of other things. Rotten wood, decomposing paper and magazines, machinery parts, torn metal structures, and animal bones.

At one section of the junk it looked like whatever cleared the area – probably a digger of some kind, Jack thought - had torn the trash pile away to reveal an open cavity under a huge pile of trash. Inside the cavity were the rusty remains of an old refrigerator, some smashed up cupboards, and what appeared to be a sleeping cot.

131

Someone had actually lived there. Hidden right underneath the junk. It must have been a long time ago, had to be. Everything looked so old.

Next to him, the armoured carrier shuddered for a moment and then fell silent as the engines switched off. But the surrounding noise was no less deafening, as no sooner had the vehicle's engine stopped roaring, than a second, much larger vehicle appeared through the roadway carved into the trash. It was a dumper truck, or so Jack thought. It looked like one of the ones used to deliver salvage to the facility, though as it pulled into the middle of the clearing, Jack realised that he had never seen one this close up. The dumpers usually tipped their finds onto the moving platforms outside of the Goods In warehouse, some two hundred yards away from where he worked, and the larger pieces would be sorted and removed before anything even reached the sorting hall.

"Daunting, isn't it?" asked a voice nearby. Jack turned to see Tyler standing just a few feet away. He had tied back his mass of dreadlocks so that they hung down his back through a hole in his jacket, and he'd also pulled a hood over his head. "We have to fill that thing before the end of each day," he said.

Jack looked at the massive dumper, with its huge open - and very empty - back. You could fit the armoured vehicle that they had travelled inside, probably twice, he thought.

"Don't worry," said Tyler, moving to stand next to him. "It'll fill up quicker than you think."

"I don't see how," said Jack.

Tyler laughed and pointed at the back of the armoured carrier. He hadn't noticed the large contraption hooked onto the side of the carrier. "We got a digger," he said. "Boots drives it and drops the heavier stuff in there, while we sift through the crap, looking for the good stuff."

They stood watching Boots and Rick unstrap the one-man digger from the carrier vehicle. As the digger hit the dirt, Jack wondered if Boots would even fit into the thing. It didn't look much bigger than a small car, and it certainly didn't look like it would be able to haul much weight. But Boots squeezed into the tiny compartment at the centre the digger, and Jack heard some clicking sounds followed by the whir of a small engine, and the thing sprang to life. It was compacted for travel, thought Jack, as the contraption seemed to unfold, changing from a strange upright column into something almost spider-like.

"We'll be out here for about a week," said Tyler. "That's how long we usually stay in one spot before being given a half day out, back at the facility, and then off to the next location."

"A week?" asked Jack. "We stay out here for that long?"

He'd thought that the expedition groups came back every night, but now he thought of the four hour journey to get to this place and realised that there would be no time to work if they spent most of it travelling.

"But where do we sleep?" he asked.

"In the carrier," said Higgins, appearing next to them. He had two rucksacks thrown over his shoulders, and dropped one of them at Jack's feet.

"That's some basic gear for ya," he said. "Mostly left over by Brody…erm… Your predecessor."

Jack looked down at the rucksack lying in the dirt.

"Thanks," he said.

"It ain't much," said Higgins. "We could have kept it all, you know. It's traditional for the dead's gear to get shared out, but we dint need what's in there so you can have it."

"You'll pick up gear along the way," said Tyler. "And anything that the facility don't need that you find out here is your dibs first."

Jack frowned. "We get to keep stuff? I mean, they let us keep things?"

Higgins laughed, almost coughing with the effort. "No, of course they don't let you keep stuff, not if it's useful to them, anyway. But if we don't put it in the back of the dumper, they don't ever knows about it, get it?"

Tyler picked up the rucksack and handed it to Jack.

"What Higgins is saying, is what they don't know about, they don't want. And out here, it's just us."

Jack looked at the digger, and then the carrier.

"But the drivers of the vehicles, surely they see if you take stuff?"

Tyler grinned. "What drivers?"

Jack frowned again.

"Ah," said Tyler. "I get it. Come on," he said. "Come look at this."

Tyler made his way around to the front of the carrier vehicle, and Jack, confused, hurried behind him, trying to fit his new rucksack over his shoulders.

No wonder none of them wants this damn thing. The straps are both ripped.

"There," said Tyler, pointing at the cab of the carrier. "You see the door?"

Jack looked at the side of the cab, and then tried to peer over the top.

"No," he said.

"No, indeed," said Tyler. "That's because there isn't one."

Jack walked around the front of the carrier, peering at the far side, but found it just the same. A sheer metal wall that ended at the front screen. The screen itself was opaque, but Jack had thought they were just designed that way to block visibility of the driver and the rest of the cab crew from the outside.

"It's automated," said Tyler. "They all are." He pointed at the dumper truck. "They can get at them from underneath, to maintain them, but there's no person in there, or even room for one, from what I've heard. It also means no one can steal the damn thing, on account of there being no controls for a human to use."

"You mean that there are no facility staff with us?" asked Jack. "Just us? We're the only ones out here?"

Tyler nodded. "Exactly," he said. "They remote pilot them, or pre-program them, or something. The carrier will remain right there for five days, and then it just goes back, on its own, after the alarm sounds. And it goes with or without us in it. And the dumper goes back every day and comes back before morning, empty."

"Not even guards?"

"Yes, there are guards, but they stay at a central camp about half a mile away from here. That's how they do it.

They set up in an area, then they carve out a hole for each of the crews. Now, you see that beacon on top of the carrier? If that starts making one God-almighty noise, you run like hell and get in the back of the carrier, because it seals shut after a couple of minutes whether you're in there or not."

"And what does that mean?"

"It means that something uninvited has moved into our sector."

"Like a creature?"

"Like predators, sure, sometimes. Plenty of those out here, but the radar doesn't look for them and they mostly leave us alone. See, the predators learn faster than people. Usually the siren means that Junkers just got picked up on the radar."

"I see," said Jack. "So, what happens if someone wants to just run off?"

Tyler smiled. "Yeah, sure. We've all thought about it, at one time or another, until we find what's left of someone who did run off."

"Oh. People do, then?"

"Sometimes," said Tyler. "Even had a guy with us about five years ago, ran with us for six months. Before Rick joined us, this guy was part of my crew. Then he decided to make a run for it and took off into the trash. Didn't even bother that we were all watching as he went. Course, he also didn't try to take any gear with him, or we would have stopped him."

"And what happened to him?"

"We found him about three months later, when we

cycled back round to the same spot, after Rick had taken his place. Higgins dug him up while we were salvaging. Found him trapped under a pile of crap with both his legs chewed off. He'd got about two hundred yards."

"Damn."

"Oh, yeah. Damn all right. That wasn't the only thing eaten. He had no hands and no face. The only way we identified him was his tags. Thought it was a dead Junker until Rick spotted the chain still hanging from his neck. Well, what was left of his neck."

Jack shuddered, and involuntarily reached into his shirt to touch the dog tags that hung there.

"You see, out here," continued Tyler. "You either have the bugs, or you have the Junkers. Both of which will kill you. And no food. Nothing grows out here, it's all lifeless and poisoned. We find bodies every now and then, among the junk. I'm guessing some of them are escapees, but who knows."

Jack nodded, his mind still stuck on an image of a body with no legs sticking out of the junk.

Tyler shrugged. "What I'm saying is. You wanna run for it, no one is going to stop you, but don't expect to take anything with you. We don't waste good gear here."

"I wasn't planning to run," said Jack, but wondered if he really was considering it. Six months was a long time to find no trace of Ryan, and he'd looked everywhere he could at the Facility. Maybe out here, he could search, but where would he even begin?

You have to start somewhere, though. Don't you? But dead isn't a start.

"Anyways, as I was saying," said Tyler. "If you hear the siren you run back to the carrier, and don't stop for nothing."

"And then?" asked Jack.

Tyler frowned "Hmm?"

"Then what happens?" asked Jack.

"Nothing. We just wait in the carrier until the drone or the troops arrive to remove the problem. Or until it just goes away."

"What if you're not inside the carrier when they get here?"

Tyler's expression turned from amused to grim.

"Then you become a vacancy."

You Again

Lisa Markell wiped the sweat from her face and stared up at the mass of twisted metal in front of her. The huge Drover vehicle had arrived just an hour before, trundling along slowly, as they always did after being left behind to catch up. By the time it had arrived, the salvage groups had already left for their individual areas and the camp had gone into overwatch.

"Can it be repaired in the field?" she asked, looking at the aged mechanic standing just a few feet away, and then at the young trooper standing next to her. Hailey Simmons had been assigned to her expedition just a few weeks before, and Lisa hadn't liked her at first but the young trooper's can-do attitude soon stopped being irritating, and now Lisa kept her at her side constantly. The girl got things done, or brought things to Lisa's attention much sooner than they otherwise would have been.

Take this drover, Lisa thought. The driver would have dumped this in the parking ground and walked away, leaving it for what? A day? Two days? Probably three days from now, when I'd want the damn thing hauling along the old roadway and clearing it for us, and we would have been delayed for repairs. Now we get the problem sorted before it's needed.

"Ah, maybe. Yeah," said the mechanic, rubbing his stubbled chin and looking at the debris jammed into the Drovers cutter. Drovers were originally designed for cutting tunnels in the earth, or even in rock, but they weren't the most robust of contraptions, and when one became no longer of use to the mining sector, they were turned into road clearance trucks, and sent out to make long gouges in the hills and mountains of junk out in the Salvage Zone.

"Maybe?" asked Lisa. "Really?"

"No problem," continued the mechanic, now looking flustered. "I can just cut that out and then we can get in to free the mechanism. Maybe a day?"

Lisa smiled. "Good. Very good. See to it, then. I need this three days from now, to clear a road to an abandoned facility we need to access."

She turned and headed back to the main control centre, a large construction built from a dozen large trucks that could just park next to each other, lower their sides and become one enclosed building. She was relieved to step out of the blistering heat and back into air conditioned rooms. She headed for the control room, right at the heart of the building, and sat down at her desk.

"Did we manage to re-fill all the group vacancies before we left?" she asked, not even looking round to see if Hailey was with her. Lisa knew she would be.

"Yes, ma'am," said Hailey. "I saw to it myself, as you asked. I picked out some healthy candidates and wrote out the cards last week. It took them a while to process, but we got the replacements just as we were leaving for this trip."

Lisa looked out across the control room, which she

always thought was surprisingly large considering it only took up the compartments in three of the trucks. A few yards away was a bank of two dozen LCD monitors, watched by two troopers, all showing different views of the various areas currently being worked by the salvage crews in her expedition group.

"Did you want to review the new replacements?" asked Hailey. "I have them right here."

Lisa was about to say no, but then chuckled quietly. The new recruit was certainly keen to please, she thought, and after how much of a relief she was proving to be, Lisa thought she should at least show interest in the girl's work.

"Sure," she said. "Throw them over here." Then she turned back to the screens again. The screen at the top right corner was flickering, and that would annoy her very quickly.

Lisa took the thin pile of cards that Hailey handed her. There were a dozen. Had she really lost that many scabs in the last few months? It was hard to tell. There were more than enough accidents out there and, of course, the occasional escapee. It couldn't be helped. But a dozen? That seemed a little high.

She flicked through the cards, checking that the current health status of each individual was marked over ninety out of a possible hundred. Healthy ones, well done again, Hailey, she thought.

It wasn't until Lisa flicked to the second to last card that she stopped and actually paid some attention to the details. Something had triggered a thought, or a recognition, and it was something on the card before, just as she looked at the last one. Lisa flipped the last card back to the top of the pile and peered at it, curious. What was it about that card that brought back a memory? For a moment she sat there, brow furrowed, just staring at the card, trying to spot what it was about it, or about the individual whose tiny photo stared back at her, that reminded her of something.

The name. Jack Avery. That wasn't familiar, or was it? She'd heard it before. But why was it so important?

Then she recognised the face. It looked cleaner, less pale, and was shaved, but there was the scar above the eyes, just as she remembered.

Well, well. So that's what happened to you, she thought.

"Is everything okay?" asked Hailey.

"Yes," said Lisa. "Fine. Absolutely fine." She handed the cards back to the young recruit. "Good choices, there."

Hailey smiled, and inside Lisa also grinned. The girl was genuinely pleased to be helpful, but that wasn't what made Lisa smile. Jack Avery, the man who had asked who she was, who they were, the man who had given himself up – a thing that no one ever did – and had caused her to remove her visor to speak to him – causing her to be demoted out into this dirty outback – was under her command.

He was one of her salvagers.

I never got answers, Lisa thought. But now I will have them.

Junk

Not Alone.

Jack stepped back from the wall of junk and took a deep breath. If it weren't for the hood that he'd managed to fashion the night before, from a scrap of dirty cloth that he found in among the trash, he'd have been even hotter. The first day had been fine for about an hour, and then the heat had started to get the better of him.

That was why they all wore hoods, he told himself that evening as he sat in his seat in the back of the carrier, his face and neck red and his head throbbing.

Not one of the other members of the crew had mentioned anything to him, but they were watching him that night as they sat around eating, talking and playing cards on a crate that they hauled out from behind one of the seats.

A rite of passage, maybe? That could be it. That they would put him at risk of heat exhaustion annoyed him a little, but he couldn't deny that these men owed him nothing, and the junk that was in the rucksack – a few spare items of clothing, a utility belt with a bunch of empty pouches on it, a crude knife and fork – they hadn't been obliged to give him them, even if they were what remained of his predecessor's gear.

It didn't matter. He'd fixed it that first night and hadn't said a word to any of them about it, and the following few days had rolled by, hard as the work was, with relative ease. Jack even thought that he caught Tyler smiling to himself when Jack stepped out into the relentless heat the next morning with a hood over his head. It wasn't great, and didn't really keep any of the heat away, but it stopped the sun from burning his already sore scalp.

Now, on the fifth day, after filling the damn dumper truck four times already, he was starting to get past the tiredness that followed in the evening, and even the aches and stiffness in the morning.

And he'd found the entire crew something rare that very morning, only twenty minutes into the start of the day. It was at the back of the caved in dwelling that had been uncovered when they had first arrived. That had been the first spot that the crew descended on the minute they started work, obviously spotting the potential that the ancient and abandoned abode could hide, and now, having found the old box behind the wall, he understood why.

He'd followed the rest of the crew over, climbed the ten or so feet up into the open cavity, and joined them in their search, but Tyler was cursing their luck within a few minutes and claiming that the makeshift home had been abandoned decades ago. Jack had picked up the half-torn and rotten remains of an old magazine that lay in the corner of the dwelling, but the pages were stuck together and most of the paper started to crumble away the second he picked it up.

"The new guy can have this spot," Tyler had mumbled, and Jack had taken his cue from that as the crew left the cavity one by one and took up positions around the clearing.

He'd stood there after they'd left, just looking at the strange cavern that had been carved into the junk, and marvelled at how long the piles of trash had been just sitting there. Centuries. And whoever lived in this dwelling twenty, thirty or even a hundred years ago, had meticulously removed and reinforced the outer walls of the cocoon inside the trash. There was no entrance, and Jack presumed that any way in or out must have been in the section of the hideaway that the diggers had already cleared. Along the walls, scrap metal had been almost woven together and reinforced with plastic covered cables and wires. The floor was constructed from sheets of metal hammered flat – probably car or machine body parts – and then, he presumed, covered in scrap cloth and pieces of carpet. The floor was covered in a mashup of something that must have been cloth or carpet but now, after all this time, it had rotted away into a brown, furry mush.

He moved away, climbing back out of the cavity and down onto the dirt ground below, and looked up at the wall of junk that was now his prospect area.

And he realised he didn't really have much of a clue what he was doing.

I can find stuff, he'd thought. Sure. I can find value junk inside this mountain of crap, but what am I looking for? Well, if what got delivered to the sorting area that had had previously worked in was anything to go by, metal and electronics were the thing. So that was where he started, hoping that they didn't send something more valuable that he didn't know about elsewhere.

Two entire days he'd ploughed through the masses of junk, avoiding broken masonry and larger chunks of rubble, relentlessly looking for things made of metal and anything that looked like electronic circuitry. That was their job, it seemed, to crawl among the debris and haul out anything made of metal that could be recycled. It was mindless, and Jack couldn't help but wonder why the hell the city didn't just send out huge automated diggers to haul the stuff away. Surely that would have been more efficient? A half a dozen men, picking away by hand, seemed a slow way to achieve what a digger could do in minutes.

On the third day, Jack had to fling himself away from the edge of the junk as the cavity, and what remained of the uncovered dwelling, collapsed. He'd been picking away at the junk wall in the area surrounding the cavernous hole all that time, pulling bits out, discarding some and keeping others, and gradually the wall had weakened. The cloud of arid dust that spewed out nearly filled the entire clearing, and as he stood up and patted himself down, he heard curses.

But then as the dust began to settle he spotted the box, now newly uncovered where it had been hidden underneath the floor near the back wall of the dwelling for whoever knew how long.

But he'd somehow known it was there. He'd sensed it, like he used to sense lost or concealed things in the ruins of the Outer Zone. He'd felt it from the moment he first saw the dark and open maw of the dwelling. There was something secret in that old place, a precious thing that someone had tucked away and covered over and not wanted anyone to ever find. Even after they were long dead.

He looked around, checking that none of the other crew members had seen it, but the dust still hadn't cleared further across the open ground away from where he stood, and he knew that the nearest to him was Higgins, at least fifty feet away. He hauled the box out from the trash that had compacted underneath the hidden dwelling, looked for a catch of some kind, found it already broken, and slowly, cautiously, lifted the lid.

There was a faint hiss, followed by a musty smell wafting out of the box, and Jack cringed and moved back a short distance, wondering what could make such a stink, but then he peered in, and instead of some nasty, rotten thing in the bottom of the box, Jack spotted a pile of small boxes, each wrapped in a clear plastic jacket and measuring about four inches across.

Cigarettes.

There were twenty packets in all, and they were old, very old.

The box must have been sealed somehow. There was no way that something like that could last that long. How long had it been since cigarettes were made? Hundreds of years? It had to be at least that. He'd heard stories of how, even long after the fall of the old world, a new industrial age had come about in the century before last, and things like cigarettes, canned food, and all manner of more basic goods had started being made again. He'd also heard how that had collapsed because of war. The cigarettes had to have been made then, because for them to come from the old world, well. Did anyone even know how many centuries ago that was? They certainly never came out of the Inner Zone if they were made there. Somehow, he suspected that such things wouldn't be high on the list of things to make for the people inside the barrier-protected city.

And so, that evening, the carrier was filled with smoke, and Jack found himself the lucky owner of a new shirt, a pair of worn but usable gloves, a tin of actual fruit of some kind, a plastic flask that could attach to his utility belt, a tough belt that he could cut up and repair his rucksack with, and even better, a pillow. He guessed that the things were mostly owned by his predecessor, and that it wasn't really much of a loss for the crew members to trade them for a share in the find, but he was happy anyway, sitting there, smoking his first cigarette for months and playing a game of cards.

They'd all heard the noise and fallen silent. Boots was the last to stop laughing, and looked puzzled until he heard the shuffling noises of movement on the ground outside.

Jack frowned, but didn't speak. He looked at Tyler, whose expression had turned serious. Tyler put his finger to his lips to indicate *be quiet*, and then sat there, listening. The inside of the carrier went silent.

There were more crunches of trodden stones from outside the carrier.

Jack looked at Tyler again, and mouthed the words *can it get inside?* But Tyler shook his head.

Jack sat in silence. Listening. Thinking.

Some kind of wildlife. Had to be. But what could live out in this waste? People probably do, though, don't they? Of course they do. Junkers. The ones that they all keep talking about. Mutants. Unclean things. Bugs.

There are a lot of things living out here, you just haven't

seen any of them, Jack. That's what Tyler already told you. But they probably wouldn't come near, probably learned from that mistake a long time ago. So what hadn't learned? Something was out there, and whatever that thing was didn't fear the carrier or the people inside it.

There was a banging sound above them, and a thud, thud, as something walked across the roof of the carrier. The sound moved above them, over Jack, then Tyler, then arrived at the top hatch, a thing that Jack had never noticed before. He hadn't even known that there was a top hatch on the carrier.

Another banging sound, and then a groan.

Was that groan made by the thing on the roof? Or was it a noise of something being moved? It sounded metallic, like a rusty box being forced open.

He couldn't know, and decided he didn't want to know.

Then the crunching sound of movement came back, and began to drift away. Whatever it was, it had decided to move on.

It probably wouldn't come back, Jack thought. He hoped it wouldn't. But he didn't sleep very well that night.

Unfortunate

Six Months Before…

An overweight weasel.

That was what the man sitting at the desk in front of Lisa Markell reminded her of. She'd seen pictures in books when she was a kid, dozens and dozens of species of creatures that no one had seen for centuries, presumed extinct, and she remembered the funny picture, and had thought that even the name of the creature was comical. A weasel. And this man looked like an over-fed one at that.

Governor Jackson was, even by standards in the city, an overweight man, and he had a nose that defied gravity. Lisa could never like him. She had decided that the moment the man began to speak to her as she stood across the desk from him, her travel bag still slung over her left shoulder and her assault rifle over the other.

"So you will replace the expedition controller - a Corporal Ranold - who we lost in that…unfortunate incident."

"Why were they all the way out there in the first place?" she'd asked. She hadn't meant to pry, not really, but sending three squads over twenty miles out of the scanable perimeter to the ruins of a town that hadn't been visited for centuries, with little backup, seemed like a frivolous waste to her. Of course, she immediately recognised that Jackson had been the one that made the decision, just by the new flush to his cheeks, and she knew she would regret it, at some point.

"I...err..." stuttered the Governor. "We needed to investigate the area. We're opening up new spots for salvage, and that seemed to be a good place to start."

But you ignored protocol, and failed to make sure that backup teams and supply lines were already in place, she thought, but didn't mention it. She'd already over-stepped.

"But that is irrelevant," continued Jackson, with an irritated glance in her direction. "It was an unfortunate occurrence."

Thirty-six troopers, three entire squads, nine fire-teams, lost. And he considers it unfortunate. No, she would never like him, and was somehow glad that her assignment meant that she would spend the vast majority of her time nowhere near the foul man and his damned facility.

Abandoned

As she sat in the back of the armoured carrier, just a few hundred yards from the Picking Factory that they were to clear and reclaim, she wondered how many other unfortunate occurrences had happened because of Weasel's orders. It was easy enough for him, sitting there in his air-conditioned building, barely ever having to step outside into the smog and pollution of the world outside, to spend lives. He never had to see the reality of it.

She wondered if the loss of the Picking Factory was something he considered a small loss, something else unfortunate. Two hundred women and children had been there, and yet the place had been guarded by just one squad of troopers. She'd wanted to read that report again, just to remind herself what she was going into, but had thrown it aside in disgust.

Not a single person left behind. That was what the report spelled out. Two hundred women and children, and a single squad of troopers. All taken by the Junkers. It just didn't make any sense to her that they should be out there in the first place, let alone so lightly guarded.

Well, if she saw a Junker today, she was going to make sure that at least that one paid the price.

"Perimeter breach in ten," came the voice of the squad leader in the vehicle at the front of the convoy.

This is it, she thought. My first actual activity in six months. She glanced around at the seven other troopers seated in the back of the APV, and her gaze paused when she reached Hailey, now kitted out in combat armour rather than her usual light armour. She imagined that the girl would look nervous if she could see her face, but they were heading into a potentially volatile area and were now wearing full Hunter armour.

It was a necessity, and Lisa was relieved that at least her troopers had that much. From what she had seen of the other supplies and equipment given to the border expeditions, the Hunter armour was a luxury.

Then the back doors were springing open, and she was the first out, power-assisted boots hitting the floor and propelling her forward as she skirted around the side of the vehicle and took up position at the very front. The carriers had swerved left upon entering the grounds of the factory, as she had ordered in the briefing earlier that day, and now they were lined up, all four vehicles in a row, just a few yards from the perimeter wall but facing the main building.

Lisa reached to the side of her helmet and switched on her zoom scanner as the rest of her squad swarmed around her to take their positions.

The facility was much larger than she had imagined, even when looking at the rough schematics that she had been sent. Eight large factory hangar buildings rose out of the dirt at least sixty feet high, and they were surrounded by old brick buildings, of various sizes, dotted around the outside of the yard.

We could have landed a dropship inside this place, she thought, looking at the vast open space to the east of the warehouse buildings, but then shrugged that idea off. She knew that the city didn't send dropships this far out. A thousand miles was much too far for them to send one of those precious flyers, and the fuel alone would make it prohibitive.

She scanned the nearest of the factories, searching for heat signatures and knowing that she would find none. It was nearly impossible, with the distortion of heat from the sun.

No easy way, she thought. A night raid and we'd see anything lit up like a candle, but with all this debris it would be deadly.

"Forward," she said into her microphone, and waited.

Five seconds later and the carriers turned and began to slowly crawl across the yard ahead of the Hunter squads. A hundred yards away and they would reach the nearest building, and she would go in there first, herself, leading her team.

And yet she knew, somehow, that this facility would be empty, completely void of life. And she also knew that she wouldn't like being the first to discover what had been left behind.

The report said that a scout drone had scanned the facility after the raid. They hadn't even sent a manned operation to go and look. Any unpleasant surprises were still there, waiting for her.

Junk

Jack lay on his new bunk in the E2 room trying to get to sleep, but the noise all around him was distracting.

They'd finally finished their five-day stint out in The Junklands, and he couldn't believe how relieved he felt when the carrier halted and the back doors opened up, spilling in sunlight from outside and the familiar waft of dry air.

They were back at the facility.

He had jumped up, hauling his stuff with him, and squinted in the bright sunlight. He'd been five days in the sun, but just a couple of hours in the back of the windowless carrier, with its low light, were enough to make his eyes start to adjust to the darkness.

They had made a good haul, Tyler had said, and he patted Jack on the back as they trudged to their room – to his new room. The tall man was smiling and nodding at Jack now, and Jack took it that he was pleased with his new team member.

Why? Well, after the third day, Jack's unnatural ability to find what was hidden started to work its way to the surface once more. After discovering the stash under the ruined dwelling, he'd gone on to find several other spots, some not even near his working area, and he uncovered piles of circuitry, some old machinery that looked like it could be rebuilt, and even an old vehicle of some kind, that Jack had never seen before. A tractor, Tyler had said. A whole damn tractor, with the wheels still on it. That thing had nearly filled the dumpster that day, after an hour of Boots struggling with its weight, and after the crew piled a heap of scrap metal into the gaps around the dumpster it was full. All before the sun had even reached its zenith.

And so it went on until the last day. A lot of the time the crew would have to spend hours digging through broken bricks and trash, just to find recyclable metal, but each day Jack managed to cut their working time short by an hour or so, just by knowing where something was hidden.

But now he lay on the bunk, trying to sleep, his head firmly on his new – if somewhat dirty – pillow, and he couldn't drift off. His mind was swirling.

It's not the noise that is distracting, though, is it Jack? It's not knowing where to go next. You hoped to see something out there, didn't you? Something that would lead you back on to the trail of the boy, of Ryan, but all there was out there was endless miles and miles of junk mountains.

And the Junkers. Who were they?

He hadn't seen one of them, but they had visited the carrier twice during the five days. Both times the crew had been tightly secured and tucked up inside the carrier, either playing cards or sleeping, and both times the noise had come from above.

He lay there in the bunk, thinking of Ryan and their last times together, and he watched the crew playing cards in the middle of the room.

During the game, Tyler turned to him. "You don't want to join in?" he asked. "Boots' got a run going here that we can't beat. We need some of your talent here, Lucky Jack."

Lucky Jack. His new nickname, given to him by Higgins after he found the tractor.

"I'm good," he said, meaning a polite no thanks.

Tyler nodded, and turned back again. "We're out to reclaim a facility tomorrow morning," he said. "They took back a Picking Factory that the Junkers stormed a while back, bout ten months or so ago, and they want crews up there to shift all the machines out. You reckon you can do some of that magic out there?"

Jack shrugged.

"Usually some good stuff left behind by the Junkers if we can get at it first," Tyler continued.

"That the place where all those kids and women got stole from?" asked Higgins. "That old reprocessing and picking plant that was right out in the middle of nowhere?"

Tyler looked at the old man, his expression grim. "I think so," he said.

"That was a nasty thing, right there," said Higgins. "Two hundred women and children, all taken. Poof, just gone, overnight."

Jack wasn't listening right up until the mention of children. Then, he was listening. Listening very carefully.

"Don't, man," said Tyler. "I don't like to think about it."

"What?" asked Higgins. "You don't like the idea of the Junkers taking them, or us going there?"

"Both," said Tyler. "You know they didn't find any bodies, apart from two of the trooper squad, and they were even stripped of all equipment. Shot with their own guns, they reckon, which also means some Junker scum out there now has firearms. I don't know. At least they didn't leave no dead women or kids behind, but it makes me sick wondering what they did do with them."

"Yeah," said Higgins. "Took em all, every last one."

Jack sat up. "Took who?" he asked.

The rest of the crew turned to him, and Tyler dropped his cards, the game no longer relevant. "The Junkers raid places occasionally, and I mean in force, like, dozens of them."

"Hundreds, some say," said Higgins.

"Yeah, well," continued Tyler. "About ten or eleven months ago there was place way out here, a Picking Factory, where they had a couple of hundred kids and some women, and their job was to sort through all the circuitry and small electronics that gets found. You know, the stuff that gets sorted here first. Well they got sent all the smaller stuff."

Jack thought about how he had spent hours dumping piles of circuit boards, wires, and small broken electronics into large tubs that were then taken away to a truck, and from there to wherever...to the Picking Factory, it seemed. Now there was a very real possibility, if Ryan had gone there, that the boy may have sorted the very stuff that Jack had packed.

"Well," said Tyler. "The Junkers usually only raid and grab supplies, and then run for it, but apparently this time they came in force and took the actual people in the factory, all of them. They don't usually do that. They normally just take stuff and go, often without even having to fight anyone. I mean, if you're faced with a few dozen Junkers charging down on you, most people just up and run like hell and come back when they're gone. This time they took everything they could carry and then some. They took the people too."

"Apart from a couple of the troopers," said Rick as he lit up yet another cigarette.

"Yeah. Apart from two or three of the trooper squad. They killed them."

Higgins coughed and jabbed at his chest. "You know, that puzzled me," he said. "Junkers eat folks, right? So—"

"There's no proof of that," interrupted Locks. He'd discarded his furry hat on the bunk at the far end of them room, the first time Jack had seen him without it perched on his head even when sleeping, and Jack could see that he had a large round bald spot on the top of his head. "No one actually got proof that they eat people, and no one has seen them doing it. Anyone found eaten out in the junk could easily have been got at by one of the bugs."

"Oh but that's what everybody says," said Higgins. "Everyone knows Junkers eat anything, including each other."

"That's what people say," said Locks. "And they also say that some of those bugs out there can talk, but that's absolute rubbish, yeah?"

Higgins shrugged. "Well, maybe. Whatever. But that's what I'm saying. If they do eat people, then why dint they take the bodies of the troopers? Or just cook em right there?"

"I don't know, okay?" interrupted Tyler. "And I don't even want to think about it. And anyway, we get to see firsthand what they left behind, because we're on clean up and reclaim duty, as of tomorrow."

That was why Jack couldn't sleep. The Picking Factory, a place that used to have hundreds of kids working in it, seemed to be the very first sign of any significance that might lead him to Ryan's trail. If there was a place that the boy could have ended up, it had to be there. Jack had found nowhere else, no other leads.

But the Junkers had raided the place, and that meant another possibility that Jack didn't want to consider. But he found it too hard not to dwell on it.

Waiting For Time

Lisa sat on top of the armoured truck and watched as the convoy of salvage carriers trundled noisily into the yard of the Picking Factory. They were two hours late, and she had been pacing back and forth for most of that time before finally settling on just sitting and waiting. It was pointless calling anyone, and it didn't matter what the delay was. They would get there when they got there.

The last truck, the one with the big grey letters E2 painted on the side, was the one she was most interested in. He would be in that one, that much she knew. She hadn't gone over to the salvagers' bunk rooms – no, that would have seemed strange. If she'd turned up there just to find Jack Avery, everyone would be talking about it. So she had been patient but made sure that the E2 crew was assigned to this duty, and now she waited.

Next to her, also looking relieved to see the crews arrive, Hailey was busy scribbling on her clipboard.

"Why don't you use a touch pad?" Lisa asked.

Hailey looked up from her scribbling and frowned. "I don't have one," she said.

"Oh," said Lisa. "I'll fix that."

Hailey nodded. "Two hours fifteen behind schedule, but at least they're all here," she said.

Trust Hailey to find a bright spot among the gloom, thought Lisa. She stood up, pushing away from the armoured wall that surrounded the flat platform on top of her command vehicle.

"And we're two hours plus behind," she said. "They better have a good reason for it."

Hailey looked up once more. "I'll find out why," she said.

Junk

The Past Comes Back.

The officer was watching him, Jack was convinced. It was difficult to tell for sure. The helmet, similar to those worn by the Hunter troops in the ruins of the Outer Zone but more worn and damaged, hid the face behind it, but that blackened and domed visor was pointing in his direction and he could almost feel the gaze upon him as he bundled his gear out of the back of the carrier and threw it over his shoulders.

The scabs stood in an inspection line with Tyler at the front. This had not been mentioned to Jack, but he just fell in line with the rest of them as the crews assembled in the yard next to their vehicles. The troop officer, and another trooper that Jack presumed was a junior officer, walked along the line and then moved away.

That officer definitely stopped at him for longer than the others, he thought, and noticed even Tyler was frowning at him. Curiosity, no doubt. If Tyler had noticed it as well then it wasn't just his imagination.

But the officer said nothing to him, just stared at him for a few seconds and then moved on. Then Tyler and the other crew leaders were called aside, moving across the dusty yard to stand with the officer. They were speaking, but what about?

He couldn't hear the conversation, so instead looked away and stood there, taking in his surroundings.

The facility was huge, much larger than he had expected. Though he hadn't known what to expect, really. The word factory made him think of the coal yard, back when he had been a kid. That had to be it. He'd expected a single crumbling building with a yard and a perimeter fence, but of course this was quite far away from the Recycling Facility, and isolated.

Why would they send so many people so far out? This was Badlands, and uncontrolled. Anything could be — and was — scurrying around out here. Junkers, whatever they were – people of some kind? And bugs. He'd seen neither, but the men on his crew had told him that they were both something to be feared.

"Like some kind of screwed up mutant," Higgins had said, when asked about the Junkers. "They might have been human once, but they were like, part machine, part animal or something. I saw it from a distance, just before the siren went off, standing right up on top of the junk and looking down on me. It had this thing, a weapon, like some kind of spear but with a nasty blade on the end. I ran for it. Something about that thing. It wanted to eat me, I'm sure of it, and the hell it wasn't afraid of the carrier or me."

It seemed hard to imagine that a human could degenerate into something entirely different, Jack thought, but then, he'd seen the Night Ones in the Outer Zone, even if from a distance, and they seemed far from human.

Maybe that was what the Junkers were like? The Night Ones. He tried to remember the time he and Drogan had been caught out in the ruins near the Ashlands. The night they had been chased. The last time he'd ever seen his friend.

Just Run

Many Years Before.

The camp fire was roaring. Drogan had seen to that. Out in the reaches near the Ashlands the air was bitter cold all year long, even when other places were baking with the summer sun. Jack had never liked going that far out, but his friend insisted on it when things were tight and they had found no salvage to trade for a few weeks.

And this was one of those times. They'd searched further and further out in the last few weeks, after heading east from The Crossing, and they'd even gone into areas that neither of them had travelled before, but the picking had been getting harder and harder.

That was the one good thing about the borders near the Ashlands. There was still plenty to be found, for those willing to risk going anywhere near the creatures that lived in the ash wastes. And if you lit a good fire, bright and hot, those things left you well alone anyway.

He'd always wondered why that was. The Night Ones, as many folks called them, were humanoid but far from being living people. Jack suspected that once, centuries ago, they may well have been people, but the pale skinned and rotten creatures that screamed and howled in the frozen ash wastes were nothing like people now.

Until that night, while the fire roared and Drogan cooked the two skinny rabbits that they'd caught a few hours before, Jack had only seen them from a distance.

But the wind was stronger than usual, gusting in across the crumbling ruins and blowing so hard that he'd nearly toppled over several times.

Then, later, when the darkness of night came and the screaming and howling began to resound from across the ash wastes, one almighty gust of wind blew through the broken remnants of the building they had taken refuge in and the fire just went out.

And the next few minutes were the most terrifying of his life.

He heard, more than saw, Drogan hurrying to relight the fire, and Jack scrambled toward the noise and tried to help. But it was no good. The wood that they had found was wet on the inside, and only the outer layers had took light. Now they just couldn't seem to get the thing to catch again, even when Jack used his body to block the wind, hoping that Drogan could at least get something going.

But Drogan stopped.

"We have to get the hell out of here," he said, and in the moonlight, Jack's vision now adjusting to the lower light that only the moon provided, he could see real fear in the man's eyes. They had travelled for nearly four years together, side by side, scavenging in the ruins and trading at the hovels, and Jack had never once seen Drogan look frightened, even when they had had to face down a gang of rovers three times their number.

But now the moonlight showed Jack a face full of fear.

They scrambled around the camp, grabbing their gear and stuffing it in packs, and a minute later were jogging alongside each other, away from the already chilling campfire.

"This was stupid," Drogan had said. "I should never have brought us out here."

"It was only the fire," Jack had replied. "If that hadn't gone out we'd have been fine."

Drogan didn't rely. He just continued to trudge alongside Jack.

"And anyway," continued Jack. "We found a tonne of stuff to trade, and we can just go further into the ruins for a couple of miles, find a place with higher walls, and make another camp."

"I suppose," said Drogan. "But I still think that—"

There had been a flash of movement from their right that zipped past Jack and slammed into Drogan. The man cried out and went down hard, struggling to his feet a couple of seconds later.

Jack already had his machetes out and stood there, on the spot, next to his friend, turning left and right, scanning the darkness for more movement.

"The hell," cursed Drogan, finally getting to his feet.

"What was that?" asked Jack.

Drogan shook his head. "I don't know," he said. "But let's not hang around to find out, eh?"

And so they had continued on, moving faster now.

And it was a few minutes later, just as they began to spot the outlines of larger ruins in the distance, the walls faintly lit by the moon, when the scream resounded from just a few feet away.

"Run," shouted Drogan, taking off at full pelt in front of Jack, and Jack had followed, urging himself onwards as fast as his feet could carry him, his lungs screaming for air and his muscles protesting at every lunge forward.

Jack caught up with Drogan and passed him, but not by much. He didn't want to push on, didn't want to split up with his friend. But then, as he ran onwards, he felt, more than saw, movement all around them. There were no more screams, but the gaunt figures that loped alongside them at a distance were not silent anymore. Growls and hisses assaulted his ears.

And then there was another flash of movement next to them, and Drogan vanished with a startled cry, going down onto the hard road with a slam that Jack heard. And he also heard something crack.

Drogan cried out, and then the cry turned into a scream.

Jack turned back, swinging his machetes at the darkness around him, but nothing came near him. There was a mass of movement ahead of him, right where Drogan had gone down, but Jack couldn't make out what it was.

Figures. Dozens of them, crawling all over each other and pushing, shoving, trying to get to Drogan.

"Run, you idio—" came the last thing Jack would ever hear his friend say, the words cut off as a gargling, bubbling rasp replaced them.

But Jack had hesitated for a moment, not wanting to leave his friend to die. Whatever those things were, the Night Ones, surely he could fight them.

He ran at the mass of bodies, hacking at anything that moved, until a few remaining creatures ran from him, leaving a dozen or more of their kin lying dead. He'd seen red for that few seconds and stormed into the creatures with a rage that he didn't know he had. Life, death – none of it mattered. Drogan was in trouble.

And then Jack was panting, his chest heaving with exertion as he tried to breathe, but Drogan was on the ground in front of him, and Jack could see there was nothing at all that he could do to help his friend.

So he'd turned and run that night, not even stopping to pick up any of the gear that had once been his friend's.

Someone else could have that if they dared.

Someone else could find Drogan's equipment if they really wanted to face the creatures out in the Ashlands. Because Jack vowed that he would never return.

Junk

No. The Junkers couldn't be like the Night Ones, Jack thought. He hoped. They couldn't be. Night Ones would never have known how to use a weapon to kill the troopers left behind at the Picking Factory. The things he'd seen that night were no more human than a rabid rat. They had been things twisted beyond recognition, dead but not dead, pale skinned and gaunt, their eyes hollow black pits that were lifeless.

And if there were Night Ones out here in The Junklands, then the people running the Recycling Facility surely wouldn't have left so many people out here unguarded.

But that doesn't answer your question does it?

Why had they left all those kids and women out here? It didn't make much sense to him. It was almost like asking for them to be taken. It had to be…what? Five hours from the main facility. And from what he had heard from Tyler and the others, they had only manned this place with a single detachment of troopers.

And the bugs? Nasty long-legged things that darted over the junk like it's a flat path, and very fast, or crawling beetle-like things, hidden away deep inside the piles of debris, nesting and waiting to be uncovered. That's how Higgins had described them, and Jack hoped never to meet either of those.

All these things went through his mind as he stood there in the blazing sun, looking out across the massive facility that they now had to clear. Rows of huge monolithic buildings lined the centre of the vast, dry, open space, and beyond that, where the perimeter wall stood crumbling, with huge gaps collapsed to the ground, smaller buildings stood.

There has to be a hundred buildings here. How are you possibly going to find any trace of Ryan? Had he been out here when the place was attacked? It sounds likely, doesn't it? This is the place to start looking, after six months of finding nothing in the Recycling Facility. A place to start.

But what if you do find something? What then?

"Okay, listen up," came the deep boom of Tyler's voice, drawing him from his daze and snapping him back into the present. "We got dealt the far compound, where the big machines are, and after that we have the living quarters and the outer buildings on the far side. That's us for the next five days." Tyler squinted in the bright sun and scratched his chin. "Usual drill, though we're being told that the carrier will be moving over there." He turned and pointed at the large open space between the huge central buildings and what looked to be some kind of hangar.

"Five days here?" snapped Higgins. "That long just to clear out a few machines?"

Tyler shrugged. "What do you know?" he said. "I guess there's more here than I expected. More than just a couple of machines, anyway. Maybe we'll find something sweet in all the rot? Never know. Let's get back on board and wait."

They headed back over to the carrier and Jack stood at the end of the line, waiting to climb on-board. Higgins was muttering something to himself about wasting time, but Jack didn't catch all of it. He was too busy looking past the crew, over to where the officer and the other troopers were standing.

The officer was watching him again.

You Again

It was definitely him, Lisa thought. He's less scruffy than he was when he gave himself up, speaking to her that day at the back of the armoured carrier in the middle of the Outer Zone ruins. But she recognised him instantly. He was tall, though not as tall as some of her men, and he was built well. Strong, even though most of the prisoners were underfed.

Now she had found him again, she was unsure of what difference it made. She'd hoped for something, whatever it might be, when she caught up with him again, but she didn't know what. And it wasn't like she could just initiate a conversation with him, ask him the questions that were bugging her. It wasn't the done thing.

I have to just watch and wait, she thought. Watch and wait for the right moment.

The man probably didn't even know it was me, that I'm the same one he surrendered to. Lifting her visor would have solved that, but she remembered that doing just that was exactly what had landed her this wonderful job out in The Junklands in the first place.

And what about that? She thought that she would be angry with the man when she finally met him again, thought that she would blame him for everything that had happened to her since then. Why had she shown her face in the first place? Why make any form of contact? It didn't make sense, not to her, anyway.

And now, having met him again, she didn't feel angry at all. The guy was in a much worse situation than she was. She'd sleep in an air conditioned armoured transport with a bunk tonight, and he would be bunked down with a bunch of stinking scabs.

He won't have found his boy, either, will he? She thought. All this time, and he has probably found nothing. There were no kids at the main Facility, they never took them there. Most of the ones that came out here were sent to the Picking Factories, like the one they stood in right now.

Had the boy been here?

Damn it, she cursed silently. Why the hell should she care about a boy she'd never met? There were hundreds here when the raid happened, she knew that much. Hundreds taken by the Junkers. And what had happened to them? Dead? Were they killers, these things that lived out in the waste? They'd killed troopers - that much she knew - but children and women? Were those things even human enough to know the difference?

It annoyed her immensely every time she thought about it. Governor Jackson had sent them all out here with just one squad of security, just twelve troopers, and they had been taken, captured by the Junkers. The troopers were either killed or also taken, and that foul creature, Jackson, shrugged it off as unfortunate.

No, he didn't actually say this incident was unfortunate, she thought. That had been the disappearance of three squads, months before. But she could bet that it would be his reply if she'd asked.

Maybe I can find some clues out here, she thought. Maybe those people are retrievable.

That would be an achievement.

Junk

The Past Comes Back.

He found it on the second floor of the last workshop and just stood there, staring at it.

Three days ago they had entered the first warehouse. As Tyler had said, E2 crew was to do the last three warehouses and then all of the outbuildings on the north side of the facility, and that included a number of workshops and smaller factory buildings as well as the area that had been used as a dormitory.

They'd entered the first warehouse, Jack at the back of the crew, carrying a heavy shoulder load of cutters and some matt sheeting. Tyler was up front with Higgins next to him, the other men following. They'd all stood there for a few minutes, gazing around the massive interior of the dilapidated old building, just looking, in awe of the massive installation that they were apparently supposed to take apart.

The floor was flat concrete and, apart from a few crumbling bits of masonry in the corners, was well swept and barely cracked. The ground was worn and looked like it had been well trodden over the years, and in some spots the bare ground even appeared smooth. If there had been doors on the building then there was no evidence of them now. Huge open spaces, looking out onto the dusty ground outside, let the sun blaze into the interior, and Jack had been surprised that the ground wasn't covered in sand and dirt from outside. But somehow it wasn't.

And the sprawling array that was the picking plant sat smack in the middle of the wide-open space. Large hoppers lined one wall, with belt-fed conveyors coming out of the bottom and leading across the open ground, splitting in several places before passing raised platforms that lined long stretches of belt.

Where the kids would have stood and sorted stuff, Jack thought.

The raised platforms were rusted and cracked, and behind them, stacked up high, were metal bins with wheels on the bottom. Mini dumping trucks for whatever the kids must have been taking off the conveyors lines.

He stood there, the dry wind buffeting his back and the heat of the sun burning his bare arms, and imagined what the place had been like when it was active, when it was busy with dozens of children sorting through the crap that must have been sent there. In his mind, the conveyors were moving, making a clunk clunk noise as each section bumped over the supporting joists. And he imagined a row of young children, from the very small right up to teenage years, lined along the platforms, poking around in the junk that passed and throwing what they found into the metals bins behind them.

He saw other children, two at a time, pushing the metal bins away to one corner of the warehouse and then pushing another empty into its place.

They were dirty kids, filthy and covered in the grime that rubbed off onto their hands from the junk passing along the conveyors, and their faces were smeared with dust and sand that blew in from the outside.

"Well, we better get started," said Tyler. Jack looked up, snapping out of his daydream and saw the tall man had turned and was looking back at his crew. "We got to take all this down, cut it up and get it hauled out to the dumper."

"Dumper isn't even here yet," said Rick, coughing into his hand and then wiping it on his shirt.

"No," said Tyler. "But we may as well get on the go anyway."

Jack spent most of the three days, until they moved into the workshops along the north side, cutting up the conveyors' parts and snipping down the sides of the bins, stacking them up near the main entranceway when the dumpster truck wasn't there. By the time they left the three warehouses, and moved into the workshops, his hands were sore, even through his gloves.

On the third day they moved out of the warehouses and started with the outbuildings, and he was relieved. The heat inside the warehouses was almost unbearable, and the temperature dropped significantly when they entered the smaller, stone-built buildings.

And so it was that, just an hour before the sun went down and they would be due to head back to the carrier and rest up for the night, he climbed the six flights of stairs to the top floor of the workshop that they were emptying.

The building was filled with work benches, lines and lines of them in every room, and on each bench was a mess of mechanical and electronics parts. Wound up spools of wires, cutting tools, knives, snippers, hammers, all manner of tools — a lot of which he knew would never make it into the dumpster and would instead be hidden away inside the personal bags of many of his crew. There was just too much treasure lying around all over the place for it not to.

They'd cleared the bottom floor, moved up to the second, and the rest of the guys, led by Higgins, were busy hauling the contents down to the ground floor with ropes and buckets.

"Why don't you go check up top?" Tyler had suggested. "Give us a scoop on what's up on the last floor, ready for tomorrow. Then come down to bottom and grab a smoke."

Jack had nodded. "No problem," he'd said.

And so he headed up the stairs and onto the raised gantry that led along all of the north side buildings. It looked like an outer defence platform that spanned most of the north side of the facility, with metal stairwells in between the buildings. He wondered for a moment if they would need to take that down as well. It was, after all, made of metal, and that was the resource most wanted by the Recycling Facility. Metal and electronics.

He shrugged and stepped out of the bright sun and into the huge open interior of the top floor and looked straight at it.

There was an old stairwell at the side of the big room, though it had long since crumbled and collapsed. Inside the stairwell the floor opened up into a drop that went all the way down to the bottom floor, but that wasn't what Jack saw.

I Need Answers

Lisa watched as the man fell to his knees, but she didn't rush forward to help him. Instead she stood there, watching, as she had the whole time.

He hadn't noticed her as he had come up the stairs and out onto the gantry, and she hadn't expected him to. She was a hundred yards away, near the next building, watching out over the sprawling landscape of junk that began fifty feet from the outer wall, and she was tucked inside an alcove away from the heat of the sun.

Her combat armour protected her from the rigours of the hot sun, from most weather in fact, but only if she was fully suited. And she hadn't wanted to be at that moment. Sitting up there on the gantry, watching out for movement far away, she preferred to take her helmet off.

And so she'd seen him enter the workshop and realised he was alone.

She glanced down and counted the crew members on the ground in the yard below. It was a full crew except for him. No one else up there. He was alone.

What Jack Saw

There was some flooring inside the stairwell. Pieces of wood that had probably once been the top of the stairs jutted out from the wall like broken and rotten teeth. Just far out enough, he thought, for someone to step round if they didn't weigh too much. He would have collapsed them with his weight, but a boy, maybe one only six, seven, or eight years old, and thin, would have been able to walk around them like a ledge to the small platform at the back that would have been the eave over the stairs, a spot most likely unnoticed by most people.

But this also wasn't really what Jack had noticed. That was all small, peripheral detail that flooded in as he stared at the top wall over the hole that would have been the stairs. The wall was a pale colour, and he thought that it was coated in paint that somehow still remained after so many years. It was, after all, tucked away inside a building and away from the wind. And it was a light coloured paint, cracked and dry near the corners and edges of the wall, but the paint covering most of the flat surface was still smooth and clear, even if it was somewhat stained.

Covering most of the surface of the wall were drawings. He didn't know what they had been drawn with, maybe a piece of charcoal, or something else dark in colour. Even a charred piece of wood could have been used. The figures were all stick men, and they were busy little stick men. Two of them were sitting on a step of some kind with bowls in their hands.

Eating ant soup, he thought.

Another two stickmen were rifling through a pile of trash, and the smallest of the stickmen was throwing bits over its head.

Scavenging in the ruins.

And then there were another two, walking and pushing a cart of some kind, the smallest riding on the front of the cart and the larger one pushing with its back hunched over.

Off to The Crossing to sell the finds.

And there, smack in the middle of the dozens of similar, tiny scenes that were scrawled all over the wall, were the same two stick people.

One tall and one small, standing holding hands.

And that was when Jack's knees went from under him.

Finally, he thought. Finally I found where you went.

PART FOUR
Reconditioned

Into Nowhere

Middle of the Night.

Jack crouched in the darkness, feeling the wet drip of rainfall tapping his shoulders and the top of his head. It was a thing he had never expected to experience in such a barren place. He hadn't seen rain at all since leaving the Outer Zone, and he'd presumed that The Junklands were as dry as they were desolate.

But there he was, hunkered down in the dark, underneath a pile of half-crushed piping and what appeared to be the remains of a vehicle of some kind. A truck, he thought. They were once called trucks. Water ran down his back and seeped into his clothes. And there was that drip, drip, drip on the top of his head. That was getting annoying.

Even though he felt miserable, Jack still managed a smile – the first humour he had felt in a very long time. The junk was cluttered around him, encasing him and hiding him from the thing that now lurked just a few yards away. The metal scrap that cocooned him alone would have been a good find, when he was working the salvage crew and even more so when he was a free man, but his time with Tyler's crew was three days since and there was no returning to that.

Not now.

The creature – and that was the best that he could think of to call it – was unlike anything he had seen before. It was roughly the size of a feral dog, he thought, maybe two feet high at the back where a smooth carapace deflected the pouring rain. In the darkness, he could barely make out what colour it was –he guessed green, but maybe brown. Moonlight was all that he had to see by and it was a dim light at that. It partially lit the creature but not clearly enough for him to see all the details.

What he could see had terrified him a few hours before. He had been making his way between two large piles of trash, following the muddy footprints left by those he now trailed. It hadn't started getting dark yet but he had begun looking for a likely spot to hide for the night when the thing just appeared, rising over the top of one of the piles of trash some twenty feet away, up the slope. It spotted him and began making the most bizarre clicking noises that he had ever heard. And it was loud.

But then, with a pair of pincers as big as his arms sticking out in front of its maw, he could understand how it made such a racket. Now that it was just a few feet away, he could smell it. It gave off a stench that was like rotting vegetation, and it assaulted his senses. He was relieved that he had managed to crawl into the small space that he now occupied.

The only problem was the thing didn't seem to be going away. He'd hoped it would get bored, or forget about him, but instead it had been sitting there for maybe three hours, probing the hole that was far too small for it to get through, and Jack knew that the creature sensed he was still there. Whether it was smell, hearing, or some other sense that was alien to him, he didn't know, but every time he moved the thing chirped and clicked again, sometimes shuffling around and banging at the trash with a frustrated claw or two.

Thirty miles, he thought. Thirty miles is as far as you got, following their damn trail through the junk. And now you're stuck with Mr Clicky out there. Better than a hundred yards, maybe, like the one you spotted as you hurried away from the perimeter fence that surrounded the Picking Factory. But still not far enough.

Now what was he going to do? He had a long pole he'd managed to scavenge from the junk, but he'd already smacked the creature several times with it to no avail, and his knife had been useless. The stinking creature's shell was as hard as metal and neither weapon bothered it. He wondered if it had even noticed.

At least it's not trying to pull the junk away, he thought. Count your blessings.

The only thing I can do is wait it out. Sit here, as quiet as possible, and it should forget I'm even here. If not, maybe I'll manage to fall asleep. It doesn't look like the thing will be able to get in here and eat me, so may as well just wait it out. Of course, that doesn't help with keeping up. The trail will go cold if I'm here too long. If the rain hasn't already washed away any signs of passage.

So what is Mr Clicky? he wondered, peering out into the darkness outside, at the strange creature sitting watch over him. Some kind of beetle? Had to be. Like a woodlouse but

186

evolved beyond anything else he'd ever seen. It was huge.

The bugs he had been warned about. It had to be one of those. But the thing was huge. He'd seen bugs like it in the Outer Zone ruins, but they were tiny, no bigger than a fingernail. Was this thing one of those, mutated beyond all possibility?

He'd managed three days on foot, crawling over piles of trash, through tunnels that had formed accidentally when large chunks of junk were dropped on top of more junk, and then, when he did find paths through the debris, he was able to make some real ground. But open space was uncommon and it was mostly piles of trash that shifted under him when he tried to climb over it. The paths in between the mounds of junk were often the only way to travel at any kind of speed.

The salvage crews would go mad for some of the stuff he had seen in that time. Tyler would go nuts.

But the ones he was following seemed to be heading along a route that he suspected they might have used before. The ground looked well-trodden in a lot of places, the trash compacted from boots walking over it maybe hundreds of times. At least he'd thought that. But then, for no apparent reason, the tracks would go right over the top of one of the piles of junk. And that really didn't make sense if you could go around.

He'd watched them, the first night, from an alcove underneath an old overturned truck. And they hadn't seen him, he thought. They hadn't noticed him watching their movements. There were at least a dozen of them, and they appeared to be human, though it was a little difficult to tell with some of them.

Junkers.

They camped up inside a huge broken pipe. He had no clue what the pipe was used for originally, but it was easily ten feet across inside. The Junkers built a fire and huddled away from the rain and the wind that seemed to have picked up the hour before they made camp. And so Jack hid inside the back of the overturned truck and watched them through a tiny gap in a side panel.

And he watched and listened.

And now he was probably miles behind them, worrying about whether he would be able to pick up their trail again, and thinking that they would be long gone. If he was stuck out here, with no tracks to follow, he would die.

I can't sit here. I need to come up with an escape route.

But then he looked through the tiny gap he had crawled through, straight into the face of the clicking monstrosity.

Damn thing is watching me.

He looked around once more, having searched the tiny alcove a dozen times already. Bricks and some broken, rotten wood held up the compacted ceiling on one side, and more crushed metal the other, leaving a cavity that was not much bigger than him. There was nothing to use against the creature. If he'd had distance on the thing he could maybe try throwing stuff at it, but he'd seen the shell on its back and figured that bricks would be no good to him. They'd just bounce right off as the thing trundled towards him.

And you don't even know how fast it can move. If it's anything like the bugs that were sometimes uncovered when you were scavenging in the Outer Zone, it could probably run over all this junk and be on you in seconds.

He picked up the nearest chunk of masonry and banged it down onto the point of his metal pole. The pole already had a wicked-looking point on the end, which would serve well if he had to fight something human and fleshy, that could be pierced and stuck with it, but the damn bug was spear-proof.

You already tested that several times, and Mr Clicky nearly yanked it out of your hands.

"Why don't you go bug someone else?" he said aloud, though with the noise of the rain hammering down he doubted if even a human could have heard him. But the bug probably would. If it had ears.

But the creature responded anyway, clicking away with its mandibles and jittering. Then it hammered on a large chunk of rock that blocked one side of the entrance. It seemed frustrated.

You and me both, Jack thought.

Then the creature hammered again, and this time the rock shifted.

Jack jumped back, nearly panicking. There seemed to be a pause in the bug's activity as it calculated what had just happened, somehow understanding that what it had done had actually worked.

And then it hammered again. The rock shifted, though not as much as it had done the first time, but it was enough to excite Mr Clicky out there. The creature reared up, heaving two sets of front legs onto the rock and started banging harder, chirping angrily as it did so, furiously trying to rip away at what was keeping it from its dinner.

Jack grabbed at his sharp pole, noticing now that as Mr

Clicky reared up and hit the rock, it exposed the underside of its belly. That area was still plated, but if he timed it right he may be able to jab it in one of its joints.

He waited, aiming the point of the spear through the hole, just a couple of feet away from the angry bug. Then it reared up once more, about to hit the rock with as much force as it could muster.

As it did so, Jack stabbed outwards, aiming for the area at the edge of the belly plate, where it met the creature's front legs. He felt the end of the spear hit something hard and cursed as the shock went through his arm, the spear vibrating with the impact.

He cursed again, hauling the spear back into the hole, and watched as the creature tumbled backwards, vanishing from the ledge just outside his hidey hole. There was a clatter and a shriek that pierced his ears and made his head throb.

Then silence.

He waited for the creature to reappear, and he was sure that it would. As sure as he was that he was going to die inside that nook, under the fallen building and the dilapidated vehicle.

But you took the chance, didn't you? When she offered you the chance to run, to go after the hope that you might find Ryan, you took it and ran.

He'd been standing there, he remembered, staring at the stick men scrawled all over the wall when the voice from behind startled him.

"He was here, wasn't he?" she'd said, and Jack had jumped and then turned to see the troop officer standing in the archway that led back out into the bright sunlight and out of the workhouse. He had stammered to say something but nothing came out.

"You were looking for a boy," she said, staring straight at him. She'd removed her helmet and held it at her waist, and Jack had seen the insignia on her shoulder and the coloured stripes. The officer continued to stare at him, and now he realised, almost inexplicably, that it was the same trooper that had stood at the back of the armoured vehicle when he had surrendered all those months ago in the Outer Zone.

The same woman.

She stood looking at him, expecting an answer.

"Yes," he said. "He was here."

He glanced back at the pictures on the wall behind him and then back to her. She was peering at them, and Jack saw what he thought was recognition of some kind.

"He drew those?" she asked.

Jack nodded. There was no mistaking the boy's drawings. Even though they were stickmen, they had a certain unique style to them that brought them to life. He'd recognise them anywhere. He'd sat staring painfully at the pictures in the back of his magazine for months.

"Yes," he said, finally.

Then she'd looked away from the pictures and her glance shifted to behind him, to the wide open hole in the side of the building that looked out onto the panorama of junk mountains, stretching out into the distance for as far as was visible.

"If he was here," she said. "Then the Junkers took him

out there."

Jack turned and looked out into the distance.

But where out there? The land was an endless sprawl of trash and rubble.

The officer turned away and walked over to the balcony facing into the facility. "Do you see out there, where there is a pinnacle of rock jutting upwards? About five miles from here, through the canyon of trash," she said.

Jack looked out and searched for the pinnacle and eventually spotted it.

"There's a collapsed building lying against it. Do you see that?" she said, still not turning to face him, and still looking at the interior of the Picking Factory, where right now the crews were climbing into their trucks for a break. Where he would be expected.

"Yes, ma'am," he said.

"Well, we were out that way just a few days ago, while we were scoping this place and making sure it was safe to send you guys in to reclaim everything." She turned now, and leaned against the railing, looking straight at him. "That was where we found the most recent signs of Junker movement."

Why was she telling him this? It was no business of his. But still, he'd looked back out towards the pinnacle of rock and the collapsed building that was leaning against it. For a brief moment he wondered how long the building had been there, but then brushed it aside as trivial.

"If someone wanted to find the Junkers, I think that's where they would have to start, don't you?" said the female officer.

"Yes, ma'am," Jack said.

"Hmm," she said, and pushed away from the railing, turning to face the stairwell. "If someone wanted to go out there and look, they could do that, if they went soon. I'm the only guard on this stretch of the wall, and I'm about to go grab something to eat and change shift with another trooper. It's very bad practice to leave a wall unmanned and unguarded, but there's no threat nearby at the moment, and the drones are currently a long way from here. And I don't think I saw anyone up here. The whole crew is down there, taking a break for a while."

Jack had felt his heart thumping in his chest. He'd need supplies, but knew he couldn't go and fetch them. He would have to survive with what he already carried and find what he needed out there. He had his pack with him, on his back. It had some things in it, but not much. There was some food, enough for a few days, maybe.

You've done it before, he'd thought. You've started from scratch before a number of times and you always managed to get by.

When he was a mile from the facility, he'd looked back as he stopped on top of a pile of metal sheets that would have been a goldmine of a find to one of the crews. His chest was heaving with exertion.

And she had been back there again – the officer – even though she'd walked off and left him to make his choice – run or stay. She'd gone back up onto the wall to watch him go.

You know, she probably watched you the whole way, he'd thought. Watched you running across the open ground and then into the trash. Maybe she had a hand on her rifle, wondering as you got further and further away if she had made a mistake. She could have stopped it right then but didn't. And you would never have known it was coming because you didn't look back, not even once.

Jack sat inside the nook, under the huge rock, and wondered why the officer had let him go. She didn't have to, and it would have got her in a lot of trouble if she'd been caught. Then he wondered how she had ended up out in the Junklands. She'd been one of the Hunters in the Outer Zone just weeks before.

And then he noticed that Mr Clicky hadn't climbed back up onto the ledge.

And Further Into Nowhere

Jack strained to listen. The bug was shifting around down there, or something was. He could hear it clattering against the rocks and the trash, rattling noises erupting every few seconds. The noises seemed to be getting more frantic, he thought. The thing was still moving and still there, but it wasn't climbing back up onto the ledge to pester him.

Do I go out? He wondered. Do I risk it?

He tried to peer over the edge, but from his hidey hole all he could see was the end of the ledge, and it was easily twenty feet down to the ground from there. He couldn't picture if it was steep or sloped.

The creature shrieked, and Jack heard it clicking its claws together, most definitely alive. But still he grabbed his spear from where it had landed on the floor nearby, crawled forward through the gap, and slowly made his way to the ledge, breathing deeply as his nerves crackled.

Damn thing is waiting for you to come out, he thought, as he stood halfway between the bolt hole and the edge. So he waited a minute longer, listening to the thing shrieking, unsure whether to go forward or try to make a run for it without even checking what was slowing Mr Clicky down.

Yet it doesn't sound as near as you first thought, does it? Sounds like it's down on the ground.

Jack took the last few steps and tentatively peered over

the edge, spear pointed out in front of him, expecting the bug to jump him at any moment.

But it didn't attack, and he could see why. Below him, the crumbled rock and rotten wood was sloped down to the ground to the path that he had been following through the junk. And there, smack in the middle of the path, lying on its back and wriggling around furiously, was Mr Clicky.

Jack laughed, and started to climb down the slope, all caution now gone. The stupid thing was wedged in. It had fallen off the ledge when he had hit it and then tumbled down into the path and wedged itself between the junk. And it was on its back, belly exposed to the sky as it thrashed around with frustration.

As Jack approached, the creature's shrieking intensified, and it tried to kick its legs and right itself, but he could see that it wasn't going anywhere.

He looked down at it, wondering if he could stick it with his spear and remove the problem, but decided against it. The thing could become dislodged and come at him again, and then he'd be right back where he was before, hiding in the hole.

Jack left the creature, jumped down onto the path and moved away as quickly as he could. He'd been hours stuck in that damn hole, and he was more than likely a long way behind the Junkers he'd been following.

But how long had it actually been? You were stuck there for quite a while and the Junkers would surely have kept moving, unless they camped up near here or their destination wasn't far away.

Only one way to find out, he told himself. Get moving

again.

He looked behind him, through the gap in the junk piles, and in the distance, a long way off, he could still make out the vague outline of the pinnacle of rock and the fallen building, highlighted in the moonlight. It was what? Thirty miles behind him now? Maybe only twenty, it was difficult to judge. But after nearly being caught by the Junkers that first night, before he'd even reached the pinnacle, he'd followed them all this way until Mr Clicky slowed him down.

But to where? They had to be going somewhere. Unless they were nomadic? They could be. Back in the Outer Zone there had been the Scavs, nomads who stayed in one place for a short amount of time before moving on. Maybe the Junkers were like that? He had no way of knowing, but what he did know was that they had taken over two hundred people from the Picking Factory, and those people had to be somewhere out here. And Ryan with them.

And he also now knew that Junkers were most definitely not like the Night Ones.

He moved quickly through the junk piles, picking up the trail where he had left off, and was surprised that he was able to do that. He'd expected the rain to wash away most of the signs of passage, but there were still things to be spotted if you were someone able to notice the small details – a rusty pot that had fallen from a pile of junk, its clean underside shining in the sun. A muddy boot-print, filled with rain water, or a cast-off bone from some dead animal, the few remaining shreds of meat not yet rotten. All of these things told him a story of passage that someone less attentive to detail would surely miss. It was enough for him to pick the trail up once more.

As the sun rose, slowly lighting up the hills of trash with a metallic shine, following the trail became easier. Darkness had hidden a lot of things he would otherwise miss. But with the light, the blistering heat returned.

The rusty pot was clean enough on the inside to be used to scoop up some of the rain water, and Jack drank deeply as he continued to walk, wishing that he had something to catch more rain in as the day went on. The sun was relentless, glaring down and heating up any metal lying around, and a number of times he touched something only to pull his hand away in surprise at how hot it was.

The water from the downpour was gradually vanishing in the heat. Small wafts of steam rose from the ground, but as hard as Jack searched, following the trail, there was nothing discarded in the junk that looked like it would hold water other than the rusty pot.

At least I can keep that full, he thought, but every time he found a pool of water in the dirt, or a piece of junk that had retained some of the downpour, he drank it all. There just wasn't enough.

As nightfall came again, he looked up at the walls of junk and tried to figure out where to camp up, where to hide from more bugs while at the same time avoid being spotted by any Junkers that may come by. He had to presume that the Junkers probably sent out patrols and the group he had been following was just that. And if there was one patrol there would be more. Of course there would be more. As for bugs, he had only met Mr Clicky so far, but he was sure there must be many more around. He had to hide before sleeping.

He eyed the hill of rubble and trash he stood at the foot of, looking for potential hazards, things that might collapse and avalanche down into the path. He saw none, so he made the slow climb up the junk to the summit. It was a hundred feet of hard climbing, and there seemed to be few footholds that would stay still for very long, everything shifting and sliding under his weight, but eventually he hauled himself up to the top and peered out over the landscape.

Still more endless junk. Miles and miles of it.

Here and there were features that stood out from the trash, but not many. Behind him he could still just make out the pinnacle in the distance, and to the east there seemed to be a huge open space of some kind, but it was too far away to make out any details other than a lack of junk. There was just a void. North there were three derelict buildings that dotted the landscape, one of which he thought may only be a few miles away.

Far enough to get to in an hour or two, but too far to make for shelter tonight, he thought.

There was nothing to the west or the south that stood out until darkness came. Jack had crawled back down the slope ten feet and had discovered an opening in the trash. He crawled into it and found himself sitting in the front of the shell of yet another rusted vehicle of some kind. It was one of the four-seater ones that were so common, or at least they seemed to be out in The Junklands. If anyone had found one of these back in the Outer Zone it would have been cut up and used as scrap metal, but they were all over the place out in the trash.

After shifting stuff around to block the entrance the

roof still hadn't caved in, so Jack settled down, glad that some of the seat padding hadn't rotted away but still feeling cold from the rain. That much he hadn't felt in a long time. The freezing feeling as night came and you were still wet from the rain.

As he watched, darkness descended upon the land. He started to make out what may have been a light in the far distance.

No, there was more than one.

Lights. There were definitely lights out there.

He could see them.

Add To Basket

Lisa stared at the screen, her eyes fixed on the acknowledgement button blinking in the middle of the panel. This was what she'd worked for, wasn't it? What she spent these last few years placing herself in harm's way for.

It was right there on the screen. All she had to do was click and it was done.

Four tickets, paid and covered. Two for her parents and two for her older brothers. The youngest brother, Alex, was also enrolled in active duty, still in his training period for the next year and posted at the main complex in the city. But if she kept it up, he'd be finishing his training on arrival at the new world, and she would be posted somewhere...somewhere out there.

It occurred to her that she hadn't the slightest clue what security forces or even combat forces were needed on the new world. The rockets would burst up into the atmosphere, connect with the Orbital Station, and unload onto the Ark ship which eventually left, bursting out into space and away from the dying planet forever, carrying its precious cargo of CryoSleep passengers along with a mass of raw material supplies.

Off in the direction of the new world.

And that was the last they were heard from.

She remembered being told during her youth that there

was a computer somewhere in the city that kept communications with the new world, but it was so far away that messages and information took years to get there and back, so it was reserved for critical information.

But that was all she knew.

The Ark ships left and that was the last that would be heard about them for the next fifty years, which was the time it took for the massive mechanical behemoths to cross the vast distance. Every year a new one was built from scratch, assembled in orbit and sent on its way.

That reminded her of the headlines that were everywhere, all over the city: HALF A CENTURY TO ALPHA CENTAURI.

She had liked that when she was a kid. Loved the way it sounded. The way it kinda rhymed.

Ten thousand credits per ticket was nearly a year's wages for most people, including those such as her, but she'd done it, finally. Her parents had always said they wouldn't leave without the kids, without her and the boys, but that would be fine. She would reassure them that she and Alex would be coming on the next one, or the one after that, and she would show them the figures on the screen the next time she spoke to them, which was when?

Lisa frowned. When did she get screen time again? Another two days, she thought.

The screen beeped at her, and she jumped slightly. Daydreaming and deep thinking had distracted her for a moment. It wasn't like she got the chance to do that very often.

DO YOU WISH TO CONTINUE?

She clicked YES, checked the screen that followed hadn't changed, and then clicked ACKNOWLEDGE.

Then she sat back again and gave a very long sigh. Forty thousand creds. Gone. Just like that.

Oh my god, she thought. Twenty-five thousand people went on the Ark every year. She frowned and tried to do the math. A quarter of a billion credits. She shook her head, not able to even contemplate that kind of money. Was there even that many credits?

She watched as the reservation acknowledgement screen appeared, confirming the places were booked and ready, then she looked at the departure date. One month from now her parents and brothers, all but the youngest, would leave the planet forever.

The Ark was a one way trip.

Next year, she thought – hoped. Next year it will be me.

The door opened behind her and Hailey stepped inside the office.

"You busy?" Hailey asked, seeing Lisa leaning back on the chair and apparently deep in thought. "I can come back later."

Lisa blinked and then looked up. "No. No, you're good. Come in," she said.

"Um. We got something a little strange being reported," said Hailey.

"Oh?" Lisa said, now interested. Strange or interesting didn't happen very often in her new job. She'd discovered that within the first few weeks.

Hailey stepped further into the room and handed Lisa

two sheets of print-out paper, and then she shook her head. "Well, it looks odd to me, and I couldn't find any similar reports, so I thought I'd better bring it to you. Seems that crew E2 – the one that the recent escapee was from – has had their vehicle tampered with."

"Tampered with?" asked Lisa. She knew the carriers were always coming back with damage, but that was normal. It was a harsh environment they worked in.

"Yeah. I don't know. Seems odd. We get a lot of intruder reports when the crews are out there, especially when they're camped up and shut down at night and it's quiet, but this time the crew chief...erm...Tyler, says that the hatches on the vehicle have been tampered with again. The 'again' part is what made it sound odd. Apparently he's reported it several times in the past, but I can't find a record of it."

"Should be reports if it's happened before. Maybe the Chief is mistaken about it being reported?"

Hailey shook her head. "No, he says he reported it about eight months ago, and about six months before that, but heard nothing back."

Lisa leaned forward, switched the screen back on and started hitting keys. She read the results on the screen, tapped a few more keys to change the search words, but still found nothing. "Nothing there," she said. "It didn't get reported."

"Okay," said Hailey. "But he insisted it was. No matter, I guess."

Lisa sat and read through the report, noting the mention of scratch marks. "I'll take a look at it later," she said.

After Hailey left, Lisa discarded the report and went back to staring at the screen that had just cost her forty thousand credits.

Could have bought an apartment in one of the plush spots in the city for that much, she thought. But why bother? No point buying a place when your entire family was intent on getting off world and you're stuck out here anyway.

Maybe I can buy a place in the new world, she wondered.

The Trail

A cold breeze woke Jack, and he struggled to move from his huddled position at the back of the buried car. He shivered and then pushed the stinking rug that he had pulled over himself away, tossing it to the other side of the car's interior. Dozens of tiny bugs fell away, falling into the foot-well of the car and scurrying off into dark corners or through holes.

An itching feeling irritated him, and he reached down to his leg and scratched. A dozen or more tiny bite marks had appeared, dotted around his lower calf, and Jack cursed himself for not covering that area. He stretched and climbed up towards the hole that would have been the back window of the car, but now acted as a porthole to the outside, exposing little of the metal cocoon he had used as a hideaway for the night.

He was surprised. He'd expected it to be colder during the night, maybe even rain again, but it hadn't, and now the heat of the morning sun was cooking the heaps of metal outside the car, the high temperature permeating through the metal and into the body of the vehicle. As he reached forward and touched the rim of the back window he pulled his hand back, startled at how hot the metal was.

You're damn lucky you slept on that stinking rug, he thought. Otherwise you could be covered in burns by now.

He considered trying to find something thinner than the rug, but still cloth, to carry with him. He was going to have to sleep out in the trash a lot, and if the damn stuff heated up like that in the morning he was going to cook.

The sun blazed down on the mountain of junk outside, and Jack peered out of the hole and across the expanse. The lights had been to the east, he thought, and there had been a lot of them dotted across the landscape, but they had been a long way off, tens of miles away in the very far distance, if not further.

Because the distance is out here is deceptive, he thought.

Jack climbed out the back of the car and crawled carefully down to the bottom of the junk slope, where the ground was bare and the path led around the side of the mountain that he had camped on. He took note of the position of the sun, glanced back to spot the rock pinnacle in the far distance, and turned to the path that led at least somewhat eastwards.

Had the lights been over near where the huge empty space was? That made him wonder. He hadn't been able to see clearly what the empty space could contain. It was, as far as he could tell, just void of trash.

Could there be something over there in that space? A town, maybe? Surely not. If it was that obviously in the open then Hunter patrols from the Resource Facility would have spotted it long ago and probably wiped the place out.

Jack made his way through the debris, along the winding path, stopping only occasionally to look at something in among the trash. After four hours of walking, in what he thought was an easterly direction, he had found nothing of real interest. These corridors, as he now thought of them, had been travelled by the Junkers so much that everything that wasn't buried underneath the mountains of metal and rubble had been picked clean.

It was as the sun was at its highest that he heard the voices in the distance, a way up the path ahead of him. Jack glanced around, hurriedly searching for an escape route or a hiding place, and realised that the path he had been on for a while now only had two directions that he could go in. There were no side paths or splits in the junk piles. The path ran almost straight behind him for a hundred yards, and ahead, where the voices were coming from, it curved away to the right. Whoever it was that he could hear approaching could only be just around that corner, barely a hundred yards away.

He made out multiple voices conversing as the noise approached him, and a near panic set in. He turned and started scrambling up the slope, hunting for a hole or crevice to hide in, climbing higher until he could just make out the heads of a dozen individuals approaching along the path.

A dozen.

Not just a couple. There were a dozen, maybe more, and they were armed with long spear-like weapons with blades at the ends.

He wouldn't stand a chance against them with just his own spear and a knife.

Then he spotted it, only ten feet away, across the slope from him. A hole in the trash, maybe two feet across. He leapt forward, not caring if he made any noise. The people approaching – Junkers, he presumed – would catch him anyway, if he were spotted. But the ground under him didn't shift or make much sound as he clambered across and looked down into the hole.

Just darkness.

A pipe of some kind, or a shaft. He wasn't sure but he didn't have time to question it, so he quickly sat, swung his feet into the hole, and lowered himself inside, holding on to the edge of the pipe and hoping that his feet would hit something solid that he could stand on.

But there was nothing underneath him, just open space. Jack hung there, listening to the voices as they approached, his hands screaming in protest at having to bear his entire weight.

I'm not going to be able to hold on like this for long, he thought, and looked down. Whatever was below lay in absolute darkness. But how far down did it go?

Does it go a long way or are you a few feet from the bottom?

"But did you see how many showed up last night? I didn't see you at the camp fire." he heard. The voice was still somewhat distant, maybe thirty yards away, and the hollow that he now hung in seemed to deaden the sound from outside. The voice was male, and sounded young – maybe that of a young man in his fifteenth or sixteenth year.

"I did," replied another, this one older and female. "Quite a turn out. I was there, I was just on watch at the perimeter."

"They even came all the way from out in the crags," continued the young man.

"Exactly," said the woman. "That's why your da and I

were on guard duty."

There was a pause in the conversation and Jack winced as he felt numbness in his fingers. Even after only a minute or so he was already struggling to hold himself up.

Maybe I should drop something, then I could hold on here longer, he thought. But didn't move.

"They're dangerous, aren't they?" asked the young man. "The crag tribes?"

Another pause. The voices were moving past Jack's hiding place and further away.

"Yes, they are. But stop," said the woman. "Look, Roan."

Another pause.

"Someone got this far." said a different voice. This one was male, and deep, almost a growl.

"Footprints go all the way along here and then disappear."

"You think they're around here, still?"

"No, I think they skittered over the junk and went somewhere else, maybe an hour ago. Maybe not so long. Could be just minutes, but it's damn hard to tell. But they came this way."

"Outsider? Or that old crackpot?"

"Outsider, I'd say." said another new voice. "Looks like it might be the one they spotted, if you ask me."

Spotted. That didn't sound good. They're looking for you now.

"So, what now?" asked another woman.

"We go back," said the last man. "We know they came this far but we can't track over the trash, at least not in this area."

Then there was noise again, and more talking, but the voices were becoming distant once more, heading back in the direction that they had come from.

A few minutes later, Jack decided he'd hung there long enough and pulled, trying to haul himself up.

And that was when his fingers finally slipped and he plummeted down into the hole.

Not Alone

The Watcher watched.

And from his perch between the two columns of stone, which marked the entrance to what had been a building many centuries before, he saw much.

He watched the group as they made their way through the pathways that led between the debris. There were twelve of them, and he thought that it was too large a group. These people, those who lived in the trash town hidden inside the wall of the great hill, covered over by debris, didn't usually travel in groups this large. Three or four was enough. This was too many. This was three groups, travelling together instead of keeping a good distance that was proper, drawing less attention from the flying demons that scoured the land before the digging people came.

Foolish indeed, he thought. But of no matter. They will come and they will go, and then it will be quiet once more, and you can sit here for a while, until you find the mushrooms you seek. Then you can go home and fill your belly. As is proper.

Foolish indeed.

But he shrugged again, irritated. They were noisy, this group, these three groups as one. They chattered, and that was not good. The young ones were being allowed to talk also, and that was not proper. The young should learn the way before they were allowed to speak of it.

And this other one, the one that was walking in the other direction. Who was this? Not of the trash town people – no. This one was of the digging people. This one, as it made its way along the winding path, rounding the hill and heading to a collision with the too big group, was also alone. Foolish.

Except you are also alone – always – are you not? Yes. But that was wise.

The loner was a stowaway, a runner, he thought. Another one of those. More foolishness. They never live, he thought. The digging people belong with their machines and being told what to do, not out here where there was no food that doesn't want to be eaten and nowhere comfortable to lie down and rest aching bones.

At this, he thought of his bed. Two days on this perch, thinking about where the mushrooms may be. Was that how long he'd been there? Two whole days and two whole nights. Yes, likely that much. And the bed would be cold but it would soon warm up.

And he was tired.

But he still watched the one that would soon meet the larger group.

That would be interesting.

He frowned, and then he smiled.

That's where the mushrooms are, he thought, glancing away from the noisy people and over to the great mound of trash across from the one on which he was perched. Inside this old building, and then down into its dirty guts, and then along the corridor, passing a few rats that would fill the pot, and then into the other side of the building, the bit that was hidden even when all the debris wasn't covering it. The mushrooms were in there.

And they're good ones. Big ones.

But his gaze shot back to the single traveller once more, and again the Watcher watched.

The man had stopped. What was he doing? Yes, he was listening. No doubt he'd heard the noisy noisiness of the larger-than-it-should-be group, coming along the path towards him.

Oh, so you've got ears then, have you? Got ears and you can hear them coming. But what will you do? What will you do now you know they're on their way?

Think they will eat you if they catch you? Well, I suppose they could, but that would be unusual, wouldn't it? They don't normally eat digging people, though digging people seem to think they do. Maybe it's a ruse? A joke upon you and the digging people, just to scare you away from all their wonderful trash and junk? Because there isn't enough trash and junk to go around?

Now the man was climbing, heading up the trash pile opposite, and he wasn't looking back, and still hadn't seen the Watcher. The man stopped at a hole, a pipe, and looked down.

Go on. In you go, thought the Watcher. Be the fool and hop on in there. Down to where the mushrooms are. It's a long way down there. A long way.

And the man did, but first he glanced around for other places to hide and looked straight at the Watcher. And the

Watcher, for one moment, wondered if the man had seen him, but the man seemed to pass his gaze right across the Watcher without recognition and then looked up the path, to where the group approached, and then back down at the hole.

And then he lowered himself into the hole and hung there.

Ah well, at least digging one over there isn't stupid enough to just hop into the pipe and break his legs. What would it be? Ten? Twenty feet? Thirty feet or more, most likely, right onto the hard ground, and the pipe would be wet or greasy, all covered in crap. He wouldn't be able to climb back out if he was to fall in.

The Watcher saw the group pass by, walk a further twenty or thirty feet, and then stop. One of them was checking the ground, searching.

Oh, you've been caught, now, digging one. Ready for the pot, or maybe not. They've found your trail and they'll find your hands clinging onto that pipe.

The Watcher listened to the chatter of the group, noting especially the words of the youngest.

Crackpot, am I? Is that what the young one thinks? Or what all of them think? Well, we will see about that young one if he ever gets sick. Yes. We'll see if he doesn't just stay sick.

The group turned back and started moving quickly away along the path from where they had come.

Oh, how disappointing, thought the Watcher.

After ten minutes of watching, and deciding that the man had either fallen to his death or daren't come back out, even after the group of trash people were long gone, the Watcher hauled himself to his feet, pulled out a long, wicked looking knife, and turned into the darkness between the columns to make his way down into the derelict factory, hidden underneath the mountains of trash.

Mushrooms and a digging one, he thought. Both waiting in the darkness below.

Secrets

The scratch marks were all over the side of the carrier and up on top. Lisa hopped down from the carrier, landing hard on the ground and thinking that she should just use the ladder next time. Shaking herself off, she went back to examine the panel on the side of the vehicle.

She'd tried every key she had, and had even gone through some of the ones in the fob storage, but nothing seemed to open the storage nooks that were welded into the sides and the top of the carrier. She even tried a different carrier and different keys, but nothing fitted.

The scratch marks aren't deep, she thought, peering at the long, dark gouges. They looked deliberate though, not like an animal had clawed the vehicle. They were made by something metal and sharp.

Eventually she shrugged and gave up. She didn't know what was meant to be stored in the compartments and, if she was honest with herself, she didn't remember ever noticing them before.

Just Junkers trying to steal stuff, she thought.

She walked back across the maintenance hangar, pacing along the wide path that led down the centre and walking past several other carriers currently in for maintenance before arriving at the other thing that she was here to see.

A new carrier – though new was certainly not what came

to mind when she saw the state of the pile of crap that had arrived.

She knelt and peered under the side panel of the armoured carrier, cursing. It had arrived just hours before and been dumped in the corner of the hangar. Who dumped it there she didn't know, as there was no signature sign-off on it and no record other than the log from the Trans. And it had arrived three hours before she and her expedition had driven in the main gates.

All she had was a printed report that she'd found on her desk. One with no signature.

It was a wreck, basically. It needed so much work that she wondered if it was worth the time to even repair it. Half of the body plates had massive holes in them, the underbelly of the beast was so rusted that she thought the bottom could drop out of it at any given moment, and the engine was half melted.

What engagement the thing had been in, she didn't know, but she suspected that whoever was driving it at the time had landed themselves in some deep trouble. Apart from the rust, the rest of the damage wasn't gradual wear. No, this was heavy weapons impact.

Who the hell in the Outer Zone, or near the city, even carried weapons capable of doing this much damage, other than those that were driving it? No one that she knew of.

But she had no choice. There was no returns option on a replacement vehicle, though she supposed if she really wanted rid of it she could roll it over to the recycle warehouse and just get them to tear it apart. At least that way it would go back.

But she needed new vehicles. Some of her existing rolling stock was almost falling apart.

Lisa picked up the inspection sheet she had tossed on the ground and went over it once more. It was late, and she needed to sleep, but if she at least finished with the inspection she could dump the sheet on the desk with the mechanical guys and work would start the next day. She pulled a chair from the desk nearby and plopped down on it to go back over the details, squinting in the harsh cold glare of the overhead light.

The hangar was empty. All of the repair and maintenance staff were asleep, just a hundred yards away, as was everybody in the facility at this time of night, baring the perimeter security. So when the far door opened with a long, grating creak, Lisa almost jumped. She looked up, peering across the large open space in the centre of the hangar, down the walkway that ran between the parking bays where her expedition's vehicles were now lined, and was surprised to see Governor Jackson and one other figure walking swiftly into the building. She was about to stand and greet them when she heard Jackson's voice cut sharply through the quiet.

"Make sure there is no one in here," he snapped at the tall man walking alongside him. "And make it quick."

Lisa frowned. Why would he need no one to be here?

She didn't like Jackson, and tried to avoid him as much as was possible. There was something unpleasant about a man who could shrug off the deaths and kidnappings that befell the people under his command on a regular basis. He was cold. Sure, even her job required a certain level of ability to be ruthless, but Jackson had taken this skill to a higher level. He was icy cold.

She hesitated and found herself puzzled that she was taking a step to the side and hiding – yes, hiding out of view from the two men. Why do that?

Because this is suspect, she thought.

It's what? Midnight? Early hours of the morning? And here is the governor, out of his bed and on the other side of the facility. You can step out at any time, it's not like *actually* hiding, she thought.

The man who accompanied the governor walked around the perimeter of the hangar, forcing her to edge around the new vehicle as he passed.

The fool didn't even spot her as he walked within ten feet. But then she had stayed very still after she stepped back into the shadow of the armoured carrier.

This is not good, she thought. Now you're really hiding.

But then it was too late, and she had to stay hidden, otherwise how could she explain where she had been? She had to continue to remain unnoticed.

She watched from the back of the carrier as the governor's assistant – Rogen, was that his name? – walked around the hangar and then returned to the middle, where Jackson waited impatiently. Lisa wondered if Jackson ever did anything patiently.

"Which one is it?" Jackson asked.

Rogen looked flustered for a moment, rustled some paper in his pocket and took it out, peered at it, and then spoke. "E2 crew. It should be in…bay 34."

Then Jackson was pacing away from the troubled

assistant, scanning the rows of vehicles as he walked.

E2. That's the crew Avery had been with, thought Lisa. And it was the scratched one. Why does he need that vehicle? Why is he even interested in any of the vehicles? The idiot never comes out here – doesn't need to. And it shows, since he can't even follow the aisle numbers.

Finally, after doubling back and going round in circles several times, the two men found the E2 crew carrier, and Jackson stood peering at the side of the vehicle for a moment.

"Well, open it then," he snapped.

Rogen stepped forward, fumbled with some keys and then leaned in to the side of the vehicle.

Open what? Lisa wondered. Are they going for the scratched storage panel?

But as she peered around the side of the carrier, straining to see what Rogen was doing, she saw him pull open the very same panel that she had been unable to open and turn back to Jackson, shaking his head.

"What?" snapped Jackson. "It can't be empty. You must have the wrong panel."

"I checked it. It's—"

"Get up on the roof and open the one up there," hissed Jackson, his voice still low.

He doesn't want to be heard, thought Lisa.

She watched as Rogen scrambled up the ladder on the side of the vehicle, clambered over the top, knelt down, and unlocked the compartment on the roof.

"It's here," said Rogen, and hauled out a worn satchel.

"Good," whispered Jackson. Now get it down here, and don't forget to lock the compartment. No one else needs to get into it. "Hurry, you fool. I want to get out of here."

"I'm coming," said Rogen, hurrying to climb down the ladder, but he slipped and dropped the satchel, which fell to the ground next to Jackson with a loud bang. "Sorry," said Rogen, his voice barely a whisper.

"Idiot," hissed Jackson. "If anyone heard that they might come to investigate. Let's get out of here."

After the two men had hurried out of the building, and shut the side door behind them, Lisa went over to E2 crew's carrier and climbed the ladder. She sat there, on the roof of the vehicle, staring down at the locked compartment and at the scratch marks all around it.

What the hell just happened here? What could possibly be held in a salvaging carrier that the governor would want?

Somehow this new and puzzling discovery made her feel very uncomfortable.

Mushrooms and More

Even in the darkness underneath the trash, edging slowly through the ruin of the ancient subterranean building, the Watcher could see well enough. He'd wondered about that once, about how he could see just as well at night, or in any darkness for that matter, as he could in the day. But after so many years it was a trivial thought, something that he took for granted as he stepped over broken masonry and small pieces of trash that had fallen into the interior through gaps in the roof.

You could find all manner of interesting things down underneath the trash if you knew where to look, and the Watcher always knew where to look.

Though this time he had struggled to sense where the cavity was, where the huge gap underneath the trash opened up. He'd known it was there, and he'd sensed what grew there, but he just couldn't seem to find a way through. The entrance that he'd found led to a wall of trash, stacked up in four different openings, and he knew one of them would lead to the interior and guessed the others wouldn't. But he was old, very old, and he didn't want to haul the trash away from all of the entrances just to find the one that led down into the dark.

He'd normally listen and eventually discover which it was before even moving a single piece of junk, but the day had been much too busy with noise to do such. First the groups of trash people moving about through the paths, forcing him to stay concealed, and then the single digging one turning up.

No coincidence, that, he thought. They are all looking for you, the little sneaky intruder that shouldn't have lived long enough to make it all the way over here to their territories.

And now they are searching for you to stop you finding their secret-but-not-so-secret towns. They will think you are going to go back to your digging people and tell them, and bring the fire from the skies and troopers with guns. But they are fools. The digging ones' rulers already know where the stupid trash towns are and avoid them. They already know, don't they? Of course they do. I've seen the flying metal things – the searchers – the other watchers that come and go. They go near the trash towns and then they leave.

But what could he do? The trash people didn't like him, didn't enjoy having the Watcher around at all, except to trade healing with. Oh, that was for sure. They didn't like coming to visit him unless one of them was sick, and then he was their best friend.

He could tell the trash people where the digging one was if he wanted to, but it would not be fun that way. Wouldn't be polite, either. After all, had the digging one not found and climbed into the tall pipe? He'd found the very answer the Watcher had been seeking. To turn him in now would be rude.

And the man was probably hurt – maybe dead. If he was hurt, the Watcher would have to help him in some way, out of gratitude, but if he was dead? Well, that would probably be more convenient.

He'd spent an hour pulling the trash away from the entrance that faced the direction of the pipe and found what he was looking for. Under the trash was walkway and a brick floor, and he knew immediately that it was the upper floor of the building into which he sought entrance. Another hour and the entrance was clear, the darkness below now accessible.

He'd searched many old ruins over the years, maybe even hundreds, and he always came away with something interesting. This time, mushrooms. That was what he had guessed was hidden below. Precious, ripe, large spore-heavy mushrooms that could be cultured near his home and grown into many more. And he'd been right. Four floors down, after climbing down a long and rickety stairwell, he'd found the first patch growing in the darkness. There was some light down there, seeping through tiny gaps in the trash above, but not much. Just enough for mushrooms to grow.

He left the patch where it was, not wanting disturb it before harvesting, and headed further into the interior.

There were ancient machines in the main room of the building, which was a vault-like space both vast and cold.

Yes, real cold, thought the Watcher. In this blistering heat there were still places that were cold. Like his home.

The machines lined up in the huge chamber were similar to many that were rusting in the trash. Vehicles, he'd heard them called. These ones were coated in a thick layer of dust and grime, but he rubbed some of it off and saw underneath that the metal body of the vehicle was shiny and new. He could see well in the dark, but not well enough to make out the colour of the vehicle.

Such a prize, he thought. Glimmering new machines. Others would love to know the location of such things, but he wouldn't tell them. Much better to leave them here, untouched and undamaged, forever.

The Watcher smiled to himself. If the trash people or the digging ones knew of some of the things he had found under the junk they would be astounded. One more reason not to tell a soul.

He found the digging one in a heap at the bottom of the pipe – the chimney – and was surprised to find that he was still breathing. The man was unconscious, no doubt knocked out from the fall, but he was very much alive. He checked the man, searching for injuries, and saw that one of his legs was lying at a strange angle.

Broken, he thought. Or dislocated. Ah well, I guess the mushrooms will have to wait until I return.

He started to unload his pack and search for something to cobble together a stretcher with.

Finders Keepers

I need a bit of old tech.

On a clear and dustless day, if Finder sat at the very top floor of his home, on the flat surface between the huge metal cones that were used to store water, he could see for miles and miles.

To the north, the endless desert stretched into what seemed forever – wisps of sand churning and drifting across the near-flat surface that hummed with a heat haze, a flatness only broken in a few places by the skeletal metal structures that jutted up here and there through the hard ground. In all other directions he could see the inheritance of Junkers. The endless piles of trash, some rising hundreds of feet into the air, broken only by the winding chasms that twisted and turned in between the great mountains of debris.

On the clearest of days, the ones that didn't come very often, he could even see all the way to the black river, in the south, and catch just a glimpse of the edge of the wasteland and the swamps beyond. But that was the darkest of places, and a reminder that not far from the Junkers' tiny corner of the world there lay poison and rot.

And there was the other swamp, the round one, not far away – the one that had formed inside what Finder thought was an unnaturally circular gap in the trash. It was where old Haggerty, the medicine man, old RootMan, lived.

He found himself up on the flat roof quite often, even though it was a hard climb. It was only six floors from his own tiny room, but those six floors were difficult. Even so, he still rolled out of his rough bunk before the sun rose most days and made his way up the fifteen ladders and one hundred and seventy rungs that it took to get there, and there he sat, the cool night wind blowing his face as he watched the sun rise over The Junklands.

His home, and that of a number of other orphan children, used to fly among the stars, OldMother told the kids. He would sit there with the others, in the story circle they formed each night before she sent them off to bed, and listen as she made up countless tales of space pirates and heroic adventurers that lived in the very rooms where he slept. In every story, the hero would win the battle, get the princess and fly away across the galaxy in the very house he called home.

He thought that maybe the tales could well have been true, but he doubted that pirates had flown in it, and there were probably no heroes in the crashed and ruined craft's history, but it *had* been a ship of some kind. Now, as it had been for hundreds of years, its nose was buried under fifty feet of dirt and the back of the ship pointed a hundred and fifty feet up into the sky. Most of one side of the ship had been replaced by junk metal panelling and scavenged windows, all bolted or welded on over the years.

So he lived in a spaceship that hadn't been to the stars for probably hundreds of years, and it made for a strange kind of house, even in a town where buildings were made entirely of junk. The original main walkway leading through the middle of the ship, from the engine room at the back to the crushed main deck, was almost vertical, only barely sloped where the ship leaned against the outcropping of rock that had become its bed, and the floor of his bedroom would once have been one of the walls.

And the four huge, cone-shaped jets at the back of the ship, which he supposed would once have spat out fire, or plasma, or whatever else was used to propel the behemoth machine through space, were used to collect and store water.

He liked to sit up there, and would have all day, but he could already see the first signs of movement below as folks opened their doors and windows to let the air in. It got very cold at night, but in the day the heat could sometimes be unbearable, and any ventilation through the junk-built metal structures, which the Junkers called home, helped a little.

But he couldn't sit there all day. He was expected by the leader, FirstMan. And he had chores to do.

He stretched, stood up, and made his way back to the hatch. In a short while there would be a gathering troupe at each of the gates, and normally he would be going with them, but not today. Today he headed through the bustle that was the lower quarter, winding his way through the shanty maze of metal shacks that was the market and up the exit on the far side of town.

Then it was out into the swamps.

There was no gradual build of wet ground, no sparse vegetation growths to show that the swamps were getting closer. They just appeared. Ten feet away the ground was barren and dry, and as hard as rock, and then the water's edge. And it was a strange place. There were plants. The swamp was one of the few places in The Junklands that Finder knew harboured life of any kind. Life as in plants. There was plenty of the other kind. Bugs and critters were all over the place, and he always held his spear tight as he travelled, just in case a skitterbug came crawling out of the trash. They were the worst. They were big and their shells were hard, but if you knew how to point a spear as they approached you could catch them and flip them right over on their backs before they got to you. He'd done it many times.

But today he got to the swamp's edge and started to make his way up the long slope towards FirstMan's encampment without seeing a single bug.

But what he did see as he approached the edge of the swamp was the old RootMan, heading off along the edge of the swamp in the opposite direction, and he was in a hurry, it would seem. He had someone with him – Finder could see a pair of arms flopping around over the sides of the stretcher that he bore.

Strange, Finder thought, as he watched the old man struggle with the stretcher. RootMan didn't normally take people back to his shack. If someone was hurt he'd go and visit them rather than take them in. And he wasn't one for visitors, either.

Finder shrugged, thinking it odd but realising that he would be in for a scolding if he got waylaid and offered to help. So off it was, up the gravel slope, to the where FirstMan lived.

It was strange house, Finder thought. Situated outside of the main settlement, perched in a large, unnatural alcove of junk that must have formed from the cavity of some monstrous metal structure that he couldn't identify, the building wasn't a building at all. It was made up of several different vehicles, set out in a circle, each of them identical and each with the open doors facing in towards the marquee tent that had been erected in the middle. FirstMan lived in the centre, with his strongest warriors guarding the entrance.

The two warriors at the entrance nodded at Finder as he passed through, his face a regular one in FirstMan's den over the last few months, ever since he had found the weapons cache for them. It was what he was good at, what he had been taught by his father before his father had been lost to him. He was Finder.

"Ah, there you are," said FirstMan with a genuine smile. He was seated on a chair near the desk at the back of the marquee, one of his legs up on the metal surface and the other on the ground. A cloud of wispy smoke rose through the air in front of him as he exhaled. FirstMan liked his smoke.

"I was hoping you'd be on time," he said. "I've got something else I want you to search for, if you are up for the task."

Finder nodded, honoured to be called to service by the great leader of the Junkers. "Yes, sir," he said, not forgetting his manners.

"Good. Good," said FirstMan. "I need you to come with me and some of my men to a place a short way from here. It's an old tech place, and we've been looking for it for months. Now we've found it, we can't find what we expected to be there."

Finder frowned. "Something old?"

FirstMan nodded. "Very old, young Finder. Very old. It's old tech, but it's something very important to our cause."

Finder studied FirstMan, searching for a snippet of knowledge that would tell him something more. "It's something that will help you see much further?"

FirstMan grinned. "You're intuition is quite unnerving, Finder. Yes. I know there's no point trying to keep it secret from you."

"I won't be able to find it if I don't know what it is," he said. "And knowing makes it easier."

"Yes," said FirstMan. "But keep that knowledge to yourself, would you? Knowledge can be invaluable, but it can also be dangerous."

"Yes, sir."

"We're looking for a stash of circuit boards, specifically ones for remote controllers and automated systems. That probably doesn't make much sense to you, but we need it if we're to succeed. It's all that's stopping us from using what we have to finally make our move. Think you can take a look?"

Finder nodded. "Of course."

It's Not Here

"Sorry," said Finder. "I don't know if it's just me or maybe the thing isn't here."

"Damn it," cursed FirstMan, kicking the dirt ground as he paced the yard. He'd been sure they would find something here. The records showed that equipment like that was stored and made at the factory. FirstMan knew it should have been there.

Others gathered around the large clearing in the ruins of the industrial complex. It was miles from the junk towns, and had taken nearly two hours of travelling to get to on foot, and FirstMan had high hopes that the boy would prove useful, as he had on other occasions. He was convinced if the boy couldn't find it then no one would.

Finder stared at the ground. Failure. It was a bitter feeling, and one he had felt many times before. This would have been a good time to not fail, and he'd known that. Back when he'd been with his father – well, the one who he'd thought of as a father – it had never been about failure. The man had taught him so much, and even the slightest of thoughts about him churned a pang of sickness in the boy's stomach. He had disappointed his father a few times, and known it when it happened, even though the man rarely scolded him. It was about praise, mostly. But that was all gone, now. His father was gone.

"It's not your fault," said FirstMan, placing his hand on the boy's shoulder. "I wasn't blaming you. I'm just frustrated that we didn't locate it."

Finder felt the pain ebb away and looked up, hopeful, and he did see something in FirstMan's eyes, something like the glances he had received from his father. "If my father had been here, and this thing you need was here, he'd have found it. He was a master at finding things."

FirstMan nodded. "And if our plan goes through, then one day you may be able to return to the Outer Zone and search for him," said FirstMan. "But we don't have him here, and that is unfortunate. Though it's strange for someone such as me to even contemplate how you manage to find things the way you do and that there may be someone out there who is more masterful at it. It's a little unnerving to watch."

Another man, taller even than FirstMan, scratched his beard a few feet away. This man Finder knew as RightHand, but he'd heard that the man's real name was Waylan. He was FirstMan's most trusted companion. "You know, we could try and capture one of the salvage crews," he said. "If I remember right, there were a lot of good scavengers among them. If anyone is going to know where to look it will be them."

FirstMan nodded again. "Maybe," he said. "Maybe we should. Other than that, we just have to keep the people out here and keep searching the place foot by foot. And honestly, I don't think the scavengers are any better than the Junkers. The boy's ability is not a common thing. I think we have to scour the whole place. Again."

RightHand winced at this. "This place is vast," he said.

"Must be a square mile, maybe two. It could take years, and we don't have that."

"No, we do have time," said FirstMan. "We do have years, if necessary, but I don't want to get old and die not having tried our plan."

RightHand nodded his agreement.

"Okay," said FirstMan. "We need to head back if we want to be back at the towns before dark. And we still need to hunt down that damn intruder."

RightHand grinned. "Last message I heard was that a group found traces of the intruder's presence about two miles from the swamp, out towards the crater, but they didn't find him. Or her. Whoever it is, they're good enough at hiding that even the Junker patrols are missing them."

Finder felt something tingle at the back of his neck, something he'd felt before. He listened intently, knowing that he should probably move away while the two leaders talked.

"They actually found traces that close to the towns?" FirstMan asked. "You never said anything about that."

RightHand shrugged. "I figured we have enough people searching. Worrying you about it wasn't going to get the guy found. And it's only one person."

FirstMan frowned. "One person could be a Spec Op from the Tertiary Station, and that could mean trouble. *End of game* kind of trouble."

Finder found some of the terms confusing. But then he always had found the leadership group of the Junkers to be different to the rest of the clans and most of the trash town people, somehow. But the mention of the swamp made him wonder about the RootMan and whoever it was that had been on the stretcher.

RightHand shook his head. "Tertiary wouldn't send a Spec Op out after us. They think we're dead anyway, you saw the report yourself. Why a Spec Op in The Junklands?"

FirstMan turned to the boy, a thoughtful expression creeping across his face. "You've found people before, haven't you, Finder?"

"Yes, sir," said the boy.

"Hmm, so you're ability works that way too. Think you could find a stranger, an intruder, if we took you to the last place he'd been seen?"

"Near the swamp?"

"Yes," said FirstMan

"Well, I was going to say, but didn't want to interrupt..."

"Say what?"

"When I was coming to meet you, this morning, I saw RootMan, old Haggerty, pulling a stretcher with someone on it."

FirstMan stopped smiling. "Old Root took someone in? He never wants visitors."

"You gotta be kidding me?" cursed RightHand

"No, sir," said Finder. "It may not be this intruder, but RootMan had someone on a stretcher. I don't know if they were alive, though."

"Goddamn old man plucked the intruder right out of the junk?" cursed RightHand. "Right under everyone's noses and then hid him? That would be so like him."

"You think? Why would he do that?" asked FirstMan. "What use is a stranger to him?"

"You don't know the guy," said RightHand. "I have to talk to him a lot whenever we want medicine, whenever someone gets sick. We've got barely any med supplies left and his damn concoctions seem to work, even though I dread to think what goes into them. He's always playing a game, always has to get one up on you. This would be just like him. Hide some damn stranger, just because he can. Just for fun, I reckon."

FirstMan chuckled. "Well. Let's head back and pay ourselves a visit to the swamp, shall we? See if Finder here is just what his name suggests."

Strange Fellow

Jack nearly screamed as the pain shot up his left leg, but he clenched his teeth and waited for the pain to go away. It didn't, not completely, but at least it dulled to a throbbing ache.

He looked around and was immediately confused. He wasn't in a dark pipe, or a hole in the ground. Instead he was lying on a bed of some kind, in a room only just big enough to fit the cracked and rusted metal cot. It was much too small for him, and he presumed that the owner, whoever that was, was either a kid or a very small person.

Light streamed in from above him, but he didn't want to move his leg just so that he could see. A window, or just a hole. A breeze blew from somewhere up there. Just a hole, then.

"You don't want to move that leg so much," called a voice from nearby.

Jack was silent, not knowing what to say. This stranger, whoever they were, hadn't killed him, and from the pile of junk dumped on the ground just a few feet away he could see that they hadn't robbed him either.

Not yet.

There was silence for a moment.

"Hey," called the voice. "Are you deaf? I know you're

awake." It was an old man's voice, Jack noted. Not a child.

Jack coughed. "I'm sorry," he said. "I was just...where am I?"

A laugh came back. The person was in the room next to his, that much he could tell, but as he strained to arch his back and look around, Jack felt his knee twinge.

It's the knee, he thought. Not my lower leg or ankle.

"It's not broken," said the voice, as though reading his thoughts. "Was just dislocated."

"Is it bad?" Jack asked.

"No. No," said the stranger. "Couple of days and you'll be up again. Maybe even one day. I put it back into place before I hauled you here. I thought it was broken when I first saw it, and that you were dead or something. I saw you fall down the chimney."

Jack frowned. "Are you one of the people who I saw? It was a chimney?"

"No. No," said the stranger. "I was just watching. And yes. Chimney of an old building hidden under the trash. Lot of those around this way."

Then Jack squinted as the man's head appeared a few feet away, leaning into the room.

He was small, as Jack had guessed, maybe only Jack's shoulder height, and he appeared as old as Jack could imagine. Maybe older. The man's beard came down to his belly, which was rounded and stuck out from the rest of his scrawny body. He was dressed in rags, and Jack guessed there were probably thirty or forty different items of clothing tied and stitched together like patchwork. He couldn't see the man's feet – the patchwork clothing hung

239

down to the ground and looked like some bizarre multi-coloured robe. The man grinned at him, and Jack was surprised to see a full set of bright, clean, shiny teeth. It was an odd sight to see, bright teeth in the middle of a grimy and unwashed face.

"What's your name, then?" asked the old man.

"Um...Jack."

The man frowned for moment. "Hmm...okay," he muttered, and then turned and left the room. Jack imagined that he had looked disappointed but couldn't guess why. "Not Bob, then?" asked the man.

"No," said Jack. "Jack."

"If you say so," came the voice again.

"Who...Who are you?" asked Jack.

"I'm the idiot that hauled you back here instead of fetchin' mushrooms. But I'm going to remedy that now. I won't be long. Don't try to move or you'll screw your leg up proper and I'll have to chop it off. Don't want that, now, do we?"

Jack was about to answer, but he heard a creaking noise beyond the door, and then a slam as a door shut, and then silence.

What a strange fellow.

What Dreams May Come

Then and Now

The hammer swung close to his head, barely missing him as it crashed into the wooden planks that lined the pit. It had been a close one, certainly the closest in a while. But the man was unskilled and over-reached every time.

Jack darted back, kidney punched the guy once with a quickly clenched fist, and then stepped back again, pacing around the arena to face his opponent once more. And the guy was struggling already. The hammer was too heavy and he had started off too quickly, lunging time after time with shots that he probably thought were good ones, but to Jack these were easy dodges. The hammer was a slow weapon and, even unarmed, Jack knew this was a battle he would win, even if the guy gained some sense and dropped the huge, heavy mallet.

I'm dreaming. I have to be.

But the man didn't learn. Still he came on, staggering from the shock that the single sharp kidney punch had caused but still determined to hit Jack with the hammer. Once more, Jack dodged, and this time he back-handed the man as he stepped away, smashing his knuckles hard into the side of his opponent's head as he moved swiftly away and put distance between them once more.

But when he turned he wasn't facing the same man, and the figure wasn't falling to the ground unconscious, like Jack had remembered.

And he was no longer in the fighting pit, hearing the jeering crowd as they chanted the name of their champion, JumpingJack, JumpingJack over and over.

His name. No. His name back then.

His pit name. Or was that pet name?

Now he was standing on the hard chipped concrete ground of the old train station once more. Ryan would be hiding where he had been told to, just a few dozen yards away, watching fearfully as Jack was encircled by the gang.

There were six of them.

And they were the ones who stole the boy's shoes.

I have to be dreaming to know that. The boy, he told you that these were the ones who stole his shoes. But he told you after you fought them. Not before.

So this had already happened.

This must be a dream.

But it didn't feel like it had already happened. The gang was spreading out, circling round, trapping him in and closing, slowly. They would strike as one, he knew. They were a group that hunted together, and they knew how to work as a team. They were dangerous.

But they had no idea what was coming and how dangerous their single opponent was.

And you were sure that you would die back then, weren't you?

There were six of them. Too many. You'd never fought

six before. But you still drew just one machete and started hopping on your feet, circling back, hopping forward – testing them. Hop, hop, hop. Dancing, almost. A way of moving that earned you a nickname, once.

And this was it, he thought. I am dreaming. This was it. In one moment the guy to the right, the one dressed in the ripped leather jacket with the blue splotch across the front. Paint maybe? Blue gunk, whatever it was. You never did know. He would rush you. And then the rest would come in. You'll go past him, that's what happened, and he didn't expect it. You grabbed his arm as he swung the bat at you and you spun round, swapping places with him even as your other hand brought the machete across his throat. Then down with your other hand to fetch the second blade from your belt.

The man leapt forward, and Jack side-stepped. The bat came swinging down right where he had been a second earlier but he was already moving forward, one hand grabbing and pulling the gang member's arm, pulling him past him. The other hand brought up the machete and swept it across the man's exposed throat as he went by.

And this was as the rest of the gang moved in, but they didn't get what they expected, did they? Instead of you backing off fearfully, easily trapped, they got their own guy, stumbling forward with spurting blood all over them. They crashed into each other to get back, one of them tripping. And it was that guy that took the next machete cut.

Jack moved past the second man, who was already bleeding out rapidly on the floor. He lifted his machete to strike the third man.

But it wasn't a gang member.

And he was no longer in the abandoned train station.

Where was he now?

Alone.

He still had his machete in his hand, but he was alone now and in the dark.

No, not alone. In the dark of the tunnel.

His stomach churned.

No. Not the tunnel.

Not that again.

He didn't want to see what was in the tunnel again.

"Hey," came a voice from the darkness.

Jack stumbled away, trying to avoid the voice. He didn't want to see who it was, what it was.

But wait. Those things hadn't talked. They couldn't.

Dreaming again.

"Hey, wake up."

The things in the tunnel had no voices, no vocal chords at all, no minds, no speech. Nothing. They were empty creatures, driven only by animal instinct. Once human – maybe – long ago. But not then, not now.

Jack felt something slapping the side of his face, but he couldn't see what it was in the darkness. He tried to bat the hand away, but it was persistent.

Then sunlight burst into the scene and lit up the tunnel, and he could see them all around him. Dead things that didn't stay dead. They approached, stumbling toward him, the nearest just feet away.

Still a dream.

244

Then he sat up, nearly banging his head on the low roof of the tiny room in the shack.

"At last," said the voice, and Jack's vision swam, hurrying to catch up with the next scene. He wasn't in the tunnel, wasn't in the old rail station, and not in the pit.

"I wondered if you was going to sleep forever," said the old man.

Then the dream left him, and Jack remembered where he was. In the shack, somewhere. In a tiny room with a rough bed. His leg dislocated at the knee. Yet it didn't hurt at the moment, and didn't seem too bad as he moved it.

"You, err…you like mushrooms?" the old man asked him, offering him a bowl filled with some greenish, greyish sludge. It looked foul, but the smell was fantastic.

Did he like mushrooms? He couldn't remember ever eating them before. Or had he? He thought maybe he had.

More Secrets

Lisa frowned. Then she stopped frowning, realising she had been doing a lot of that lately.

"It's not there," Hailey said, banging on the table. The woman was frustrated. She didn't like not being in control of the computer system.

Lisa leaned forward and started tapping the keys, waited for the results, and then stood back. "Maybe there's a problem with the system?" she asked.

"Nothing that I can find," said Hailey. "I put three other reports in at the same time, and they are all still in there, I checked. The one on E2 is gone, like...well, someone got rid of it."

Jackson, Lisa thought. Or Rogen. One of them. Both would have the clearance to remove the records if they wanted to. And it made what she had seen the previous night even more strange. No, not strange – it damn well put the chills up her. Something was going on that was not legitimate, but she had no way of knowing what it was.

Unless she figured out how to open the hatch next time.

The scratches. What was with the scratches? She'd checked in with maintenance and they'd said that the scratches would go when they gave the carriers their usual blast cleaning, a process they used to clear out all the crap that the machines picked up out in the dirt and grime of

246

The Junklands. The guys over in maintenance had told her just an hour before that the carriers had scratch and dents marks on them all the time, and that they promised to clean up E2. She wouldn't even know the marks had been on it, they'd said. They'd promised.

But Lisa hadn't been bothered about the marks being removed. What bothered her was that she couldn't find out if other carriers had come back similarly marked.

Happened all the time, maintenance had told her.

"Let's just move on to the next issue," said Lisa.

Hailey turned to face her. "Doesn't it bug you? Not knowing?"

Lisa nodded. "Yeah, sure," she said. "But it's not important. I want to know where we're headed tomorrow."

Hailey turned back, tapped at the keyboard, and peered at the screen. "Sector thirty-two," she said. "Just another salvage op."

Lisa sighed. "Nice. At least I can work on my tan."

Two hours later, Lisa tossed the scruffy paperback book she was reading onto the floor next to her bed and sat up.

Sector thirty-two, she thought, unable to take her mind off Jackson's little espionage mission in the hangar. That's just one hop over from the last, where E2 was tampered with.

Maybe whoever did it will try the same again. And I'll make sure I intercept it. Then I'll know why.

She sighed. Wanting to know why was what had gotten her into trouble the last time, but she couldn't help it. As if thinking of her time in the Outer Zone sparked some memory she wanted to recall, Lisa reached down to the cabinet at the side of her bunk, pulled open the second draw down, and took out the magazine that sat on top of the pile inside. It was old and scruffy but she still treasured it. You couldn't get stuff like this back in the Inner Zone, not relics of this kind. The magazine was ancient.

There was a faded picture on the front, showing a huge building called Grand Theatre, and outside the building were crowds of people queuing to get in. But what she peered at wasn't the coloured cover. It was the two stick people drawn near the entrance of the building, right next to where the queue entered a large, ornate doorway. The stick people – an adult and a child – were holding hands and walking into the building in front of the crowd.

She put the magazine back in the draw and pushed it shut, then thought back to her current dilemma. She didn't like Jackson, the governor of the facility. He was up to something.

And she wanted to know what it was.

Open Up

The Watcher heard the banging and woke. Other noises should have alerted him much sooner, but hadn't, and he cursed himself for being slow.

You're getting old, he thought. You don't hear or see things the way you once did.

And someone was rattling at the front door.

He stirred, sat up from his bed, and stretched. In the other room he could the heavy breathing of the stranger, the digging man, and nodded.

Still here, then. Sensible.

The Watcher trundled across the wooden floor towards the front door, frowning at the noise being made, interrupting his sleep.

"Come on, RootMan," called a voice. One he recognised, wasn't it? Yes. FirstMan's second in command. Right-Hand, Tight-Man, or something like that. Trouble, was what he was. "We know you're in there."

Do you tell the stranger to hide? He is surely what they are here for. No. You're too late. You're at the door and they'll kick it down if you keep them waiting for too long. Ah well, at least you gave the digging man a day of rest. And his knee would fix soon anyway, if they don't beat him too badly.

The banging continued.

"Alright!" called The Watcher. "I'm coming. Don't break my door!"

"Get this door open, you old fool," came the reply. "I don't have all night."

You don't? Don't have all the time in the universe for your foolishness? You could stay out there for an hour or two and nothing much would change. Always in such a hurry to go nowhere in particular and then disappointed when you get there.

The door creaked loudly as the Watcher pulled it open. He blinked at the darkness outside, but then smiled as his eyes adjusted to the dark and he saw the face of RightHand stared back at him from the gloom.

"Well if I never," said the Watcher. "A visitor." But then he saw other shapes moving in the darkness. "Many visitors."

Of course, he'd sensed they were there before he saw them, but he didn't want them to know that.

If they think you're old and stupid, they'll leave you alone. They won't be bothered with you. It always seemed to work. Except when that other man was involved.

Then FirstMan stepped out of the darkness and into the dim light that seeped out of the cracks in the building, cast only by the low lamp that burned inside the entrance. The Watcher liked dark places to hunt and search, but he also liked to keep his home lit.

Yes, that man. More trouble than most trouble.

"Hello, Haggerty," said FirstMan, also smiling. "I'm sorry to bother you in the middle of the night, but it would appear that news has reached me to suggest that you may have a visitor staying with you that is of great interest to me."

The Watcher, Haggerty, frowned. "Well, now," he said, his bright, toothy grin spreading wider. "Who could have told you that then?" And he thought back over the time since he brought the digging man to the shack, but couldn't recall seeing anyone other than the search party that he had avoided out in the trash lands.

"Oh, I don't think it's important who told me," said FirstMan. "But I do think it's important that you allow us to speak to your visitor."

The Watcher peered at the dozen other Junkers gathered along the edge of the swamp. "You mean to accost my visitor?" he asked.

"Oh, let's not be so harsh, now," said FirstMan. "We just want to know who it is and why they are here. Make sure they're no danger to you or anyone else."

"Humph," muttered Haggerty and nodded his head towards the shack. "Go on in, then," he said. "Not that I can stop you anyways. I suppose I should consider myself fortunate that you even knocked in the first place."

"I wouldn't have dreamed of any other way," said FirstMan. He too nodded, but this time to RightHand.

RightHand stepped into the doorway and Haggerty moved outside, walking along the wooden platform that jutted out over the swamp. FirstMan followed him and they both looked out over the dark water and waited. There were noises inside the shack, things being moved, doors opening, cupboards opening and then closing, and then a minute or two later RightHand stepped back out into the night.

He looked confused. "No one in there," he said.

FirstMan frowned and turned to Haggerty. "Where did your visitor go?"

Haggerty shrugged. "I guess they just up and took off while I was asleep. If they was even there in the first place."

"You said you had a visitor," said FirstMan, now seeming irritated.

"Did I?" said Haggerty "I thought it was you that said that."

FirstMan turned to his men. "Spread out," he ordered. "They can't have gone far." And then he stalked off, ignoring the old man.

RightHand stayed for a moment and stared at Haggerty. "You should be careful," he said. "Hiding a potential enemy is not going to help any of us, including you. And it's bad enough out here as it is."

"Thank you," Haggerty said. "For the advice. I shall consider it when I next have visitors."

After the group had gone, Haggerty went back into the house and peered into the small back room that Jack had been asleep in. The bed was empty, and the pile of gear that he had found with the man's unconscious body was also gone.

But there were no signs of how the man had got out of his shack.

Well done. Well done. Right under their noses, as well. Even skipped past me.

I must really be getting old.

Out of Here

Finder watched from the top of the junk pile, a hundred yards from the edge of the swamp, staying back as he had been told to by FirstMan. He didn't see why it could be dangerous. Old Haggerty wouldn't hurt him. They were friends, or so he believed, and whoever it was that he'd seen the old man helping towards his shack had certainly been in no condition to be moving.

But he did as he was told, as always, and sat there in the darkness, just listening and watching as FirstMan and RightHand spoke to the old man. He couldn't hear what was being said, but he saw RightHand move into the house.

To go fetch who is in there, Finder thought. And he wondered who the man could be. If it was a man. There was that as well. It could be a woman. But none of that mattered. It wasn't a Junker, so it had to be someone from the facility, or maybe a Farlander, or worse.

A trooper? No. The person lying on the stretcher hadn't been wearing the grey armour they wore, the sort that he could so vividly remember. Of course, it could be one of the salvagers going runaway. But, from what he heard, they don't usually get very far and no way did they reach this far towards the Junker towns.

But this one had caused all kinds of worry in the towns, with Junker patrols and warrior packs going out every day to find the intruder. The intruder had been spotted at a distance a number of times but they hadn't caught up with them. Whoever it was was too good at hiding.

Finder remembered someone he once knew that was good at hiding. The one who taught him.

It was with these deep thoughts that he sat there, waiting patiently for the group to be done with the old man and the visitor. He did wonder if they would kill the intruder, but even with the rumours of how ruthless the Junkers were, he had never actually seen them treat anyone badly. He remembered when he had joined them, not long ago – just half a year ago – with all the others from the Picking Factory.

He'd been in the last picking warehouse in the facility, the one nearest the sleeping quarters, standing up on the platform and looking at the constant flow of junk rolling along the conveyor.

There were half a dozen others on the platform, all leaning forward and grabbing things from the trash, throwing them into the bins behind them. He remembered vividly reaching forward and taking the rusty wrench from the flowing trash when the sirens went off.

He'd never heard the siren before, and he stood up, shocked and surprised to see the rest of the kids running down the steps and over towards the other end of the warehouse. They stopped there, not far from one of the open entrances of the building, all huddled together.

He ran down the steps, half a minute behind everyone else, and was only part of the way across the open ground when the strange figures crossed the compacted dirt outside.

He'd never seen a Junker before that day, but had been told all kinds of nasty tales about them and what they did. Mostly that they were really half-human monsters that ate people, but seeing them then, up close, he wondered if any of the stories were even close to being true.

Sure, they were ragged looking and covered in dirt. But they seemed to be wearing armour that was similar to the facility troopers, and they even carried weapons that looked the same. The tales he'd been told were of spear wielding savages.

And then the siren stopped.

He stood there, not knowing what to do, as the Junkers entered the building, a dozen of them spreading out and scoping the corners. Some of the kids nearly bolted and ran, but others grabbed them and stopped them.

Finder had just stood there, in the middle of the open space, not knowing where to go. And they had let him stand there.

Then the three facility guards walked into the warehouse from the other side and headed towards the Junkers.

It had puzzled him at the time. They had met in the middle. No blazing fights, no killings, no blasters going off. At the time he'd thought he'd better run and get under cover, because where he was standing was a prime spot for catching a stray blast.

But the two groups spoke, and one of them even laughed.

The women and children that worked in the facility had been made to walk then, and it seemed that it was a walk that took days, because they slept in different shelters along the way, guarded by either the Junkers or the troops from the facility.

And not once had he seen anyone being hurt or even pushed.

As he sat there, in the darkness, waiting for FirstMan and the other to be finished at the shack, he smiled, thinking of how little he had known back then. He smiled and stared at the shack perched on the shore of the great swamp.

And then he noticed the figure moving through the junk below. He stopped smiling and sat perfectly still, not moving, not making a sound. He altered his breathing, remembering everything he had been taught in an instant. Slow and shallow. Slow and shallow.

The figure was moving quickly, dodging along the winding path between the great piles of junk, and whoever it was, they were limping.

Then it dawned on him exactly who it was.

The intruder.

"They're over here!" Finder shouted. "Over here!"

Hunted

The voice, so close by, made Jack jump. But it was clear who the caller was shouting about. He paused only for a moment, glancing up the trash mound and seeing a small figure dart back into the darkness and into hiding.

Even if he wanted to silence whoever was up there, he wouldn't be able to. His leg was screaming at him to stop moving, and the climb up there would be too much. It was the best he could do to double his efforts and press on, following the path and hoping to spot a hiding place along the way.

Except now he knew he wouldn't have very long to do it. In the distance, back in the direction of the shack at the edge of the swamp, he heard voices calling out to each other, and the rattle of junk falling away as the group of men who had gone to the shack in search of him started taking chase. They would be much faster than he on this terrain.

He pushed on, stumbling along the path that was anything but straight. It wound around large, dark shapes that he couldn't identify, and they slowed his progress. He was at a huge disadvantage out here.

They will know where they are, and they will know the territory. Every last bit of it, probably. You're a fool to even think that you can outrun them or hide from them. Hell,

257

you could be running right over the top of a hidden base for all you know.

But what if they catch you? What will they do? Eat you? The old guy from the shack, the one that took you in, seemed harmless enough, though you can't really know that.

Had he turned you in? No. He hadn't. The conversation outside the shack wasn't a welcoming one. They knew each other, all of them, but the old man hadn't been enthusiastic about letting them into his house and finding you. He'd even been sarcastic about it.

He didn't turn you in. He just gave in because he had to. No choice.

Jack stumbled and nearly went down. The voices had stopped behind him but he could hear them coming. A dozen of them at least, mostly following the same path he was on but closing much faster than he could move.

They'll be here soon, he thought as he rounded a corner and came to a large clearing in the junk. Across from him was a gaping hole in the darkness, a spot much darker than everywhere else. A tunnel of some kind?

He had no choice. He laboured across the clearing, stumbled up the small slope of trash at the foot of the hole, and started to climb, grimacing as his leg twinged with pain. He rolled further into the darkness, relieved that it seemed to slope away from him.

And then he lay there, about ten feet inside, in almost utter darkness, and waited for them to come, hoping that if he stayed still and quiet they would pass him by. It was by no means the best place he'd found to hide over the years, but it wasn't too bad.

He lay there and listened, hearing boots trudging over the ground outside – some of them passing by the hole and heading further along the path. But others, he thought, had stopped not far away. He could tell that less pursuers were moving around outside.

He held his breath for a second and then started slow breathing. Slow and shallow.

Even if you're standing just a few feet away you can still hide.

It had worked on the man who came into the shack, like it had with others, dozens of times before. The man came into the shack and walked right by you. Three steps into the opposite corner and he'd walked right by you again as he came out. No movement. No sound, and he hadn't spotted you. The darkness inside the shack had helped, but to stay perfectly still and blend in, that was the trick. And then out the front, right behind him, just feet away. No noise. Careful steps. Three figures outside, all facing the glare of the old man's lantern. But they were far enough away, over near the edge of the walkway. And they were slightly blinded, and not able to see you slip away, as the man who had searched for you blocked the view of you stepping out behind him.

When they didn't think you were there, it was easy.

But now, as he lay there in the darkness, he wondered how long it would be before they found him.

It was all very well moving quietly and making a quick escape when they didn't think you were there, but when they were hunting a moving escapee on their home ground it was an entirely different thing.

And that voice. That bothered him.

The one who had called out. The voice was so familiar, but yet he couldn't place it.

In the silence he played back the voice in his mind, stepping back a few minutes to hear it more clearly.

And then he was back in the Outer Zone, searching through the ruins of the cinema. The boy had wanted Jack to show him it after he'd told him all about how people would gather there to watch some vast moving picture. He'd explained how they all sat in rows of seats and watched the lit-up wall with images on it, and the boy had marvelled at how such a thing could even exist.

"Can you show me?" Ryan had asked him, and even though it was three, maybe four, long days of travel from where they were, he'd still taken the boy and stood outside with him as Ryan looked up at the crumbling remains of the vast building. Most of it still stood, even though the inside of the building was almost completely gutted and stripped.

It was still an impressive sight, hundreds of years after the magazine photos had been taken.

Jack had shown Ryan the pictures in the magazine of the exact same building. He thought it had to be the same one. The details were so similar, even if most of the gleam and shine and the bright lights were missing.

And, of course, the boy had found another magazine in one of the rooms at the back as they both scoured around the building, Ryan looking avidly for some new find but Jack only wandering around, knowing that he had searched the place thoroughly already.

It had been the magazine that Ryan had drawn the stickmen in. The one he gave to Jack and the one they boy was so pleased at finding for him. Now lost.

"Over here!" Ryan had called. "I've got something! Over here."

Over here.

That voice.

It was older, but not much different.

Not much different at all.

The hidden stranger on top of the mound of trash, the one that had given him away and called down his pursuers, was Ryan.

It was him.

Jack lay there for a moment, in the darkness of the hole, playing back the voice over and over, knowing that he was right.

Then he crawled to the edge of the hole and dropped down onto the ground, raising his hands as the four men standing the other side of the clearing raised their guns.

And then it occurred to Jack that Junkers weren't supposed to own guns, let alone the assault rifles that all four of these men carried. And the armour. It was Hunter armour, wasn't it?

One of the men stepped forward and a light shone in Jack's face.

"Who are you? What are doing you here?" asked the man, and Jack recognised the voice of the man who had spoken at length to the old man in the shack.

"I'm looking for someone," Jack said.

"I asked who you are," said FirstMan. "Are you from the Recycling Facility? You a trooper? Spec Ops?"

Jack was confused. They thought he was military? One of the Hunters or facility guard. He didn't know what a Spec Op was.

"I was a salvager," he said. "I don't work for...I mean, I'm not from the Inner Zone."

"Then why are you out here in our territory?" asked FirstMan.

"I'm looking for someone. A boy. Ryan."

Another figure moved into the dim glow of light behind the spotlight, a smaller figure maybe shoulder height to the men, but Jack couldn't make out who it was.

"Ryan, you say," said FirstMan. "And you're definitely not from RAD or TSO?"

Jack shook his head. "No. I don't know what those are, or who they are, I was just...I had to get out and find—"

"Jack?" asked a young voice. The person behind the men. "Is that you?"

Jack's heart nearly jumped out of his chest and he took a step forward, only to step back again when the four men raised their guns higher, aiming at him now.

"Is that you, Ryan?"

The figure behind the men moved forward.

"Yes, it's me," said Finder. "It's Ryan."

PART FIVE
What lies below

Trapped

Jack sat, staring at the ground inside the cage, not paying much attention to any of the movement around him. People of the Junktown came and went throughout the day, and the cage that he now called home was sitting smack in the middle one of the larger, more open courtyards in the warren city that was hidden in the junk. Jack had seen a lot of that city on his way in, though he had been bound and gagged the whole time.

Endless covered paths wound through the mountains of junk, and along each of the many paths, there were doors attached to the walls. From the outside, the streets and alleyways looked like walls of junk until you saw a home or shop hidden behind it through an open door. The Junkers had made their homes not only amongst the trash, but out of the trash, carving deep holes into the very junk mountains above and the depths below. And there were far more people than Jack could have imagined. Hundreds, maybe even thousands, of them.

He was taken along many of these alleyways as his captors guided him to where he would be held, and saw not only houses, but shops and large open places where resources were kept. At one point they passed what appeared to be the side of a massive old stone building, jutting out of the trash, and it reminded him of the Grand Theatre back in the Outer Zone, except this was used as a marketplace. There was an area where dozens of large metal containers had been stacked on top of each other, and Jack could see makeshift stairs and platforms built to reach the topmost containers. People were living inside them.

The cage that was to be his home, it would seem, was sheltered from the rain but not nearly as hidden from the elements as many of the Junker dwellings. There was only a rough mattress to sleep on and small boxed in hole in the ground to relieve himself in. At least the cage was dry. There was that. The cage was maybe twenty feet across both ways and tall enough to stand up in, and Jack had spent a lot of time pacing around the perimeter with only his thoughts to entertain himself.

They fed him, if you could call the grey slop, which was passed to him in a dented metal bowl three times a day, food, but he wasn't going to complain. Jack had the impression that most of the inhabitants of the Junktown ate the grey slop. They had little choice, he thought. And honestly, it actually tasted good if you ignored the lumps. Where they mushrooms or some kind of animal? He wasn't sure. He didn't really want to know.

He had visitors, though, and those visitors took away the monotony of his incarceration. And anyway, he'd been there before, hadn't he? Well, maybe not exactly there, but he had been in a cage similar to the one he now called home, and that had been somewhat smaller. But that was many years ago.

One good thing, though – he wasn't expected to fight every other day, and there were no jeering crowds. No blood-soaked floor.

Just the solitude of the cage and the quiet of his own thoughts.

He wasn't expecting to be let at out all.

The cage had held a lot of slaves a year before, Old Haggerty had told him. Until FirstMan had arrived, with his troopers, and set them all free, killing the mob of slavers that had held the Junktown in thrall for years. But there were no others now. The cage was reserved for criminals to stay in while their fate was decided. Jack had been the only one in the cage during his stay.

He had three regular visitors. The one they called FirstMan, the leader of the Junkers, came at least once a day and questioned him endlessly about his past and his reason for being out in the Junklands. The man didn't seem to believe him at first but gradually became less hostile and more curious. Jack thought he may even like the man, under different circumstances.

"I'll probably let you out tomorrow," FirstMan said before leaving each day, and Jack wondered after the third day if this was something that would ever happen. He suspected that his imprisonment was to be long term.

His second regular visitor was the old man that lived in the shack at the edge of the swamp, and his were the least expected of visits. The old guy checked Jack's leg every day and muttered to him about mushrooms quite a lot, or other junk that he had found, as though it may be of interest to Jack. Then he just left. He only ever stayed maybe ten minutes at most.

Jack liked the old man, apparently named Haggerty, for some reason, even though it became obvious to him during those visits that few Junkers did. Jack thought that Haggerty had an honesty about him that was refreshing. Oh, not a kind of non-lying honesty. Certainly not. Jack suspected that half of what Haggerty said was a lie, or simply misleading, but when it was time for him to go, there were none of the formalities that even the Junkers used. No hello, no goodbye. Not even a nod. The old man simply stood up and left, often cursing at someone nearby to get out of his way, even if they were nowhere near him.

And then there was the third visitor. Ryan.

The boy came half a dozen times, during the daylight hours, and often sat there at night until he was scolded by one of the Junkers and sent to bed. From Jack's 'cell', which had once been some sort of shipping cage for animals, he could see the building that was Ryan's home in the distance, poking up towards the clouds.

Jack couldn't believe it was an actual spacecraft of some kind. They never made real ones, he'd thought, and had believed that his whole life. Sure, there were the Ark ships that left every year, he remembered that much from his youth, but they were built in orbit, or something like that, built next to a space station, a kind of building that hung in the air, high up outside the atmosphere, in space.

Jump shuttles rocketed up into the sky hourly from the Inner Zone. He'd even seen them in his earlier years, on the few occasions he'd been close to The Wall. They burst up into to sky with a roar and then gradually vanished into the clouds, the roar of the ascent diminishing over a few minutes until all that was left was a plume of fumes dissipating in the sky.

But no, Ryan insisted that the metal monstrosity leaning against the rock outcrop was, in fact, once a ship that had flown in space.

They talked about a lot of things, he and Ryan. And when the boy left to sleep, or eat, or do his chores, Jack felt both relief and joy as well as guilt. It was as though they had never been apart. The boy chattered and chattered, bringing him more drawings that he had done, entire books full of them. They had a lot of scrap paper in the Junklands, as well as card and other materials scavenged from the mountains of trash, so much so that Ryan had two dozen or more wads of sewn together paper with his own drawings in. The paper alone would have brought a fortune in barter in the Outer Zone, but it was a common material in the Junker town.

But, with all these visits, Jack wondered if he would be stuck in the cage for weeks, or even months.

They don't trust you, you see. Not Ryan, he will always trust you, it seems, even after you let him down so badly. He doesn't think you did, and you're lucky for that. Very lucky. He could have been angry with you and he wasn't. No, it's not his trust you're missing. The Junkers don't trust you. And why should they?

But things were different today. Jack could sense it. He had the ability to pick up on such things. Jack looked up from the dirt to see FirstMan strolling towards the cage, with that ever-confident swagger he used, and

Jack's spirits lifted. Even if FirstMan was trying to conceal it, Jack had noticed the ring of keys hanging from the tall man's belt.

Hope.

There was no greeting like there usually was. FirstMan just jumped straight into the conversation that he wanted, like they had been talking for half an hour already.

"I apologise for keeping you in such a fashion but we have no spare quarters or buildings that were secure enough to keep you in one place," FirstMan said. "You seem to be quite good at slipping by people, and getting out of places undetected, and I couldn't have that until I was happy to let you go."

"That's okay," Jack replied. "I understand."

"You do?" asked FirstMan, surprised. "I thought you'd be angry. I have the security of all these people to consider, and few resources to achieve that goal, but now Ryan and Haggerty, and RightHand, have convinced me that you're not a spy, I don't feel I have the right to hold you any longer."

"It's fine," said Jack, thinking that he'd been kept in worse places. Maybe not much worse. Where was this going, though? He wondered. Freedom wasn't coming without a price. He could sense that already.

"I have a proposition for you, Jack," said FirstMan.

There it was.

Keep it calm and friendly, he thought. Play the game how he wants to play it. Just be yourself.

Jack frowned.

"I know it seems strange to keep you prisoner and then offer you a job," FirstMan said. "But after your little escape trick, back in the swamp, and after everything that Ryan has told me you are good at…well, I find you to be quite a talented individual. If you would be interested in working with us, maybe helping us locate certain things, I think we could make it worth your time."

Jack thought in silence for a moment, and could sense that First Man was about speak again. "Okay," he replied. They had kept Ryan alive all this time, and they were probably both his and the boy's best option for survival at that moment.

FirstMan grinned. "Oh," he said. "That was easier than I expected. I was anticipating having to haggle and persuade." He stepped forward, unlocked the cage door and pulled it open, gesturing that Jack could leave.

Jack stepped out of the cage and stood up straight, stretching. "You've kept my boy safe all this time, and more importantly, he's alive."

FirstMan tilted his head to one side. "Well, not just me. You can thank the rest of the folks in the towns for that," he said. "He was brought in with a large group, a couple of hundred kids and women, quite a while ago. They became part of the community, so it wasn't done as a favour to you."

"I know," said Jack. "But he's alive, and that's all that matters to me."

"He's not actually your son, is he?" asked FirstMan. "He has always claimed he was, but I sense not."

"No, he's not by blood," said Jack. "But we kind of adopted each other when he was much younger. He may as well be. Always has been, I think."

"Good," said FirstMan. "A kid needs a father, I always say. I lost mine when I was young, so I know the hole it leaves."

They were silent for a few minutes, both considering their own thoughts and what they had just learnt of each other. Jack thought that maybe the man wasn't so bad after all. He could put his faith in worse.

"So you'll take my offer then?" asked FirstMan.

Jack nodded, his lips pursed. "Sure. What am I looking for?"

FirstMan paced the floor next to the cage and then closed the door and flipped the lock shut, as though putting that part of history to rest, locking it away for good.

"I need you to find me some old tech," he said.

Follow Your Orders

A year before

They moved through the mountains of trash like ants, scurrying between dirt mounds, navigating the pathways swiftly, even in the dark. There were no spotlights or torches. These figures moving rapidly towards the hidden settlement wore grey armour, with full face visors that showed no view of the people underneath, and gave no indication that built into the helmets were full spectrum enhancements that meant to them it may as well have been the middle of a bright, sunny day.

There were guards at the entrance to the Junktown. Three of them huddled against the inside of a wall made of rusted, stacked up cars, but they didn't see the squads of troopers approaching, or hear them until it was too late. The first fell when he tried to lift his weapon, and the other two didn't know what happened before their worlds went dark.

Two hundred yards away a tall, lean man covered with tattoos awoke to noises outside. He pushed aside the young woman that lay on the bed nearby and struggled to his feet. Something had woken him, he knew, and it was something that shouldn't be there, but now, as he listened, he heard nothing.

The girl opened her mouth to speak but the man

271

raised his hand, indicating that she should remain silent. She said nothing, not daring to anger him. She had seen what happened to people who angered the ruler of the Junkers.

He got up, grabbed the large axe that lay next to the bed, and stood listening.

There. There it was again. Almost a coughing sound that was sharply cut off. But then there was no more.

There was movement outside in the town streets, and that displeased him. The curfew he had ordered meant no one was allowed to leave their huts after sundown, and if they did they would be cast in with the slaves. But, sure enough, he heard someone running across the hard dirt in the large clearing outside.

He trudged towards the entrance and peered outside into the dark. It was not raining so the sky was clear. It hadn't rained for weeks, and the ground outside was beginning to crack. Even the deep well spring was running slower.

No movement, and he was about to step outside when he saw it. A flicker of red across the clearing.

He squinted, frowning, wondering if it was only in his mind, a memory from a day, long ago, when everything had fallen apart. It had started with those flickering red lights.

He closed his eyes for a moment and re-focused.

No. There it was again — a flash of red across a panel of rusted metal.

Escape. Leave now. That was all that he could do now. Out here, so far away from where he had come from, he had thought they would not follow him. But they were here again, weren't they? Curse that fat man for backstabbing him after he had sent him all that good stuff. If he ever had the chance to...

No time for that, he thought.

He turned and ran back into the hovel, grabbed his bag and his knife and shoved the blade into his belt. The back door was fifty yards away, down the passage that led deep into the trash, and it came out in an undercut area near the back wall of the town. He had hollowed the entrance out years before, knowing that if he needed a quick exit that he would need to be unseen. It had to be one that no one else knew about. So he had gradually carved his way from the very back of his hut and through the trash until he made a tunnel that came out near the wall.

He ran down the passageway now, leaving the confused girl behind him. She would slow him down, and he was done with her anyway. Another mouth to feed later on that wasn't needed.

He slammed into the makeshift door at the end of the passage and heaved it open. A second later he dropped down into a shallow cave. But he didn't stop. He kept moving, jogging in a crouched position. The cavernous space was large but not high, and he was too tall to stand upright down there in the dark, and would probably bang his head on the ceiling if he did.

He passed one of the struts that he had put in place to hold the roof up, and then another, counting four such columns before he reached the outer wall and the ladder that led both up and down. It only led down if you knew how to lift the hidden floor panel, and he paused, thinking of the treasure hidden far below this spot, things he could use to barter if desperate, but he couldn't carry them and didn't have the time. If he wanted to escape it had to be now.

He heard the shouting begin above him, and the noises of resistance in the main town square. Some fool was fighting back, he knew. Some fool that would only end up dead or shocked into submission.

He had been a king once before, when the grey warriors came and destroyed everything and took him to their prison. He had eventually escaped even then, but he remembered. Now he would not wait to fight them. He'd learned.

He pushed the hatch up and hauled himself out onto the ground outside.

Dark figures moved around the gate a hundred yards away, so he crouched and headed in the other direction, running low to the ground as he dashed for the nearest pathway into the junk.

He was ten yards from the freedom of the trash that surrounded the town when two figures stepped from the darkness and aimed their rifles at him. He slowed and stopped, and he was about to raise his hands when he saw a flash of bright blue light as one of the figures waved a scanner in his direction.

Then there was a moment of silence before the second dark grey figure raised their rifle higher and Jagan saw the red light as it burned into his eyes. Then the world was gone to him.

Inside the town, Corporal Ranold stood just to the side of the main clearing, one hand pointing his assault rifle outwards as he scanned the clearing, the other touching the panel on the side of his helmet.

"Target Alpha eliminated, over," came the voice of team one's commander, a Squad Leader named Waylan.

"Good," replied Ranold. "That's all four primary targets down. Watch out for more resistance and stand by for further orders, over."

Ranold changed the channel and immediately heard the laboured noise of his superior, the Governor, wheezing over the radio. Ranold wasn't surprised. The man had been in charge of the facility for more than a decade, and the air near the factories was polluted to the extreme.

"Governor Jackson," said Ranold. "This is Corporal Ranold, over."

"Ah, corporal," said Jackson. "You have good news, I hope?"

"We have hit the location specified and all named primary targets are eliminated, sir, over."

"They're all dead?" asked Jackson, sounding surprised. Ranold found this irritating but he kept his mouth shut.

"Yes, sir," replied Ranold. "All the targets you specified are dead, over."

"That's excellent news, corporal," said Jackson. "You may now proceed to cleanse the rest of them. I want the whole area clear of vermin."

Ranold coughed, but was thankful the filter on his

radio would cut that out. Had he heard correctly? The trash town had maybe a three or four hundred people in it, he knew. They had scanned the area using drones before the assault, and most of the people were held in slave pits or cages. Women, children, the old and the weak. He'd seen the images.

"Sir, can you repeat? Over," he said.

"I said proceed to remove the rest of the population there, corporal," said Jackson, "I don't want the problem returning in a few years, so they all have to go."

Corporal Ranold paused for a moment. No. He had heard correctly. The Governor had ordered that he and his men slaughter the settlement.

"Sir, wouldn't it be better to order a roundup and bring them in? Over," he asked, but he already knew the answer.

"What was that?" asked Jackson. "You're questioning my decision? Don't be silly. Have you any idea of the cost of such an operation? Better they are put down now, corporal. Follow your orders and then find that cache of tech. That is all you are to bring back. And don't bother to come back if you don't find it."

Almost Right

Old Tech

"You were almost right," said Jack. "It's not here."

They stood side by side in the large clearing that FirstMan had brought them to, the boy still much shorter than Jack, even though he had grown quickly in the two years that had passed. Jack placed his hand on Ryan's shoulder and nodded. "You already knew that when we were on our way back here, though, didn't you?"

"Almost?" asked Ryan with a sheepish grin. "I wanted to find it for them, but it didn't matter how hard I concentrated, nothing came. I can't do what you do. Not always. It just doesn't come every time, like with you. I just kept getting an urge to search further out."

Jack nodded, though he wasn't surprised in the least that the kid had picked up some of his talent during the time they had spent travelling together. He thought that something like that must rub off on those around you. It certainly had on Drogan, though his old – now departed – friend had been more unpredictable with his results. And when he thought back, hadn't he himself gained the ability from travelling with that old man, when he had been very young? It wasn't a natural ability. That much was for sure.

"Sure you can, if you try," Jack said. "And maybe further out is precisely where you should be looking? Maybe you were right but didn't follow your guts?"

The boy frowned up at him, and Jack let go of his shoulder and turned to scan the horizon, ignoring the crumbling buildings nearby. They were wrong about those. The whole complex had been used for manufacturing electronics at some point in the past. A very long time ago, Jack thought. But most of what had been there had been taken, or moved to somewhere else. Not all of it had travelled far.

He squinted in the bright sun and tried to ignore the figures standing a hundred yards away, watching them. FirstMan and his troops. He wasn't yet sure about them, especially one now called RightHand, but Ryan seemed to think they were okay, seemed at ease around them. But they weren't Junkers, Jack knew, or they hadn't always been. He didn't trust their past, whatever that may be. He also found it distracting having them standing there, watching hopefully. This thing they were here to find was important to them.

His gaze wandered over the horizon, passing skeletal structures that had once been a city. Many other buildings would have stood between each of the towering ruins but had long since crumbled and collapsed, leaving these odd, vast towers, tottering on the edge of extinction themselves, dotted around the landscape like lonely teeth in a rotten maw.

Two of them caught his attention and drew him towards them, and he knew that one of them held the thing they were there to find, but he couldn't decide which it was or what was unusual about the other. Two ruined buildings, and one that he needed to search, but both had something to hide. They both looked guilty, he thought.

"So do you think it's here, then?" asked Ryan. Jack turned back to look at the boy, noting with a little amusement how his hair had been left to grow long and how it now curled up near his shoulders. Needs cutting, he thought. Was that a slight hint of impatience he saw in the boy's expression? Maybe.

"Yes," Jack replied. "I think it's here, but we're looking in the wrong place. It was moved at some point, a long time ago, but not far. It's further out, though, in one of the distant buildings."

Ryan looked hopeful at this. "But, where?" he asked, looking out at the far buildings.

Jack pointed at the first, a tall building, half collapsed but still rising maybe half a dozen floors from the ground, and then at the second, much more squat in comparison. Both were at least a mile from where they stood. "See the tall spire," he said, "and see that one that's already collapsed in?"

Ryan nodded.

"It's one of those two," Jack said. "I'm sure of it."

"But which?" Ryan asked.

"That's what I want you to tell me," said Jack. "Look at them. See if you can spot what I can't."

Ryan did as he was told, staring off into the distance, first at the shorter building and then at the collapsed one. He frowned. It was there, that gut feeling, just as

Jack had always said it would be, but both buildings called to him. It was a strange feeling to have, and Ryan had never felt it as Jack described it while he had been with him. It wasn't until he had been living with the Junkers for a few months that he started to really understand how things called to him. He only had to learn to listen to his instincts and spot the signs that were right in front of him.

He stared hard at the taller building, sensing something hidden there that had been long forgotten, and feeling that people had recently been there but not discovered the secret that was hidden within. Had they been there looking for it? He couldn't tell, but he knew they had been disappointed when they left.

The second building – the much smaller ruin – felt entirely different, though. It had been a very long time since anyone had ventured there, so long that he felt it could maybe be decades or centuries. "I don't know which it is," he said.

"Hmm," mumbled Jack. "Me neither. But you get something from both?"

"Yes," said Ryan.

"Want to make guess at it?"

Ryan shook his head.

Jack turned back to stare at the tall building.

Recently searched, he thought. Not recent as in months, but maybe a year. A group stayed there. The other building. Not searched since the days of the old world. Untouched. Something is hidden there, though, and he knew that would bug him. The taller building was

280

what his gut now said.

"It's the tall one," he said, turning back to Ryan.

"You think?" asked the boy, and for one moment Jack questioned his instinct. "I thought that too!"

"You know, we don't have to stay," Jack said, his voice low.

Ryan looked up at him, frowning.

"We don't have to stay with these people. We'd be fine on our own again, just like we used to be. We could just strike out, there." Jack nodded towards the buildings in the distance.

"I don't want to leave," said Ryan. "And you won't, if you stay."

Jack smiled. "If I stay?"

"If you don't head off out there alone," said Ryan.

"Boy, I lost you for over two years... nearly three," said Jack. "Nearly never found you. I won't let that happen again. If it means getting used to these..." he waved his hand at the group gathered fifty yards away, "junk people, then that's what it means."

Ryan grinned. "They're called Junkers," he said.

"Junkers, yes. I'm sure I'll get used to them."

They stood silent for a minute, the time passing slowly as they both struggled to find the right thing to say. Finally Ryan spoke. "So, the tall building," he said. "That's where we need to look?"

Jack nodded. "That's where your FirstMan's gadget is," he said.

All Out of Cache

A year before

They couldn't find the equipment cache. Ranold had the entire troop out for two days, searching the area and questioning the captured Junkers, but no one knew where it was. It was hidden, and only Jagan had known where he kept his stash.

He stood in what the Junkers called The Throne Room, staring around at the mess. The place that Jagan had called home was trashed, turned over and over by his troops, the floors pulled up, the tunnel that led out the back exposed, but they found nothing. Wherever Jagan had kept his stash of goods it was well hidden. The Junkers couldn't even tell him where Jagan went, most of the time.

That was something that niggled at the back of his mind. He had always been given the impression that the Junkers, the savages that lived out in the junk and wastelands were precisely that – savages – but they were polite, they built homes hidden in the junk, and they taught their children to read and they had laws. It was tribal, sure, but this was no savage society.

And he had orders to kill them all.

He'd seen the expressions on the faces of his troops

when he informed them of the Governor's command. Not a single man or woman wanted to obey. Not one. He wondered, thinking about how they had reacted, if any of them would even follow the orders. He imagined the situation escalating into something messy, a fight between the squads, those that would carry out their orders and those who refused to murder innocent civilians.

Because they all saw that these people weren't monsters, and they'd all seen the school of a hundred or more children, sitting in a large circle inside the hollowed out hull of an abandoned sailing ship, their grubby, dirty faces, fearful of the troopers but bright eyed and keen to learn the magic of reading and joy of singing songs.

And they'd all known that those frightened faces thought the troopers were the bad guys. And he supposed they were, or could be. But more importantly they could *not* be, as well.

No. He thought. There would be no fight. Not one of his troops would obey that order. They had all spent time capturing vagrants in the Outer Zone, but their orders were to capture alive, not kill. This was an entirely different thing.

And there was this problem of the equipment cache. Whatever Jagan had been keeping here was important to Governor Jackson, and that man wanted it, but they couldn't find it.

And that conversation hadn't gone well.

"Sir, reporting that after forty-eight hours we are unable to locate the cache," he'd said.

Silence on the other end of the radio. But then Jackson finally spoke.

"Keep looking," he said.

"Yes, sir. We have supplies for maybe two more days before we have to head back."

"No, corporal. You can take supplies from that Junker scum. You will erase them anyway, once you are done. The only reason I allow you to let them live, for now, is because you insist you need to question them. But that isn't working, is it? Find the cache and bring it back. You are not to return until you locate it."

"Yes, sir, but what if we don't find it?"

"Then you keep searching until you do."

Keep searching until you do find it.

Ranold looked at the massive bed that sprawled over a large area in the corner of Jagan's throne room, the pillow, rugs and fur turned over. If they'd captured him instead of killing him, as ordered, then maybe they'd have found it by now, but that was another thing Jackson had demanded without argument.

The man simply had no grasp of operations or how to achieve a goal. Well, Ranold thought, maybe he did, but his methods were ridiculous and self-defeating.

Waylan entered the throne room from the outside and Ranold turned to him. He noticed that the weather had changed, and the sun was shining down on the huge open ground outside Jagan's abode.

"Hey," said Waylan, a keen expression on his face. "You know, they have an underground mushroom farm here."

Ranold frowned. "A what?"

"Seriously," said Waylan. "It's massive. Must be an old warehouse, covered by the junk ages ago. It's huge inside and dark. Just a bit of light shining through some gaps. It's bigger than that reclaiming building back at the facility."

Ranold shook his head. "So much for savages," he said.

Waylan's expression turned serious. "We can't kill these people," he said. And there it was, the first spoken acknowledgement of what they all knew.

"I know," said Ranold. "But if we don't, and we don't find that cache, then we can't go back. Jackson was quite clear."

"What's he gonna do?" asked Waylan. "Demote us all?"

"He'll court martial us if we go back having disobeyed orders," said Ranold. "He was quite clear about that."

"Then I won't go back," Waylan said nervously.

Ranold frowned. "What?"

"I won't go back," repeated Waylan.

"What do you mean?" asked Ranold. "What will you do?"

"I'll stay here," said Waylan.

Ranold was surprised by this and stood silently for moment. Waylan seemed to take this as an indication to go on.

"Look," he said. "These people need help. They've

spent the last few years under the grip of that idiot, Jagan. He killed them if they disobeyed, and you don't even want to hear the other things he did."

"I know what he was like," said Ranold. "You remember I was a grunt when we took down his pit fighting operation in the Outer Zone?"

"Yeah," Waylan said. "Of course. I forgot. But anyway, these people need someone to take charge and rebuild, man. Come on. Wasn't that our dream anyway? Sure, we wanted to do it out in the new world, but we've found it right here. And, oh boy, you wanna see the good stuff that's just gathering dirt around here. I mean old tech, generators, appliances, all sorts of gear. We could have power up and running in a matter of days."

"Junk is not a good reason to stay out here," said Ranold.

"Yes, I know," said Waylan. "But did you know there are over a thousand Junkers here and in the surrounding area?

"What?" said Ranold. "That many? A few hundred, I thought."

"I spoke to some of the elders. Now they're starting to think we won't kill them all, they're talking, and they told me over a thousand. There's about twenty hidden settlements. C'mon, man. You wanted to start anew, to build something meaningful and not have to follow orders. We don't have to go to the new world to do that. We found it right here. This is what you said your dad wanted. What you wanted."

"What of the others?" asked Ranold. "Not everyone

is going to want to stay."

"I think most, if not all, will. But we'll deal with it," said Waylan. "Right here. This is important."

Right here, thought Ranold. And I like mushrooms.

Hidden treasures

Now

"How does it work?" asked FirstMan as he walked beside Jack. They hadn't taken Jack's words on faith, and he thought that FirstMan believed him only because Ryan believed, and he made a note to ask how the boy had gained such trust among these men.

"What?" asked Jack.

"The way you and Ryan find things," said FirstMan. The man was older than Jack had expected, probably older than Jack by a decade, and he bore the scars of combat to show for it. Deep lines etched one side of his face, which Jack suspected may be shrapnel wound scars, and there was mark on his chin that looked like it had been very deep. "You just stand there and then you know where stuff is," said FirstMan. "It's quite unnerving."

"It's not really just standing there," said Jack, finding it awkward to explain. "I can somehow read my surroundings and...sense? I think that's the best word, sense, what happened before, just by the signs left behind. You ever hear of something called dowsing?"

FirstMan nodded.

"Well," continued Jack. "It's sort of like that but

looking for more than just water."

FirstMan was silent for a moment. "You can find clean water?" he asked, now even more keen for answers.

"It's all around us," said Jack. "And that cage you kept me in?"

FirstMan frowned.

"Well, that hole to take a dump in probably drops straight down into an underground river," he said. "But yes, it's sort of like dowsing, for something other than water, and without the stick."

"But you can sense it all the way over there?" quizzed FirstMan, indicating the tall ruin that loomed over the flattened landscape just a quarter of a mile away. The mountains of trash weren't present in this area of the Junklands, but there was still plenty of junk strewn about, just not mountainous amounts of it.

"It's something I picked up from an old man, back when I was a kid, just by watching him work," Jack continued. "You think it's odd, what I can do? You want to see a crooked old man smelling the air and then finding an old stash of tools three floors down in a cellar five miles away."

FirstMan stopped walking and looked at Jack with an incredulous expression. "You're serious?"

Jack laughed. "Very," he said. "I was maybe eight years old, about Ryan's age, really, and we were out in the middle of nowhere, not far from the Ashlands, and places where people don't go and shouldn't go, and he stood for half an hour, smelling the air. All I could smell was that ash smell. You ever been out there?"

"To the blighted lands?" asked FirstMan. "Yes, a few times, but we were always geared up. You can't smell anything in full suits of combat carapace. Dismal place, though. Full of things that should be dead."

Jack nodded. "That's the place," he said. "Well, the old man stood there for ages and then just started walking. Didn't speak a word. We went for half a mile, him stopping every few minutes to sniff, then another half mile, and so on and on for about five miles. Eventually we stopped at a ruined building, just like all the other thousands of ruins out there. Nothing to distinguish it from any other. Then he sniffed again, nodded, pointed at the ground and told me to dig. Plopped himself down on the floor a few feet away to roll a smoke and watch me."

"And you found tools?" asked FirstMan.

"Pristine tools," said Jack. "Boxes and boxes of the damn things. I dug where he pointed and opened up a stairwell that nearly collapsed under me. Three cellars deep the place was, and full of cobwebs and spiders and all kinds of nasty stuff. He made me build a wheel cart from scratch just to haul the stuff back to The Crossing. Never lifted a hand to help with any of it, either."

"Harsh," said FirstMan.

"Yeah, but I learned a lot," said Jack. "I learned a lot and I learned it fast. I was his slave, and I got paid with food and little else, but the talent I learned from him was worth that price. You know, he could stand still in a room while talking to you and just vanish. Still talking, just somehow not visible, and yet not leave the room. It took me a long time to realise that most of it was about what was in your own mind. He had this theory that he went on about a lot. He thought that people used to be able to do many more things that were forgotten and that you just had to remember how to do it."

"Sounds strange, but amazing still," said FirstMan.

Jack laughed. "Yeah, it does. He said his ability to vanish was just a matter of making someone else forget he was there. The old guy was pretty screwed up."

They arrived at a wide, open ground across from the target building. The huge space appeared to have been some sort of plaza. The ground was covered in broken slabs that still bore faded colours and patterns that Jack couldn't make out clearly. Across the other side of the plaza was the rusted carcass of a tank, with its gun long collapsed to the ground.

The group of armoured troops that FirstMan had brought with them, all geared out in Hunter combat armour, the origin of which was still a puzzle to Jack and a question he was itching to ask, started forward, heading towards the tall building. But Jack felt something uneasy in his stomach, something urgent, and it wasn't the need to relieve himself.

Something was not right here, but he couldn't place what it was.

"Wait," he said, lifting his hand and signalling the men back. A few stared at him questioningly, and then looked to FirstMan for orders. But FirstMan waved them back.

"Problem?" asked FirstMan.

"I don't know," said Jack. "Something odd. Something makes me nervous."

Jack turned to Ryan. "Buddy, get back over there near the building and keep out of the way." Then he turned back to FirstMan. "Just in case."

Ryan didn't wait to question, and jogged back to the building opposite the taller spire, and stood peering around the edge of a crumbling wall, the curiosity too much to just hunker down and hide.

Jack stared at the front of the building, and at the junk strewn around it. There was a very definite area, maybe fifty feet wide, in front of the building that was completely clear of junk. The ground was still dusty, and dirty, but there was a section up on the dais in front of the building that was...

That was it. That was what was wrong.

"Everybody get back under cover," Jack said as he peered at the patch of ground and stooped to pick up a stone. He waited until they were all behind cover, took a dozen steps forward, and threw the rock. He waited two seconds to confirm that the stone had fallen inside the open space, and stepped to the side, putting the ruined tank in between him and the clear spot.

There was a click, a series of beeping sounds echoing across the plaza, then a grating sound, followed by a continuous tick, tick, tick that didn't seem to stop. Eventually he edged forward and peered around the edge of the tank. In the middle of the dais, where the clear spot had been, was a gun turret sticking up from the ground. It was pointing directly at where the stone had landed and was furiously attempting to shoot it.

But it was out of ammunition.

FirstMan arrived next to him, the other troopers following. The leader peered at the angry gun as it shifted and tried to track anything else in the locality, again repeatedly firing nothing at whatever it had decided was a target.

"Well, that could have been messy," said FirstMan, turning to Jack. "I think maybe I'll just trust whatever strange talent you have from now on," he said.

Jack peered at the man who led the Junkers. There was something unusual about him. "Who are you, anyway?" he asked.

FirstMan frowned at him. "What do you mean?"

"You're not like the rest of the people out here," said Jack. "You and your men."

FirstMan smiled. "So not just good at finding things, then," he said. "You spot far more than I'm comfortable with, Jack."

Jack shook his head and smiled back. "I'm no threat, you know that," he said. "But you didn't take that armour from dead Inner Zone troopers, did you?"

FirstMan grinned back. "No, it was issued to me," he said, deciding that he liked this man, Jack, and considering that the man would have just saved their lives if the defence gun had been packing ammunition, he thought he could trust him. "I'm Ranold. Previously Corporal Ranold, of the Inner Zone RAD. Though I prefer the Junker term FirstMan, if you wouldn't mind sticking to that in front of other Junkers. All of my men are ex-RAD as well. But we're all Junkers now, and we've worked hard to unite the tribes into one."

Jack looked puzzled. "Then why are you out here?"

"It's a very long story," said FirstMan. "And one that we should tell another time. When we have what we came for."

"It will be below ground level," said Jack, indicating the building with a nod. "Probably in some kind of storage. I think there was a battle in this area, a long time ago, and the tech was moved and secured." He turned and started towards the front of the building.

"So a bunker, you think?" replied FirstMan, following him.

"A bunker," replied Jack. "Though I doubt it's locked. Just well hidden."

"Then let's go find it, shall we?" said FirstMan.

Into The Old World

Jack stepped carefully over the pile of rubble that blocked most of the entrance to the building. Once, he thought, the entrance hall had been a grand affair, a sprawling and large open space with huge panel windows surrounding it that providing a stunning view out into the plaza that he also thought would once have been beautiful. He'd seen the tiled floor in the centre of the plaza, and although it was now broken, and overgrown with weeds and even a few trees poking up from the cracks, the tiles were still colourful.

He glanced back, as he stepped down onto hard ground, and looked out of the gaping holes that must have held single, massive panes of glass. How anyone could have made such things was puzzling to him. There had been a man at The Crossing that made glass, but it took a lot of recycled bottles and scavenged broken pieces from the ruins for him to smelt anything of size, let alone something to fill the huge holes in the side of this building.

Such were the losses of history, Jack thought. But maybe they can still make it in the Inner Zone, maybe someone still has the knowledge. They have to. He'd seen the glass panes on the Trans, and in the windows of the large buildings in the compound where he had been sorted with the rest of the captives.

But there was no one to replace these out here, he

thought. He glanced towards FirstMan, who stood just a few feet away and was searching the ground and the room ahead of them, and then he looked into the once plush foyer of the building.

There was an abundance of broken wood and cracked plaster covering the floor, and as he glanced around he saw other things – bones, rags, and bits of metal. A fight had taken place here at some point, and much of the debris had been left untouched since then. Jack frowned. There were two sets of stairs and two open shafts where lifts had once been, and there were a set of doors beyond that, but no sign of a way down.

"Search the upper floors," ordered FirstMan, and Jack looked up to see RightHand heading up the left set of stairs, followed by one of the other troopers. Another pair headed up the other stairs, while the rest remained at the open entrance, looking out into the junk and ruins beyond the plaza.

"Where do we look?" asked Ryan. The boy was picking at a pile of broken wood and plastic a few feet away, where Jack imagined a desk of some sort would once have been. Ryan picked out a long pole of plastic, turned it over and then dropped it back into the pile. He stood up and frowned at Jack.

"We need to go down," Jack said.

Ryan glanced around, checking first the lack of a way down the stairs and then at the few doors that lined the back of the hall. "Through there?" he asked.

Jack nodded. "Has to be," he said. "I don't see any other way."

Ryan didn't look convinced. "Are you even sure there is a down? Doesn't look like one to me. No stairs."

Jack walked over to the nearest lift shaft and peered down. Darkness below and more rubble. He could vaguely see what he thought was the bottom, some thirty feet below, and what looked like the top of the lift itself. There was a large pile of metal cable collapsed on top of it and a small hatch that was already open, revealing darkness inside.

"The lift goes down further," he said, and then noticed that Ryan and FirstMan were already next to him, also looking into the darkness. "But why would they build a level that only the lift accessed?

FirstMan shrugged. "I've seen worse designs," he said. "You should see the conversion facility over at the RAD grounds." He shook his head and looked puzzled. "Utter mad chaos."

Jack turned to face him. "I saw that place, or at least the entrance to it, when I was captured," he said. "What do they do there?"

FirstMan looked back down the shaft and then upwards. "You really want to know?"

"I'm just curious," said Jack. "I saw someone causing trouble and they got dragged off that way."

FirstMan smiled, but there was no joy in it. "Well that person is about the unluckiest you ever met," he said. "They...recondition people who are a problem, mostly violent criminals and troublesome captives from the Outer Zone. Brainwashing, or should I say, Resetting."

"They actually do that?" asked Ryan.

FirstMan turned to the boy, seemed to consider whether he should be telling the youngster such things, but then continued. "They do indeed. And if you ever happen to be unlucky enough to bump into the HAC — that's Heavy Assault Corps, then you'll be looking at the results of that...facility. They stew up their minds. They don't get rid of violent tendencies, in fact I'd say they increase those, but they make them like obedient dogs."

"Nice," said Jack.

"Absolutely," said FirstMan. "I had the unfortunate pleasure of having to escort a detachment to a drop off at a clearance zone, once. Not a single one of them spoke, the whole two-hour journey. They just sat there, looking straight ahead into empty space."

Jack looked back down the shaft and finally noticed the set of rungs studding the wall at one foot intervals. They seemed to lead both up and down, and he could see that they went all the way to the bottom.

"That's our way down," he said, pointing.

FirstMan frowned, but then saw what Jack was pointing at. "You want me to send my guys down there?" he asked.

Jack shook his head. "No, me and Ryan can handle this. Better off without a lot of heavy boots stomping around down there. Also, I don't know if those rungs will take the weight of that armour you guys are wearing."

FirstMan nodded, reached to his waist and pulled away a radio handset. "Well this is my spare, if you know how to use it? Yell if you need us."

Jack took the radio, clipped it onto his belt and then turned to Ryan. "Want me to go first?"

"No way," Ryan said as he sat down, swung his legs over the edge of the shaft, and shuffled towards the ladder. "I'm gonna find the loot way before you can sniff it out."

What Lies Beneath

Jack followed the boy down the shaft, squinting as his eyes adjusted to the darkness below. He could just make out Ryan, about fifteen feet below him, as the boy dropped down onto the top of the lift. A quiet, dull thud echoed faintly up the shaft as he landed. Jack thought he heard something else, a clattering noise of some sort from far above them, and wondered what RightHand and the others were doing up there.

He glanced upwards to see that the shaft rose high into the building and then darkness, and thought for a moment that now would not be a good time for something to drop down from that height. With this he sped up, taking the rungs two at a time and hoping none of them would break. Finally he hopped onto the top of the lift and looked down the hole that he had just seen Ryan disappear into.

"It's okay down here," said Ryan, looking up at him from inside the lift. "There's…ah…the remains of someone down here in the corner, at least I think it was a person, but it's really old and dusty, so try not to step on it. I nearly did."

Jack started to lower himself and then peered down into the hole once more. He saw the boy kneeling on the ground, and a moment later there was a spark and a flicker of flame as Ryan lit a makeshift torch made from a scrap of wood with some cloth tied to it.

Good lad, Jack thought. You haven't forgotten the things I taught you, even if you haven't gotten rid of that reckless adventurer streak. Not a bad thing, really.

Jack dropped down into the lift, felt the structure shudder and then settle once more, and watched as Ryan stepped out into the opening outside the lift. Jack stepped forward, moving beyond where the boy stood. "Okay, now I go first," he said, grinning as Ryan frowned with annoyance. "Just in case something is down here."

In answer to that, Ryan flashed his knife in the torchlight. He held it tightly in his other hand and smiled back. "I'm ready for that too," he said.

Jack nodded and took out his own knife, thinking again that he was glad the FirstMan had put his gear aside instead of sharing it out among the Junkers. He knelt down next to the lift. "Can you shine that over here?" he asked.

Ryan knelt beside him and lowered the torch to the bottom of the lift, peering and trying to spot whatever it was that had caught Jack's interest. The torchlight was dim, maybe lighting up twenty feet from the spot with a yellow, flickering glow, but it was enough for the two of them to see underneath the lift, and to see there was nothing underneath it but a concrete floor, half a foot lower than the floor inside the lift.

"What?" asked Ryan.

"Bottom floor," said Jack, standing back up and looking around the room outside the lift. "Means unless we find a stairway or something, this is the lowest level and we don't need to search any lower down. Also means that with the open shaft and decent ventilation its ok to leave that flame lit."

Ryan looked confused for a moment, looked at his torch burning in the darkness, then he seemed to realise what Jack meant. *Gas below ground.* His mouth turned to a silent *oh* and he nodded.

Jack already suspected that what they were looking for was not far away. Glancing around the large room, he saw piles and piles of boxes and crates, all seemingly filled with cables and rusted gadgets, some of which looked similar to the thing that FirstMan had described. But he knew it had to be a sealed package that he took back up with him, or the circuit board would be useless after so many years exposed to the elements.

He stood in the darkness, watching as Ryan walked around the room, uncovering more boxes as the light from the torch explored the unknown. There was a set of double doors at the other end of the room, a single corridor with three doors leading off it, and another door in the far corner.

But which of them leads to what we want? he thought. Where does the trail lead us?

Jack looked at the smaller corner door, thinking. That it was probably a storage room for cleaning materials. Seemed to be the obvious choice. He glanced at the three doors. One of those, maybe? But, no. The double doors led somewhere else, maybe into a larger storage room. He judged a direct line from the lift opening to the double door, envisioning someone wheeling a trolley out of the lift and directly across the room. He glanced at the floor, peering through the scattered pieces of debris and broken plaster that had fallen from the ceiling and onto the worn concrete. The paint marks had worn away over the centuries, but there was still a trace of them. Deep lines crossing the gap between the lift and double doors, those painted in yellow. The other lines, three of them and much thinner, heading to the corridor and the three doors, and then a blue line weaving its way across the floor towards the smaller door.

He tried to twist his brain around the image on the floor and closed his eyes for a second. In the darkness inside his mind he saw an image of the Sorting Room, where he had been sent down one corridor along with some of the other captives, and others had been sent down different corridors. Coloured lights marked the different destinations and this was somehow similar to that. Then the image was gone, and he saw an automated factory, with small metal robots making their way around the different machines, delivering parts and picking up new ones. This was an image of the Picking Factory, he thought, but one from long ago. Where the image had come from he didn't know, maybe one of his old magazines, but as he opened his eyes he saw, just for a moment, a ghost superimposed on the cluttered and dusty room in front of him. A large robot with a trolley following behind it moved out of the lift and drifted forward, its wheels skittering over the flat, unobstructed floor and ignoring the real debris that was there now. It rolled forwards, heading across the room towards the double doors, following the painted line. It slowed until the doors opened and then sped through them into the interior of the next room. Then the ghost was gone.

"That way," Jack said, pointing to the double doors, and Ryan turned from the box over by the smaller door, which he was peering into, and looked towards the doors. The boy's mouth opened a little, and Jack waited for the questions, but then Ryan just nodded, accepting Jack's intuition. He dropped the box and started forward, holding the torch aloft to light the way.

And that was when the loud crashing noise came from far above.

Intruder

RightHand peered into the darkness of the third floor, aiming his assault rifle high into the rafters. As he had discovered on the second floor, after he and his men negotiated the crumbling stairway, the levels of the building were built with an odd ceiling cavity, maybe four feet thick, that was filled with rusty cables and piping. Many of the pipes had cracked and fallen, and were probably the cause of the collapsed ceiling, most of which now lay on the floor of the large open space at the top of the stairs, but much of the cabling still hung down from above like some crazy plastic and metal spider web.

This probably isn't going to take very long, he thought, as he looked out across the rubble covered floor.

There weren't any side rooms or corridors on this floor or the one below, just a large open space, and he also thought that by the state of the stairs they would only be able to access two more levels, possibly just one. He glanced among the rubble, which was mostly broken masonry and rusted metal, and decided there was nothing worth risking going out into the room for.

It would probably collapse if you did, he thought.

Across from him, fifty feet away, there was movement, and he watched as one of his men came up the other set of stairs, glanced around the room without leaving the safety of the stairs, and nodded once at him.

"Move to the next floor," he said into the microphone balanced near his chin. The other trooper nodded, looked up and then moved away, heading up the stairs to the next floor.

But the next floor wasn't like the previous ones at all, and RightHand frowned as he looked out of the stairway entrance into the vast room. Here, much of the ceiling and probably most of the upper floors had collapsed downwards and was now piled up, filling more than half of the space of the original room.

He took one step forward, signalling for the men in the opposite stairway to stay where they were, and edged into the room to look upwards.

There was something too regular about the debris, he thought. He didn't know what it was, but the cabling, panels and masonry weren't stacked up as though they had just fallen there. Some of it, he mused, almost looked as though someone had put it there, exactly as it was, maybe as some form of barricade.

And he kept thinking that right until the bug crawled out of the gaping hole in the ceiling above and dropped down to the ground, chittering and clicking at him.

Before the thing moved more than a few paces, RightHand fired his weapon, a single shot into the front of the creature that tore away a large chunk of its carapace and imploded its face.

Damn bugs, he thought, Let just hope there's only one of the—

Another bug dropped from the hole in the ceiling, and then another, and another.

What Lies Above

FirstMan's eyes went wide and he stepped back from the lift shaft, snapping his gaze upwards and then to the stairwell. The rifle shot had pierced the air with a muffled snap that he heard even a few floors below where RightHand was. The assault rifles were silenced, almost, but if you were only twenty or thirty yards away, or inside a building, they still made an audible noise.

"What's up?" he asked, tapping the microphone attached to his collar, just below his chin.

"We got a few bugs up here," came the reply from RightHand. Then a moment later there was aloud *thud* from above and then RightHand was cursing.

"Damn it," came the voice over the microphone. "Back up. Down the stairs. Get the hell out of here!"

FirstMan reached to his waist, instinctively grabbing the assault rifle that hung from his shoulder strap.

"What's going on?" he asked, the microphone still active.

"Bug nest!" came the reply. "Damn thing just fell from the ceiling."

FirstMan glanced back down the lift shaft, wondering how far into the building Jack and Ryan had gone. "Jack, you there?" he asked as he moved to the bottom of the stairwell and readied his weapon, waiting for RightHand and the others to get down the stairs and pass him.

They won't be able to get out if there's a lot of bugs, FirstMan thought. No way will they be able to get back up here in time. There was a lot of noise above him. Gunfire, running boots on hard stairs, falling debris, clicking monsters, and then the sounds of something heavy falling with a crash, and brickwork crumbling, bouncing off rusted metal floor panelling.

Oh damn, he thought, as he heard the upper floor begin to collapse.

He moved quickly towards the open doorway as the troopers reached the bottom of the stairs. "Jack, can you hear me?"

No reply.

Visitors Revisited

Tyler turned over the smashed-up pipe and peered inside. It was starting to get dark, and he thought about turning in but knew that if they didn't fill the dumper that they'd hear about it when they got back to the facility in two days. But the pipe was empty, as he'd expected. He cursed, dropped the pipe, and looked across the clearing to where the other crew members worked.

It had been over four weeks since Jack had gone off into the Junk and they still hadn't replaced him with a new member of the crew, and it was showing. Tyler told himself that it wasn't Jack's unnatural ability to hunt down the good stuff, but it sort of was. But with one man down on the crew it meant a larger share of the dumper to fill for each of them, and dammit if they hadn't been posted out into the deep north scavenging field, where the junk mountains were smaller and there were definitely less pickings to be had. Why they even bothered to send anyone out there was beyond him.

And why change their next location at such short notice? wondered Tyler.

Jack's disappearance puzzled him the most. The man had never given any indication that he was a runner, and that he planned to take off, though Tyler had noticed the change after the conversation in their bunkhouse about the people that had been taken from the Picking

Factory, and he had certainly thought Jack was particularly quiet when they actually got to searching and reclaiming the place. Quiet and preoccupied, somehow. Had it been his fault for sending Jack up to the top floor of the workhouse? No, he didn't think so. Guards should have been on the wall and would have spotted Jack making a run for it. How that had happened was puzzling.

He stood back up, groaned at the ache in the bottom of his spine, turned, and decided the grief of a scolding when they got back would be worth it. He was done for the day. As he crossed the open space towards the carrier, he saw Higgins turn and peer at him.

"We done?" called the old man.

Tyler nodded and called to the others to stop before he climbed into the back of the carrier and slumped down on his chair. His back was throbbing, right down deep at the base, near his ass. Old age, he thought, though he wasn't really that old. Working out in the Junklands aged a man faster, he thought. Unless you were Higgins. He tried to ignore the niggling pain, took a deep breath and closed his eyes.

The other crew members climbed into the carrier over the next few minutes, each one clattering the door as they came in and making even louder noises as they dumped their stuff and dropped into their own seats. Finally he heard the door clunk shut, followed by a series of clicks as the bolts were pulled over.

Time to rest, he thought. He was hungry, but food could wait. First just a few winks.

He sat up, startling himself, and looked around,

glancing immediately to Higgins. The old man was sitting up, looking towards the roof, but gave Tyler a quick glance and touched his finger to his lips to indicate silence. He had slept for a while, he was sure of it. That hadn't been just a minute or two.

And there it was, that familiar sound up on the roof. Tyler frowned and listened intently, trying to judge what could be making the noise. So far, they'd only found the scratches left behind and never anything else, and without staying outside when the carrier door was shut there was no way for them to watch their visitors. No one was willing to do that.

A few minutes later, after a lot of noise from above, there was a thud on the ground outside and the sound of something moving away quickly across the dirt.

The crew — all of them awake now — sat in silence for a long time until Tyler spoke.

"What are the bets the top compartment is all scratched up?" he asked. The other men nodded in return.

"I'd say that was pretty much a done deal," said Higgins, looking up at the ceiling. "Guess you better file another one of your reports."

Tyler chuckled. "Not that that is going to do any good. I don't think they believe me."

"Must do," said Rick. "They see the scratches every time."

"Until maintenance covers them up again like they were never there."

Rick shook his head. "I don't get that."

"What you mean?" asked Higgins.

Rick pointed at the ceiling. "Maintenance always hammer the panel back out and sand it off until the marks aren't there and the panel is shiny and new again, only for the scratches to turn up on a different spot the next time. They don't bother with all the rust holes and cracks in the outer plating of the rest of the vehicle, why bother with a few scratches?"

"I have no idea," said Tyler. "But it's really starting to bug the hell out me. I want to know why something keeps fiddling around up there."

"Or someone," said Higgins.

Tyler looked at him. "Or someone. Whatever or whoever it is only seems to like messing with us. No one else reports it, unless we just don't find out."

"Which also makes me wonder," said Rick. "If it's always us, then how the hell does it know where we are every single time? I mean, we travel for miles onto the next zone, but it always seems to track us down."

"Could be something stuck in that compartment that it can smell for miles and miles," said Higgins. "Like it's an animal or summit. Maybe something is dead in there."

"Enough dead things out here for a critter to smell without having to track down our carrier," said Tyler.

"Hmm, still don't make much sense," muttered Higgins

"We could try and prise the compartment open," said Rick. "Have a little nose at what's in there."

"We don't have the gear to open it," said Tyler. "It's

313

at least and inch thick, I reckon, and none of us have the tools to bust it open. At least not without some alarm going off. You wanna be the one to explain that to those that we must obey?"

Rick shrugged. "No, I guess not."

"Hey," said Boots, a man who rarely had anything to say. "May we should set up a trap for the critter."

Tyler frowned. "What kind of trap?"

Boots frowned and then shrugged. "Don't know, just thought it might be an idea."

Tyler looked down at the ground, squinting. A trap, he thought. Well, maybe not a trap, but some way to record who was out there or to scare them off. Something.

That was worth thinking about.

Trapped

Jack looked up and coughed as the dust settled in the room. He could see Ryan through the gloom, standing a few feet away.

"You okay?" he asked.

The boy nodded and brushed some crumbling pieces of rubble from his shoulder. Above them the floor groaned. Jack heard the hiss of the radio.

"Jack, you there?" came the voice of FirstMan.

He grabbed the radio and pressed the button on the side. "I'm here. What's going on?" There was a moment of silence, then some crackling, then another voice.

"We found a bug nest," came RightHand's voice.

"Stay right where you are," said FirstMan.

Jack looked over to the entrance where they had entered and saw that beyond the archway a pile of debris had collapsed into the large room. "We're trapped down here," he said. He stared at the fallen pile of junk and rubble, thinking that he and Ryan only just managed to avoid being crushed by running through the double doors. That had been too close.

Ryan turned to him, frowning, and stood up, taking two steps towards the entrance.

"Don't go any closer," said Jack. "Just in case it

collapses any more."

The boy stopped. Jack looked at the ceiling, noting the steel girders that crisscrossed above them and the metal plating the lay on top of that. Someone had wanted to keep whatever was in this room safe, he thought. What was it that was in here? Was it what he came to look for? There was a lot junk in the room, piled up in boxes around the outside, and in the centre of the room stood half a dozen tables pushed together. Upon the tables there was an assortment of circuit boards, wires, tools, cables and smaller boxes.

Jack grabbed the nearest box and peered inside it. Nuts, bolts, clips – all manner of small junk that was mostly metal. Still a treasure trove, though.

"We may as well get comfy in here," he said as the first sounds of gunfire rattled from above them. He thought that among the snaps of shots from the assault rifles the soldiers carried, he heard clicking noises. Mr Clicky's friends, he thought.

"Jack, you still there?" came FirstMan's voice on the radio.

Jack paused, but then pressed the button. "We're still here," he replied. "And still stuck. Looks like a lot of crap just caved into the room next to us, but were fine. We're trapped in a vault down here. Room is full of junk and gear."

"Good," said FirstMan. "It'll take us a while to clear out these bugs. There's a lot of them—" The radio crackled once more and Jack missed the words that followed. "—gave you. Over."

"Okay," Jack replied, guessing the general message. He turned to Ryan and located the boy on the other side of the room. He was holding a box from underneath one of the tables and peering inside it.

"There's all kinds of good stuff in these boxes," said Ryan, as he held up a rusted wrench. With a good clean the tool would be serviceable, Jack thought, and he started to search through the items collected on the tables. He had a feeling about this room. This was where they were meant to end up, but maybe not quite in the circumstances that they got there, trapped underneath who knew how much collapsed rubble, with a nest of Mr Clickys above them.

The gap underneath the debris didn't look big enough for Mr Clicky to get through, so Jack relaxed a little and turned to look at the pile of boxes lined along the far wall.

"Look what I found," called Ryan, a second or so later. Jack turned and found that Ryan was holding up what appeared to be a large handgun. Jack walked around the tables and took the weapon from the boy. He brushed the dust off it. It was old, and the magazine seemed to be missing, but Jack hadn't seen a weapon like it before. It was made from some sort of dense plastic, or another synthetic material that wasn't metal, with two square holes at the end of the short barrel. He put it down on the table. "See if you can find some of the ammo magazines that go with it," he said. "But don't mess with it until I've given it a good clean up."

Ryan nodded. "Sure thing, boss," he said, and began shorting through another box. "There's two more of them here."

Jack nodded. "Nice find," he said. "They're for us. Call it payment for services rendered."

Ryan grinned at this and placed the other two guns on the table next to the first. "Let's just hope there's some ammo for them in here."

Jack turned to the wall where the boxes were stacked up, his gaze drifting over the unreadable letters that had worn away over time, but he stopped at a box with a yellow label still stuck to one side. Squinting in the dim light, Jack moved over to where the box was, nestled among the others, and started lifting some of the boxes off, coughing as dust wafted everywhere. "Damn," he cursed. "This stuff really hasn't been messed with in a long time." Something small, with a lot of legs, scuttled over the top of the yellow label box and dropped down into the gap behind. A bug of some sort, maybe even Mr Clicky's babies, thought Jack, but he ignored it and concentrated on the yellow label box.

All of the boxes were made of plastic, Jack noticed. He hadn't seen something like that for a long time. If left sealed shut, the boxes down in this cellar would keep their contents safe from the ravages of time. He swept a space on the nearest table clear, then hauled the yellow labelled box out of the stack and plopped it down. The top was stiff, but eventually there was a hiss and a pop as the plastic lid came away in Jack's hands. Jack dropped the lid and peered inside.

"Bingo," he said.

"You found it?" asked Ryan. "Damn. I was hoping to beat you." But then he held up a six inch knife that was still in its holder. "But I got this. And this box here looks like the magazines for those guns. There must be forty clips or something like that."

"I think your find is better than mine." Jack smiled at the boy's enthusiasm. "We're going to be down here a while," he said. "So we may as well keep searching. You, know, for anything of interest. We do, after all, get first claim on this. Especially since we already found what FirstMan wants."

Ryan's grin widened.

Jack looked around the room. It had been a long time since he had seen so much stuff in one place that wasn't on its way through the Recycling Facility. Maybe that place in The Crossing, old Racket's place.

Drogan would have loved all this, Jack thought.

Don't Eat That

Jack waited at the entrance to the hovel, watching the bustling road outside while still keeping an eye on Drogan's back. Inside the building was a mess of old electronic junk that Jack had seen dozens of times over the last few years, ever since he first hooked up with the older man at the junction outside the remains of the New Stadium settlement. That had been the day he gained a new friend, a shotgun, and also saw the fall of a settlement that had barely begun to thrive.

Hunched over on the other side of Drogan was Racket, an old man with only one eye over which he wore a large round lens attached to a leather strap. Jack always thought the strap looked much too tight. The lens made Racket's one remaining eye seem five times bigger than it really was, and Jack had often wondered if he could see at all without it.

Drogan was a man who knew just where to trade for most things – especially anything that even vaguely resembled old tech. From circuit-boards out of the back of old TV sets to the guts of a rusting, rotten computer, he would insist on taking them to Racket, and Jack had to admit that the old man would certainly pay top coin if the object happened to be of value to him for one of his projects. What those projects were, Jack had no idea. He had never seen beyond the entrance room of Racket's building, but knew that the rest of the building, considering its size, could hide quite a lot.

Racket had a lot of resources at his disposal to pay for anything they found. Enough, Jack mused, to cover the costs of employing a thug to stand outside all day, and few could do that.

"What do you mean, you can't give me a good price?" Drogan's voice bellowed from the room behind him. Jack glanced over at the thug, standing a few feet away, and the man looked back. They both shrugged. This was usual, Jack thought.

Drogan knew what he was doing, and Jack had been in the other room a number of times to witness the conversation between his friend and the old man as it got a little heated, but Drogan was used to getting what he wanted, and persistence was his middle name. He'd keep on and on, and eventually Racket would give him a little more. They all knew that Racket was bound to try his luck with at least one thing that Drogan was trying to sell him.

Drogan and Racket were old friends and Jack had learned that this was the way they spoke to each other. The anger was only feigned, pretend.

Ten minutes later, Drogan came out with a grin on his face. We won this time, thought Jack.

"We ready?" Jack asked.

Drogan nodded. "Sure. Let's go get some food."

They wandered through the market, Drogan walking a few feet ahead of Jack, occasionally stopping to glance at something on one of the stalls, but mostly leaving things alone.

The pedlars were almost as persistent as Drogan, constantly waving things in Jack's face as he walked by. He was used to this, keeping his hands by his sides and shaking his head as continued on his way.

They eventually made their way to the east side of the market where the food places were. "What's it to be?" asked Drogan. "Rat roasted, rat fried, rat soup?"

"Fat lot of choice," said Jack. He'd rather not touch any of it, but he was hungry and they had few supplies after their last expedition. Drogan stopped at one of the stalls where small rodents of some kind – probably still rats, Jack thought – were skewered and roasted over a fire pit. He had to admit, the smell was pretty good when you were that hungry.

Drogan started haggling with the seller, so Jack stood back, watching those around him, and he noticed someone out the back of the tent. The chef had his back to them, preparing more of their catch. The man wore a long smock, stained with blood, and it turned Jack's stomach. But it wasn't until the man reached out for another skewer that Jack noticed the purple mark on his arm. It was only small, no bigger than a fingernail in size, but it was there – a purple mark surrounded by slightly grey skin and a black spider mark, trailing away along the man's forearm. The man must have sensed Jack's scrutiny, because he glanced up and pulled down his sleeve, looked at Jack once, then turned back to his cooking.

Jack put his hand on Drogan's shoulder. "Let's leave these," he said. Drogan frowned but then he saw the serious expression on Jack's face and nodded.

The food pedlar frowned. "What? You don't want anything now? I was doing you a bargain."

They walked away, ignoring the curses from the man behind them.

No Time to Bug Out

FirstMan took a deep breath and lowered his assault rifle, watching as the last bug kicked and writhed on the ground a few feet away before finally lying still. There must have been a hundred dead bugs littering the ground outside the front of the building and in the foyer by the time RightHand and the rest of the troopers had finished wiping out the nest. He shook his head.

I've never seen so many in one place before, he thought, but then, no one really comes here, do they?

At least none of his people did.

The industrial complex was too far out, and too near The Crags. FirstMan wondered for a moment if the crag tribes visited this place. But then, he thought, no nest such as this would have grown to such a size, and remain undiscovered, if it had been near the Junktown. And the crag folk would have eaten them.

He grabbed his radio, coughed to clear the dust from his chest, and spoke. "Jack, you still okay down there?"

"Sure. We're good. Still stuck down here and not going anywhere soon," came the reply. "But I think we may have found what you're looking for."

"Really?" asked FirstMan, as he walked back towards the building. "That's good news. Bad news is I think you're buried under a quite a lot of debris."

"Yeah, figured as much from the mess down here," replied Jack.

"Seems that it was a large nest, and it collapsed from above," said FirstMan. "It took out a couple of floors. May take us a while to get you out of there."

"We'll be okay," said Jack. "But don't take too long."

FirstMan turned to RightHand, who was standing a few feet away, looking around at the dead bugs and then at the collapsed rubble. It now filled the area where the stairs and the lift shaft had been. "I guess we better get digging," he said.

They're Back

Corporal Lisa Markell stood staring at the scratches on the side of the carrier, puzzled and a little amused. It had been over a month since she had watched Jack running off into the junk, and several weeks since she had spied the Governor poking around the vehicle bay, and in that time she had almost forgotten about the scratches and the compartments that had been tampered with.

Thankfully, she had badgered Mechanical to sort out a key fob that opened pretty much all of the compartments on any of the vehicles in the bay, and she had managed to do it – as far as she knew – without Jackson finding out. That, she thought, would be that last thing she wanted. She'd seen the report the last time they were sent to the facility. Hayley had dug it up for her.

Even though Jackson didn't bother with the normal formalities of talking to each trooper about their performance levels, as was usually required, he also didn't bother removing the officers' report summaries from the batch that she used to rate her troops. If she kept up her current performance level she could be reassigned within months, maybe just a couple, back to the Inner Zone or at least a closer facility.

No, alerting Jackson to her suspicions was the last

thing she wanted. Better to investigate, take notes, and make a full report when she was moved on and out of his clutches and ability to harm her career.

But here were those very same markings on — and it seemed even more unlikely — the same carrier. E2 crew. And they had been reported by the crew leader, Tyler, as they had before.

Except this time she'd been looking at Tyler's report on the screen when it had been deleted. She'd watched as the entry disappeared from the screen less than two hours after it had been put there.

Lisa coughed, wiped the sweat from her face, and swiped the key fob over the panel next to the compartment. There was a slight click and a beeping noise from the fob, and the compartment popped open.

Hayley, standing next to her, grinned and gave a quiet "Y*es,*" as the door swung open slowly. "We're in."

Lisa pulled the door open, glanced around to make sure than no one but she and Hayley were nearby, and pulled out the small package stuffed inside the compartment. She placed it on the ground, pulled her scanner out and swiped it over the package.

Nothing. No signs of live electronics or life, not that she was expecting any.

"What is it?" asked Hayley, trying to peer over her shoulder.

"Don't know yet," Lisa said, as she pulled back the dirty cloth that wrapped the object. Inside something metallic glinted in the bright sunlight.

What Lies Outside

Three hours later, Jack squinted at the bright sunlight as he dusted himself down. He was standing a dozen feet away from the ammo-less gun turret outside the front of the building. Three hours in the dark, waiting for FirstMan and the troopers to clear the way down to them, was a long time, and in that time he and Ryan had managed to sort their way through most of the treasure that was buried in the room below. He had tried pulling away some of the junk blocking the doorway but heard the debris above it groan in protest. It was too risky.

So they were stuck in there until FirstMan and the other troopers managed to clear what had fallen into the lift shaft and some of the room beyond that.

He'd thought, given time, if they'd been stuck down there, with no help from the outside, that he'd be able to gradually make a tunnel of some sort through the debris, but he saw little need since FirstMan and his men needed what Jack had found more than he needed them.

But what happens to me now? he thought, wondering if his usefulness was spent.

But he was still alive, and FirstMan was sitting on a pile of rocks near the broken pavement that had been churned up by nature as it forced its way up from underneath. The man was examining the contents of the yellow label box and nodding

"Perfect," FirstMan said after a few minutes. "Just what we needed, and even some replacements, if necessary." He held up one of the sealed packages stuffed into the box. "At least one of these, if not more, is gonna be in working condition. Excellent job, Jack."

"So," said Jack, peering at the man whom he still wasn't sure he trusted. "You going to tell me what it is you need these for?"

FirstMan looked up at him and the looked back down at the box, "That's a long story. Where do I start?"

"At the beginning?" suggested Jack.

"Well," said FirstMan. "As I said before, we used to work for the facility, or should I say we used to work for the RAD. Me, RightHand, and all my men, were Inner Zone troopers, sent out here to run missions clearing out zones ready for scavenging. Basically, doing whatever Governor Jackson decided was needed. His dirty work. Sometimes we were sent out here to find a group that was particularly troublesome and were raiding the outer lying facilities."

"Like the Picking Factory," said Jack.

"Yes," said FirstMan, nodding. "Just like the Picking Factory. When we got here, we took out the group that was trouble, but we found far more than we expected. Thousands of Junkers out here, and as you can see they're not the monsters that we were told about."

FirstMan paused in thought for a few moments.

"We were given orders to wipe the entire place out,"

he said.

"What? Kill them? All of them?" Jack asked, stunned.

FirstMan nodded, his expression grim. "Yes, all of them."

Jack looked away, disgusted. He'd only met Jackson, the Governor of the facility, once, and he hadn't liked the man. He remembered how Jackson had looked at him like he was a piece of dirt. But, to someone like Jackson, Jack supposed he was just dirt.

"So you mutinied?" asked Jack, looking at FirstMan.

FirstMan frowned, but then smiled, seeming a little embarrassed. "Well, yes. I suppose you could say that, but I wouldn't consider it mutiny, as such. Maybe changing sides. You see, my father was sent out here, to the facility, many years ago, when I was very young. I know that he worked with the salvage crews, but I don't know which, or under whom. I do know that I never saw him again.

"We had money problems, you see. My father was ambitious. I wouldn't say he was greedy, but... Well, I wouldn't know for sure, but he ran up debts that he couldn't pay off. So they arrested him and sent him out here is punishment. My mother went to a workhouse, and we were lucky we managed to stay in the Inner Zone and not get kicked out into the ruins like so many."

"Sorry to hear that," Jack said, remembering his own father vaguely. He wasn't sure if he felt the same loss that FirstMan felt, though, having been abandoned by his own parents when he was a just a child.

FirstMan paused and then looked at Jack. "Sorry, I didn't mean—"

"No, it's fine," said Jack. "Carry on."

"Well the choice between killing a few thousand people out here and disobeying orders wasn't a choice to me, nor was it to any of my men. These people needed help." FirstMan stopped talking for minute or so, and just stood there, staring at the ground.

The man's hiding something. But what? Jack thought that he was probably telling him more than he wanted and making sure he didn't tell him too much.

But he's telling you because he wants more from you.

FirstMan sighed and looked around. None of the other troopers were nearby. They were too busy helping Ryan and RightHand empty out hidden treasure trove on the floors below.

Finally, he spoke. "That circuit board can be used to fix a drone that we managed to capture, or should I say the Junkers managed to capture a long time before we joined them. It was sitting among the trash when we found it. The old guy, Haggerty, he told us a story about how it was sent to take pictures of the Junktown, and the old chief – one of the ones that we took out when we came here – shot the thing down from the sky. It had been in the trash ever since.

"Well, we had a look, and one of my guys is a pretty good tech, a dab hand at fixing stuff up. He managed to get it working, apart from the navigation. And that's what these boards are – a navigation system that can link in to the satellites still in operation by the Inner Zone."

Jack frowned. "Satellites? Like in the sky?" Jack remembered seeing pictures in an article in a magazine about such things, but believed them to be a thing of centuries ago, of the old world.

"Yes, exactly," said FirstMan. "We can use it to guide the drone if we can get it working again." FirstMan looked Jack in the eyes. "One of the things that we carry on the troop carriers, in case of extreme circumstances, is an EMP device. An electro-magnetic impulse explosive. It can take out electronics within a half mile radius, with very little damage to structures and even less damage to people. If we have this drone working, we can use it to take out the outer wall defences at the Recycling Facility."

"Why would you need to do that?" asked Jack.

"So that we can invade the place and take over."

"What good would that do?" asked Jack. "Why would you want to take over the place?"

FirstMan watched him, no longer wary, and Jack thought that somehow he'd already decided he could tell Jack everything. "Because from there we can control all of the facilities this side of the Trans. It's the hub. The only connection from the Junklands to the Inner Zone."

"So you just want power?" said Jack, puzzled. "You want to rule out here?"

FirstMan was shaking his head. "No, sure, yes. We want to take over, but not just so that we run this place. It's not all about power. But I guess it sort of is."

"Then what?" asked Jack. "Why bother. Why go to all that trouble?"

"Because if we take over the Junklands, and all the facilities, it'll choke the Inner Zone, and they'll no longer be able to send their Ark ships without dealing with us. They need the resources out here and, if we control that, then we will have something to bargain with."

Jack was confused. All this talk of taking over, of bargaining, of bartering with the Inner Zone. "But why would you need to do that?" he asked, but somehow he already knew the answer. There was a bigger plan here. Something much grander in scale than he had first thought, and his respect for this former soldier was growing with each new enlightenment.

"The Junkers," said FirstMan. "All these people. If we control the flow of resources, then we can barter. We can bargain a ticket off world. For everyone."

"Why tell me all this?" asked Jack.

"Because you asked," said FirstMan.

"But, you actually think you can trust me enough to tell me the whole plan, why?" asked Jack

"Because you have Ryan to look out for, and you have someone you care about, like I care about these people. It's someone to fight for."

"Fight?"

"Yes," said FirstMan. "I told you because we need someone to carry a targeting beacon into the Recycling Facility, so that the drone can locate the power plant we need to take down to lower the outer wall defences."

"You want what?" asked Jack.

"I want you to get captured and taken back into the

333

facility with a beacon hidden on you. I want you to be the target for the EMP," said FirstMan.

PART SIX
What lies ahead

The Pits

Years Before...

Jack's heart thumped in his chest. He breathed deeply, wincing at the pain that shot across both sides of his ribcage.

It wasn't normally like this. The fights had never winded him – at least not since the first few, when his body had protested the unexpected over-use of muscles and tendons. He chased his breath, trying to calm his nerves. His thoughts flailed.

Something has changed, hasn't it? But what? What was different this time? You never failed to entertain them, not even that first time, fumbling, stumbling around, expecting the next moment to be your last. But it hadn't, had it? It hadn't been the end, and this mustn't be, either. Them. They must have changed. Not you.

He was down on one knee in the dirt, wobbling, trying to stay upright as he stared down at the hard floor of the fighting pit. His vision blurred in and out, one moment clear, another moment washed and wavering as sweat dripped from his forehead and stung his eyes. He noticed, above other things, that his hands were swollen. Fresh blood painted them red. Not his blood, though.

He blinked, peering at his fingers, flexing them, thinking them damaged somehow after the endless pummelling he had put them through in the last few minutes. They would ache, but that would be tomorrow or the day after. For now, they were fine. Most of the blood – drying even as he stared – belonged to the motionless figure lying on the ground. Little of it was his.

His gaze shifted from his throbbing hands to the unconscious body of the pit fighter he had just beaten, and he ignored the raucous sounds from above.

This one had been meant to finish him.

He had been lined up to die.

After dozens of fights in the pits, this one had been a test, and he was supposed to lose. They hadn't given him a weapon. He had nothing to fight back with apart from his bare fists, and the man he faced held a machete and was armoured in leather and metal, like that worn by many of the spectators – the slavers.

Jack leaned forward and plucked the machete from the ground. For a moment, his mind flashed back to minutes before, and he remembered the other fighter's crazy, staring eyes, his unnatural speed and strength.

There had been no fear of death in those eyes.

Jack had seen insanity.

The man had been drugged, no doubt, Jack thought. Drugged and then drugged again. What was thrown into the pit had no humanity left in it, just animal instincts and basic desires. His opponent had only wished to cut him limb from limb.

And, Jack thought, he had seen a look he had never witnessed on other pit fighters' faces. Hunger.

A flesh eater.

The noise from the crowd above slowly washed over him, pulling him from his thoughts. They were cheering for him, yelling and screaming at him to finish it. But he couldn't force his body to move anymore.

Let them do the final atrocity, he thought. I've done enough.

"We have a victor!" a familiar voice boomed from above. "Bring him up, boys!"

Jagan, the slaver king. Despot ruler of the pits.

They'll kill me now, even after that, Jack thought, and he forced himself to look at the body in the middle of the pit. One cut with the machete would do it. Just one, and then…

He didn't get the chance to finish the job. The grinding sound of the cage being lowered into the pit tore his weary attention from his opponent long enough for the cage to reach the ground. Jagan was not known for his patience. Time was up. All Jack could do was stagger forward and stumble inside the cage as it thudded down. The dirt floor of the pit moved swiftly away, his stomach churning as they hoisted him upwards, and then rough hands pulled him from the cramped cage and dragged him before the fiery haired leader of the pit slavers.

"Well, well," boomed Jagan. "It seems I underestimated you. What have you to say?"

Jack merely shook his head and shoved the machete into his belt. They hadn't taken it away. That was a good sign, he thought. If they allowed him to keep it, and left him alone, that would be good.

"Got nothing to say?" boomed Jagan, then his voice lowered. "A silent killer. Interesting." Jagan seemed to consider Jack for a moment, and Jack's mind scrambled for something to say before the giant lost patience and ordered him dead. Before he could say anything, Jagan spoke once more. "Well, you bested one of our finest, it would seem, and he'll not be pleased when he wakes up." Jagan moved a step closer to Jack. "Or maybe he shouldn't wake up? What say you? What fate will you give him? Do you want to go back to the pens with the rest of the cattle, or you could take his place in the prize cages where only the very best of my gladiators live?" Again, Jagan paused, waiting for a response. "You can take his cage, and his slaves, if you want."

Jack nodded. Anything but the slave pens, he thought. He didn't like the idea of taking the madman's cage, and dreaded what he would discover there, but if it meant his own space away from the cramped and diseased conditions in the slave pens then he would have to take it.

There was a thud, and Jack turned to see two of Jagan's men dumping the barely moving, semi-conscious figure of his crazy opponent on the floor a few feet away. Jagan lifted his hand and pointed at the man. "Then it's decided," he said.

Jack's eyes opened wide, and he took a stumbling step back, surprised and confused. Was Jagan suggesting he should kill the man? He wondered if he could do it, but his hand instinctively went to grip the machete now tucked at his waist. Then, before he could step forward, Jagan reached down, grabbed the madman's hair, pulled his head back, and sliced open the man's throat with a knife. The semiconscious man gargled on his own blood for a few long moments as the pool spread outward, across the ground. Finally, he lay silent.

"His cage is yours, now," said Jagan. "You." Jagan pointed at a warrior standing a few feet away from Jack. "Show him where he is to stay."

The thug nodded and signalled for Jack to follow him.

"And somebody clean—" his words ended there, and Jack looked up, puzzled to see Jagan frowning, looking up into the sky. He didn't finish what he was saying. Instead he stared at the clouds in confusion.

Jack had thought, even when he had been fighting in the pit, that he may have heard the distant sound of thunder approaching, but this storm was not what he had expected and was of an entirely different nature. But it was still a familiar sound. A distant thud, thud, and a hum, deep and gut-wrenching. He knew it well.

"Dropship," said several voices at once, just as the word formed in Jack's mind. One of the men nearby pointed eastwards, and Jack turned to look in that direction, as did many others. He saw the huge bulk of the dropship appearing like a phantom in the distant sky. It hung there, grey and ominous, first appearing like some great, dark thunderhead before its form solidified as it approached, heading across the skies towards them. It was lowering, slowly, drawing closer every second, doubling in size as it raced in their direction. Barely twenty seconds passed and the massive machine was upon them, lowering into the open grounds of the pits just a few hundred yards away.

"Weapons!" bellowed Jagan, then he turned and walked – almost absurdly casually, considering what was coming – toward the nearby building that was his court and home, where his throne was. Around him, the thugs and the crowd dissipated, scurrying for their own makeshift, shanty abodes, grabbing weapons that leaned against walls or hung from hooks. Shouts went up as the warriors assembled.

Jack stood, a little stunned, wondering what he should do. The man he had been told to follow was now pacing back towards him, carrying two spears. He threw one at Jack and walked past him. Jack clumsily caught the spear and gripped it tightly.

Are they really going to try and fight a dropship? he thought. Are they mad? Yes, idiot. You already know how crazy these people are. The question is, are you mad enough to join them? And was the ship even coming for them? It might not be.

But as Jack watched, he knew it wasn't going to move on. He watched as it came closer, descending as it came, and as he had estimated, it was heading towards the ground that was flattest, just north of the pits.

Dust filled the air, blown from the hard, dry ground, as the behemoth touched down. Soon, vision had been reduced to twenty feet as a cloud of smog threw a veil over the entire camp. Jack choked as his throat dried up, and he snatched at a scrap of cloth that hung from his shirt, using it to cover his mouth. A blast of hot wind hit him, churning up even more dust.

"They wouldn't attack us, would they?" asked one of the thugs nearby. "They wouldn't come for a fight here?" The man took a step back, his expression nervous.

Jagan appeared once more and the thug fearfully re-joined the line of warriors waiting for him. The huge, red headed giant was now fully dressed in scavenged metal armour, and he carried a long spear with a wicked looking blade in one hand and an axe in the other.

"If they do," shouted Jagan, "We'll give it to them."

Someone has to go

Now...

Something stirred in the murky depths of the swamp, sending a thin stream of tiny bubbles up to break the surface of the green tinted water. Ripples drifted away from the lines of movement, causing the reeds and the strange blue flowers that floated upon the surface of the swamp to shudder.

Thirty feet away, Jack sat upon a large rock that overhung the water. He wasn't far from the path that led up to where FirstMan's camp lay, hidden in the open quarry, but Jack had no interest in going up there today. He'd spent enough time up there the day before, going over FirstMan's plans and hearing, time and time again, why he was the one that needed to go. Jack looked down to where Ryan stood, skimming stones out into the distance and bouncing them off the strange twisted trunks of the trees that grew only in the deepest parts of the water.

The wildlife and fauna of the swamp was unlike anything Jack had ever seen, and he thought it would be more at home on some distant alien planet than here in the Junklands. Most of it seemed warped or rotten in some way. But the strange growths still clung to life, and they had a beauty that was unnerving. The colours were somehow more vibrant than they should be, and even the twisted boughs gave an illusion of movement that was entrancing if you watched for too long.

The boy had been silent for a long time but finally spoke up. Jack could sense a hint of anger in his voice, and he figured it was justified.

"But, you've only just got here," Ryan said. "You've only been here a few weeks." He looked across the water and threw another stone, watching as it bounced half a dozen times on the surface of the swamp before ricocheting off a tree thirty yards away.

"I know," said Jack. "I know it sounds crazy, but if you listened to FirstMan then you'd understand why they want me to go." He waited for a response, but Ryan was silent. "If anybody else hands himself in," Jack said, "they'll just kill them. You know that."

"I know," said Ryan. "I also know that they might kill you too."

"I don't think they will," Jack said, his mind drifting to thoughts of the officer whose name he didn't know. The woman who had first taken him captive in the Outer Zone and had then set him free, running into the junk, just weeks before. He wasn't positive, but he didn't think she would kill him. He only had to hope that she was the one in charge when he handed himself in.

Jack sighed. Ryan was right, though. It did seem crazy.

"Why don't they just attack the base?" Ryan asked, frowning.

"Because too many people could be killed," said Jack. "There is a defence system around the base. They need to get through that first. If I go in, they can use me as a target for their weapon. It shouldn't harm me. It explodes high above the ground, but it needs a target to follow, and it needs to be specific. They can't get anyone close enough to use it, otherwise. A lot of people will die if they attempt a frontal assault. Hopefully, this way it will only knock out the electronics, stun the guards, and not kill anyone. I'll be inside the detention centre, and it won't hurt me in there."

"You hope," said Ryan.

Jack nodded.

After Jack had gone, Ryan sat on the rock staring across the water. He understood, really; he did. He knew Jack was doing this for him – for them. Jack had even suggested, hadn't he, that they didn't have to stay with the Junkers. They could go it alone. Ryan wondered now if he should have just taken the offer, but it'd been he that convinced Jack to stay, and he that persuaded Jack he would like FirstMan and the Junkers when he got to know them.

His fault that Jack was about to risk his life for them all.

Ryan turned a large pebble in his hand, over and over, staring at its worn surface. Jack had agreed to go back to the camp, back to the facility, because he wanted to help. He wanted to make the world safe, or at least safer for Ryan.

People have to sacrifice themselves, Ryan thought, just so that others can live better lives. The thought angered him. Why did it have to be Jack?

There was a snap of twigs not far behind him, and Ryan spun around, reaching for his spear. But when he saw that it was Haggerty, the old RootMan, he left the spear leaning against the rock.

"It's you," Ryan said.

"Aye it's me," Haggerty said. "Well that's some welcome, isn't it, boy?"

"Sorry," Ryan said, but there was no enthusiasm in his voice.

"He is going to do it, then?" old Haggerty asked. "He's going to be their bait?"

"Yes," said Ryan.

There was silence for a minute as neither knew what to say.

"He'll be back," Haggerty said finally. "You do know that, don't you?"

Ryan ignored the old man, and sat looking out at the water.

"He will," said Haggerty as he approached and leaned against the rock. "He is a special one."

Ryan frowned. "What you mean?" he asked.

"I mean he's not like most," said Haggerty. "When I took him in and helped him with his knee... When they came to take him, he just vanished, you know, like magic."

"He is just good at sneaking," said Ryan.

"Yes," said Haggerty, "and sneaking is what's needed, isn't it, boy? You just mark my words. You just listen and heed me. He'll go in there, and he'll walk out. You'll see I'm right."

"I hope so," said Ryan.

The Pits

Jack forced his protesting legs to work as the sound of the armoured vehicles streaming toward the area grew to a roar. He spun around, looking for somewhere to run, an escape route, anywhere, even one that may be temporary. He needed to hide. There, he saw it. Not far from where he stood was a drainage entrance in a ditch behind the wall of one of the shanty buildings. It led into shadows, and who knew where, but it was dark and enticing.

Some of Jagan's warriors rushed past him, and the sound of gunfire erupted nearby, that sharp crackling noise that he had heard many times before. But this was more intense. It wasn't the noise of one rifle firing but the cacophony of many. Jack's head swam, still recovering from the fight in the pit, not completely in control of his own senses. His vision wavered, blurred by the streaks of movement from those rushing toward the invaders. Jack heard the bellow of Jagan's voice, urging them on, but barely seconds later, several of the warriors rushed past him once more, this time in the other direction. One of them stumbled towards the entrance of the nearest building, and almost made it, but just as he was about to run through the entrance, something slammed into his back and sent him sprawling to the floor, where he lay, twitching.

A dart. Jack could see it, sticking out the back of the warrior's neck.

Tranquilizers, Jack thought. They're taking everyone.

Jack glanced at the crooked spear in his hand – a thing that clearly identified him as one of Jagan's men – and therefore a target. He couldn't have that, and thought that it would probably break if he tried to use it against Trooper armour. He threw it aside. He still had the machete.

He ran towards the open sewer entrance, but slowed before he got close. The way was blocked by a large pile of rubble. He panicked and looked around, trying to find somewhere else to run to. Directly across from him was another hut, and Jack forced himself forward, scrambling across the floor, his machete clenched in one hand. There was the sound of many boots on the ground, and more gunfire, as he rolled into the dark interior of the building and looked straight into the eyes of one of the slave girls. She was hiding in the corner of the room, just feet from the entrance, her eyes bright with fear. Jack scrambled to his feet and looked further into the interior, searching for means of escape.

He was about to run but stopped. He glanced back at the girl hiding in the corner. "Let's go," he called, reaching out to her. "We need to leave."

The girl sat there, stunned, just looking at him in terror. He ran forward, grabbed her wrist, and tried to pull her, but she resisted, pulling back.

Jack let go, frowning down at her, before turning to run. She would not leave. The fear was too much for her, and there was little he could do. Cursing and hating himself, he took off, running through the building, but as he ran he noticed movement on all sides, and he slowed, stumbled, and came to a stop with his knees in the dirt. He was surrounded by cages like the one he had been held in.

A slave storage house, he thought, as he looked at the nearest cage and noticed that it was tied with a rope that was knotted much tighter than anyone in the cage would be able to unravel. They were too weak. He looked down at machete in his hand and then back at the rope. Outside gunfire continued to drown out the noise of battle-cries and screams, but no one had entered the building after him. The slave girl still crouched near the entrance, but now she was staring at him.

And a dozen pairs of eyes stared back at him from within the cage. Young, old, but all frail. They had no way to escape.

Taking a deep breath, and hoping he wasn't releasing a pack of ferals, Jack hacked at the rope again and again until it fell away, and the door swung open.

But no one moved inside the cage, they just sat there, staring out at him, not comprehending their own freedom.

You can't make them leave, he thought. Not if they don't want to move. You can't make them try to make a break for it.

Then he frowned. But you can at least give them the choice. Jack moved further through the building, ever closer to the opposite entrance. He stopped at another cage, also filled with people, and quickly hacked at the rope that secured the door. Then he moved on, leaving the door to swing open. Another dozen feet and he swung at another rope, and then another, fearfully glancing at the entrance and hoping that none of the grey warriors streaming from the dropship would rush through it before he was done. He could still hear the rage of battle outside and hoped that enough of Jagan's men still fought the grey Hunters to delay them just a while longer. The slavers could die, or be captured, and he wouldn't care, but he had to open all the cages before he could leave.

It was the least he could do. Give them a choice, a chance, even if they were too weak or unwilling to take it.

Finally, he was at the last cage, and he stopped to glance behind him. Some of the slaves at the front of the building were tentatively edging out of the cages and Jack shook his head, realising they were all too frightened to move very quickly.

"Get moving," he shouted. "This is your chance to escape here. You only have this one chance!"

This seemed to rouse a few of them, and several pushed their way out of the cages and looked around, but still they made no effort to leave.

Until one of Jagan's warriors stumbled into the entrance and fell to the floor, dead. There was a large burn mark in the centre of the man's back that seemed to burrow all the way through his body, and at the sight of this possible fate, the crowd of stunned slaves sprang to life. Jack looked back as he approached the far entrance and hesitated, but the fleeing slaves had no intention of being cautious. Two younger men ran past him and out into the sunlight.

Jack watched, terrified of going out there, waiting to see the young slaves fall, but the two men kept on running. Someone shoved him aside, and Jack stumbled into the wall next to the entrance. He turned, expecting to have to defend himself, but there was no assailant. Whoever had shoved him was trying to get past him and out into the open.

"You're welcome," he muttered as the man ran out into the light.

Jack stumbled forward, crouching low, staying among the crowd of fleeing people. All around him, people flooded out from buildings. Many of them looked like escaping slaves, unarmed and afraid, running in whichever direction they could. He dodged in between people, tripping, almost falling several times, but he managed to stumble away, running for the perimeter of the camp.

Then he saw it at the far end. A gaping hole in the ground – the Subtrans entrance. A few figures were running towards it, desperately trying to find a place to hide, and the dark inviting stairway was the only place that Jack could see that offered any hope. He pushed himself on, urging his tired limbs forward, and felt something brush past his shoulder. A man running a few feet in front of him jerked and fell, tumbling onto the ground. Jack didn't slow down. There was no way he could help the man, and as he passed him a few seconds later, he saw a dart sticking out of the man's back. A stun dart. It had barely missed him.

"I'm sorry," were the only words he could say as he ran past, but already the man's eyes had glazed over. Jack ran on, trying not to bump into others that fled, and he almost fell down the stairway that led into darkness.

The shadows enveloped him, and he heard and felt others rushing down the stairs alongside him, colliding with each other, cursing, falling. Jack moved to the side, fumbled until he found the railing that ran down one side of the stairway, and staggered down into the dark, still trying to keep his balance as bodies rushed past him. Some of them, he thought, falling, only to be trodden on by those behind.

Eventually the ground levelled out, but there was no light in the ancient ruins of the Subtrans. He could sense panic among those who had got this far. They had nowhere else to go. He moved through the darkness as his eyes strained to adjust.

Think, think where to go. There must be somewhere. There *had* to be somewhere way down here to hide. Eventually he made his way to the platform and looked down the dark tunnel. He could barely see a thing, just some vague outlines of cracked pipes running along the walls, and beneath his feet, old and rusted rail track that hadn't been used for centuries.

And the rail track led somewhere. It led further away from the slavers and from the Hunters. Jack started down the tunnel with both hands in front of him, one still tightly clutching the machete.

Jagan's Tale

Years before…

Jagan slammed the hammer into the Hunter's helmet with such force that it buckled and smashed. The trooper crumpled to the floor, one side of his head a bloody mess, but even with such a grievous wound the man held on to the last moment of his life, struggling to back away as one half of his body was consumed by a switching spasm.

Jagan ignored him. There was no way the trooper was going to reach his weapon, which lay a dozen feet away. The man was no longer a threat.

And neither were the other three Hunters, their bodies broken, lying still upon the ground. Jagan took a step back, heaved in a deep breath, lifted the hammer once more and brought it down upon one of the motionless bodies. He reached forward, and was about to take the automatic rifle the Hunter had carried, but as his finger circled around the trigger he felt a warmth and glanced down at the grip. The trigger had lit up, a red flashing light blaring a warning. Two seconds later a piercing sound began to emit from the top of the rifle.

Jagan grunted and tossed the rifle through the entrance of the hut, and not a moment too soon. There was a loud crack and a hiss, and smoke wafted from the entrance.

A sensor, he thought. He glanced around. Nowhere to go and nowhere to hide. They would find him soon. His gaze stopped at another body lying in the corner.

It was one of the slaves. The man had a dart in his shoulder and another in his leg. Jagan thought for a moment that he recognised the man, but he shrugged the feeling off. It didn't matter. The important thing right now was what he should do next. There was no visible escape route, and they would be on him soon. Much of the camp was already overrun, and Jagan knew that he had maybe a minute to do something, to hide or escape. Something.

But what?

Disguise, he thought. He had to hide his identity. He was going to be caught, there was no avoiding it, but he could still influence what happened when he was.

Cursing, Jagan knelt next the slave, saw the knife on the floor next to him, and snatched it up.

The hair. That would give him away.

It had to go.

He cursed. His whole empire in ruins in one day. All the work building it over the years. His army, his pits, his gladiators, his slave empire.

Everything gone.

And now he even had to cut off his damn hair.

Jagan reached behind his back, pulled the long braid of bright red hair around his shoulder, then reached up and began to cut. The braid came away, but it wasn't enough, he knew. They would still recognise him. He grabbed handfuls of hair and cut away more until there was barely anything left on his scalp. Then he snatched up another assault rifle lying on the floor next to one of the other dead Hunters. He pressed his finger to the grip, waited for the high-pitched noise, then dropped the rifle onto the pile of hair.

The effect was just what he needed. The flash of energy that surged through the weapon, a powerful enough spike to knock a man unconscious – maybe even kill anyone trying to steal the weapon – set the hair alight. There was a flash of flame and acrid smoke wafted up as the hair burned, removing the evidence.

But it still wasn't enough, he knew.

Jagan staggered over to the dead slave, turned the man over, and began to strip him of his jacket and his trousers. Jagan was a big man but this man looked almost his size. Maybe the clothes wouldn't fit so well, but it was better than just stripping naked. The seconds ticked by, and Jagan watched the entrance, expecting Hunters to storm the hut at any moment, but he managed it. He had just finished pulling the coat on, after roughly dressing the dead slave in his armour, when a shadow moved across the entrance.

Jagan scrambled backwards, until he reached the back of the hut, and then dived to the dirt. There he lay, keeping as still as he could, waiting to found, his eyes shut tight. He vaguely saw the shadows moving around, saw them poking at the bodies and finally settling on the body of the slave.

No way to know, he thought. He couldn't hear the Hunters in their silent suits. He could only hope that his ruse would work.

Only one way to find out, he thought, as he sat up and rubbed his head, feigning confusion, trying to act concussed.

The two nearest Hunters raised their weapons and aimed them at him. There was a moment as he sat there, mouth wide open, unable to speak, and then he heard the sharp crack and felt a jolt in his chest. He looked down, frowning, and saw a dart sticking out from where his heart was.

It's not that bad, he thought. Not so painful. Just a wasp sting. But then his vision began to blur, and the room started to spin, and he felt a rush of tingling spreading through his limbs and his cheeks.

And then came darkness.

The Pits in Chaos

Years before...

Jack huddled in the pitch black of the Subtrans station with his back against the crumbling concrete wall. A cold breeze blew down the dark tunnel, and it carried a musty smell that was both old and unpleasant, reminding him of hidden places where things that should no longer be alive dwelt. But there were few noises from the tunnel. The only sound was the quiet moans and whispers of others who had sought refuge in the depths.

From where he hid, Jack could see a dim light coming from the stairwell that had led him down into this dark place. Minutes before, dozens of others had clambered down those stairs with him, jostling each other, panicking to escape the chaos above ground. It had seemed pitch black, as he had stumbled with the others, but now, after he had sat for a while, getting his breath back, his feet trying to find something stable to stand on, he could see that the sunlight from above had managed to creep its way down to the platform.

He had tried walking along the track, into the darkness, hoping to discover some other way to leave, maybe miles of underground tunnel to escape along and find some way back to the surface. There were ruined Subtrans entrances all over, and he had thought he could make his way to one, but he'd tripped over some rubble and fallen. He knelt there for a few minutes, feeling his way around, before he decided that the tunnel had collapsed, and he headed back once more to find a spot on the track among the other escapees.

There were a lot of people huddled there, afraid, and the noise that came from above did little to allay those fears. As Jack looked around him, he noticed a familiar face in the dim light, that of the slave girl he had seen in the building with the cages. There were other faces too, some that he vaguely recognised from the cells he had opened.

At least some got out, he thought, sighing deeply. But it will all amount to nothing if the Hunters come down here.

He clinched the machete at his side, vowing that if they did, he would take at least one of them with him.

Who are you kidding? If they do come down here, chances are all those hiding here will be taken or killed.

But an hour passed, and the sounds of gunfire and shouts from above ground ceased, and then, just as he was thinking that it may be over, a tremendous gust of wind blew down the stairway into the station. The people gathered in the darkness cried out in fear, and Jack wondered for a moment if some new and terrible weapon was being used, but then he recognised the wind and the noise.

The dropship.

A deep humming, rumbling sound came from above and then the wind ceased. His ears popped as the dropship sped away, the air in the Subtrans being sucked up the stairway as the dropship rocketed into the sky. He felt the breeze along the tunnel increase and saw a rush of dust billowing out of the tunnel behind him as it was sucked up the stairway.

And then silence.

Nothing, not even a whimper from those around him. After a few more minutes, Jack finally stood up, climbed back up onto the Subtrans platform, and edged his way through the shadows towards the bottom of the steps. He looked up the stairs, squinting in the bright daylight. No movement. No shouts. No noise.

Nothing.

He began to slowly make his way back up the stairs.

"What are you doing?" asked a voice from the shadows.

"I think they've gone," said Jack.

"You'll give us away," whispered another voice.

"No," said a different voice. "He's right. That rush of air. That buzz. That's them leaving. They've gone. Maybe."

Jack paused at the foot of the stairs.

"But Jagan's men may still be up there," another voice called.

Jack coughed. "Then stay down here, in the dark, if you want to hide," he said, and then he started up the stairs.

He emerged to a changed landscape. Where once there had been huts and shanty buildings dotted across the entire area, now there were only collapsed ruins.

More ruins to match those across the entirety of the Outer Zone, Jack thought, as he stood at the top of the stairs and scanned the vast area. Not a single human being stood as he made his way through the camp. He found

358

some of Jagan's men, lying dead in the dirt, and quickly stopped to strip them of weapons, valuables, clothing, and armour. Most was burned beyond use, charred by the blasts of the Hunters' rifles. Soon the slaves that had escaped, and whoever else had been hiding down in that tunnel, would be up here, and he did not want to be around when they started fighting over the spoils of the dead.

I need to get away from here, he thought. Get away while I still can.

He stood for a moment, scanning the horizon, trying to get his bearings from several larger ruins in the distance, all landmarks that he knew. It had been weeks since he had walked free, weeks stuck in those pits, and it would take him time to re-adjust.

Time to go, he thought, and started off in the direction of The Crossing.

Jagan's Tale

Years before…

Jagan cursed as the Hunters pushed him roughly to the ground. He was ready to stand up, bellow at them, and fight. Every part of his soul wanted to tear them to shreds with his bare hands.

But you can't, he told himself, taking a deep breath. Keep control, he thought. Keep control.

He slowly raised himself from the ground, squinting around the huge open space. Nearby, a dozen other captives struggled to their feet, and twenty feet away another group was emerging from the back of an armoured vehicle. More vehicles poured out of the massive dropship, which now took up half the space in the vast yard. As his eyes adjusted to the light, Jagan saw that he was in some sort of industrial facility that was surrounded by tall buildings with glass windows. Real glass windows.

He got to his feet and stood silently, watching the Hunters as they pushed and manoeuvred groups of captives out of the armoured trucks, herding them onto the ground where they were ushered into small groups. Jagan's gaze stopped at a man in the group next to his. Two of the Hunters were speaking to him, and Jagan recognised him as his own lieutenant – Leon. He couldn't hear the conversation, but Leon was looking around the crowds as he spoke to the Hunters. Paranoia brought many thoughts to Jagan's mind, but the most prominent was his lieutenant was stabbing him in the back. They were searching for him, now that they had destroyed his army. So far, his feeble attempt at a disguise, just rags and a short haircut, had worked. Why the Hunters that found him hadn't killed him, anyway, he didn't know.

They had been in a hurry, he thought. They'd dragged him out before retrieving their dead. They hadn't been interested in the supposed slave they found.

Jagan took two steps to his left and edged behind two taller captives, his nerves twitching. He was not only surrounded by any number of his own men but also countless slaves. Any of them could recognise him. He crouched to the floor, grabbed some dirt, and rubbed it on his face and his hair. No one seemed to be paying much attention to him at that moment.

But that could change, he thought. He needed to look as different as he possibly could. Other than the fact that his hair was now gone, it was difficult. He was a large man.

To Jagan's relief, the Hunters moved on to another group, passing him by.

How it's Going to Work

Now...

"All you have to do is swallow the chip," FirstMan said with a smile. He and Jack sat in one of the larger side rooms in FirstMan's compound up on the hill. The room was filled with tech salvaged from the ruins, stacked high on shelves and littering the workbench in front of them. Three of FirstMan's troopers stood in the room, but they were busy tinkering with tech that Jack couldn't identify, and he wondered if they were even listening. A fourth man sat at the table opposite them.

Jack frowned. "Just swallow it?" he asked. "Surely it'll just come back out in a few hours?" He cringed at the thought.

FirstMan shook his head, stood up and turned to man sitting on the other side of the table. "This is Hyde. He's one of my tech guys."

The man nodded at Jack. He was short and stocky, and his beard was thick and wiry. On the table between them was a drone. It was much smaller than Jack had imagined.

"Hyde has been working on getting the drone functional," said FirstMan. "And now, thanks to the new circuit board, we have it working. But we need someone to go in there and act as a guidance for the drone. I want that

362

to be you."

Jack peered at the drone with uncertainty.

"Let me explain about the chip," Hyde said, scratching his beard. "When you swallow it, it will activate and attach itself inside you before it reaches your stomach." He pointed at his throat, and then traced a line down his chest to just above his stomach. "Then it sits there and waits until it picks up the transmissions constantly buzzing around the facility. There are computers using wireless connections and radio communications – everything. It all has a signature that is specific to the Recycling Facility and is basically what we use to encrypt everything."

"Encrypt?" asked Jack, puzzled.

"Disguise," said Hyde. "It means that anyone listening to radio transmissions at the facility, unless they know the encryption codes, would just hear garbage. We, of course, know those codes. As soon as you are within range of the systems the chip will detect its location and reactivate and send a pulse signal to us."

Jack didn't understand a lot of what the man was saying, but he understood the need to swallow the chip. When he was picked up by the Hunters he would be searched, possibly interrogated. Any kind of tracking device would be confiscated, but not one that was hidden inside him.

"I know how the detection systems work," said the man. "So, I've programmed the chip to avoid them. You'll be able to go in there, and they'll probably lock you in solitary in the detention centre. That's standard procedure. That will put you in the building right next to where the computer suite is. In fact, it's just thirty yards away. That computer suite handles all the security systems, including those in the solitary cell block where you will be. The chip will activate, and it will open a relay that we can use to target a missile that will take out the perimeter defence system and the drone defence system that protects the base."

"When that happens," FirstMan interjected. "We can hit it."

"Yeah," said Jack. "That. That's the bit that I'm not so sure about. This chip, you say, acts as a beacon for some nasty explosive?"

FirstMan shook his head. "Yes, sure. It's an explosive. But not the kind you're thinking of. This is a pulse weapon. The most damage it will do to a person is stun them or knock them out. It's an electromagnetic charge. It will temporarily knockout electronics and computers, and therefore take out the perimeter fence, which, as I explained before, is electrified."

"Then you can make your move and raid the facility." said Jack.

"Yes," said FirstMan.

Jack sat staring at the table. The chip was small, no bigger than a fingernail. He picked it up and turned it over. "Okay, let's get this done," he said.

"Excellent," said FirstMan. "Good man." He smiled, stepped forward, and held out his hand. "Welcome aboard."

Muster

Now...

Ryan hurried through the open gates, the bundle bound for the school thrown over his shoulder. If there was one thing he didn't mind doing it was being a carrier. He didn't like being stuck in somewhere, unable to move around, and taking on the role of a carrier, delivering small stuff from place to place for anyone who needed it and would pay a fee, was the ideal choice for him.

But as he moved through the warrens of Junktown, heading towards the school building, he noticed an increase in activity.

There were a lot more people rushing about than usual. And many of them were armed.

He stopped in the middle of one of the busiest thoroughfares of the hidden junk city and looked around, watching those hurrying about him.

Three men passed by, all carrying long, sharp halberds built from metal scrap. One of them was trying to strap armour pieces to his shoulder as they walked, and he struggled to keep up. Across from the three men, an older man – one of the smiths that usually spent most of their time building doors, braces and other structural metal objects from scrap – was hammering out what looked like it would be a shield.

Another group of warriors – three women and a younger man – rushed by, heading in the direction of the town's centre.

Ryan frowned. Something was kicking off already. Something important was happening, and he wanted to know what it was.

This is bound to have something to do with what FirstMan wanted Jack to do, he thought. It has to.

He turned away from the path to the school and followed the group of women and the younger man, trailing them through the crowds of people. They headed directly through the busy town centre, avoiding the usual traders and market folk, and climbed the walkways that led to an area called The Moot.

Ryan turned a corner, edging around a large group of warriors mustering at the entrance, and saw the gathering. FirstMan was standing with a group of his troopers, surrounded by a large number of Junker warriors, and next to him was RightHand. Jack was nowhere to be seen.

Ryan moved through the crowd, heading as directly towards FirstMan as he could until a hand grasped his shoulder. He turned to see the face of Ruben, the old warrior that lived in a warren house at the foot of his own home. The man was a friend of their teacher and often looked out for the school.

"No place for young ones today, boy," said Ruben. "You need to get off back to your work, away from here."

Ryan frowned, trying to think of an excuse he could use, but came up with nothing. Just as he was about to give up, a voice interrupted them.

"It's okay."

Ryan turned to see FirstMan standing next to them. The tall leader nodded, and Ruben let go of Ryan's shoulder and took a step back.

FirstMan turned to Ryan. "But he is right about this being no place for young ones, Finder. What is it that brings you here?"

"Jack," said Ryan. "Is he… Where is he?"

"He left for the facility already," FirstMan said. "They went earlier today, to get a head start on us, so that Jack is in place, where we need him, when the time comes. We're joining him very soon."

Ryan didn't register the words for a moment, and just stood there, silently trying to get his head around it. Jack was already gone. He had already left. When they had spoken earlier…that had been Jack's version of 'goodbye for now'. And all he had done was act like a spoiled, stroppy child. He hadn't thought it was going to happen this quickly. He'd thought he had time, weeks, at least days.

"I can fight," said Ryan.

FirstMan smiled. "I know," he said. "But you're too young for this mission."

"But—"

"And too valuable," interrupted FirstMan. "I can't have my best finder being at risk. I need you for a great many other jobs, Ryan."

"I can help, though."

"Not this time," said FirstMan. "I know you want to,

but the best thing for you is to stay here and be ready when it's over. We'll need all the finders we can muster when we take control of the facility."

"I can—"

"No," said FirstMan, his voice changing, gaining a sharper and more commanding edge. "This is not the time."

Ryan sighed, nodded, and turned and headed for the school.

Jagan's Tale

Years Before…

Governor Jackson scratched his head and stared at the screen. He leaned forward, tapped the keyboard a few times, shook his head and turned to face the man in the seat opposite.

"Eight different incidents," Jackson said, chewing his lip. "Eight in just two months of being here."

The man in the seat sat in silence, staring back at him. The prisoner was immobilised, his hands and feet bound with pulse locks set to stun him if he moved too quickly, or if Jackson decided to press a button on the device in front of him.

"Just eight months," Jackson continued. "It's a problem, don't you think?"

The man continued to stare at him for a moment, then grinned. "What do you care what I think?" he replied, finally.

Jackson, stood, rubbing his hands together. "Oh, it does speak. It can communicate in ways other than with its fists. I was beginning to wonder."

"Screw you," said the man.

Jackson shook his head. "I don't think so. I don't think you'll be doing any such thing anytime soon." He stood up and paced the floor, glancing at the screen every few seconds, mumbling his thoughts to himself.

"Jagan," Jackson said, his smile widening as he noticed the surprise on the prisoner's face at his mention of the name. "Not a common name. And it would seem you were something of a leader, prior to coming here, and something of a troublemaker."

Jackson paused, looked at the man, expecting another retort, but he was disappointed when Jagan simply stared at him.

"I could order you killed, you know. From those eight incidents, I've had four guards injured, twelve workers also, and finally the worker you argued with this time is now dead."

Jackson waited again, but there was still no reply.

"Out here, I'm in charge. The rules, and the punishments for breaking them, are dictated by just myself. If I ordered one of my guards to take you outside and put a shot through your head, they would do just that. No questions."

The prisoner frowned. "What do you want?" he asked, and Jackson was pleased that the glare filled with hatred was now showing some signs of nervous tension around the edges. The huge, muscled monster of a prisoner was just the same as any coward when faced with their own vulnerability.

Jackson sat back down and patted a pile of papers stacked on his desk. "Have you heard of Junkers?" he asked.

Jagan nodded. "Sort of," he said. Just some scum out in

the junk.

"Good," said Jackson. "Well, I consider them to be my biggest problem, even more so than a thug like you. I need to deal with them, but I don't have the spare military force to take them all out. Damn things are crawling all over the Junklands, thousands of the stinking wretches."

"Where do I come in?" asked Jagan, and Jackson could see a hint of hopefulness in his eyes.

Good, he thought. Let's give him a little more.

"You have experience…governing over a rabble, I hear. Slaves, thugs, all sorts. In large numbers, apparently. That is a considerable skill, I think, and a shame for it to be wasted."

Jagan coughed. "This is a trick."

But Jackson shook his head. "No, no. Not so much a trick as maybe a possible way that we can both benefit from me not ordering your immediate death. Consider it an employment opportunity and a way to improve your current situation tenfold."

Jagan sat silently.

"It will also involve you leaving this place, alone," said Jackson.

This got him the reaction he wanted. Jagan went from sitting with a confident slouch, to leaning forward, his eyes eager. "Tell me," he said.

Jackson nodded. "I hoped you would see reason."

"I'm listening," said Jagan.

"Good," said Jackson. "Very good. Well, I have need of someone with your skills. I need them to go out there, into the junk, meet up with the Junkers and become one of them. I need to be informed of their actions, and I need attacks on my facilities to be…minimalised."

"What do you mean?" asked Jagan.

"Well, if the attacks were to stop altogether, I think that the Junkers would suspect, but if they were kept to a minimum, and allowed to happen under the correct circumstances, then I could ensure that the inconvenience they cause is…reduced."

Jagan peered at him for a moment and seemed to consider the proposition. "You want me to go and take over out there and be your lackey?"

Jackson laughed. "I wouldn't exactly say that. If you subject them to your will, and help me achieve my goals, our contact will be infrequent. You will be left alone to rule them how you see fit."

"But there must be a catch," said Jagan. "You're not telling me everything."

"That is correct," said Jackson. "I'm not. And the part I've withheld is…sensitive. You see, the Junkers have a source of something I want. Tech equipment from the old world, hidden in places all over the Junklands. They seem to be able to find it, while it eludes my salvage crews often. If you were to…take over, then we could trade in such items. And I would be eternally grateful."

"Grateful," muttered Jagan.

"I would pay very well," said Jackson. "Goods and possibly in other…things that I can acquire. You see, you would be left to your own devices out there, as long as we had an agreement that the intrusions into my operations were greatly reduced. Do you want your freedom? I could ensure that anyone coming from the Inner Zone in search of a certain red headed ex-bandit leader would…find the trip unfruitful. Why, they could never have existed on my records. Such shame for the justice court to lose an important criminal entity forever, but you know things are dangerous out here, accidents happen, people disappear."

Jagan seemed to be considering the offer, but Jackson knew the man was playing the part. Wouldn't want to seem too keen now, would he?

"And if I say no?" asked Jagan.

"Accidents happen. People disappear," Jackson repeated.

Finally, Jagan nodded. "We have a deal."

Risky Business

Back again...

Jack stood about twenty feet away from the dust covered metal monstrosity, staring at the rusting panels and the dimly glowing outside lights. He could hear muffled voices from inside, but only faintly, and he smiled as he made out the deep tones of someone he knew. Of course, that the carrier would currently be home to people he knew was obvious to him. Highlighted clearly, in large white figures on the side of the vehicle, was the assignment number: E2.

"You okay?" asked a voice nearby. Jack turned to see FirstMan approaching, and behind him were RightHand and several of the other troopers that had defected to live with the Junkers. One of the men moved past him, heading towards the carrier.

"Yes," Jack said, wondering if he was. Being back at the carrier was unnerving, and it seemed like months or even years had passed, when in fact it had only been a few weeks. He had started to become accustomed to freedom once more, and the idea of being incarcerated again was not a welcome thought.

If this all fails, you could be a slave for good, he thought. Or a pile of dust. It had better not fail.

They watched as the trooper approached the side of the

carrier and quickly scaled up on to the top, moving toward the middle of the roof before bending down to examine something that Jack couldn't see.

The roof panel, he thought.

"What is he doing?" Jack asked, his voice low. He didn't want to alert the men inside that there was more than the single intruder on the roof, remembering how he had sat inside the vehicle with the rest of them, musing over what made the noise.

"A delivery for Jackson," said FirstMan.

Well, I certainly have something to tell Tyler this time, he thought. If I get the chance.

The trooper on the roof jumped off, landing heavily on the dirt ground, but he didn't falter, moving swiftly back to the main group as FirstMan stepped forward.

"You just have to wait here," said FirstMan. "And that will be the most unpredictable part of it. I can't help much with this part. But if they follow standard procedure, you won't be harmed. You'll be identified quite quickly. I'm sure they will be very curious and keen to talk to you. You remember that you must stay silent for as long as possible. Not a word, maybe act stunned or confused. Then they will take you to the facility and the detention centre. By the time they get around to interrogating you, the attack will already be happening and this should all be over."

Jack nodded.

"Sir," said a low voice from a few feet away. One of the troopers nodded at FirstMan and indicated the device he held in his hand.

A tracking device of some sort, Jack thought.

"Their scout drone is on its way," said FirstMan. "We've got about five minutes, so we need to hike it out of here."

"Okay," said Jack, not knowing what else to say.

"Remember," said FirstMan. "Stay calm, and don't reveal what you carry. Try not to eat until you're in the compound – preferably within the prison block. They will take you there quite quickly, I believe. Do you remember your story?"

Jack nodded again. "I was captured and held prisoner by the Junkers but escaped."

"Good," said FirstMan. He stepped forward and placed his hand on Jack's shoulder. "And luck be with you. I'll see you when we take down the facility. We will have much to celebrate."

Then they were gone, quickly heading into the shadows and moving away through the trash at speed, leaving Jack standing in the dim light cast by the outer lights on the carrier.

Jack breathed deeply and gave a sigh. He looked up at the empty, black sky. He had never actually seen the drones before, having always been inside the carrier when they came. Would they be low to the ground or high up? He had no idea. And he didn't know if they were even silent until he heard the distant humming.

At first, he thought it might be an insect hiding in the trash. He had certainly heard enough of those, but this sound was different – deeper and more metallic, like the hum of a very quiet engine.

Then a light blazed across the clearing where the carrier was parked, and a dark, bulky object, drifting at head-height, loomed out of the piles of trash and sped toward him. It was illuminated by a dozen small lamps that shifted their focus rapidly, producing a dazzling, whirling effect that obscured the shape behind the lights until it was directly above him.

Jack stood, transfixed, wondering if he should raise his hands in submission or just stand there. Indecision made the choice for him.

The drone hovered above, then went higher as Jack stared at the lights, then a blinding flash illuminated the area. His vision blurred, shocked by the brightness of the light. Another flash, then another. Jack's head began to ache, then a wave of dizziness came over him.

He fell to the ground, already unconscious before he hit the dirt.

Not Again

Now…

Corporal Lisa Markell stood frowning at the screen.

"Hold off," she said, tapping the drone operator on the shoulder, just to make sure he heard her command and followed it. She was very aware of how much firepower the drones carried and that just one shot would kill a target. She had always thought it was a good job for those in the Outer Zone that the drones' range was only a few kilometres or there would be nowhere to hide. As it stood, the things weren't very convenient or useful for tracking down and capturing Junkers, who seemed to be able to evade them at even a few minutes' notice.

"Scan in," she said, and a second later the camera view on the big screen in the ops rooms zoomed in on the figure standing in the dark next to the carrier.

"Should I light it up?" asked the operator.

"Yes," said Markell. "Lights only. No firing."

The operator nodded, and Lisa frowned as the screen brightness intensified, the spotlights on the drone illuminating most of the area around the figure standing outside the carrier – one of *her* carriers.

Dammit, she thought, and for a moment she was worried that she had said it aloud, but no one in the ops room showed any signs of hearing her. It was him, the one she had let go. He was back again, and he looked a lot healthier than he had when he left. How could that be? She hadn't a clue, but there he was.

This could potentially cause her problems. If the man was taken back to the facility, as all protocols suggested he should be if he wasn't eliminated, he might inform Jackson that she had let him go. Why, she didn't know, but then why the hell was he even back here, anyway? She could command the operator to put him down. Kill him. The officer would do so without question.

And that would be the end of it.

Except she couldn't do that. Curiosity scratched at the back of her mind. Why was the man back? How was he looking healthier rather than more ragged? How was he even alive? She had let him go presuming she would never see him again, that he would either find what he was looking for or die trying. The odds in her mind gave her an image of a corpse decaying in the junk.

"Stun him," she said, realising that until she knew why he was back, she wouldn't be satisfied, but there was the problem of the cameras. Even though they were miles from the facility, every machine, including the drones, had cameras that would record and send everything back to the central computer system, where Jackson could see them. If she brought the man in, she knew Jackson would look at the videos. Any slight hint of hesitation on her part would draw suspicion that she didn't need.

But she wanted to know anyway.

I just have to wait until he comes around, then I can ask him, she thought.

A chill ran down her spine, and her mind wandered over possibilities. There was something not right here, something she wasn't seeing.

Yes, Again

Now...

Jack woke abruptly, feeling a throb of dull pain at the back of his head. He opened his eyes and found himself staring at a solid metal wall. Instinctively, he reached up to touch the ache, but he regretted it a moment later. There was a large lump there, and blood had dried on the wound. He cringed as a spasm of sharp pain shot down his back. He blinked back the pain and tried to focus.

How many times had he been in this situation? It was getting to be all too regular, almost familiar, and he sighed. He was tired of it all.

He wondered for a moment if he was in some kind of prison cell, but the ground was shifting underneath him, vibrating, and a low rumbling noise filled the confined space.

Was he on the trans system? It had to be the same one that had brought him from the Inner Zone to the facility, so far out in the world, out in the wilderness. He was still struggling to remember where he was, but he had the distinct feeling that being on the trans would be bad. He wasn't meant to be there. He thought for a moment, and then it came to him. The compartment was much too small, but like the cells on the trans, there was little light. Only a thin strip of daylight shone into the compartment. Whether it was from outside, or from within the interior of the vehicle that now transported him, he didn't know, but he suspected the light was natural; sunlight from outside.

This was where he was supposed to be. Caught once more, on his way back to the facility. So far, all was good, apart from the bump on his head. That would hurt for a good while.

Rubbing his head again, and glad to find that it hurt less the second time, he pushed himself up onto his elbows and looked around. He would not be able to stand in the compartment, and he was sure that it was not built for transporting people. Maybe a cargo hold? There was no such compartment in the carriers, that much he knew. He had spent enough time inside one.

So this was another vehicle.

He frowned and tried to recall what had happened. He remembered standing outside the carrier, waiting for the drone to arrive, and then the bright lights, but not much after that. The throb of his head abated somewhat, and it was only then that he realised the side of his head was also bruised and sore.

He'd fallen. He remembered he'd fallen when the drone came. Maybe it'd stunned him, like one of the pulse weapons the Hunters used in the Outer Zone, but he didn't recall.

Having hauled himself up into a sitting position, he leaned against the wall. The vibrations running through the floor did little to help the headache. He needed something to lean against. Where a few hours ago he had felt set and ready to go, now he was drained of all energy.

Jack sighed.

Well, this is the stupidest thing you've ever done, he thought. Or was it? No, he'd done some pretty crazy things in his youth, hadn't he?

There were a number of situations he had found himself in. His undoing, throughout his life, it seemed, was to find places where there was trouble and throw himself into it. But this was the stupidest, surely?

No. This maybe came second, he thought.

Dangling from a rope came first.

The Dark and Empty Places

Many Years Before...

Jack lowered himself slowly down the cord, peering into the darkness, and then looked back up at the hole above, where three eager faces stared back at him.

"You okay, man?" shouted a man called Casey. He was the scruffiest of the three, with long greasy hair that stuck to his head and an overgrowth of beard that had a mind of its own, poking out at odd angles. He always seemed to be the most eager to put someone else in the way of danger rather than himself.

Jack sighed and held on tightly to the rope, cursing at himself, wondering why the hell he'd hooked up with the three men. It wasn't like he didn't manage fine on his own. Sure, it had been a harsh winter, and for a while, he'd thought that maybe his fate would be like one of those that he sometimes found in the ruins, lying there alone in tattered blankets, having frozen to death. But he always did manage.

It was something about the unlikely trio that had attracted him. That was what he told himself. That and a run of good luck that had come in the time he had been with them, which was what? Two months? Time seemed to pass so quickly.

Casey was as scrawny as he was annoying, but he couldn't deny that the man had a gift, a knack that surpassed even Jack's ability to find stuff. More than once it had led them to trouble, even into the occasional fight to keep what they found, but Jack thought that that was Casey's way. The man didn't discover things by himself, he merely spent his time in places where people talked a lot, and he overheard when the others were planning an expedition and made sure he got there first.

The other two – Bron and Sturgess – were little more than Casey's thugs, his gophers. They never questioned Casey and did as they were told, even though they were both twice the size of the old man. But neither of them had many brain cells. They liked it easy, seeming to prefer to follow the lead of the man who barely reached either of their shoulders. Jack knew not to mess with those two. They were much bigger and he suspected fast, as well. Bron certainly was. He'd seen the man in action, not long after they'd met, when Casey told Bron to remove a competing scavenger. Bron had done as he was told with a frightening efficiency. Now here was Jack, also doing as he was told, dangling from a rope over a hole in the bottom of an old factory.

They'd found stairs, but they had been blocked with rubble, and Casey was convinced that it was much easier for one of them to go down the hole in the middle of the main floor. "It's not far, maybe forty feet down to the ground. Easy. Why don't you go check?" Casey had given him a look, the same one he always did when he wanted his way.

"This is ridiculous," muttered Jack.

"What was that?" called Casey from above. "Didn't

quite make you out there, boy."

"Nothing," replied Jack. "I'm good. Nearly there."

"You're the best man for this job," Casey had said. "These two lugs are way too heavy and would break the line. And I seen you climb. Seen you climb just like a spider."

Jack looked back up. Casey was still peering down from the bright sky above.

At least it was still daylight, he thought. Though the daylight didn't reach far enough down into the darkness below.

"Don't worry," called Casey "Rope is still proper secure."

He wondered, as he reached three quarters of the way down the rope, if Casey had decided to be rid of him, just drop him into a hole and be done, but he couldn't think of a reason why. No, he climbed like a spider, as Casey said. And that was useful. But he still didn't trust the three men, and several times he had considered just waiting for the right moment to head off on his own, but then Casey caught wind of a recently uncovered underground area. Jack hadn't been able to resist.

He made his way slowly down the rope. It was easily a drop of sixty feet or more, three floors maybe, though he was now getting close to the bottom. He tried to squint and see into the collapsed rooms on either side of the shaft, but the glare from the sun above was destroying his dark vision.

He was just feet from the floor when he heard the first noise. He froze, dangling there on the rope, looking down into the dark. As his eyes adjusted, the darkness split into different objects. There was movement down there. A lot of it, shapes shifting in the shadows. He willed himself to move, to climb back up the rope, but found himself frozen and it wasn't until he felt a tug and on the rope that his limbs burst into action and he began to climb once more. Now he began to panic.

"Something's down here," he'd shouted, and looked up.

Casey was leaning over the edge, frowning. "What you mean?" he called, as Jack reached the halfway point on his journey back up the rope.

Something was pulling on the rope down below, and Jack glanced down. Barely ten feet behind him, clawing its way up the rope, was a creature Jack still had nightmares about. Its features had been human once, but now its face was shrivelled and sunken, its eyes so far receded into its skull that they were hardly there at all. Teeth that were cracked and broken snapped together rapidly, gnashing at the air between them.

They only came out at night, he knew, but this one was determined, this one was intent on crawling into the daylight after him. There was a curse from above, and Jack launched himself upwards, pulling as hard as he could, his muscles screaming from the abuse. Then he saw what Casey was doing. The man had seen past Jack now, and spotted what was chasing him up the cord, and he'd drawn a knife and was cutting at the rope.

Jack hauled himself further.

Faster, you idiot, move faster, faster. But he could feel the creature below him gaining distance, scaling the rope behind him. Jack managed to reach up with one hand and grasp at the broken ground just as the rope gave way, and

387

the creature below him plummeted back into the darkness, screaming in frustration as it fell, leaving Jack hanging by one hand, swinging in the air. Rough hands reached down and hoisted him out into the sunlight, where he lay for a few minutes, just trying to get his breath back.

"You were going to cut me loose," said Jack, leaning over onto his side. He glared at Casey.

"No, no," said Casey. "I was holding on, waiting 'til you was up. I didn't cut it all the way."

Jack looked from Casey to Bron and Sturgis. The two big men were frowning, looking intently at Jack.

They're waiting for you to make a move on Casey, he thought. And then he thought better of it.

Let it go. Just move on. Tonight. Head off on your own. It's better that way. It always was. Whenever you get involved with others you always end up in some sort of trouble.

Once More into the...

Now...

Jack hadn't noticed the vehicle carrying him coming to a stop. It could have happened hours before. He'd drifted in and out of groggy consciousness several times already, so when tingling in the side of his face started to bring him round, it didn't occur to him to wonder whether the vehicle was still moving or not.

After a moment, he lifted his head from the cold metal floor and cringed as a rush of pins and needles spread slowly into his cheek. His dazed mind, barely able to focus, was vaguely aware that there were noises outside until they reached the back of the vehicle, right next to where he was being held. There were voices and then banging on the panel near his face. Then there was a clunk, and another clunk, much closer, right next to him.

He rolled onto his side as the wall he had been leaning on fell away and swung open. A blast of air and desert heat rushed into the small compartment. The light was blinding, and he closed his eyes as he felt rough hands pull him from his prison and out into the daylight. He was lifted to his feet, but his legs still refused to function correctly, and he staggered, firm hands holding him upright.

"Be still," said a voice. "Give him a moment." The voice was muffled, as though spoken through a visor, and Jack's eyes began slowly to adjust to the bright daylight. He made out the shapes of three armoured figures – facility security forces – gathered around him. Beyond that he saw familiar buildings and a dirt roadway. The figures and his surroundings went from a blur to a slow clarity. He focused on a group standing maybe thirty yards away and felt some slight relief as the face of Tyler and the other E2 crew members registered in his brain.

"You are the one that escaped several months ago," said one of the troopers. She stood a few feet away, regarding him. Jack looked at the officer. She had opened her front visor and he could see it was the same woman officer that had let him escape. She looked stern and curious.

She let me go, he thought. She's probably thinking I could cause her trouble if I were to open my mouth.

"I don't remember much," he said, hoping the lie was convincing. "I haven't been able to remember much over the last week or so. And everything before then is gone."

The officer squinted at him and he wasn't sure if she believed him. She stood there, not answering.

"I think I may have banged my head," Jack said.

The officer nodded, then turned to the other troopers. "Make sure to escort him straight to the detention centre and then file the necessary report." Then she turned and paced away.

Jack watched as she went.

I wasn't convincing enough, he thought. Haven't had a lot of practice with lying, recently.

Then he was being ushered forward by the troopers, one of them pushing him and another walking alongside. The third trooper walked ahead, moving along the dirt road and up the hill towards what Jack recognised as the detention compound. It was a good three hundred yards further along the dirt track, and it took maybe half of that distance for his legs to start responding to what his mind was trying to tell them. His body was battling every step of the way.

Must be side effects of being stunned by the drone, he thought. Or doped. Maybe they doped me.

The three troopers escorted him to the concrete compound, and one stepped in front of him as they reached the entrance. Jack noticed that his own hands were bound by pair of electronic cuffs. He couldn't remember them being put on him.

Had to have happened while I was unconscious, he thought. He followed numbly, still trying to focus.

One of the troopers spoke to another pair of facility staff inside the entrance of the detention building, and then there was more trudging, this time along internal corridors. They turned left, then left again, and then right, onto a corridor with a row of a dozen small doors, half of which were still open. The other half were closed. He was guided into the fourth cell on the right and instructed to sit. He looked around, spotted a bed, and stepped forward, slumping down onto it. He turned to look up at the guard, who stood over him while he removed the cuffs. Jack was about to speak, but before he could, the guard backed out of the room. The door shut firmly with a clunk and a hiss, and Jack found himself in near darkness once more.

So, he thought. Solitary, is it.

He wondered why they deemed it necessary, but no sooner had he had that thought than he noticed a glowing

391

pale light on the ceiling that was gradually becoming more intense.

Watching Over You

Now…

Jackson tapped his fingers on the desk, impatiently watching the video screen in front of him. The image was grey and flickering, and concentrating on it was giving him a headache. He coughed, turned to look out of his office and then looked back at the screen. It was taking too long, as it always did. The crew were busying themselves, checking over the vehicle, but not quickly enough, in his opinion. He wanted them done and out of there. It was already getting dark outside and soon the shifts would change, and that was when he needed to be moving.

"Patience," Jackson muttered. It will be time soon enough. You're just on edge, keen to see what the next delivery will bring, and to see if the deal was being upheld. It had been too long since a delivery. Removing Jagan should have increased productivity, not decreased it. He didn't like it Not at all. He leaned back in his chair, folded his arms, and pondered the image of the maintenance bay.

The mark on the side of the E2 carrier was there, but he couldn't be sure that it was the correct one, a deliberate mark. At least not until he got a closer look. He cursed, hammering at one of the keys on the keyboard, wishing that the zoom on the maintenance bay surveillance camera would go closer, and at the same time he made a mental note that he should have it seen to. The cameras on all internal buildings should be replaced with more functional ones. They were, after all, his eyes on the whole facility.

As he sat there, looking at the screen, the image clarified for a moment, and he leaned forward, squinting. Yes, there it was, almost as if answering his demand. A clear double scratch mark that couldn't be made by some critter. No claws crossed over in such a way. Jackson sat back again, smiling. He wouldn't have to go down to the bay until much later, when the lights were down and no one was around. The marking was clearer now.

"Excellent," he muttered, and tapped at the intercom on the other side of his desk. "Rogen," he said, and waited. After three seconds – almost long enough for him to have the urge to repeat the process – the intercom crackled and the puny, hesitant voice of his assistant replied.

"Yes, so sorry, sir. I was busy."

"Really," Jackson said. "Busy, at this time of the evening? Why, I thought you would be at the canteen already."

"No, sir," replied Rogen. "I was just relieving myself."

Jackson coughed. "More information than required."

"Sorry, sir."

Silence for a moment. "We have an…errand to run this evening, Rogen. Ten of the clock, prompt. You understand?" said Jackson.

"Yes, sir," said Rogen. "Not a problem, sir. I—"

"You will need to arrange the usual set of guard shifts to allow for our visit to be private."

There was a pause, as though Rogen was hesitating. "Yes, of course, Mr. Jackson. Of course, I can arrange that straight away."

"Good," said Jackson. "I have excellent feeling about this delivery," he said, and he released the intercom button.

Yes, he thought, leaning back in his chair once more. I am indeed having a good feeling about this one.

Unseen Unheard

Now...

Ryan crouched low behind the wreckage of a half-crushed vehicle, his body tucked behind the pile of broken concrete at the back. Part of the roof of the vehicle stuck out at an odd angle, providing both cover and darkness as he watched the long line of Junker warriors pass by. He knew a lot of the faces that passed him, and he could hear their conversation even though it was all in hushed tones. Not one of them had spotted him – or would. He was getting too good at this.

But it wouldn't be easy to follow them. He would need to wait until the very last were almost out of sight, before moving forward, or he would have to navigate around other paths, guessing their route.

I could go alone, he thought. Take a route around them, head through the junk hills and be there before them.

No. Too risky. There were more than bugs out there to worry about. He could only range so far away from the junk town before starting to move into territory that was much too dangerous. And the closer he got to one of the facilities, the more chance there was of being spotted by a patrol of troopers, or worse, an active drone.

No. Patience was key, here. That much he had learned

from Jack. There was a time to rush, to get to some place in a hurry, but when it came to stealth the key was not making mistakes, not rushing forward and risking giving yourself away. If any of the Junkers spotted him he would be chastised and sent back, and FirstMan would hear about it. If he was caught because he went on ahead of them, well, no one would probably hear of it, and he'd never see any of them again.

And let's face the truth of it, he thought. You don't even know why you're following, do you? You can't change what's going to happen. Jack was already out there, probably already captured by now and on his way to the facility, just where he was supposed to be for the plan to work. You're just a tag along, and an unwelcome one, at that.

But what happens when it all kicks off, when the defences of the facility go down and hundreds of Junkers rush in? War is what will happen. And in the middle of it will be Jack.

That thought set Ryan's mind racing with questions. How could he help? Was he just going to be a witness? When everything went crazy, was he going to run in there, like an idiot, and hope to help in some way?

And where was FirstMan anyway? Ryan had expected him to be leading the expedition, but the man had been absent for nearly two days.

I don't know, he thought. I really don't know.

On my Orders

Now…

FirstMan knelt in the trash and peered over the ridge. From his position, overlooking the open expanse between mountains of trash and the facility three hundred yards away, he could see the whole theatre of his operation. The flat, bare ground started just yards away, down the slope of junk. The entire distance between the defensive barrier and where he and his men were hiding was almost completely void of debris, having been cleared years ago to allow a good distance between the trash mountains that were the wealth of the Junklands and the main facility. It was a killing ground, and unless his plan went exactly as he wanted it to, that was what it could become.

FirstMan sighed. Even with the protective combat armour his own men wore, they were vulnerable. The Junkers wouldn't stand a chance against the perimeter defences. The guns, even though they were sparsely placed – maybe a hundred yards apart – were powerful enough to cut a man in two, ablative armour or none.

The drone strike meant everything. Jack's position in the detention centre meant everything. Of course, that one was the biggest uncertainty. From the trash mountains, they couldn't see far enough into the facility to know that the man had been taken there, it was mostly hope.

Mostly.

"Well?" FirstMan asked, turning to Hyde, the tech trooper kneeling beside him.

"I'm still picking up the signal," said Hyde, nodding. "And the feedback delay, and trajectory of point of origin, suggest that he is definitely inside the detention centre." Hyde grinned at this.

"Excellent," said FirstMan.

"Only one slight hiccup on that," said Hyde.

Always, FirstMan thought. Always there is something not quite how we want it to be.

"Go on," said FirstMan.

"Well," Hyde continued. "If the estimate is correct, they've put him in the left wing."

FirstMan frowned. "Why would they do that? He's not brain fried. One look at him and you know he's not."

"We know that," said Hyde, "But they appear to have decided otherwise."

FirstMan considered this for moment. "Does this cause us a problem?"

Hyde shrugged. "Technically, no. It's still more than close enough to take down the grid. The problem is, when the magnetic locks in the detention block stop working, our friend Jack may find himself in company that isn't the most stable."

FirstMan crouched low, taking cover behind an overhang of rebar as he looked over the space between them and the perimeter fence.

"Unfortunately, he will have to deal with that," said

FirstMan. "He's tough. Tougher than I first thought."

Hyde nodded.

"He'll be fine," said FirstMan. "Let's get prepped, hunkered down so we're ready for dawn."

FirstMan looked around. On top of the pile of trash, keeping under cover using the front of a vehicle that jutted out, RightHand also knelt and had been spending the last hour using a viewfinder to scour the perimeter. The rest of his troops, at least the ones armed with shock rifles, had spread out further along the ridge, and behind them, hiding amongst the trash, his larger assault force was waiting. The Junkers themselves lay low in the valley of trash, mostly huddled in small groups, some of them lying down, catching some needed rest before the assault.

FirstMan squinted through the viewfinder.

"Is the dampener working?" he asked RightHand. The man glanced at him and looked behind them at a small machine another of their techs was monitoring, using it to hide their presence.

"I hope so," said RightHand. "If it isn't, then they're being very lax with the perimeter watch."

FirstMan peered through the viewfinder again, scanning the perimeter, checking the towers, the walkways. He remembered walking those boards himself. They called them *the boards*, but it was a concrete and metal structure, with towers every hundred yards or so, and underneath that was a mesh fence charged with enough power to instantly kill a man.

The towers also held scanning equipment that should, right now, be alerting the admin office to mass intrusions on the perimeter.

That was what the dampener was for. To hide them.

There was no big light display given off by the defence wall; the fence merely hummed. If they stood within a few yards of it, the static was tangible and would make their hair stand on end. If they went too close...well that was another thing entirely.

Fortunately, there was a gap between the boards and the fence, and anyone patrolling the top was far enough away, but he swore that some nights his legs had felt numb after guard duty, and that had to be something to do with the power running underneath.

He now saw only one guard making their way around the boards, slowly walking the perimeter, just like he had. They would walk it ten times, all the way around, before their shift was over.

Only one guard per post at one time. They always used to have two, but Jackson had sent three companies of security troopers back to the Inner Zone a few years before, all to cut his budget. The man was naive, but then no one had ever tried assaulting the base, so maybe Jackson wasn't as naive as he thought. It didn't matter. It would all backfire on him now, FirstMan thought.

If this goes to plan.

"Target is locked," said Hyde. "I have a firm on the chip location, and it's immobile, as we instructed."

He's probably asleep, thought FirstMan. And so, the waiting begins. FirstMan shifted to try and get comfortable.

Three hours later, he watched as the perimeter guard walked down the ramp and out of sight.

Change of watch, he thought, nodding. Double the number of troopers around the perimeter fence for the next few minutes.

He waited some more, until the new patrol climbed the ramp and started their long walk around the boards.

"Wake everyone up," FirstMan said. "I want them all ready in ten minutes."

"Yes, sir," said one of the troopers nearby. The man signalled down to one of the Junkers below, and after watching several more head out to wake everyone up, he nodded at FirstMan.

"Situ on the drone," said FirstMan.

"Drone is in place and ready to launch," said Hyde. "Inbound time to launch will be fifteen minutes after your call."

"Launch and begin inbound journey," said FirstMan.

"Drone launched," replied Hyde.

FirstMan looked through the viewfinder at the perimeter fence, and he traced along it until he spotted what he was looking for. One of the drone bays. There was a dozen of them across the base, but this one was the only one in view. He needed it to remain inactive. The guns were bad enough, but at the first sign of an assault, those drones would launch and it would all be over.

But if the missile is on target, those things will never wake up, he thought.

As the first hint of colour touched the horizon, moments before the dawning of a new day, FirstMan smiled. "All units move to your designated place and be ready to launch assault on my order."

402

This is it, he thought. This is where it all begins.

PART SEVEN
Another man's Gold

Waiting Room

Now...

Jack was whistling.

The absolute lack of noise or any other form of stimuli within the cell had begun to irritate him over the last hour. And there was that tune he'd heard Ryan humming. It was stuck in his head, now; it wouldn't go away. The boy said he'd been taught it in his schooling lessons at the junk town, and he'd sung it to him. Even though Ryan had forgotten most of the words, it was enough, and now the tune was well and truly embedded.

It was occupying his mind, he told himself. Distracting him from the uncertainty of what was coming – or what should be coming but hadn't started yet.

Jack looked around the room for the hundredth time. All it contained was the bed and a toilet with a small sink next to it. The cot was uncomfortable to lie on, and it wasn't nearly large enough for him. But it was, he reminded himself, better than the hard floor.

And then there was the blue light above the door. Jack

swore it stared at him. Always blue. Only once red, just as he had entered the room – delivered by the guards – and then only until the door hissed shut, sealing him in. It had been blue ever since.

From that moment, nothing had changed. The room had to be sound-proof, because there was no hint of noise from outside. He didn't know how many hours had passed. There was no window to judge by – just the blue light.

Why can't you just enjoy the silence? Enjoy the calm? Soon enough this place is going to be chaos, if FirstMan's plan comes to fruition. This moment of quiet is probably the first you've had in weeks.

But that thought didn't help at all, and if anything, it made it worse. He didn't want the quiet of the detention block; he didn't want to be at the facility at all. Out in the junklands was where he wanted to be. He'd even started thinking about prospecting for a nice location to build his own place out there. Maybe by the swamp, not far from old Haggerty's place, or further out. There were places, like the industrial complex they had searched for the drone chips, that were relatively free from junk. There had to be an ideal spot out there.

If you can survive this, he thought. If this pulse missile doesn't kill you, or you manage to avoid getting yourself shot during the attack, then maybe you can still do that.

FirstMan had said the building he was being held in would protect him from the missile, and he had no reason to believe otherwise. But something he hadn't thought about was what the hell he was going to do when it all kicked off? Would he still be stuck in there? If he got out he'd be unarmed.

Better to sit tight and wait.

Jack's stomach rumbled. How long had it been since he ate or drank anything? Hours. He'd swallowed the chip without eating first, and now he was regretting it.

Jack realised that he had stopped whistling. And now he thought of it, he'd stopped breathing as well. He was holding his breath. Why? He felt a prickling sensation run along his arms.

Like static electricity, he thought. What was that all about?

He frowned, and with that came another realisation. He was staring at the blue light, and not even a simple idle gaze. He was staring at it. Waiting for it to do something. He was convinced it was about to.

Then he was on the floor, hands scrambling to steady himself. Bright lights flashed across his eyes, distorting the room. His ears popped. There was a wave of something – was it heat? No, not heat – a shock wave of some sort of energy that his body struggled to comprehend.

He pushed himself up into a kneeling position and looked around. He reached forward, steadying himself against the wall, and looked back and found that it had been the bed that had moved, somehow bucking inwards and throwing him forward. The sheet that covered it was now tangled around his legs, and Jack could clearly see the metal of the bed had bent in the middle.

He tried to breathe and found there was no air. His lungs weren't responding. He was about to panic when his body shook in a spasm that sent a shock down his back, air gushing painfully into his throat and filling his lungs.

The missile, that must be it, he told himself. It must have happened.

Then the blue light went out and he found himself in darkness for a few seconds. There was perfect quiet once more, but then the light was back on, flashing red.

And then there was a hissing sound from the door.

Last Call

Now

"When does your flight leave?" Lisa Markell asked. The image in front of her was low resolution video. Her mother and father sat in a waiting room. Around them were dozens of other people, all carrying hand luggage and looking both nervous and excited.

"In about an hour," said her mother. "It's all running on time."

"No need to worry," said her father.

Lisa smiled. She could tell that her mother was close to crying. This was a big leap for them, leaving to go to the New World, and worse, leaving Lisa and her brother behind.

"You promise me that you'll get yourself a ticket as soon as possible," her mother said in a wavering voice.

"Yes, Ma. I promise I'll get one for me and Bob as soon as I can. Look, you'll be in cryo for a few years. By the time you wake up, you'll probably have a queue of messages from us telling you to look out for the next ship coming in. We'll already be on our way."

"I know that," her mother said. "I know but I can't help but worry. Those tickets are expensive."

Lisa leaned forward in the chair. "I told you. Another

408

two duties and I'll have the money. And if I manage to wrangle a promotion out of this, it will be even sooner. And anyway, Bob is already putting his own money aside. At this rate, I won't even need to pay the full amount for both tickets, just enough to top his up."

"I hope so, honey," said her father.

"I expect by the time we get there you should have the apartment all ready for us," said Lisa. "Have you any idea how—"

She stopped speaking as the screen went blank. The constant hum of power that was usually heard in the base cut out, and the lights went off. Lisa found herself sitting in darkness.

"What the hell?" she said aloud. It was then that she heard the screech of the alarm sirens outside, as they began to wail louder and louder in their protest.

An Unwelcome Gift

Now...

Governor Jackson paced ahead of his jittery assistant as they headed along the aisle in the vehicle maintenance bay. He'd ensured that E2 was given a permanent spot, under the pretence of making sure all vehicles were kept in their own bays in future, rather than selecting any of the ones available at any given time. It was a practical thing, he'd told the maintenance crews, and although they'd seemed puzzled with his choice, they wouldn't argue with him. What it meant for them was probably more walking between jobs instead of having vehicles queued up in bays next to each other. They would now need to walk to where their next maintenance job was already parked, potentially all the way across hundreds of yards of bays.

Jackson, of course, cared little about the extra work he'd created for them. What he cared about was that it meant the vehicle he had an interest in was directly opposite the clearest CCTV camera in the building, and he could peep as much as he liked.

"Catch up," Jackson said as he paced along the floor of the maintenance bay. His assistant jerked forward, awkwardly catching him up and obviously out of breath. They turned a corner and finally reached where the E2 vehicle was parked.

Jackson came to stop in front of the vehicle and peered up at the platform on top.

"Well?" he asked, glaring at Rogen, who just looked confused. "Get up there!"

Rogen hurried forward and clumsily climbed the metal rungs attached to the side of the vehicle. The man was sweating, and Jackson knew he disliked heights. Even though these vehicles were not as tall as a building, even being 10 feet up would put Rogen into a nervous state. But the man was more frightened of Jackson than his own phobias, and he managed to make his way to the hatch at the top.

Jackson grinned as he watched the man crawl nervously across the top of the carrier. There was a certain pleasure, he found, in the discomfort of others, and his assistant was a most wretched man who, in Jackson's mind, deserved it.

There was a scraping noise, followed by clicks and then a cough.

"I've got it," said Rogen. "Um. Oh."

"What?" said Jackson.

Rogen coughed. "I don't think this is quite what we were expecting."

"What do you mean? What's in there?" said Jackson.

"You may want to come and have a look for yourself," said Rogen. "I don't think I can touch it. It's...well...awful."

The idiot, thought Jackson. Can't even carry down a package. He lumbered forward and climbed the steps, finding himself already sweating by the time he reached the last rung. He pulled his heavy bulk up onto the top of the vehicle and stepped onto the platform, striding quickly forward across the flat roof, scowling at Rogen, who stood off to the side of the open hatch, holding his nose.

"What?" asked Jackson.

Rogen shrugged and pointed at the open hatch.

Jackson looked down into the small compartment. Before his mind could register the object that he was looking at, the smell hit him. "What in hell's name is that?" he said, cringing.

In the compartment, wrapped in a dirty rag, was the small body of something long dead. Fur stuck out at odd angles, and at the bottom of the rag a tail stuck out, curling back over the rag like a tiny snake.

"It ah…it looks like a dead rat, sir," said Rogen.

"A dead…" Jackson's face flushed bright red and he could feel his cheeks tighten. "Why the…" Then he frowned. "The impudent fools. How dare they do this? This is unacceptable. An insult. There will be consequences for this," he said. Then, as he turned to head back to the ladder, his fists clenching and unclenching, all the lights in the building went out. Jackson was about to curse when he heard the warbling sound of the sirens outside.

It's Happening

Now…

FirstMan leapt over a pile of discarded scrap and hit the ground running. The perimeter fence was now less than a hundred yards away, and although the spotlights that would normally be tracing across the open ground that he now ran across were no longer operational, he could still see clearly enough. It was not yet dawn, but a hint of sunlight edged over the horizon. Within the next half an hour, that orange glow, which silhouetted the entire facility ahead of him, would be blazingly bright.

Fifty yards, and he kept going. Beside him, keeping pace, was RightHand, and he could hear the footfalls of many others as they rushed across the open ground. He had ordered radio silence unless there was an emergency, otherwise he knew there would be a cacophony of chatter among the Junker groups. Since arriving at the facility, he'd known that communications shouldn't be picked up, not with the dampener in place, but they were on open ground now and moving out of the dampener's range. Most of the facility's systems were down, but that didn't mean that every radio in the complex was dead. Some would have survived the pulse.

As the fence loomed before him—ten yards, five yards, and then right in front of him—he became aware of the shrieking sirens inside the facility. Other than their constant wail, there was little other noise.

Surprise was still within their grasp. The facility guards would still be trying to pinpoint the problem and figure out what had triggered the alarms and killed the power. Those near the impact point would be stunned and confused. It would take several minutes before they figured out what was going on, and by then...

He slowed as he reached the fence and pulled out a set of heavy iron cutters. He took a single deep breath, looked briefly toward RightHand – who nodded – and clipped the first links on the fence.

No blast of power. No buzz. He was still alive.

"All teams, open it up," he said into the radio as he rushed to cut the wire. One long line of cuts, all the way down to the ground, and then two cuts sideways, opened a hole as the weight of the chain links pulled the wound open. He heard others doing the same, hurriedly making holes in the mesh, then pulling it open to make an entrance wide enough to move back through, should the power come back on.

Then he moved through the gap, dropping the cutters and drawing his weapon. RightHand followed him, never more than a few steps behind, and behind him, other troopers started to move quietly but swiftly through the gap, flooding into the facility.

The sun had still barely shown its face, and darkness filled the spaces between buildings, and the invaders took advantage of it, moving into the shadows, keeping to the sides of buildings like a swarm of scurrying rats.

Over four hundred warriors from the junk tribes accompanied him on this assault – a number that would easily leave the defenders outnumbered by five to one. Only his men – all former facility troopers – carried firearms. Surprise was still their best tactic.

FirstMan moved along the side of one of the buildings, watching the shadows, doorways, and alleyways.

Why had Jagan never attempted an assault? The thought came to him without a warning, and with no reason. But now he wondered. The tall thug had controlled as many warriors as FirstMan did now. Maybe more, since FirstMan still hadn't been able to unite the crag tribes – something that Jagan had managed to do. The perimeter fence with its drones and turrets, now powered down and useless, was a massive deterrent, true, but with a little ingenuity, Jagan could have done it. There were enough intelligent Junkers. He cast the thought aside. Not now. It was a question for another time.

FirstMan moved along the side of the building, edging toward the roadway. Soon most of the guards would be out of the buildings and searching for intruders, and he wanted this over as quickly as possible.

He tapped the communicator attached to his helmet. "All units ensure any firearms are switched over to concussion. I want as few casualties as possible. Repeat, switched to stun, only. We're here to take over, not to slaughter."

With that done, he stepped out from the side of the building, raised his own assault rifle, and aimed at three startled facility troopers just ten yards away, pulling the trigger multiple times in three sharp bursts.

Lights Out

Now...

Lisa stumbled forward in the darkness that engulfed her room. She felt her way to the door and turned to the left, reaching out to the rack on the wall.

Was there enough time to put her armour on? She didn't think so. And besides, she wouldn't find it all in the dark. Most of it would be lying strewn across the floor, where she had left it. She grabbed the handgun from its hook at the same time as she pulled on the handle of the door. It was heavier than usual, and she had to lean into it.

"Damn power-assisted door," she cursed, but the door eventually pulled open and she was greeted by near darkness outside in the corridor. Only the red emergency lights highlighted the walls and floor. She stepped outside and started along the corridor.

It must just be a power cut, she thought. But that wouldn't explain the noise coming from outside – a distant warbling of sirens – that she had heard prior to the lights going out. It had been enough for her to grab a gun before investigating.

Maybe an explosion in one of the power stations? That might explain it, but her nerves told her otherwise. Something was very wrong.

416

She was near the end of the corridor when another figure darted around the corner. Lisa lifted the gun quickly, aiming, but held back when she heard Hayley's voice.

"It's me," Hayley said.

Lisa lowered the weapon and hurried forward. "You made me jump," she said. "What the hell is going on?"

She passed Hayley, heading for the main corridor.

"I don't know," Hayley said. "I just woke up. There was a loud noise."

"Yes. I heard." Lisa moved quickly along the corridor. The whole building was illuminated by just the red emergency lights, but she could see clearly enough. "Some sort of explosion, maybe. Let's go find out."

They hurried further along the corridor and turned into the junction where the dormitory wing met the main corridor. Lisa didn't slow down, heading for the main entrance that would lead them past the conference centre. Other doors opened around them as they passed. Curses followed from the unlit rooms.

The Chaos That Follows

Now…

Jack sat on his bunk, still frowning into the darkness as he peered at the single red light on the door in front of him.

Was it already over? he wondered. Was that it? He sat scratching his head, feeling numb. He'd expected something far more dramatic. He'd thought maybe the bomb would take the roof off; kill him, even. FirstMan had said that he would be safe inside the building, but he hadn't really believed it would work out that way. It was, after all, a missile – a bomb.

Somehow, he was disappointed. Relieved, certainly, but disappointed all the same. Bombs, in his limited experience of them, were much more devastating than this. They made craters like the ones found out in the Outer Zone ruins, fifty-feet wide and twenty feet deep, the debris cast outwards for miles. And then there were the old bomb sites, the *really* big ones, ten times that size. He'd seen one of those from a distance but never up close. You never went close to the old bomb sites. People got sick when they did that.

He listened but heard nothing. Not that he expected to. He'd seen how thick the walls were and didn't expect to hear what was going on outside. There was a thud from somewhere nearby, as if in answer to this puzzle.

Something hitting the wall, he thought, or maybe someone. Then there was a distant shout, muffled, and it ended abruptly.

He pulled himself up onto his feet, shook off the dust, and walked towards the door.

Where did all the dust come from? he wondered. I'm damn covered in the stuff. And yet there was no damage to the room, or at least no apparent damage. Now that he looked more closely, he could see hairline cracks had appeared along the edge of the door, and some of them crept across the walls.

What had FirstMan said?

Fry the electronics.

That was it, and that was all, or so the man had insisted several times. It seemed otherwise, but Jack wasn't going to complain. He was alive.

And he had no idea what he was supposed to do next. There was no plan for that. He had no instructions to follow the missile hit. He had done his job.

Do I just sit here and wait?

A buzzing sound shook him from his thoughts, and then the single light to switched to green.

What did that mean? Green. That wasn't one of the two colours he'd seen. Green meant something different.

Green always meant go, didn't it?

The attack must have been a failure, he thought. The power is back up, and at this very moment, all those people rushing toward the perimeter fence are dropping like bugs, mown down by the defences. Drones were launching, weapons firing.

Damn it.

He couldn't stay. If the attack failed, and he was left there, they would eventually find out that he played a part in it. He had to get out.

But he couldn't find the urge to rush. Instead, Jack edged toward the cell door and tentatively reached forward to touch it, expecting a shock or something in reply. But there was nothing.

Unfortunately, there was also no handle on his side of the door.

They were magnetic doors, he thought. There was no handle on the outside, either – just a button. He looked at the small square hatch in the middle and then back at the light. It's worth a try, he thought, and he grabbed the edge of the hatch. There wasn't much to get his fingers around, but he was surprised at how little was needed. The door shunted part way open with the slightest pull, but it left him with only a foot or so to squeeze through. Beyond the door, red emergency lights flashed in the corridor.

He peered through, unsure whether to brave it out there or not. A scream from down the corridor answered his concerns, and he stepped back into the darkness. A shape rushed by, dressed in orange overalls.

Goddamn it, he thought. Another of the prisoners?

Then Jack remembered who else they kept in the prison block. Those who had recently lost it and gone crazy, either from sickness or just the work itself. This was where they were kept until they got over whatever it was that was troubling them. Solitary. Locked up with only their own thoughts.

Sometimes people snapped, and they would be kept in the detention block until they either calmed down and could be sent back to work, or, well...he didn't know what they did with those that didn't recover, but he couldn't imagine it was very pleasant.

Now that he thought of it, had he ever actually seen anyone go back to work? Maybe one or two, but most that had been taken in had never been seen again.

More yells came from outside, and two more figures ran by. There was a scuffle along the corridor and a snapping sound. A weapon was fired, followed by the thud of something heavy falling to the ground, and then more yelling.

Jack waited a few more moments before he finally peered through the gap, and he edged around the corner so he could see down the corridor.

One of the orange figures lay on the ground and appeared to be out cold, and beyond that, about ten feet further up the passageway, one of the security troopers lay against the wall. His head jutted out at an odd angle, his neck broken.

There was no sign of the other two orange overalls or the weapon that had been fired.

Jack looked around for anything he could defend himself with but saw nothing. He slowly made his way along the corridor, leaning against the wall, stepping over both bodies, his eyes darting over everything as he kept to the darkest areas.

Finally, he reached the entrance of the detention block,

and stepped cautiously out into the foyer. The windows of the main entrance had been smashed out, and another security trooper lay dead on the ground. This one had been shot many times.

Somebody was getting trigger-happy, he thought, and he pictured one of the crazies in orange overalls with a firearm. It wasn't a good image, and it didn't encourage him to move on, but he knew he had to.

Maybe they will provide some distraction for the guards while I escape, he thought. Of that he could only hope.

He moved through the entrance hall, ducking behind the desk and peering out of the main windows there. He was about to leave, planning to crawl along the edge of the room where there was a row of chairs, but he spotted something underneath the desk, something that made him move back.

Better, he thought. There, lying on the ground, maybe discarded before it could even be used, was another handgun. One of those used to stun prisoners – or worse. He grabbed it and turned it on its side, examining the switch on the top. There were no markings, nothing obvious, but he was sure the switch determined whether the gun stunned or killed. There was no way to know.

Looking away from the gun, and out onto the road outside, he decided that it was best left to fate. Either setting would have to do, right now.

He thought of FirstMan, standing in his tech room, explaining the assault they planned and Jack's important part in it. The man had assured him they wished to take the facility with as few injuries as possible on both sides.

But now there was at least two more people out there, armed and totally out of their minds.

This is More Important

Now...

Lisa sprinted along the main corridor, almost colliding with the opposite wall as she hurried towards the armoury. It was a small room that ran alongside the main ops room, with a double door that opened out onto the central corridor. As Lisa reached the doors and slammed the release button, she heard Hayley behind her, breathing heavily.

"Is that weapons fire out there?" Hayley asked.

"Yes," Lisa said, hitting the release on the door a second time, this time somewhat harder. The door shunted slowly open.

"And the main power is down," Lisa said.

"What can that mean?" Hayley asked.

Lisa didn't answer. Instead, she pushed through the gap in the doors, not waiting for them to open all the way. She hurried forward, momentarily stopping at the bank of combat armour suits hanging in their cabinets, and decided that there was no time. She grabbed the nearest assault rifle on the rack, checked to see if it was charged, and turned back to the main doors.

"Better than handguns," she said. Hayley nodded and grabbed a rifle from rack, also checking the power cell.

Even in the dim emergency lighting, Lisa could see that Hayley was terrified. Training or not, the young officer was not combat experienced.

"Is it an attack from outside, do you think?" she asked.

"I don't know," Lisa said. "It could be a worker revolt." Then she shook her head. "No. they wouldn't be able to smuggle weapons away."

"Maybe it's just our guards firing," Hayley said.

Lisa wasn't convinced. "Too much of it for a few guards suppressing unarmed workers," she said. "We'd best go and find out."

They left the armoury and jogged along the corridor towards the main doors. Gunfire could still be heard in the distance, and not just that of the odd weapon. No, Lisa thought. Not workers. But it was confusing. Some of the gunfire was dull, like concussion shots, but then it would be answered by sharper snaps of fire. Deadly shots. Someone out there wasn't trying to stun, and that could only mean one thing. They were firing at an enemy that needed to be killed. The rules were clear – you didn't kill workers unless absolutely necessary.

"Shouldn't we be geared up?" Hayley asked, hurrying behind her. "If we get shot—"

"We don't have time," Lisa interrupted as she reached the main entrance. "Just keep your head down. Stay under cover."

The doors ahead slowly opened as she got within a few feet, and the heat from outside hit her in a dry wave. It was barely dawn, but even at this time of day it could be hot outside. They stepped out onto the dirt road, and Lisa regretted not putting on the armour, even though she knew there was not enough time. The suits had built in temperature control, and she wouldn't normally even consider stepping outside without being geared up.

Lisa turned in the direction of the heaviest gunfire, off to the south, and started down the road, weapon raised, scanning the buildings ahead. Hayley stayed close to her, crouching low where there was any form of barricade.

A concrete wall ran along the front of the admin building, all the way to next junction, and the pair used it as cover as they made their way towards the perimeter fence.

"The fence must be down," said Hayley.

Lisa frowned. That was what was different. The gunfire was one thing, but since they had stepped outside she had noticed a change but couldn't place it. The lack of hum from the generators and the fence.

She turned to look at the large square building directly across from where they stood, on top of which was the communications tower and the power relay for the perimeter fence. Normally there would be an audible hum coming from the relay, and a trio of bright blue lights flicking on and off, but the lights were red and there was no noise. From her position, at the edge of the barricade, she could see down the sloped road that led into the centre of the workers' area, To the right of that was one of the barracks; to the left, the prison block. Lisa could smell acrid smoke coming from somewhere.

Then she saw it. There was a blackened mark down one side of the outer wall of the prison block, as though the building had been burned from above, and yet there was little structural damage. All along the front, the panel glass windows been smashed out.

Some sort of bombardment? No, she thought. The damage was minimal except for the power being out.

The power was out, and the fence was down.

"This is a full-on assault," she said, pointing at the burn mark. "Someone targeted and took out the power, and with that, the drones and the fence."

Hayley looked alarmed. "What do we do?"

"The only thing we can do," said Lisa. "Go and help with the defence."

The flash of gunfire was barely visible in the growing daylight, and there was movement between some of the buildings further down the road.

"Come on," she said, stepping out from behind the barricade just as Governor Jackson and Rogen burst from the alleyway next to the power relay. They hurried up the road in the opposite direction to the fighting.

Lisa took a step towards them. "Governor," she called.

Jackson stopped in the middle of the street, his eyes wide, but then he recognised Lisa and slumped, leaning over and panting heavily. The man was clearly unfit for running.

"Officer Markell and…your assistant," he said, in between breaths. "How very fortunate. You two will assist me."

"Sir," said Lisa, "the perimeter fence is down—"

"Yes, yes," interrupted the governor. "I've seen on the monitors. There's been a breach. We're under attack. There is something important I must do. Documents, data the needs to be safe if this place falls, which from the number of attackers I've seen, may be an imminent problem. You will accompany me."

He started forward, half jogging, half stumbling, followed by Rogen, who glanced at them with a panicked expression.

Lisa turned to Hayley and shrugged.

"The perimeter?" asked Hayley.

"We have our orders," Lisa muttered.

They both turned to follow the two men.

When the Time is Right

Now...

It had been structure of some kind, Ryan thought. But that had been long ago. He wasn't sure what kind of building. It certainly hadn't been made of stone or wood. Large chunks of broken concrete and metal girders met in criss-crosses buried among piles and piles of trash that obscured most of the steel, but it was still easily visible from his perch thirty yards away.

The trash ended in open flat ground that stretched for several hundred yards before it came to an end at the perimeter fence with towers dotted along the outside.

He'd been able to see more clearly a few minutes before, when the ambient light from the glow of the spotlights that surrounded the massive facility had partially lit the ground – and even the trash, to some degree – almost to the spot where he hid.

Some of the Junkers had seen him as he quietly made his way toward a view of the facility, but they must have thought he was meant to be there, because none of them questioned it, and with that in mind, he decided he only had to avoid FirstMan or RightHand, maybe some of the troopers.

But what would they do, anyway? Send him away? They

were all busy, and he was left alone. He had climbed up the girders until he almost reached the top, where only the very tip of the frame poked out from the mountain of junk, and found a small, flat area where he could hide and watch the proceedings. He didn't know what he'd been expecting when the drone approached, the sound a low hum in the distance. Under pale spotlights and the dim glow of the sunrise, he thought the drone would have to fly over the facility. But it hadn't. He never even saw the thing, it was that far away, but he did see the missile.

It happened so fast – a flash of movement across the sky, then a loud *whump* noise as it hit something inside the facility.

All the lights in the sprawling facility began to flicker, and then they went out. The constant humming noise, that he had barely noticed before, ceased, leaving an eerie silence. The entire facility had been buzzing furiously with noise the whole time, but it was so faint that it was almost imperceptible until it was no longer there.

His senses were alert now, and he knew what he was looking for as hundreds of shadows emerged from the junk and swept across the open ground. He wondered then if there might be traps on the ground between the junk and the facility's outer fence, but told himself that FirstMan, RightHand and the other Troopers would know if there was and would have done something in preparation.

It was irrelevant, now that they were running across the open ground. Part of him wished he could be among them, but he wasn't even supposed to be there, and it had taken a lot of patience to stay so far behind the mass of Junkers that had headed through the passes, all the way to the facility. He was good at hiding, keeping eyes diverted from himself, but fighting? He didn't know. Taking out a bug in the junk was one thing. To kill a man?

Gunfire erupted within the walls of the facility. Shots rang out, echoing through the trash canyons, followed by shouting. Ryan thought of Jack. He was in there, right now. He may be locked up somewhere, but the battle would soon reach wherever he was being kept.

But he knew that Jack was alive. He knew it for certain. It was gut instinct. Jack was in one of the buildings, somewhere, still trapped, but he was at least alive.

Ryan reached down to the medical pack he had found when the pair of them had been underneath the building that they found for FirstMan, where they also discovered the handgun at his waist, among many other treasures. They had found the tech that FirstMan had been looking for, and in return FirstMan had looked away as he and Jack took what they wanted from the hidden storeroom.

The medical pack was old, probably centuries old, but it was high-tech. He'd opened the case a dozen times already and looked over the injectors and dispensers inside their sealed packaging. This, he knew, was valuable stuff — healing medicine far beyond anything that could be made now, probably by anyone. And they were all clearly labelled.

Ryan looked toward the facility and the dozens of holes in the fence. It was all abandoned, now that the attackers were inside. No one was there to stop him crossing the open ground and sneaking inside. Jack may need him soon, and he may need the medical pack.

Ryan checked the pack was still securely strapped to his chest, then twice checked the magazine was slotted

431

correctly in place in the gun. He put it back in its holster and began to climb down the junk.

Overrun

Now...

FirstMan stepped out from behind the building, his rifle raised. "Drop your weapons," he shouted. Normally only those close by would hear his voice through the helmet, but a few seconds before he had switched on the helmet's external speakers and they were much louder than a human's normal voice.

The three facility guards spun around, and FirstMan was sure they would have opened fire if it was not for RightHand and the dozen other Troopers moving out from behind the building, spreading out as they moved from the shadows and onto the road. It was still dark in a lot of places between the buildings, and the sun was still low on the horizon, but emergency lighting had illuminated the front of the guard duty building.

But the light levels mattered little here. These Troopers were wearing helmets, and FirstMan knew that they could not only see him and the men behind him but probably the other three dozen Junkers moving silently along the side of the building behind him.

Still they hesitated, and one glanced to the other two, looking for their reaction, but they slowly lowered their weapons to the ground and stood with their hands in the air.

FirstMan wondered if he had worked with any of these Troopers; if they had even been under his command before. They could be new, but it was unlikely. The men would have recognised his voice, he thought, and it was obvious that they would also know the armour he wore – that of an officer. But they wouldn't know the Junkers. He had to move quickly and spread his forces across the facility. If he could do that, maybe all contact incidents would end the same way. The three guards were obviously confused at the mixed group of troopers and Junkers, but they would recognise the Arc rifles he and his men carried – firepower far superior to any of the rifles guards would carry, and reserved only for expeditions that were deemed dangerous.

These men knew they were not only outnumbered but outgunned.

"Move back into the depot and stand down," FirstMan said, edging forward. With a flick and a wave of his hand, he indicated that RightHand and his men should secure the area, but two of them would follow him. The three guard troopers backed through the door. FirstMan glanced around and then looked at them. "This is over already for you," he said to them. "There is no need for anyone to get hurt. Now, I'm gonna leave you in here, but we will be watching you, so you will close the door, and don't leave until you are told you can come out."

The Troopers looked even more confused.

"My name is Captain Ranold. You may already know me."

All three Troopers nodded. The one standing nearest the door even saluted but then awkwardly lowered his arm.

"In there, and quickly."

434

They closed the door behind them, and FirstMan, tapped the radio on his headset. "All units give me an update," he said, as he scanned the area up the road, the buildings, and behind them. He listened to reports coming in from Junker squads as they moved through the facility. There was some gunfire coming from south of his position, but it ended quickly, and the group leader – one of his own troopers – called in to inform him that the situation had been dealt with.

He didn't like the sound of that. 'Dealt with' could mean there had been deaths. He hoped it wasn't the case. "Any injuries?" he asked and waited. There was a chorus of *none* and then the final group replied *two injured, no fatalities either side.*

FirstMan paused, then spoke again. "Good. Proceed to move through the facility. Be careful. No one's been killed so far, and that's the way I want it to stay. On both sides."

Hidden Things

Now…

Lisa cringed as she heard more weapons fire from coming from across the other side of the facility. The sharp snap of assault rifles echoed between the buildings. With the hum of the generator and perimeter fence absent, the noise was strange.

She couldn't remember a single time anyone had needed to fire a weapon inside the facility, at least not since she had arrived there. It had never been required. The workers were placid, most of the time, drained of all will to resist.

Now, the place was in chaos.

She followed Jackson and his assistant along the roadway, Hayley at her side. They both held their weapons up, scanning corners of buildings along the main road as they headed towards the admin building, but the fighting was still concentrated at the south of the facility.

The noise was spreading all along the perimeter, now, ending abruptly in places and escalating in others. How long before it spread to the whole facility? The guards could never have been prepared for this level of attack. Most of them would have been asleep when it started and slow to react.

She cursed again, wishing she'd grabbed a helmet with a

communicator before she left her quarters. Not being able to hear the comms channel was frustrating.

Jackson hurried into the admin building, pushing open the sluggish doors. He didn't stop to check for intruders, rushing along the main corridor with his assistant almost loping behind him. Instead of heading into his office, Jackson jogged a dozen yards further, to the next door, took out his key fob and jabbed it at the middle of the wall.

Lisa had never been in this room before, and that thought made her frown. She hadn't paid any attention to it. All the other rooms around she was familiar with, and in her mind, they swallowed up all the space. But there it was, a door she had no recollection of.

A facility lock-up, she thought. It had never been opened while she was around. This was Jackson's domain only. After speaking quietly into the panel on the wall, the door slid slowly open, and Jackson walked in.

She had barely entered the room, glancing around and seeing only a few shelves with metal lock boxes stacked on them, when Jackson barked his command. "Officers, take that green box and these two cases." Jackson thrust two compact, metal cases toward Hayley, who looked puzzled. The young officer lowered her weapon, then let it drop to her side so that she could hold both cases. Lisa reached down and picked up the green box, finding it surprisingly heavy. She too was now rendered ineffective, but with a hand still free she was not letting her rifle go.

Governor Jackson grabbed two more cases and shoved them into Rogen's hands, then picked up another case, this one black and equally heavy-looking. Then he was moving again, hurrying out of the room and heading along the main corridor toward the other end of the building.

"Follow me, quickly," he said, leaving the door wide open. Hayley opened her mouth to say something, but Lisa shook her head and followed the two men.

"What's so important in these that we need to move them, sir?" Lisa asked. "Surely they are more secure in the lockup."

Jackson only turned only briefly, and he looked irritated. "Facility data. Important document storage devices. It's not your concern," he said. "But I must take them away from the facility, lest they fall into the wrong hands."

Jackson stopped at the double doors at the far end of the admin building and turned to Lisa and Hayley.

"You two go first. Make sure there is no one out there. We need to get to the SubTrans as soon as possible."

Party with Insanity

Now…

Jack stepped through the broken doorway, carefully avoiding the large shards of glass scattered across the ground. It was nearly dawn, and the glare of the sun was just creeping its way up from the horizon. It was still quite dark along the road, where the buildings cast long shadows, but he knew that would change very quickly.

Jack had seen the sun rise many times across the wasteland, and he knew that within the next half an hour, maybe even just twenty minutes, it would go from a dim dawn to blazing bright. But while it was still half-light, he would have to tread carefully. He glanced in both directions, wondering which way to go – and which way the two crazies could've gone. But then he heard a shout from nearby.

He hurried left, along the front of the building, gripping the gun tightly, and glanced around the corner. One body lay in the dirt half-way along the alleyway that ran next to the detention block, and there was a struggle going on further down.

That was all he picked up at a first glance before he ducked back out of sight. He took a deep breath and slowly leaned out again, gun raised, ready to fire. At the far end of the alley, one of the crazies stood up. A second Trooper lay motionless at his feet, and Jack realised that the insane prisoner had such a small grasp of his situation that he had used a live firearm to beat the Troopers into unconsciousness rather than fire upon them, and it must have happened quickly, because both Troopers were armed and Jack had not heard any nearby gunfire.

But there was gunfire coming from somewhere, a distant rattle that he thought must be coming from the perimeter.

The invasion had most definitely started.

He lifted his handgun, judged the distance of forty feet, and, without a second thought, fired the gun. The handgun hissed in his hand and the escaped prisoner was thrown from his feet, the blast hitting him directly between the shoulders before he could even sense that Jack was there. The man crumpled, falling forward and rolling onto his side. Jack hurried along the side of the building and slowed as he approached the body. The man had fallen face down, and Jack could see a dark blast mark on his back. There was a moment of guilt, but Jack noted the two bodies of the very dead Troopers and shrugged it off.

The man would have killed more if he had been left to carry on, Jack thought, as he turned and headed back towards the nearest Trooper. He now knew which setting meant stun, and he switched the handgun power off. He shoved it into his belt and reached down, grabbing the assault rifle that lay discarded in the dust. This one he had seen used more recently. An Arc rifle, he thought was the name. FirstMan and his men carried them, and one of them had even taken the time so show Jack how to ready and fire one. He quickly set the weapon to a short-range stun – not trusting his aim enough long distance — and hurried back to the main road.

Now what? he thought. You must think quickly. move fast. Either you make a guess or you hope the other crazy makes himself known. But there was no sound nearby; no more fighting to alert him other than what was going on in the distance, near the perimeter fence.

I need to alert Tyler and the others — let them know that this isn't a fight they need to involve themselves in.

That decided, he took off, jogging along the road in the direction of the scavenger block, aiming the assault rifle in front of him and checking every alley as he passed each building.

He was just rounding the corner at the junction before the road led down to the residential area when something glimmered in the sunlight to his right, moving fast. Then, before he could judge that it was a reflection on the window of the opposite building, he was sprawled on the floor, rolling, dropping the assault rifle, his brain barely managing to register the flash of orange overalls as something large collided with him. He shook his head and pushed himself up onto his arms, his senses reeling. The figure rushed towards him again. Somehow the attacker had missed him the first time, delivering a glancing blow rather than a full-on body-slam.

It was the second prisoner, Jack realised, and he had come from above. The crazy must of jumped from the roof of a building. Why had he been up there? Jack didn't know, but the man had dived on him from above, as he attempted to do so a second time, right then. Jack rolled and kicked out a foot in the direction of the orange blur, one last attempt at defending himself, one learned from the pits, many years before. Leg straight, foot flat. The man's chest hammered into Jack's heel, and Jack felt a sharp pain run all the way up his side. The man's own body weight propelled him forward, reeling over the top as Jack rolled away.

There was a crack as the man hit the ground, and a gasp of breath. Then Jack was up on his feet, reaching for the assault rifle, but the weapon was yards away. He grabbed the handgun, still stuffed into his belt, but then slowed as he lifted it. The man wasn't moving.

Jack edged forward, switching the gun back on and flipping the mode switch to what he now knew was stun, his heart thumping in his chest as the weapon charged and then blinked to life.

He fired, hitting the prone figure in the side. The body jerked, reacting to the surge of energy, but then lay still.

Jack moved slowly forward, still not totally convinced the crazy was out cold. He rounded the body and shivered as he realised why the man wasn't moving. Somehow, after Jack had kicked the man during his dive attack, the inmate must have landed badly, and his neck had broken. Jack sighed and lowered the handgun.

Well, that's those two dealt with, he thought. Not quite what you had in mind, but over, nonetheless.

He grabbed the assault rifle, glanced back once at the body in the middle of the road, and started off again in the direction of the residential blocks.

A Case of the Unknown

Now...

The SubTrans building was the northernmost structure in the facility, and it was large enough that it could be seen, perched in its raised position, from nearly any place within the perimeter. It seemed miles away to Lisa as they jogged along the road towards it. The fighting hadn't reached this end of the facility yet. Everything was still concentrated on the south and the east side, though Lisa thought that it had moved away from the perimeter and deeper into the maze of buildings.

Whoever was assaulting the facility was winning, she thought as they made their way toward the turning before the road reached the SubTrans building. Lisa tried to judge from the noise just how far the uprising, or whatever it was, had spread, and she wished again that she had grabbed a helmet with a communicator, so that she could talk to the other positions and get some idea of how bad the situation was. Soon, she thought. I can drop Jackson off at the SubTrans and then turn back, try to help.

There was an armoury directly across from the SubTrans. It was only a small one, a safe cache underneath the guard outpost that overlooked the entrance. She could get a communicator from there. There should even be guards there; maybe they would be able to update her, fill her in on whatever was going on.

But as they rounded the corner which led toward the sloped entrance of the SubTrans building, she saw that the outpost was empty, abandoned. The door was wide open.

Dammit, she thought. They seriously ran from their post? No, maybe not. Maybe the guards had done what she wanted to do and headed straight for the conflict. Not everybody was trying to run away from the battle. At least the guards must have headed towards the trouble.

"Quickly," Jackson shouted as he jogged up the slope towards the arch, but instead of going into the office next to the entrance, Jackson carried straight on, hurrying into the terminal building. Lisa and Hayley gave each other confused glances.

What was he doing? she wondered. There would be no Trans in the station. They only came when new deliveries or new recruits were being sent. But Jackson hurried into the building anyway and then out onto the single platform. He took a sharp right, jabbing light switches as he went, until he reached the end of the platform where an archway opened out into the maintenance bay.

Lisa had never been into this part of the SubTrans building. She frowned, realising she had never been back since the day she'd arrived. What could be back here that was so important?

She followed Jackson through the maintenance bay and all the way to the end of the platform, where it disappeared through a closed off doorway. Somewhere else beyond the maintenance bay? Other than the large closed gates, only a single door led through to whatever lay beyond.

Jackson jabbed at the security pad on the wall next to the door and cursed impatiently until the door hissed open. He didn't hesitate after it opened, stepping through into the darkened room.

"Quickly," he said as the lights began to flicker on in the room. "Bring me the cases."

Lisa and Hayley put the cases they had been carrying next to the two Jackson had placed on the floor.

"You two guard the entrance to the platform," he commanded. "And make sure nobody comes in. I must get the Maintenance Trans ready so we can leave." The large man then scuttled towards a control panel on the other side of the room, barking commands at his assistant, who rushed over to pick up two of the cases.

Leave? Lisa thought, and she frowned again. The track that came into the SubTrans appeared to end in this room, and there, parked next to the railing that marked the end of the line, was the smallest Trans she had ever seen. It was barely bigger than the driver's cab on most Trans, though it bore a small operating platform at the front with what appeared to be a cluster of cameras and mechanical arms pointing down towards the track.

"Sir, surely we need to go and help?" she asked. "Surely we don't want to leave? We can stop whatever is happening and secure the facility again."

"Not this time," Jackson shouted as he reached the panel of controls. "I saw them on the cameras. There's hundreds of them. They've taken the perimeter fence down. How they managed it, I don't know, but it's completely out, along with the drone defences and the turrets. This is an invasion, and they are well armed, and we have lost most of our defences."

Lisa glanced at Hayley, then to the SubTrans entrance and then the dark tunnel that loomed at the other end of the platform. They were leaving? Abandoning the whole facility? She couldn't believe Jackson was so spooked that he was running so quickly. There was something wrong with all this, something he wasn't telling them. The man was panicking. If this was just an attack by some Junkers, losing the outer defences was bad, but they had over a hundred Troopers inside the facility. They could take it all back. The attack could be repelled. She knew it could.

Jackson wasn't telling her everything.

"Sir, I strongly suggest I assist with the defence," she called.

"You will do as I command," Jackson yelled. "You stand here and guard until I get the Trans ready." He turned to Rogen, who was still ferrying he cases over to the Maintenance Trans. "Will you speed it up.? Come on, with those cases."

Jackson knelt next to the large green case and flipped open the top.

"I don't get this," Hayley said, keeping her voice low so that only Lisa heard.

Lisa just shook her head. "Just do as he says. Then, when he's gone, we can go and help." She listened and heard Jackson hissing commands at Rogen. The governor must have thought she couldn't hear them from across the bay, but she could just make out what they were saying.

"That's it. Put all those in the Trans," Jackson said. "I'll be there in a moment. I just need to set this correctly so we have enough time."

"Is that what I think it is?" Rogen asked, and Lisa noticed his voice waver.

"Yes," said Jackson. "Shut up."

Stand Down

Now…

FirstMan kicked aside a broken chair that lay on the floor between the two smashed doors at the entrance to the Admin block. The mechanism that opened the doors seemed to have gotten stuck in a loop, and the left door was opening and shutting, opening and shutting, slowly but constantly. The door on the right wasn't moving, but whirring and clicking noises came from the wall next to it, and he could see a chunk of debris was stuck behind the door.

He stepped into the foyer before any of the other Troopers, but he was followed closely by RightHand. The man had barely been three feet away since they first breached the perimeter fence, and FirstMan wondered if it was RightHand's own fears that drove him or if he was just being protective.

The building was darker, further in. The foyer itself was lit by the glare of the bright sun, but the main corridor leading from the room had no windows, and only the flickering of emergency lighting illuminated the passageway. There had been a struggle here already, that much he could see, but he also knew that none of his task force had gotten this far, so this was internal chaos rather than a defensive struggle. Had some of the inmates of the facility taken the opportunity to fight for their freedom? He had no idea. There were no bodies, and no signs of weapons fire, but there was plenty of debris. The foyer and the corridor beyond looked as though a storm had blown through it.

"All units call-in," he said into the comms. He stood there, looking up the corridor, waiting for his team leaders to reply. The calls came in, in rapid succession, and it wasn't all good news. Mostly the defence had fallen quickly, either stunned or surrendering, but now he listened as three different reports came back to him with fatalities. A dozen Junkers were down, three of whom were dead. Nearly twenty of the defenders were wounded, and lastly one of his own Troopers had taken a shot to the face and was in a critical state.

And we don't have much in the way of medical support, he thought. Unless we take the rest of the facility quickly. The med bay was on the other side of the very building he stood in, and that, it seemed, was now his major priority, alongside capturing that damn pig of a governor.

Thirty yards along, a left turn and then right led them to the entrance of the main ops room. Target number one. This was where any remaining command would be, he thought, but he wondered if there was even anything left that resembled such.

He crouched low and moved to the doorway leading into the ops room. Leaning forward, he pressed the button on the wall that would open the doors. There was a satisfying hiss as the two doors shunted open, disappearing into the wall panels and filling the corridor with a blast of bright light.

"Back the hell out," shouted a voice, and FirstMan

immediately ducked lower, scanning the room for the source of the defender. He saw three – no, four – figures in the room, all behind desks that had been dragged across the floor and rearranged into a defensive barricade in the middle. Computer terminals and power cables littered the ground where they had been abandoned.

"That you, Ranold?" shouted the same voice. FirstMan recognised it this time. How could he not? Major Bryant. The man had commanded the facility security forces for years. "You got a hell of a damn nerve."

FirstMan turned quickly back, checking the positions of his men with a glance. RightHand was behind a desk just a few yards away, but most of the troopers were crouched against the wall out in the corridor. They had line of fire on some of the room, but only he and RightHand had a view that covered the entire room, which, as with most of the Admin block, was lit only by emergency lighting. He considered the room, glancing at the rows of desks, tables and cabinets. There could be any number of Troopers in there; a dozen or more could easily be hidden under cover, yet maybe it was only the few he thought he had seen.

"This doesn't have to get nasty," called FirstMan. "Not if you don't want it to go that way."

"Damn you, Ran," Bryant replied. "I never would have taken you for a traitor. Even when I was told you all went AWOL, I didn't think it was clear."

Bryant's voice came from the back of the room, over near a set of cabinets that lined the wall. Another set of identical cabinets faced the wall. He was sure that was where Bryant was.

One concussion grenade could fix this, he thought. But

what a waste of good Troopers. If he could only persuade the old man to stand down.

"Sir, if you are willing to lay down your arms, we can discuss this," said FirstMan.

"My arms?" shouted Bryant. "You attack my goddamn facility, kill my men, and you want me to just stick my hands in the air and beg for mercy? Not on this day, or any other, soldier. You want this facility, then you'll take it inch by damn inch, with blood."

FirstMan smiled. The man had always been stubborn. "No, sir, no begging required. No one is being killed. If you will simply stand down, you will be detained, unharmed, until we can organise transport to take you back to the Inner Zone. We already have—"

But he didn't get to finish the sentence. The initiative was lost before he could react.

"Fire!" shouted Bryant, and FirstMan saw movement from several corners. Three other Troopers broke cover, along with Bryant, to fire a volley through the room and into the corridor. FirstMan heard a thud as one of his men hit the deck, but he didn't have time to check on him. He raised his rifle and started firing, and with that, the guns behind him in the corridor followed.

A flash of heat shot past his face, and he felt it even through the visor. Bryant and the others inside the room were firing live, and his men would still be firing to stun. Both would damage the room and the equipment within, but only the live shots could kill. He ducked back, then leaned out to aim and fire. Then he did it again. The third time he saw one of the defenders fall, and he heard another go down at the same time. He still couldn't get a bead on

451

Bryant; the man was in near full cover behind the cabinets.

A flash of blue shot up the corridor, and FirstMan heard another of the defenders go down.

"Just Bryant left," snapped a voice in his ear. "But he's in there thick." It was RightHand, talking through the comms. The noise in the room was deafening, even if only one man was left defending it. His own Troopers continued to blaze shots all over the room, sending furniture flying, computer screens crashing to the floor, and wall panels collapsed in.

For moment, he met RightHand's eyes, lowered his rifle and signalled the group to rush the room. RightHand nodded back and signalled to the men behind them, his gloved fingers indicating three seconds, then two, the one, then go.

The blasts from the corner intensified as they rushed in. RightHand went to his right, ducking behind a row of desks that hadn't already collapsed, still firing into the back of the room. FirstMan went straight forward, then bore left along the back of the cabinets. A burn of heat singed his left side, and he realised that firing live, Bryant could fire even through the cabinets, not just round them. Stun shots had no such ability.

He rushed forward, leaned around the corner, and heard a grunt as Bryant fell back from a surge of shots coming from the row of desks where RightHand and another trooper were firing.

Then he saw the major, slumped back against a cabinet, stunned but not out cold. The man was still pointing his weapon towards the desks. FirstMan lunged forward, getting just feet from the major, and aimed his weapon at the man's face.

"Stand down, Major," he shouted.

For a moment, the major stopped firing and looked surprised to see FirstMan so close. He thought the major was going to surrender, and the weapon lowered just a few inches, but then Bryant grimaced and spat at him as he pulled the trigger again, unleashing a volley of fire that clattered against the back wall.

FirstMan fired.

It was over. The major slumped back, unconscious. FirstMan glanced around. The room was completely trashed. Barely anything would be recoverable. Three other bodies lay unconscious on the floor along the back of the room, all of them armoured but wearing rookie insignias.

It seemed the major had been caught unprepared for the fight.

"Sir, we have a problem," called one of the Troopers. The man was kneeling hunched over a figure at the other end of the room.

Damn, he thought. I just lost another one of my men. His stomach churned as he wondered who. Every one of them was worth a hundred others, each having followed him out into the Junklands, giving up their lives in the military, and each having fought at his side numerous times.

He walked over and crouched by the prone figure.

It was then that he realised that the injured man was not just any of his men, but RightHand.

"Waylan….no," his whispered as he sank to his knees. He looked at the wound in the centre of his friend's chest, and then into the man's cold, lifeless eyes. There was nothing that could be done.

RightHand was already dead.

"Sir, Team 4, here." A crackling voice spoke in his ear. "We have a visual on Jackson heading into the SubTrans building, repeat, we have a visual on Jackson moving into the SubTrans building. Three other targets accompanying, two are Troopers. Over."

FirstMan sighed, still unable to grasp what had happened. This was not how it was meant to be. He and RightHand had plans. Waylan had been the one driving most of this. The man had ideas for everything. Now he was gone.

"Sir, this is Team 4, please respond. Over."

FirstMan stood up, his head still lowered, and pressed the comms button on the side of his helmet. "First, here. All teams converge on the SubTrans building. First there goes for the shot. Disable Jackson. Disable all targets." Then he paused for a moment, looking back at his dead friend. "Use ultimate force if necessary. Over."

Hunted

Now...

Jack dived behind a wall a dozen meters from the first residential block, his eyes stinging with sweat that hadn't been brought on by just the heat of the sun that now blazed down onto the facility. Behind him, the fragments from the corner of the concrete building rained down and scattered across the ground, blasted away by the Arc rifles of the two Troopers that he had nearly run into.

He'd had barely a second or two to react, his instinct to hold fire, to try and get them to lower their weapons. Now, as he buried his head and tried to stay low behind the wall, he wished he'd just fired. At least he had the decency to have the weapon set to stun. They certainly didn't.

For a few seconds the barrage of fire ceased, and he heard boots on the ground, heading across from their position to his. They were coming in, probably presuming they'd already hit him. He rolled over several times, covering himself in dirt and dust, but managed to end up a dozen yards along the wall, well away from where he had been, and only just in time. The first of the two Troopers jumped right over the wall, firing as he went, but thankfully aiming at the spot where Jack had been hiding a few seconds before. The second, maybe a more cautious Trooper, went around the other way, aiming and firing toward the corner of the building.

They realised their mistake before Jack could use the advantage. He raised his weapon and fired, but both Troopers dived for cover before he could hit either of them.

I'm screwed, he thought. Totally screwed. He ran once more, this time heading for the other corner of the building, just a few yards away. These guys were a much better shot than he was. They were well trained and used to their weapons. Apart from a few hours' training with one of FirstMan's Troopers, Jack had little experience with assault rifles. A machete? Sure. But guns? No. Few Outer Zone wanderers ever owned such things, unless they were scavs, and those folks weren't sharing what they managed to get hold of.

Should have spent more time practicing with the damn thing, like FirstMan suggested, shouldn't you? he thought. Knowing how to flip firing modes and shoot a piece of junk thirty yards away was one thing. Hitting a moving target that was trying to blow your face off? That was entirely different. He wondered, for only the slightest of moments, how many Junkers were dead.

But he didn't get to think for very long. He felt the heat rush by as he made the corner, almost falling flat on his face. He stumbled, glancing round for more cover, and spotted a large metal container further along the alleyway between the buildings. He started running.

Boots thudded on the ground behind him. Damn, they're persistent, he thought. He'd hoped that if he ran they might just let him go, maybe stay at whatever post they were supposed to be at, but these two weren't leaving him alone.

Another rush of heat blasted by as he ducked behind the container. He looked around, his thoughts shifting between standing and fighting and just keeping on running. He couldn't stop. They were firing live rounds, and there were two of them. He knew this was it. He'd never take both out. He ran on, keeping to the wall along the side of the alleyway, hoping that the container would cover him for enough time to make the next junction.

It was twenty yards, then ten. Jack found himself unconsciously switching the rifle from stun to live, but he switched back again as he reached the corner. Then, just as he was about to round the corner, a blast hit the ground next to his right foot. He stumbled and rolled forward, thankfully around the corner, but still onto his face. The rifle once more fell from his grip as he reached out, trying to avoid smashing his skull on the concrete ground.

He reached for the weapon but wasn't quick enough. The two Troopers appeared around the corner, both rifles aimed directly at him. Jack tried to raise his hands, to show he was surrendering, but both Troopers aimed right at him.

"Drop them," came a voice from nearby. The two Troopers spun to their right, turning their rifles in the direction of the sound.

Now, Jack thought. Use this. Quickly. He forced his hand to reach quickly for the weapon, pushing the shock and fear that was bubbling in his gut aside.

But as he raised the weapon he saw that the two Troopers were lowering theirs. Jack frowned, raised the rifle, but instead of firing, he watched as half a dozen other armed Troopers – FirstMan's men – walked out of cover. A dozen Junkers followed behind them, and Jack could see that most of these now carried rifles or handguns.

There were several sharp cracks, and the two Troopers jerked and fell to the ground, stunned.

Jack stood up, one hand raised, and was relieved when the lead Trooper lifted his visor to show a grinning, bearded face.

It was Hyde, the Tech Trooper that had given Jack the chip to swallow.

"Damn, it's good to see you," Hyde said, patting Jack on the shoulder. "We were worried you might get taken out before we could overrun the place."

Jack nodded. "Me too. Look, I need to make sure that my friends here are ok. Did you hit the bunk houses yet? The ones for the carrier crews?"

Hyde grinned. "Already taken care of, my friend. We secured the whole area already, with no resistance." He tapped the side of his helmet, turning away from Jack. "Yes, sir," he said. "Acknowledged and on our way."

"What's going on?" asked Jack "What do you want me to do now?"

Hyde turned back to face Jack "End game time. Come on. Stick with us, and grab one of those helmets so you can get on comms. The governor has been spotted heading for the SubTrans. We gotta make sure he doesn't get out of here."

Deactivated Dream

Now…

Ryan crouched behind the wall as a trio of Troopers ran by. He closed his eyes for a moment, willing himself to slow his breathing, just as Jack had taught him, and hoped his cover was enough.

It was. The Troopers were too pre-occupied with the chaos all around them. In the alleyways and the buildings across this whole side of the facility gunfire and shouting echoed, and the three Troopers rushed towards a building nearby and ran inside. Gunfire followed.

That was his moment, and he took it, kicking away from the wall and racing across the dirt road as fast as he could, one hand gripping tightly to the medical pack on his chest, the other holding the small handgun. He ducked into an alleyway and made his way along the darker side where the sun cast a shadow over a third of the tiny path.

At the end of the alleyway he found himself in a small clearing between the large concrete buildings. Several more alleyways led away from the clearing, giving him half a dozen options of which direction to head in, but he noticed them second to the thing that was parked in the middle of the clearing.

A drone.

It was not much shorter than he was and maybe three metres across, perched upon a low concrete platform in the middle of the clearing. Next to it was a charging station and a covered alcove with a computer screen in it. Ryan didn't know much about those, but both Jack and FirstMan had explained what they were. Some way to communicate with the drone, to tell it what to do.

He stood still, just looking at the thing for a minute or so before he noticed the thin wisp of smoke rising from the charging station.

The drone's power source had been fried in the attack, Ryan thought. He thought back to when Jack was explaining it to him, and even though he had been angry at the time, and not really listening, he was surprised at how much he remembered. That was what the missile was meant to do. The electronics would be broken all over the facility, and that included this drone.

He walked round to the front of the drone and peered at what he thought was its face. It kind of even looked like a face, in an insect, bug-like way, with half a dozen camera lenses pointed out in different directions and a central dome that looked like a funny hat covering them.

He had expected wings. The drones flew, and he could see how they would do it with the jets sticking out at various angles, but the physical reality of the thing somehow didn't match what he had seen in the sky when the missile was fired. It looked like it should be clumsy, rather than graceful and smooth in flight.

I wonder if it could carry a person? Ryan thought. Maybe. If it could hold the weight of a missile, maybe it could hold someone who wasn't too big. Not too heavy. He imagined, for a moment, himself flying over the junk, holding onto the top of the drone, controlling it with some sort of steering stick like he had seen in abandoned vehicles.

A noise from one of the alleyways shook him from his strange daydream, and Ryan turned to see several of FirstMan's Troopers passing by the other end of the alley. Then, briefly, he saw Jack run by.

He was about to call out, shout Jack's name, but then thought better of it. He left the drone, and his daydream of flying, held the medical pack tightly, and started running along the alleyway.

Time to Leave

Now…

"We're ready," called Jackson. He crossed the SubTrans maintenance bay and headed over to the small Maintenance Trans. Rogen had finished loading the cases into the small compartment and stood a few feet away from the steps that led up to the cab. The man was fidgeting, and Lisa could see he was nervous to the point of nearly exploding.

She checked the entrance to the building one last time, then glanced at Hayley. The girl was frowning, not even looking in the direction of the doorway that she was supposed to be guarding, but she did look back at Lisa, nodding toward the large green box on the floor next to the Trans track, half way along the platform.

Hayley started toward the Trans, stopping at the steps next to Rogen, and they waited as Jackson hauled himself up the three metal steps and into the cab. Lisa looked back down at the building's entrance, thought for a moment that she could hear voices out there, and backed toward the Trans.

"Sir, you've left one of your cases," said Hayley, pointing toward the green box as Rogen stepped up onto the Trans. The gangly man was looking at the control box that would seal the door.

"Leave it," said Jackson. "That stays." He turned back to the controls of the Trans, flipped a few switches, and smiled when the vehicle hummed to life. "Officer Markell, if you would be so kind as to untether the Trans from the power feed."

Lisa nodded and walked to the back of the Trans. Several thick cables were plugged into a large box built into the floor. She knelt and unplugged each cable, frowning when the first was automatically reeled in by the Maintenance Trans, the cable winding up into a box on the side of the vehicle until only the plug itself poked out of a hole in the chassis. It was after she had untethered the second cable, and it had also been reeled in, that she noticed the sound coming from the green box a dozen yards away.

Bleeping. Roughly every second or so. No, not roughly. The box was emitting a quiet bleep every single second exactly. She frowned and walked over to the box.

"Officer Markell, the box is to be left, and we all need to embark upon the Trans and leave right now," Jackson said in his most commanding tone.

But Lisa looked down at the green box. There was a timer on the top, and the sides of the case had been pulled down. The timer read 7:52, then on the next beep 7:51

"Sir, what is this?" Lisa asked. "Is this what I think?"

A detonator, she thought. But to what?

"It is indeed what you are probably thinking it is," said Jackson. "And before you step further out of line and ask, it is very necessary."

Lisa turned back to the Trans. Hayley was standing on

the steps now, and Lisa saw that Rogen was twitching frantically.

"If you are coming with us then we are leaving right now," said Jackson. "Unless you wish to throw your life away on some foolish errand."

Lisa started toward the Trans. "What do you mean, throw my life away? Just what kind of detonator is that? What are you doing?" She saw that Hayley was now slowly lowering her hand and reaching back to her rifle.

"This place must be neutralised," said Jackson. "I have no choice. It must be unmanned when we return to reclaim it."

"Unmanned?" asked Lisa. She glanced at the green box – a bomb, she thought. "What kind of explosive is that?"

The Trans hummed louder, and she saw Jackson now had his hand on the accelerator, ready to go.

"You can't leave that here," said Lisa. "You can't just kill everybody. There are over a hundred Troopers – officers – over a thousand workers."

"It is necessary," said Jackson. "And I am not staying. Now, follow your orders!"

Lisa faltered, unable to get her head around what Jackson was willing to do. Something to knock out the facility, make it unusable by the enemy, maybe, but to neutralise everyone?

"I can't do that," Lisa said, raising her rifle. "I can't let you blow this place up with everyone in it."

At this, Jackson's expression changed, his eyes squinting at her, glaring. He seemed to understand that he was no longer in control. She would stop him, she thought. She would make him disarm the bomb. And he now seemed to have realised it.

Jackson drew the handgun before Lisa could react. He was never armed, she thought. She had never seen him carry a weapon. But this was small, something that could easily be concealed, and as the man rammed his hand down on the accelerator, he fired wildly out of the door. Rogen was caught off balance as the Trans lurched forward, and he fell out of the door and tumbled down the steps, hitting the railing as he went. As the Trans sped up, heading away from them much quicker than Lisa had expected, Rogen fell onto the track.

Lisa fired at the Trans but then stopped. Hayley had been at the foot of the steps when the Trans had started moving, and while Rogen had tumbled out of the cab, she had stepped forward and grabbed the rail next to the door. She also nearly fell away as the Trans sped up, threatening to unbalance her, but she released her rifle and grabbed at the door with both hands.

Lisa aimed but couldn't get a clear shot. Hayley was in the way as she and Jackson struggled in the entrance.

The Trans was almost at the tunnel now, and Lisa ran along the track, trying to catch up, but it was going too fast. There was the sharp crack of a gun going off once more, and Hayley fell from the cab. Jackson disappeared as he fell backward into the cab, and Lisa could only watch as the Trans vanished into the tunnel. A moment before it disappeared into the shadows of the tunnel, she aimed at the back panel, where the power supply would be—

Too late. The Trans was gone, as it gained full engine power and passed into the tunnel, speeding off into the darkness.

Lisa rushed along the platform towards the prone figure of Hayley. The girl had fallen from the cab and hit the tunnel archway as she fell. Even as Lisa approached she could clearly see that one of Hayley's legs was bent at the wrong angle.

She crouched down and carefully rolled Hayley over. She cried out when she saw the large blast mark in the middle of Hayley's chest, one that would prove fatal if she didn't get medical attention.

"I'll get help," Lisa said, and went to stand, but Hayley grabbed her by the arm, shaking her head.

"What?" asked Lisa. "I need to get you a medic."

"No time," Hayley said, her voice strained. "The bomb."

"Yes," I'll stop it. I'll get Rogen to stop it. Then I'll get you a medic."

She ran along the platform toward where Rogen lay, stepped down onto the track, and hauled Jackson's semi-conscious assistant onto the platform. She rolled him over and looked at his face. His eyes were glazed over.

"Rogen. How do we stop this damn bomb?"

Rogen's eyes opened for a moment, and he tried to speak, but all that came out was a gush of blood that splattered down his front. His eyes went wide as he saw that he was just feet from the bomb, and he began to twitch. Lisa noticed something sharp and metal sticking out from his chest. A piece of the railing at the back of the Trans must have broken when he fell, and he had fallen onto it, impaling himself.

"Calm down," said Lisa. "Tell me, if you can. We can stop it. Then I can get you some help."

Rogen took a deep breath and cringed. "Tamper proof. Don't know code," he whispered before passing out again.

And Counting

Now...

Seven minutes and five seconds.

Seven minutes and four seconds.

Lisa blinked. Nearly a minute had passed since she had looked at the readout on the green box, and in that time two of the four people in the room had been wounded, possibly mortally, and the fourth was now nearly a mile away along the Trans, and she was hesitating.

Nearby, Rogen had already stopped breathing, but at the other end of the platform she could still see Hayley struggling to sit up, to stay conscious.

If I go and get a medic, the time will be up before I get back, and the bomb will go off. A bomb that, from Jackson's brief description – and her own estimation of its size – would probably flatten the entire facility and possibly a large area of land outside of that.

There's no way I can get Hayley out of here in time. No way I can get *anyone* out in time. There was also no way to deactivate the thing that she could see. If she tried the keypad, she knew it would probably set the thing off early. Tamper proof, Rogen had said. It would be rigged against someone meddling with it.

Nothing to be done. Nothing that could be done. There

was no other Trans. She couldn't send it off down the tunnel. The drones were all taken out, according to Jackson, all deactivated. They took ten minutes to reactivate. Not enough time.

Just as she considered the only option she may have, she heard the boots thudding on the platform and out in the hall. She spun around, turning one-eighty and raising her weapon, but she was nowhere near fast enough. Six armoured troopers were aiming at her and two more over at Hayley, and yet more came from behind them.

Lisa shook her head and lowered her weapon, and then she recognised two people. The nearest trooper was an officer, and the insignia on the front of his chest-plate designated him as the officer that should be in charge of her unit and several others, her superior. His armour was dusty and battered, like it had been through wars and not repaired. It had to be her predecessor. There was no mistaking the markings. And that explained a few things. That explained who was leading the invasion of the facility.

The second person she recognised only when he took off the Trooper helmet he was wearing. It was the only piece of combat armour that he wore. The rest of his clothing was ragged and dirty. A long jacket with dark jeans that had been repaired many times. The man she had released weeks before, whom she had recaptured just a day ago.

* * *

"Please, you need to drop your weapon," Jack said, speaking before any of the Troopers could. He watched as the female officer lowered and then just dropped the weapon to the floor, all will seeming to leave her. Two of

469

the Troopers approached her, and she slowly raised her arms. Jack looked quickly around the Trans building, noticing the injured people: the first another female Trooper – moving, barely – and the second an older man with a nasty looking spike of metal sticking out of his chest, who didn't appear to be moving at all. "We need to get medics in here," he said.

"No point," Lisa said, pointing at the green box. "It's too late. Nothing we can do. It will all be over in a few minutes."

Everyone froze except for FirstMan, who raised his visor and frowned at her as he walked toward the box. "What do you mean?"

Lisa blinked, her mind unfocused. "It's a bomb."

"You set it?" FirstMan asked, his expression turning angry.

"No. Jackson did it," Lisa said. She appeared to be coming out of shock, now, but Jack thought there was still a sense of resignation about her. "It's tamper locked, I think."

FirstMan crouched over the box. He shook his head. "Damn it. I knew he would have something like this."

Jack walked over to where FirstMan stood, staring at the bomb, but then turned with several of the other troopers as footsteps echoed along the corridor. A small figure appeared at the corner, peering into the hall.

Ryan.

Fly Away

Now...

Ryan walked onto the platform and tried to take in everything around him. Jack was there, and safe, not dead or hurt as he had convinced himself that he would be. FirstMan was there as well, but RightHand was missing. A lot of Troopers stood around, their weapons mostly trained on a woman dressed in facility fatigues but unarmed.

He frowned as Jack rushed over to him. What was so dangerous about the woman that they all had to point guns a her?

"Ryan," called Jack. "What the hell are you doing here?"

At hearing Jack's voice, he ran to him and threw his arms around him.

"This is not good," Jack said. "You shouldn't be here."

"I thought you might be injured," said Ryan.

"We have six minutes before this thing blows," said FirstMan. "That's not enough time to get out of range. Not for any of us."

Ryan's heart started thumping. "What does that mean?" he asked.

Jack sighed. "It's a bomb, Ryan," said Jack. "It's going to go off if we can't stop it."

"Then we need to go," said Ryan. "We need to run—"

"It's too late. We won't get far enough away," said FirstMan, who looked at Lisa. "You know of no way to stop this thing? Switch it off?"

Lisa shook her head. "No. And neither do either of these," she said indicating Rogen and Hayley. Jackson is the only one who knew, and he is on a Trans, down that tunnel, and probably miles from here by now."

"Hyde," called FirstMan. The Tech Trooper moved quickly to his side. "Any ideas?"

Hyde shook his head. "No. I know just by looking at it what type it is. They made them so you can't rig them, can't stop them unless you know the code. There's no quick get out with it." He looked along the Trans track. "And no other Trans to send it down the tunnel. I know I can't stop it."

"Can it be contained?" asked Jack. "Put in a strongbox or something to deaden the explosion?"

Hyde shook his head again, as he examined the box "It wouldn't be enough. I recognise this. It's used for mining, mostly, to blow out large areas of surface rock. And as a last resort to take out a facility like this. It's meant to blow a five-kilometre radius to dust." The man's face turned pale.

"And we have just six minutes and twenty-five seconds to get away," said FirstMan.

"I was going to put it in a vehicle and drive as fast as I could away," said Lisa.

"That could work," said FirstMan. "Jacobs, Allen, go and get the nearest fasted vehicle and be as quick as hell. We'll get this thing onto a trolley and outside."

"It's tamper proofed," said Hyde. "We jolt that thing too hard and it'll go off. No way can it be driven out of this place with the roads like they are. We'd get to the perimeter if we're lucky."

Silence. No one spoke. Ryan felt dizzy. This was it. The end was rushing up to meet him and all he could think about was flying away on the drone. But the drones were dead. He knew that much. The one he had passed on his way through the facility had been fried. There was no drone to carry him away.

Then it came to him. No drones here, except the one that fired the missile. The one now sitting somewhere out in the junk. "What about the drone?" he blurted. Everyone turned to him, and Ryan felt uncomfortable.

"What?" asked FirstMan.

"All the drones were taken out," said Lisa.

"No I mean the one used to fire the missile?" Ryan said.

Lisa Looked puzzled.

Too slow. Not enough time to explain everything, Ryan thought. I have to get a grip, tell them how I see it. Not me flying away on the drone. The bomb.

"If the bomb is tamper-whatever you said, and can't be jolted, then can't the drone pick it up? I saw it. Floats like a bird. It wouldn't jolt it," said Ryan. "It could fly it away."

FirstMan looked confused as he tried to run the idea through his head. Then Ryan saw the very moment the man understood. His eyes registered hope.

"It could work," said Hyde. "It could do it. I think. I'll call the drone."

"Do it," said FirstMan. "Now, and fast, while we figure out how to hook it onto the drone" He turned to Ryan. "You're a damn genius, kid," said FirstMan.

"Will it get here fast enough?" asked Jack.

"On its way, already. ETA four minutes," said Hyde. "It'll be close, but as long as we get moving that thing out of here quickly, when it gets here we may stand a chance."

Ryan looked around at the faces of the adults. Nearly everyone he knew was here. He hoped to whatever gods existed that the plan would work. Then, as everyone seemed to be rushing around, he noticed the woman at the other end of the platform. She was lying on the ground, and she looked stunned, maybe injured, but was still moving. He patted the medical pack on his chest and started jogging toward her.

Necessary Measures

Now...

Governor Jackson clung to the control panel, steadying himself as he tried to slow his breathing, staring at the open doorway just a few feet away. He should close it, he knew, but he was terrified that if he let go of the panel he would be pulled out of the door into the tunnel and be smashed against the wall that was rushing past at a speed that was dizzying.

He looked down at his hands and saw that they were nearly white; his grip was so strong on the metal that the lack of circulation was making his fingers numb and his hands throb.

With one deep breath, he braved letting go of the side of the panel and reached up.

I must be far enough away by now, he thought. Must be. And the bomb must have gone off by now, surely. But there had been no indication of it in the tunnel. No tremor that he had felt or rush of hot wind.

But then there wouldn't be, would there? The Maintenance Trans that he was in was rocketing along at such a speed that a gush of wind would be trivial, and many times over the last few minutes he had thought the damn thing would jump off the rail with all the banging and rocking it was doing.

It wasn't meant to be used at such a speed. It was for scouring the track slowly, looking for repairs that needed to be made. He remembered, then, as he reached up to the speed control throttle, grasped it tightly, and pulled it slowly back toward him. There were dozens of pull ins along the tunnel, one every thirty or forty miles along the thousands of miles of tunnel that led all the way from the Inner Zone to the Junklands. The maintenance crew had two more of these things, one going in each direction, and they would do a stretch of track each day, taking weeks to cross the entire length of the tunnel.

Weeks in this damn tunnel, he thought. No. He could never do that. All this darkness and dank air. It was stifling. But somewhere along the track were the other Maintenance Trans, one heading in his direction and the other away, their occupants used to spending most of their lives down here in the dark, sleeping at the pull ins.

Had he passed one of the stops already? he wondered. No, not yet. But he must be close. He had to get there, had to get off the Trans and somehow contact the people in the Inner Zone. They would send a proper Trans to pick him up. One where he could sit in relative comfort and drink coffee, maybe even eat something.

The maintenance vehicle slowed, but he didn't stop it. He hadn't gone far enough, he thought. The bomb may or may not have gone off; he hadn't been able to judge the passing of time since his terrifying escape.

So, close. It had been so close.

But it was not a worry now. Only the darkness of the tunnel was a worry. As the Trans slowed to almost walking pace, he felt a shudder. He was looking at the wall of the tunnel, just a few feet away, and the concrete floor underneath the rail. There was graffiti on the walls, written by who knew who. Someone down here.

Jackson quickly reached for the open door and pulled it shut. He grabbed the throttle again and sped the Trans up so that it was travelling much faster than a man could run, too fast for anyone to jump aboard.

It was a shame that Rogen had not made it, he thought. Such a shame. He had treated the man badly, most of the time, but he still had a fondness for him. The scrawny thing was like a rodent, but he was *his* rodent, his to command. He should have been able to travel with him to the New World.

I would have liked to have someone to boss about in the New World.

But that was in the past now, and couldn't be helped. Rogen would die with the rest of them, when the bomb went off, and maybe that was a good thing. No one would remain alive to tell anyone anything.

It was another hour before he saw the light ahead, and he knew he hadn't noticed it for a minute or so. The small speck in the distance slowly grew bigger and bigger, and it was only a few hundred yards away when he saw it.

The stop off. It must be.

He grabbed the throttle once more and patted his belt where the hold out gun was holstered, checking it was still there, before slowing the Trans to jogging speed.

A small turn off on the track lay head, but he couldn't see how he was supposed to move the Trans onto it, so brought the vehicle to a stop a dozen feet before it and climbed out onto the thin path that led along the side of the tunnel. A large glass panel ran along the wall, and Jackson thought he could see a faint light behind it − a room, maybe? The maintenance drivers had to stay somewhere that wasn't on the track. There had to be rooms back there.

He reached the end of the small jetty of track and found a slightly ajar door in the wall with light shining out of it. Inside was just one single small room with a bed, a cabinet, a toilet in one corner, and the thing he had hoped for − a comms station. But what of the Maintenance Trans? There had to be some way to switch the track.

He turned back and cursed himself for being stupid. It was on the wall next to the door. He'd walked right past the small switch and lever. He flicked the switch and heard a distant humming. The lights in the room brightened. He frowned and pushed the lever and was relieved to hear a grating sound outside. Peering through the window, he could see that the jetty rail had now moved to intersect the main rail.

Excellent, he thought. Problem solved. I'll move it in a moment.

First, he needed to speak to someone.

"Hello?" he called into the stubby microphone on the comms desk.

No response.

He looked around at the few controls and noticed a green button. He pressed it and called again. "Hello?"

Twenty seconds passed, and he was about to curse when a voice came back. "Maintenance Control, here." said a deep male voice. "Is there a problem?"

"This is Governor Jackson speaking. I am in one of the maintenance stop offs and need to urgently be put through to Internal Security."

"Um, did you say *governor*?" asked the voice.

"Yes, I am governor of the NE7 Resource Recycling Facility and the Junklands operations. Hurry, this is important."

"Yes, sir. Sorry, sir," replied the voice.

A few seconds later a different voice came back. "Governor Jackson, please respond."

Jackson coughed to clear his throat. He would shut the door soon and make himself more comfortable in the stop off room while he waited, but with the door open, the air was filling his lungs with dust.

"This is Jackson speaking."

"Sir, that's a relief. This is Major Callister of the Security Corps. Our monitors just reported something disturbing and we were unable to contact you at the facility. The readout suggests there has been a major explosion of some kind near the Recycling Facility. Can you confirm?"

"Yes, I can confirm," said Jackson. "Something terrible has happened, and I only just managed to escape myself. Unfortunately, I was alone. You say the detonation was near the facility. What can your readouts tell you, officer?"

"Erm…just a moment. I'm pulling up the reading, now." said the voice. "There. Wide radius, high resonance wave, actually 5km radius, measuring at 8.5. That's very high. Right in the middle of the facility. Suggests some kind of high yield explosive. All comms are down at the facility.

What happened, sir?"

Jackson sighed. It had worked. He didn't want the man on comms to hear it in his voice, but Jackson smiled. Every damn one of them and every damn thing. Blown away. Gone. He looked over at the row of cases near the door and grinned.

"That's quite a long story," said Jackson, "but let's just say that a large explosion was set off; the facility was being overrun by savages and I was forced to stop them from taking over. If you could arrange for me to be picked up, I will provide a detailed report when I am back within the safety of the Inner Zone. I fear that it is quite dangerous where I am now."

Deal with it

Two Weeks Later…

The figure moved along the dimly-lit street, keeping to the middle, away from the shop fronts and alleyways. Even at night the place was bustling with life. The voices of shop owners haggling with customers over a price at their counters and the low hum of a multitude of discussions taking place in the shadows of the alleys and doorways built up to a constant din.

The buildings rose as high as four floors in most places, and even though it was not quite dark in the sky, the street below would have been in total darkness if not for the chain of lamps that hung from every other building, joined together with a long chain of wires that zigzagged across the rooftops.

This wasn't downtown in the Inner Zone, where the shops occupied spots along marble pavements and sported massive, spotless glass panels at their fronts. There were no suited, perfectly presented assistants waiting to satisfy the whims of potential customers.

The Warrens was an embarrassment to the establishment, and most who lived in the Inner Zone didn't frequent the alleyways and passages that seemed to follow no discernible pattern. But not everyone in the Inner Zone was rich. Even inside the barrier wall there was a lower class that survived purely on others' need for things that couldn't be purchased in the pristine shopping malls.

Jackson ducked under an overhang in front of a shop selling some form of food on a stick. He caught a whiff of whatever meat it was as he went by, and cringed. He would rather have met someplace more tasteful, like a café on the riverbank. Enough of them were quiet enough to conduct business in without being scrutinised. But it seemed that this was necessary to the man whom he was to meet.

He stopped at a junction, where the main street met a wider alleyway, and glanced first left, then right, before taking a scrap of paper from his coat pocket and peering at it. He frowned, looked over several of the signs that stuck out of the walls and pointed in various directions, and then he blinked in recognition. A sign quite a distance along the left alleyway was what he was looking for. Though, he thought with some disgruntlement, the note had said it was only around the corner.

He didn't like the look of the alley – didn't like the numerous dark places where some buildings jutted out in front of others, or where there was an access path to the back of the building. A dozen such uncertain spots lined the alley before he would reach the sign.

Necessary, he thought. It would be worth it.

But still, as he took a step into the alleyway, he stuffed the note back in his pocket and kept his hand in there, leaving the note loose but taking a firm grasp of the handgun he still possessed.

They had not even checked him when they picked him up. They hadn't even questioned the cases he carried.

He walked down the alleyway, trying to ignore the movement he saw inside at least two of the darkened alcoves, shrugging off the group of figures down a side alleyway, and finally reached the building he had been looking for. He knocked quickly, four times. He waited for a few seconds and then knocked just once more, slightly louder, exactly as he had been told to.

Then he waited.

After what seemed a lifetime of standing in the alleyway, where he most definitely did not want to be, the door opposite the shop front opened and a man dressed in a well-tailored suit stepped into the alleyway. He was taller than Jackson by six inches, and he was much thinner, even though Jackson had lost a significant amount of weight over the last few weeks. He was also much older, maybe sixty or more, with long grey hair tied back into a topknot and a short, perfectly trimmed beard that seemed almost silver in colour.

"Mr Jackson?" asked the man, giving Jackson a nod.

"Erm…yes," said Jackson.

"Come, please," said the man.

Jackson followed the stranger through the door into a small room furnished with just a table and two chairs. He sat where the man indicated and laid the case on the table.

"Show me," said the man.

Jackson coughed quietly and started to open the case. "I must say, coming to this place makes me very uncomfortable," he said.

The man simply nodded and looked back at the case.

Jackson opened it and turned it to face the man in the

suit. He seemed to consider the contents of the case – which Jackson had intentionally kept to just a small sample of what he had brought with him from the facility – for a long time.

But then the man smiled and nodded. "This is excellent," he said. "And you have much more of this?"

"Yes," said Jackson. A hundred times more, at least. This is just a small sample of what I was able to collect during my time at NE7. I assure you it is the best that can be found, considering it has been over five hundred years since anyone has manufactured it."

"Indeed," said the man. "I can see as much."

Silence fell between them for a moment.

"Do you think we will be able to make a deal?" asked Jackson. "I would like to offload all that I have, and I need to do it within a week. I am due on the next HyperTrans, you see, and I do not wish to miss that opportunity. Do you think you can find a buyer before then?"

"Yes." The man nodded. "Absolutely. I can get you an excellent price this very day."

What Comes Next

A Week Later...

Governor Brannigan scratched his head and frowned at the screen, watching the flicker of alerts coming in. This was not turning out to be one of his best mornings. Usually the list was marked mostly with grey – non-urgent requests for a response from some administration department or other – or yellow messages, which were usually of a more urgent nature and required a quick response. But they could wait an hour or two if he was particularly in need of a coffee.

The list this morning, as it had been for almost a week, was riddled with bold, glaring red entries that seemed to be breeding. As soon as he opened one, shook his head in disbelief and pondered how to handle such a situation, another red message seemed to be born.

And it was such a lovely day outside; something unusual and welcoming. He could have left a flood of grey and yellow and gone for a wander, visiting various nearby departments personally – just to increase morale, of course.

Not today, it seemed. Just like the last six.

Jackson. It had all started with the rescue of the operations governor of the NE7 Resource Recycling Facility, and it then proceeded into unknown territory and grew to be an absolute nightmare. Each day he hoped the

485

red messages would be gone, but there seemed to be more than ever.

Blown to dust. The entire facility, or so the initial reports had said. No other outcome possible. A bomb that was the last resort, a fail-safe so that the facility never fell into the hands of someone else, not supposed to be used unless all else had failed, had been triggered.

His supply of raw materials for building the Ark ships had been cut off, just like that.

Brannigan minimised the messaging program on the computer and opened his operations inventory. He quickly scanned over the levels of raw materials and electronics in stock. Same as yesterday, there was not enough to even complete half of the next Ark ship. Not that it was much of a surprise. Without shipments from the Junklands the inventory was unlikely to change. And it was already under construction, sitting in orbit right next to the one that was ready to launch. Just a hollow shell. And now it may never be completed.

A shiver ran up his spine. Maybe he should get on this one? He was overdue by four or five now. If things were about to go badly with the supply line, that Ark ship in orbit may well be the last. The thought unnerved him. He could get a ticket easily enough. They kept back a few statesman cabins just in case of emergencies.

He shook his head and flipped the screen back to the messages.

No. This must be dealt with. Another expedition was needed. At the very least they would need to re-establish communications with the other, smaller facilities out in the Junklands. There were a dozen other small factories and power plants outside of the main one that would still be manned.

And where the hell was the first expedition? There had been no communication back from them in days.

Brannigan slammed his fist on the table. They couldn't use the main Trans. The area would be contaminated well beyond safe occupation levels for years. A whole new length of tunnel would need to be built, taking the Trans around the red site and out to another location, then a new facility

It could take years.

As Brannigan put his head in his hands, about ready to rip his own hair out, he noticed a small blinking box in the corner of the messages screen.

A call. Right now. Someone wanted to talk to him, right at the time when he really wasn't in the mood for any human contact.

He sighed, hovering the cursor over the box, and read the title that popped up.

Incoming. Communications Corps. Urgent.

The Comms Corps? What hell did they want?

He clicked the button and rubbed his eyes as the picture of the operator appeared in the middle of the terminal.

"Yes?" he asked.

"Ah. Governor Brannigan. Sorry to interrupt you. I'm sure you are very busy at the moment."

"Yes. I am. I hope this is important."

"Yes, sir. I'm Major Elkand of the Comms Corp, and I've got an incoming conference request for you."

Brannigan frowned. "What? From whom? Which department? And why come through your office?"

The comms officer paused, looking puzzled. "Well, that's the confusing part, sir. And I apologise again. The call isn't from within the Zone, sir. It's from outside. A long way outside."

"What do you mean?" Brannigan asked. "Spit it out, officer. I am in no mood for suspense."

"The call is from the NE7 Facility, sir," The comms officer said. "They said they wanted to talk to you personally and no one else."

"But. What? How?" Brannigan asked, his annoyance rising. "NE7 was destroyed. No one could survive that detonation. Who is on the line, officer?"

"First Corporal Lisa Markell," the comms officer said. "One of the security officers from the facility."

"Put her through," Brannigan said.

"Yes, sir. Patching the conference signal through to you now."

A large box appeared on the screen, the usual spinning circle indicating a delay in connection. Brannigan rarely spoke to anyone outside of the Inner Zone, so the delay was normally only a second or so, but this connection took twenty seconds before stabilising. Brannigan clicked an icon on the box and the conference image expanded to fill the whole screen.

He was looking at a large table in a well-lit room, with four people seated facing him. One of the four seemed to be talking to whoever was holding the camera that was filming them. Brannigan turned the speaker volume up so he could hear what was being said.

"Are we through?" asked the man on the screen. The man squinted, then seemed to look straight at Brannigan. "Ah! Yes. Looks like it's working. Put it on the tripod and leave us, please."

The image wobbled for a few seconds, but then went perfectly still. There was the sound of footsteps on metal, then the click of a door closing.

"Can I presume that I am speaking to Governor Brannigan, High Administrator?" the man on the screen asked.

Brannigan was silent.

"I apologise. I should have introduced myself. My name is Ranold. I'm First Councillor for the North-East Republic. Beside me is Councillor Tyler, our head of public relations, and Councillor Avery, head of—"

"What North East Republic?" Brannigan said. He could feel his face turning red. "What are you talking about? There is no North-East Republic."

The man on the screen nodded. "There wasn't a week ago, when Governor Jackson, the previous occupant of this facility, attempted to kill several thousand people, but in the week that has passed, we have established much."

"Who are you people?" Brannigan asked. "Are you those terror fighters I've heard reports of? Those junk people."

"I was attempting to make introduction…" the man said.

"Introductions? Have you seized our facility?"

"No, Governor. We attempted to do so, then your Governor Jackson blew the facility up – or tried to. Fortunately, thanks to a few brave individuals among our staff, and their ingenuity under very stressful circumstances, the explosion happened roughly fifteen kilometres above the facility instead of on the ground. It was little more than an interesting firework display. Technically, *you* destroyed your facility, and we claimed the remains."

"We will not sit by and let you take—"

"We already apprehended your first group of investigators. Now, before you worry, I can assure you they are perfectly safe, and they will remain so. But, so that you know, before planning any further incursions into our territory, I can promise you that we have taken measures so that no one can come within ten miles of our new capitol via the Trans tunnel without our permission. We will be extending our control over the tunnel out to fifty miles within a few weeks."

"This is theft. It's invasion."

"No, sir, it's reclamation. This land was occupied before you arrived here, and now the Free People of the North-East Republic have taken it back. With minimal hostility, I will mention."

Brannigan was silent once more. He had no words. Nothing came to mind. There was little he could do. No transport other than the Trans could reach that far out. The Dropships certainly couldn't go out even a tenth of the distance.

"Now, we need to discuss our trade situation. We realise your dependence upon the commodities found in the Junklands is of high importance, and as much as this seems like a hostile takeover, we would rather negotiate a trade deal and a peaceful co-existence."

"Why on Earth would we want that?" Brannigan asked.

"Let me hand you over to Officer Markell, who was and still is a first lieutenant in your military forces. She has something interesting for you. Intel that was gathered by our people, nonetheless, and offered, freely, to you as a gesture of our goodwill and hope for a mutually beneficial settlement of the current situation."

The woman on the screen nodded and cleared her throat. "Governor Brannigan. I'm First Lieutenant Lisa Markell. I used to head some of the expeditions out here, and I've some critical information regarding the practices of Governor Jackson."

Brannigan's eyes narrowed. He was ready to shout, ready to curse at them all, but this sounded interesting. "Go on."

"We have evidence that Jackson has been illegally acquiring some extremely high value goods and shipping them to the Inner Zone for sale through underground methods. He has also been holding back and acquiring some components that we know are extremely difficult to acquire and critical for your project with the Ark ships. We also believe that Jackson may have made his way back to the Inner Zone and is at this moment in possession of a large amount of these goods. All indications from my investigation here point toward the attempted destruction of this facility to cover his tracks. I can provide a lot of information if you need it, but I would suggest that apprehending Jackson should be a high priority."

Brannigan stared at the screen, ready to explode with

fury, but he calmed himself. It seemed that his anger should be directed elsewhere. "What you suggest Jackson has been doing is highly treasonous behaviour, Officer. Those are some very serious accusations."

"Yes, Governor," Lisa replied. "And as I said, I have solid evidence to back them up that I could bring back with me, if a negotiation could be agreed with the New Republic. There is also a reasonable number of Inner Zone Troopers here, including myself, that need to be repatriated.

"Also, can I just say that The North-East Republic has been very helpful and open with my investigation over the last week, and the treatment of Inner Zone Troopers has been very good. After listening to the Republic's plans, as far as trade and co-operation is concerned, I think you would do well to at least listen to what they have to say. The deal the council is willing to offer you is quite exceptional. It may possibly be more profitable than holding and operating these facilities yourself."

Drawing In

Two days later...

Jackson stood in line at the bottom of the escalator. There were three people in front of him – an old gentleman, who seemed to be struggling to stand up straight, his left hand gripping a small travel bag tightly, the other holding onto the handle of a walking stick, and a young couple in front of him. Jackson mostly ignored the older man, but the young couple bugged him. They were cheerful and clutched at each other, obviously excited to be making the one-way journey up into orbit.

How the hell had they afforded this? That was what was bugging him. At twenty thousand credits per person, this young pair had to have stumped up a hefty forty thousand to be going. Rich parents, maybe? Neither of them looked older than twenty. *Had* to be rich parents.

This thought made him hate them even more than their being before him in the queue, and he couldn't stop himself from glaring at the backs of their heads, even as the security gate stopping access to the escalator lifted and a light on a nearby panel turned green. The pair squeezed each other's hands tighter as they stepped onto the moving stairway and began the long journey up to the platform, two hundred feet above.

Then the gate closed once more, and the light turned

red.

Back to waiting.

He glanced behind and then immediately cheered up. There were a hundred or more people in the queue behind him, and the thought that they would all have to wait until he was allowed to board the ship was somehow gratifying.

He looked around the massive hangar. The building was at least fifty stories high, big enough to contain the shuttle and its launch platform, along with all the extra machines needed to maintain the thing. It was the first time he'd even seen one of the shuttles up close. Sure, he'd seen them launch before, many years ago, back when he lived in the city. They were hard to ignore. One would launch and then return after a few days, the journey up into orbit being loud, the journey back down quiet enough that you could miss the shuttle's arrival if you weren't watching at the right time of day.

And only half of the shuttle was filled with people, he thought. The other half was chock full of the materials needed to build the next Ark and a stack of supplies for the one that was leaving soon.

How long had some people been living up on the orbital station, now that it was just a few days until the Ark ship left? They travelled up there constantly, so theoretically there could be people up there who had been waiting for nearly a year?

That was not a thought that cheered him, and he was glad to be leaving just as the ship was ready to head off to the new world.

The green light blinked on once more, and the old man

in front of him wobbled forward, seeming to take forever to reach the gate.

If you don't hurry up the damn gate will shut, Jackson thought. He stared at the old man's back, willing him to move faster. Every moment the old waste of space took to get onto the escalator was another moment that he would be waiting.

Calm yourself, he thought. This is it. It's almost over. He patted his jacket pocket and took a deep breath. Everything was ready. He was on his way, finally leaving this terrible place, and the rigid wallet in his pocket contained everything he could possibly need for a lifetime. He was rich beyond any of his dreams.

This is what it had all been about, all this waiting. The goods were sold, and the price had been as promised. There was more credit on the card in his pocket than any man could ever need.

The old man finally stumbled onto the escalator and wavered, his limbs protesting gravity as he was jerked forward. He reached out and grabbed the rail to steady himself, and Jackson watched as he began his slow ascent to the boarding platform.

I'm next, he thought. Just a few minutes to go. *If* that old idiot doesn't fall off.

"Governor Jackson." A metallic voice spoke from behind him. He almost jumped out of his skin, but instead he managed to hold his composure as he turned to see a squad of four Troopers standing behind a tall man wearing a long grey coat and flat military cap. It was an officer's cap, and Jackson glanced at the insignia on the man's shoulder.

IZS. Internal Zone Security.

"Yes," Jackson replied, feeling a slight sweat break out in his armpits.

They were here to escort him, surely. A man of his rank deserved such. In fact, he thought, they should have been there to meet him upon arrival and take him to the front of the queue, to guarantee his safety.

"Sir," said the officer. "Please step away from the gate and place your arms out straight."

Jackson frowned. "What? What for?"

"Please do as I say," said the officer. "And please do not attempt to reach into a pocket. Any sudden movement will be met with measurable force."

"Measurable... What is going on here?"

The officer was fast, much quicker than Jackson had expected or was prepared for. One moment his hands were at his side, and the next, Jackson found the muzzle of a heavy assault pistol pointing at his face.

"Governor Jackson," said the officer. "You will comply without further question."

Jackson found he was shaking, but he managed to put his arms out, his hands palms up. This was ridiculous, he thought. How could they possibly have found him out?

But then he saw her in the distance, standing next to two other Troopers. Her uniform was not the same as she had worn when on duty, back at the NE7 Facility. No, it was blue, like that of a senior officer rather than a first lieutenant. To wear the blue meant she had been given a significant promotion – to major, at least.

And there was only one way he could think she could have managed such a promotion in such brief time.

First was by not being dead. He had last seen her as he raced away into the Trans tunnel, leaving his poor badly wounded assistant behind, and Markell and her co-officer — whose name he couldn't remember — helpless on the platform where the bomb was.

She should be dead. They should all be dead.

She watched him, expressionless, as the officer and two of the Troopers restrained him, placing him in cuffs and a neck collar, and Jackson couldn't help but grin.

The facility hadn't been destroyed, he now realised. Somehow, they had stopped it. He didn't know how, but they had.

Jackson became aware that the officer was talking, reciting something. What was that?

"…right to say nothing. Everything you say will put on record and used in court. The IZS has a full list of charges against you, and you will be able to review them once you are placed in captivity, but the charge of high treason is the first and most prominent charge, and there is unquestionable evidence of that against you. You are probably aware of how serious these charges are…"

Jackson switched off from the man's voice, choosing to ignore it, and instead he glared at Markell.

High treason came with only one penalty.

What Lies After

One month later...

Jack leaned back in the chair next to the corner desk, where a monitor buzzed quietly. The small room had once belonged to one of the officers at the facility, but it was one of only a few dozen that shared the main compound's air conditioning, and that was a luxury that Jack was glad of.

Ryan sat on the bed a few feet away, reading a comic book that he had found somewhere in the stores. The boy had been hunting around the facility for weeks now, and he had uncovered all manner of interesting stuff, tucked away in dark corners and locked cabinets. The pile of comic books was his most treasured find.

"I notice you've been over at the medical bay most afternoons," Jack said, grinning as the boy blushed. "How is Hayley doing?"

"She's recovering really well," Ryan said. "Well, that's what the doctor says. They're not sure if she will walk again, though. I only go there because she must get bored. She seems to like me reading my comics to her. Or she just doesn't tell me to go away."

"I'm sure she enjoys it," said Jack.

"The doc says that they plan to move her back to a hospital in the Inner Zone soon," said Ryan. "But they have to do one more operation so her back is strong enough."

"I see," said Jack. "You'll miss her, won't you?"

Ryan shrugged. "She's funny. But I guess if we go to the New World, like they offered us, then I won't see her again, anyway."

"We don't have to go," said Jack. "It's all up to us, for once. No one to tell us what to do. It's a difficult decision to make. I'm not in any hurry to make it."

Ryan nodded and managed to look up from the comic. "What do you want to do?"

Jack thought about it for a while. It was a life changing decision, and he was never keen to make those. "Well, the New World is supposed to be a lot cleaner, but it will probably be a lot like the Inner Zone."

Ryan frowned. "In what way?"

"Well, for starters, there won't be anywhere near as much freedom. Unless we go out there loaded with cash, I'd probably need to find work somewhere. We'd need to find a place to live, and that will cost money."

"Yuck," Ryan said. "I know we have to start all that, now that this Republic thing is happening, but I prefer swaps."

Jack nodded. "Also, we couldn't just go live anywhere we wanted. Not like here. You know, I found an amazing spot not more than twenty miles from this place, while we were scoping out that water plant. There's a whole patch of land out there that is flat and not covered in junk. Even some trees. Well, sort of trees. They're a bit stunted."

"No smelly swamp?" Ryan asked.

"No smelly swamp, but some huge, empty reservoirs that Hyde says were originally for storing excess water from the water plant. He thinks that if the plant could be brought up to higher production, it could provide clean water for a lot of people and probably fill those reservoirs again."

"What?" Ryan asked. "Like real lakes?"

"Yeah, I think. Real lakes," Jack said. There's a lot of work to be done out there, first, though, and FirstMan even suggested that if I was interested, I could probably head the operation."

"Governor Avery?" Ryan said, frowning. Jack could sense the sarcasm hidden there.

"No," Jack said. "Apparently, that title is banned. I'd still have to keep the title councillor, since they put me on their damn council."

Ryan was quiet.

"Well, think about it, anyway," Jack said. "It's an option among many. Hell, Lisa even said we could live in the Inner Zone if we wanted to, now that all the negotiations are underway and things are less volatile, though she is leaving on next year's Ark so we wouldn't know anyone, and I'm not sure I even want to go back there."

Ryan nodded. "The New World. I don't know. I think I like this one, even if it's a bit old and worn."

Jack smiled. "Yeah. Old and worn. I know how it feels."

THE END

Acknowledgements

Thanks to all of the Jameses – Julia, for your patience and constant encouragement, and my kids, for just being you.

To my parents and my brother for not being too surprised that I write crazy fiction, and for telling me it's cool.

To Bill, Sara, Billy, Jim & Jean for taking me seriously and never doubting that I could actually do this, and for demanding signed copies when I thought that whole idea was daft.

Many thanks to Andrea of Express Editing Solutions - http://www.expresseditingsolutions.co.uk

Any typos or errors in this book after this fantastic editor went through it - are entirely my fault.

About the Author

GLYNN JAMES, born in Wellingborough, England in 1972, is a bestselling author of dark sci-fi novels.

He has an obsession with anything to do with zombies, Cthulhu mythos, and post-apocalyptic and dystopian fiction and films, all of which began when he started reading HP Lovecraft and Richard Matheson's I Am Legend back when he was eight years old.

In addition to co-authoring the bestselling ARISEN books (over 400,000 copies sold), he is the author of the bestselling DIARY OF THE DISPLACED series.

For More Info

www.glynnjames.co.uk

Made in the USA
Coppell, TX
31 July 2021